Praise for the Novels of Karen White

The Girl on Legare Street

"Karen White delivers the thrills of perilous romance and the chills of ghostly suspense, all presented with Southern wit and charm."
—*New York Times* bestselling author Kerrelyn Sparks

The House on Tradd Street

"Engaging. . . . The supernatural elements are not played for scares, but instead refine and reveal Melanie's true character. . . . A fun and satisfying read, this series kickoff should hook a wide audience." —*Publishers Weekly*

"*The House on Tradd Street* has it all: mystery, romance, and the paranormal including ghosts with quirky personalities. For me this is White's best work and I am looking forward to the sequel." —BookLoons

"White delivers funny characters, a solid plot, and an interesting twist in this novel about the South and its antebellum history." —*Romantic Times*

"Has all the elements that have made Karen White's books fan favorites: a Southern setting, a deeply emotional tale, and engaging characters. " —A Romance Review

"The key to this quirky charmer is the depth of the lead characters, especially the heroine and even some of the ghosts. Fans of paranormal romantic suspense will want to read this wonderful tale as Karen White provides a fine treasure hunt mystery with a nasty spirit inside a warm romance in which readers will say yes that they believe in ghosts and in love." —*Midwest Book Review*

"If you enjoy ghost stories with some mystery thrown into the mix, you are going to love this one. The sights and smells of the old house, along with excellent dialogue and good pacing, add up to a wonderful, mysterious, and ghostly tale." —Romance Reviews Today

"Brilliant and engrossing . . . a rare gem . . . exquisitely told, rich in descriptions, and filled with multifaceted characters." —The Book Connection

"Karen White is an extremely talented and colorful writer with tons of imagination. If you are not a believer of paranormal, you will be after reading this novel." —Fresh Fiction

The Memory of Water

"Careful plotting, richly flawed characters and a surprising conclusion mark this absorbing melodrama." —*Publishers Weekly*

"Beautifully written and as lyrical as the tides. *The Memory of Water* speaks directly to the heart and will linger in yours long after you've read the final page. I loved this book!" —Susan Crandall, author of *Pitch Black*

"Karen White delivers a powerfully emotional blend of family secrets, Lowcountry lore, and love in *The Memory of Water*—who could ask for more?" —Barbara Bretton, author of *Just Desserts*

Learning to Breathe

"White creates a heartfelt story full of vibrant characters and emotion that leaves the reader satisfied yet hungry for more from this talented author." —*Booklist*

"One of those stories where you savor every single word . . . a perfect 10." —Romance Reviews Today

"Another one of Karen White's emotional books! A joy to read!" —The Best Reviews

Pieces of the Heart

"Heartwarming and intense . . . a tale that resonates with the meaning of unconditional love." —*Romantic Times* (4 stars)

"A terrific, insightful character study." —*Midwest Book Review*

"[White's] prose is lyrical, and she weaves in elements of mysticism and romance without being heavy-handed. An accomplished novel." —*Booklist*

"A story as rich as a coastal summer . . . dark secrets, heartache, a magnificent South Carolina setting, and a great love story."
—*New York Times* bestselling author Deborah Smith

"As lush as the Lowcountry, where the characters' wounded souls come home to mend in unexpected and magical ways."
—Patti Callahan Henry, author of *Between the Tides*

More Praise for the Novels of Karen White

"The fresh voice of Karen White intrigues and delights."
—Sandra Chastain, contributor to *At Home in Mossy Creek*

"Warmly Southern and deeply moving."
—*New York Times* bestselling author Deborah Smith

"Karen White writes with passion and poignancy."
—Deb Stover, award-winning author of *Mulligan Magic*

"[A] sweet book . . . highly recommended." —*Booklist*

"Karen White is one author you won't forget. . . . This is a masterpiece in the study of relationships. Brava!" —Reader to Reader Reviews

"This is not only romance at its best—this is a fully realized view of life at its fullest." —Readers & Writers, Ink

"*After the Rain* is an elegantly enchanting southern novel. . . . Fans will recognize the beauty of White's evocative prose." —WordWeaving.com

"In the tradition of Catherine Anderson and Deborah Smith, Karen White's *After the Rain* is an incredibly poignant contemporary bursting with Southern charm." —Patricia Rouse, Rouse's Romance Readers Groups

"Don't miss this book!" —*Rendezvous*

Titles by Karen White

THE GIRL ON
LEGARE STREET

KAREN WHITE

NEW AMERICAN LIBRARY

New American Library
Published by New American Library, a division of
Penguin Group (USA) Inc., 375 Hudson Street,
New York, New York 10014, USA
Penguin Group (Canada), 90 Eglinton Avenue East, Suite 700, Toronto,
Ontario M4P 2Y3, Canada (a division of Pearson Penguin Canada Inc.)
Penguin Books Ltd., 80 Strand, London WC2R 0RL, England
Penguin Ireland, 25 St. Stephen's Green, Dublin 2,
Ireland (a division of Penguin Books Ltd.)
Penguin Group (Australia), 250 Camberwell Road, Camberwell, Victoria 3124,
Australia (a division of Pearson Australia Group Pty. Ltd.)
Penguin Books India Pvt. Ltd., 11 Community Centre, Panchsheel Park,
New Delhi - 110 017, India
Penguin Group (NZ), 67 Apollo Drive, Rosedale, North Shore 0632,
New Zealand (a division of Pearson New Zealand Ltd.)
Penguin Books (South Africa) (Pty.) Ltd., 24 Sturdee Avenue,
Rosebank, Johannesburg 2196, South Africa

Penguin Books Ltd., Registered Offices:
80 Strand, London WC2R 0RL, England

First published by New American Library,
a division of Penguin Group (USA) Inc.

First Printing, November 2009
20   19   18

 REGISTERED TRADEMARK—MARCA REGISTRADA

Library of Congress Cataloging-in-Publication Data:

White, Karen (Karen S.)
The girl on Legare Street/Karen White.
p.   cm.
ISBN 978-0-451-22799-7
1. Women real estate agents—Fiction. 2. Mothers and daughters—Fiction 3. Haunted houses—Fiction.
4. Historic buildings—South Carolina—Charleston—Fiction. 5. Charleston (S.C.)—Fiction   I. Title
PS3623.H5776G57   2009
813'—dc22   2009024592

Set in Bembo Regular
Designed by Alissa Amell

Printed in the United States of America

To Claire White Kobylt, who's known me longer than just about everybody, and who likes me anyway. Thanks for your friendship.

ACKNOWLEDGMENTS

Thank you to my readers, whose letters and e-mails inspire me to continue writing. Although—in answer to your most frequently asked question—I can't write any faster, I will continue to write books for as long as you will read them.

Thanks again to Nancy Flaherty, for the use of your name as well as your golfing and knitting hobbies for shameless use in this book, and to my brother-in-law, Rich Kobylt, for your cameo performance as a plumber. I hope you both enjoy your character incarnations as much as I enjoyed creating them and as much as readers enjoy reading about them.

To Klara Rehm and Joyce McDonnell, thank you for your time and expertise on the German language translation and for saving me from embassassment.

Thanks also to my publisher, New American Library, for taking a chance on a "different" kind of book series and for all of your support and for giving my books fabulous covers as well as for getting them into as many readers' hands as possible.

And thanks to my critique partner and talented author, Wendy Wax, and to Tim, Meghan and Connor for your support, words of wisdom, and for not slapping me silly even when I deserved it.

Last, but not least, thank you to the beautiful city of Charleston and its citizens, who welcome me warmly on each visit. I hope I have faithfully portrayed your "holy city."

THE GIRL ON
LEGARE STREET

CHAPTER 1

The milky glow of winter sun behind a sky rubbed the color of an old nickel failed in its feeble attempt to warm the November morning. I shuddered in my wool coat, my Charleston blood unaccustomed to the infrequent blasts of frigid air that descend on the Holy City from time to time to send yet another reminder of why we choose to live in this beautiful city, whose inhabitants—both living and dead—coexist like light and shadow.

I yanked open the door to the City Lights Coffee Bar, the wind behind me threatening to close it again before I'd gone through it. Glancing around, I spotted Jack at a table by the front window, a latte with extra whipped cream and a large cinnamon roll already sitting on the table across from him. Immediately suspicious, I approached the table with caution.

"What do you want?" I asked, indicating the latte and cinnamon roll.

He looked up at me with a pair of killer blue eyes that I'd spent the last six months of my life trying not to notice. His look of innocence would have made me smile and roll my eyes if I didn't still have the lingering aura of dread that had dogged me all the way from my house on Tradd Street to Market. It had been a strong enough feeling to make me pause outside the café for a moment longer than necessary, hoping to identify whatever it was. I wanted to think it was my grogginess, caused by a phone call at two o'clock in the morning after which I'd been unable to fall asleep. That would have been an acceptable explanation, but in my world—where phone calls from people long dead weren't as unusual an occurrence as most people would expect—I wasn't satisfied.

"Good morning, Melanie," Jack said cheerfully. "Can't a guy just want to buy breakfast for a beautiful woman without expecting anything in return?"

I pretended to think for a moment. "No." I unbuttoned my coat and folded it neatly on the back of my chair before sitting down, noticing that all of the women in the restaurant—including the gray-haired woman with a walker at a table by the bar—were staring at Jack and regarding me with narrowed eyes. Yes, Jack Trenholm was way too good-looking to be a writer, especially a writer of historical true-crime mysteries. He should have been bald with a gray beard, wearing thick turtlenecks that protruded over his paunch, his teeth tobacco stained from his ubiquitous pipe. Unfortunately, like so much about Jack, he didn't even try to fit the stereotype.

"So, what do you want?" I asked again as I took out the bottle of hand sanitizer from my purse and squirted a dollop on my palm. I offered the bottle to Jack, but he shook his head before taking a sip of his black coffee. Emptying two packets of sugar into my latte, I looked up at him again, then wished I hadn't. His eyes were certainly bluer than they needed to be, their intensity not needing the help from the navy blue sweater he wore. But something flickered in his eyes as he regarded me—something I thought looked a lot like concern—and it made me squirm in my seat.

"How's General Lee?" he asked, ignoring my question and glancing out the front window, then down at his watch.

I swallowed a bite of my cinnamon roll. "He's fine," I said, referring to the small black-and-white dog I'd reluctantly inherited along with my historic home on Tradd Street.

"Are you still keeping him in the kitchen at night?"

I avoided his gaze. "Um, no. Not exactly."

A wide grin spread over Jack's face. "He sleeps in your room now, doesn't he?"

I took a huge bite of my roll to avoid answering, annoyed again at how astute Jack could be where I was concerned. After having failed to foist General Lee off on my best friend, Dr. Sophie Wallen—who'd turned out to be allergic—I'd sworn to all who would listen that I wasn't a dog person and had no intention of actually keeping the animal.

"He's sleeping at the foot of your bed now, isn't he?" Jack couldn't keep the glee from his voice.

I took a long sip of my latte, studiously avoiding looking at him.

Jack crossed his arms over his chest and slid back in his chair, a smug look on his face. "He's on the pillow next to you, too, right?"

"Fine," I said, slamming down my coffee mug. "He wouldn't sleep anywhere else, okay? He'd cry if I left him in the kitchen, and when I brought him up to my room he'd sit next to the bed staring up at me all night until I brought him up there with me. Sleeping on my pillow was his idea." I slid the mug away from me. "It's not like I actually like him or anything. He just seemed . . . lonely."

Jack leaned forward, his elbows on the table. "Maybe I should pretend I'm lonely and look up at you with sad puppy eyes and see what happens."

I stared at him for a moment, suppressing the unwanted trill of excitement that settled somewhere near my stomach. "You'd end up in a crate in the kitchen." I pushed my empty plate away and signaled the waitress for another.

Jack laughed, then shook his head. "You know, one day those calories are actually going to stick to you, and you'll have to watch what you eat like the rest of us mortals."

I shrugged. "I can't help it. It's hereditary. My maternal grandmother was as slim as a reed until the day she died, and she ate like a linebacker."

"Is your mother the same way?"

My eyes met Jack's and I saw he wasn't smiling anymore. "I wouldn't know, would I? I haven't seen her in more than thirty years." This wasn't precisely the truth. I had accidentally spotted the famous soprano Ginnette Prioleau several times while surfing channels on the television, the remote control in my hand unable to flip quickly enough from the PBS station broadcasting a production of the Metropolitan Opera. The exact truth was that my mother was still as slender and as beautiful as she'd been when she abandoned her seven-year-old daughter without a backward glance.

The darkness that had been hovering over me all morning now seemed to descend on our corner table, obscuring the light as if someone had hit a dimmer switch. I fought a wave of nausea as the hairs on the back of my neck rose, and I looked at Jack in panic to see if he'd noticed a change, too. But he was too busy staring past my shoulder to notice anything else.

"You look a lot like her, you know." Jack's eyes slid back to mine and I saw his look of concern quickly switch to one of apology.

"Oh God, Jack, you didn't!" I made a move to stand but he placed a hand on my arm.

"Melanie, she said it was a matter of life or death and that you wouldn't see her or return her phone calls. I was her last resort."

I looked around blindly, searching for an exit other than the door through which I'd entered, and wondered if I could run through the kitchen before anybody noticed me. A small gloved hand gripped my shoulder as a bright light seemed to pop in front of me like a curtain being pulled back from the window to reveal a sunny day. The darkness dispelled as she squeezed my shoulder and dropped her hand, but the light remained, leaving me to wonder if the sigh and whisper I'd heard as the darkness dispelled had been only in my imagination.

I looked up into the face of the woman who'd once been the world to me, when I was too small to understand the vagaries of human nature and that calling somebody "Mother" didn't always mean what you wanted it to.

"Hello, Mellie," she said in a soft, melodious voice that had haunted my dreams for years until I'd grown old enough to believe that I didn't need to hear my mother's voice anymore.

I winced at the sound of the nickname she'd given me—the nickname I'd never let anybody call me until I'd met Jack, who persisted in calling me Mellie regardless of whether I wanted him to.

I faced Jack, and my fury easily turned on him. "You set this up, didn't you? You knew I didn't want to see her or talk to her but you set this up anyway. How dare you? How dare you involve yourself, uninvited I might add, in something that has nothing to do with you and something I explicitly made clear to you that I wanted nothing to do with." I paused just for a second to catch my breath, ignoring my mother's presence completely since that was the only way I could remain relatively calm. "I don't want to see you again. Ever."

He raised his eyebrow, and I knew we were both remembering another time when I'd said the exact same words. I leaned forward and pressed my finger into his sweater-covered chest. "And I really mean it this time."

I stood, intending to make a graceful exit, but managed instead to bump the table and spill the remainder of my latte in addition to two tall glasses of water. I slid to the next chair to escape the deluge, and while a busboy and our waitress were cleaning up the mess, my mother used the opportunity to slide into my vacated chair, effectively holding me hostage between her and the window.

She faced the side of my head because I refused to look at her. "Please don't be angry with Jack. I'll admit to using my friendship with his mother to coerce him into helping me. It's hard to say no to Amelia Trenholm, even if you're her son."

I knew Amelia, and even liked her, but it didn't stop the need I had to get out of that restaurant and away from my mother as fast as I could. Staring down at the wooden tabletop, I said, "I haven't had anything to say to you for over thirty years, Mother. And I don't think anything has changed. So if you'll excuse me, I need to go. I'm meeting clients at nine to show them houses in the Old Village and I don't want to be late."

She didn't move and I was forced to continue staring at the darkened wood of the tabletop because I didn't want to look across from me and see the reproach in Jack's eyes.

My mother folded her hands on top of the table—still wearing her gloves—and I wondered if she wore them out of habit now or still out of necessity.

"I need your help, Mellie. Your grandmother's house on Legare is for sale again and I need your professional help in purchasing it. Everyone says that you're the best Realtor in Charleston."

Finally, I faced her for the first time, seeing the dark hair swept back in a low ponytail, her flawless skin and high cheekbones, and the green eyes I had always wanted instead of my father's hazel ones. Only the hint of fine lines at the corners of her eyes and around her mouth showed that she had aged at all since the night she said good night to me when she really should have said good-bye.

"There are hundreds of other Realtors in Charleston, Mother, all as qualified as I am, and a hell of a lot more willing, to help you purchase a home. In other words, no, thank you. I don't need to make a buck that bad."

To my surprise, she smiled. "You haven't really changed all that much."

"How would you know?" I asked, needing to wipe the smile from her face.

I heard Jack suck in a breath. "Mellie, I know you're hurt, and I wouldn't have had any part in this if I thought your mother was here just to make you feel worse. But there's more, and I think you need to listen to her. She believes you might be in danger."

I resisted the urge to roll my eyes. "Right. Well, tell her that I can take care of myself. I've been doing it for more than thirty years, after all. And I'm not speaking to you, remember?"

My mother spoke quietly beside me. "I've been having dreams. Every night. Dreams about a boat at the bottom of the ocean rising to the surface after many years. There's something—evil about it." Her eyes met mine and darkened. "And it's looking for you."

My throat tightened as a lungful of air escaped through my mouth. I recalled the phone call I'd received the night before and the feeling of dread that had followed me all morning, and I had the odd sensation that I had just fallen through thin ice into freezing water. I swallowed, giving my voice time to find me.

"It was a dream, Mother. Only a dream." I slid on my coat and fumbled with the buttons with shaking fingers before giving up on them. "And I really must go. If you need a recommendation for a good Realtor, call our receptionist, Nancy Flaherty, and she'll put you through to somebody."

"I tried to reach you, after I left. I did."

I thought of all the things I wanted to say to her—all the things I'd rehearsed saying to her if I ever saw her again—but they all seemed to fall short now that I had the opportunity. Instead, all I said was, "You should have tried harder."

To my surprise, my mother slid out of her chair and stood, a printed card held out to me between two gloved fingers. "Take my card; you're going to need it. This isn't the first time it's sought you out, you know. But it is the first time you're old enough to fight it." She paused. "We are not as we seem, Mellie."

Again, I was consumed with the feeling of plunging into icy water, and I couldn't speak. I stared at my mother without making a move to take the card. After a moment she laid it on the table, and with a brief good-bye to Jack she walked away, leaving the lingering scent of orchids and stale grief behind her.

I turned to Jack again but he held up his hand. "I know. You don't want to speak to me or see me again. I get it. But I think you need to listen to your mother. Her psychic abilities are well known and she knows what she's talking about. Sure, she could be wrong. After all, you have the gift too, right? And you're not seeing anything. But what if she's right? What if you're in some kind of danger? Don't you think you should know?"

"Why would you care?" I began to move away but he grabbed my wrist.

"I care a lot more than you'd like to think."

Our eyes met briefly but I found I couldn't hold Jack's gaze. He dropped my arm and I turned around and headed for the door. I didn't have to look back to know that he'd picked up my mother's card and was now carefully placing it inside his wallet.

CHAPTER 2

I was nearly numb by the time I made it to Henderson Realty on Broad Street. I yanked open the door—my anger not completely cooled by the cold—then let it slam behind me.

"Damn." Our receptionist, Nancy Flaherty, stood with a phone headset on her head with one hand on her hip and the other on a pitching wedge. She frowned at me, having apparently missed a chip shot due to my loud arrival.

"Sorry to interrupt your chipping practice, Nancy. I'll be more careful next time," I said as I swept past her, yanking a hanger off the coatrack, my sarcasm completely lost on her. She assumed everybody agreed that golf should replace baseball as the national pastime and would therefore understand that her pursuit of perfection in the game of golf should take precedence over everything else. Including her job. "Do I have any messages?"

She didn't look up from where she was aligning another shot. "Just your nine o'clock. They're running a bit late and will be here at nine thirty."

I squared the shoulders of my coat on the hanger before buttoning up the front so that it would hang straight. "Great, thanks." I headed toward my office, then turned around and stopped in front of Nancy again. She looked up at me, her club held in midswing.

"One more thing. If Jack Trenholm calls, I'm not here. I don't want to speak to him. Ever."

"Again?" she asked, lowering her club and focusing on the ball again.

"Excuse me?"

"Right. You're not here if he calls or stops by. Got it."

I started walking but she called me back. "And you're still not here if your mother calls."

"Exactly. But if she does call and she says she needs a Realtor, transfer her to Jimmy."

This time Nancy put her club down and turned to me. "Now, Melanie, that isn't nice."

"To Jimmy or to my mother?"

Nancy shook her head. "He's back on medication, you know, following that streaking incident at the Dock Street Theater."

"Was that before or after he painted his naked body purple and orange and ran out on the field at the last Clemson–USC game?"

"After. He's a nice guy, but he needs to channel his energy to more productive avenues, I think." She shook her head. "And even though he somehow manages to be a great Realtor, I certainly don't think he's really ready or skilled enough to mix with polite society right now."

"I know. That's why I thought he and my mother would be a good fit." I didn't wait to hear an answer but instead strode back to my office and shut the door, leaning against it and drawing deep breaths.

Now that I was alone, the enormity of what had just happened at the coffee bar began to sink in. I made my way to my desk chair and fell into it, using my hands against the desk to steady myself. *Thirty-three years*, I said to myself. It had been thirty-three years since I'd last seen my mother, and then all of a sudden, on an otherwise normal day, she had reappeared in my life. I leaned back in my chair, closing my eyes. I wanted to forget the whole episode—the way she looked, the sound of her voice. But her last words kept swirling around my head like a fallen leaf that got swept up into a wind, unsure where to fall. *We are not as we seem.* I had heard those words before, of course. Recently even, in a phone call, those exact words had been spoken to me by a woman who'd been dead for more than three decades.

The phone on my desk rang, jarring me and reminding me where I was. I picked it up on the third ring.

"Melanie, I have a prospective client on line one for you."

"Who is it?" I asked, eager to speak to somebody about anything other than dreams, mothers, or phone calls from the dead.

"Her name's Rebecca Edgerton. She says she's an old friend of Jack's. But don't hold that against her," Nancy added quickly. "I don't think she realizes that you're not on speaking terms with him. Again."

I sighed heavily into the phone. "Fine. Put her through. Maybe I'll like her anyway."

I heard a click and then a soft female voice with definitive Charleston inflections. "Hello? Is this Melanie Middleton?"

"This is she," I said, curious as to how she knew Jack.

"I'm a reporter with the *Post & Courier*. I wouldn't normally call a potential source out of the blue like this, but our mutual friend, Jack Trenholm, said that you were very approachable."

I raised an eyebrow. "Did he now? So can I assume this isn't about real estate?"

"Um, no. Not exactly. I'm actually doing a piece on famous Charlestonians of the last fifty years, and I wanted to ask you some questions about Ginnette Prioleau Middleton. Your mother."

I was too surprised to realize I should hang up the phone and instead said nothing.

"To be fair to Jack, I will tell you that he told me that you and your mother have been estranged for a number of years and that you might not be receptive to answering any of my questions. But then Jack told me to mention the readership the paper gets and how people reading that you're related to the famous opera singer might bring in a lot of business for you."

My cheeks flamed red at how accurately Jack could read me. My career had been my number one priority for a long time. But he was wrong about this one thing. "Go on," I said through a tightening throat.

"Even though my story will be about your mother, I thought getting your perspective first would make this an eye-opening piece for my readers. I mean, sure, she's a world-renowned opera star. But at what personal cost? I understand she abandoned you when you were a little girl to pursue her singing career. That must have made a mark on you."

We are not as we seem. I swallowed, struggling hard to sound normal. "That's not—that's not why she left."

There was a short pause. "Really? That's not what I've heard. So, why did she leave?"

I thought back to the days after my grandmother Prioleau's death following a fall down the stairs in her house on Legare Street, and how a darkness had descended over the house and garden, silencing the summer sounds as if we'd suddenly been submerged in water. And then I remembered my mother putting me to bed, her tears hot on my forehead as she leaned over me. She told me that there were things I was too young to understand and too weak to fight, and that sometimes people had to do the right thing even if it meant letting go of the one thing they loved most in the world. I remembered the sound of hushed voices from people who weren't there; I remembered them because that was the last time I heard them. Then my mother told me that she loved me and kissed me good night. I went to sleep immediately afterward and awoke in the morning to find my father in my room, packing my things and telling me that my mother had gone and that I was going to live with him on an army base in Japan.

I forced myself back to the present. "I don't know," I managed. "You'll have to ask her yourself."

I was about to hang up when Rebecca spoke again. "Actually, I did. And she told me I should ask your maternal grandmother, a Sarah Manigault Prioleau. But records indicate she's been deceased since 1975. Do I have that wrong?"

I paused—unsure how to answer—and finally decided on the truth. "No. That's right. My grandmother died when I was seven years old."

"Then why would your mother suggest . . ."

"Good-bye, Ms. Edgerton. I'm sorry I can't help you."

I hung up the phone, my hand lingering on the receiver for a long time as I wondered why, after all this time, my mother had come back— and why she'd brought my grandmother with her.

Despite a productive meeting with my new clients and two accepted counteroffers on houses South of Broad and on Daniel Island respectively, I returned home grumpy and out of sorts. As I pulled into the old carriage house that had been converted into a garage behind my house on Tradd Street, a feeling of calm came over me. Not that I would admit it to anybody, but the dramatic restoration in progress gave me an enormous sense of pride and accomplishment. Having reached this point by accident and by the sheer force of the will of my preservation-minded friends, I was loath to admit to anybody that I actually liked the house and felt at home in it. And that I looked forward to whatever the next project might be.

I spotted Sophie's lime green Volkswagen Beetle at the curb and smiled to myself. As a professor of historical restoration at the College of Charleston, Dr. Sophie Wallen was not only my best friend, but she was also my right arm in the restoration work on my house. My smile slipped a little as I realized that in addition to being my right arm, she was also my conscience. She would no doubt worm out of me—if Jack hadn't already told her—what had happened with my mother that morning and then admonish me for not asking my mother to come stay with me while I worked on the purchase of the house on Legare.

With a sigh, I made my way through the garden gate, then up to the front door of the Charleston single house, the buttery light from the fan window above the door spilling onto the floor of the covered front porch like a warm welcome mat. Before I got my key out of my purse, the door flung open and Sophie—her untamed hair swarming around her head like wild bees and covered in what looked like white paint flecks—stood in front of me. "You're home. Just in time!"

She threw the door open wider and General Lee bounded toward me, yapping excitedly. I dropped my briefcase and purse and swooped him up in my arms, reluctant to concede that the little fur ball had grown on me as much as the house had. There was certainly something to say about living with a guy who was always happy to see you, never argued, didn't leave the toilet seat up, and could keep you warm in bed at night. At almost forty, I'd pretty much reconciled myself to a life of singleness, and I found the companionship of a dog a fair trade-off.

Sophie sneezed. "Sorry—I've been keeping him in a different room from me so I wouldn't have an allergic reaction. It's not so bad, though." She sneezed again, accenting her point.

"Let me go put him in the kitchen with Mrs. Houlihan. She always saves a soup bone for him." I walked to the back of the house and pushed open the kitchen door, depositing General Lee and greeting my housekeeper, yet something else I'd inherited from the home's former occupant.

I returned to Sophie, who was dabbing at her streaming eyes with the hem of the tie-dyed T-shirt she wore over a long, quilted skirt that brushed the top of her Birkenstocks. Of all the things I liked and appreciated about Sophie, her sense of style wasn't one of them. I reached over and plucked a paint chip out of her hair. "What's this?" I asked, holding it up between my fingers.

"You need to come see the upstairs drawing room. You'd hardly recognize it. I've been scraping away over a hundred years' worth of paint from the ceiling cornices and it's like I've discovered heaven."

I blinked a couple of times, trying to equate ceiling cornices and heaven in my mind before giving up. Instead I just said, "Great. What's next on the agenda?"

"Refinishing the floors in the whole house. They'll need to be hand stripped, so it will probably take a while, but I don't want to see a machine tearing up the wood grain on those beautiful floors."

I looked away, pretending to study the elegant mahogany balustrade I remembered staining by hand and the numbness in my lower back that had lasted for weeks afterward as a reminder. Throughout the restoration, I'd snuck in sanders, heat guns, and an assortment of other contraband modern conveniences behind Sophie's back to preserve my own. I intended for both the house and me still to be standing by the end of the restoration.

"Whatever's best," I said noncommittally as I leaned forward to stare at an imaginary smudge in the stain.

"Uh-huh," she said as she blew her nose on a wadded Kleenex before shoving it back into the pocket of her hideous skirt. She walked past me to the large main staircase and I followed behind her.

"How's Chad?" I asked, referring to another professor at the college who had originally been my client until he'd met Sophie and decided to move in with her. As just roommates, or so they both claimed.

"Don't change the subject, Melanie. We were talking about your mother."

I stopped. "Actually, we weren't. And we're not going to, either. Did Jack call you?"

"No, your father did. Jack called him."

I slapped my hand against the banister. "Great, so now all of you can condemn me for being so unfeeling. The point you all seem to be missing is that I'm the victim here."

Sophie paused at the top of the stairs and waited for me to catch up. "You're only a victim if you choose to be."

"I didn't *choose* to be abandoned by my mother, in case you didn't notice. And yes, my dad recently told me that she tried to speak with me many times while I was growing up but that he interfered. But it doesn't change the fact that she just left me without saying good-bye and without a reason why. I've gotten over it and made my own life. And there's no room in it for her."

Sophie regarded me for a long moment. "Did you ever think that there might have been a really good reason for her to leave? Have you ever asked her?"

I swallowed, knowing her questions had been my own for a child's handful of years until all my grief and hurt had finally buried even the tiniest glimmer of hope that my mother's reason for leaving had been about anything else but me.

Instead of answering, I walked past her to the double doors that led into the upstairs drawing room. "Come show me those amazing cornices."

I heard her following behind me. "Ignoring the problem won't make it go away, you know. It's always the problems we try our hardest to ignore that eventually end up biting us on the butt."

Facing her, I said, "Well, then. I guess I don't need to worry about it, do I? I don't have a problem; therefore my butt can't get bitten."

Sophie opened her mouth to say something but was interrupted by the doorbell.

As I headed down the stairs I heard her say under her breath, "Or maybe that butt bite might happen a little sooner than we expected."

I glared at her over my shoulder before I opened the door and saw my father standing on the threshold, a bouquet of pink roses cradled in his arms like a newborn.

"Hi, Dad," I said as I kissed him on the cheek. His robust appearance still hit me softly around the heart despite nearly six months of getting used to his being sober. I'd never known him this way, and we'd both been wading into unfamiliar territory as we renavigated the father-daughter roles that had been reversed when I was a child. We were like new coworkers, still trying to determine which of us got the desk by the window.

I noticed he was looking over my shoulder, and I stepped back to allow him to enter. "Come in. Are you here for dinner? I could ask Mrs. Houlihan to set an extra place."

Sophie's voice sounded a little forced. "Hello, Colonel Middleton. I've got a stack of receipts for you, so don't leave without getting them from me."

My dad, the trustee for my former client Nevin Vanderhorst's house and estate—of which I was the only beneficiary—was responsible for overseeing the costs of the restoration. And for playing referee between Sophie and the rest of us mortals working on the house—whose need to employ authentic materials and processes wasn't nearly as rigid as hers.

I glanced from one to the other, realizing an undercurrent of communication was going on between them, their forced words making it clear that they didn't want me in on the secret. I looked at the roses. "Are these for me?"

"No," he said at the same time Sophie said, "Yes." I closed the door behind me and put my hands on my hips. "What's going on here?"

Again, they exchanged glances, confirming my suspicions. Finally, my father cleared his voice and spoke. "Pink roses are your mother's favorite."

I stopped to think for a moment. "Why on earth would you be bringing Mother roses here?"

I stepped between them so that they couldn't make eye contact and faced my father. "What did Jack tell you that would make you think Mother would be at my house?"

Sheepishly, he placed the bouquet on the hall table. "I spoke to him this morning before he met you for breakfast. He was pretty sure that after you listened to what your mother had to say, you would invite her here to stay with you. I, uh, assume things didn't work out the way Jack thought?"

"That would be a real good assumption." I stepped back to include Sophie. "And you bought into this, too?"

"Your mother convinced Jack that you were in danger. We all thought that would make you listen to her."

I walked across the marble foyer, heels clicking with my agitated steps, and into the restored drawing room with the stately mahogany grandfather clock that dominated one side of the room. I flopped down into a French sofa with faded yellow silk upholstery—returned from storage to be reupholstered—then stood again to fluff the cushions. "You all thought that after more than thirty years of avoiding her I might forgive her in fifteen minutes and invite her to live with me? Are you all out of your minds?" I walked around the room, straightening pillows, dusting off the tops of picture frames with my index finger, and rewinding the clock—anything to keep from using my hands to squeeze the breath out of somebody's throat.

Sophie sat down on a Chippendale chair, her Birkenstocks looking out of place next to the delicately carved ball-and-claw legs. Quietly, she said, "I saw the phone out in the hallway, Melanie. Something's up, isn't it?"

Sophie was one of exactly two people—Jack being the other—I'd confided in about my peculiar "gift." My ability to communicate with the dead never felt like much of a gift because it had caused more trauma in my life than anything else, but it was reassuring to know there were others out there who believed you when you told them that your dead grandmother liked to call you on the phone to let you know there was trouble in the air. Unfortunately, my father was not one of them.

"Wait a minute," he said. "Nobody mentioned any hocus-pocus. Your mother told me she'd been having disturbing dreams. That's all, nothing about phone calls from dead people. You know how I feel about that, Melanie. It's not healthy to think that stuff's real."

I sat down in a chair identical to the one Sophie had chosen and put my chin in my hands. "Dad, I'm not having this conversation with you. Especially when I should be asking you about those flowers. Mother left *you*, remember? She dumped me with you and then left. So if you're bringing her flowers because you still have feelings for her, I think I might have to throw up."

My father cleared his throat again, something he always did when he was nervous, and managed to look hurt. "I brought them because I thought they might help a bit with dealing with what happened to her mother's grave."

Both Sophie and I turned to him. "What are you talking about?" we asked in unison.

"Oh, you haven't heard? It was on the twelve o'clock news this afternoon. They said somebody vandalized St. Philip's cemetery this afternoon. I was about to change the channel when I heard them mention the name Sarah Manigault Prioleau. Apparently, hers was the only grave that was disturbed."

Sophie stood. "That's your grandmother, right, Melanie?"

I nodded, the odd sensation of drowning sweeping over me again. I turned my head, catching the pungent smell of salt water. It faded softly, making me wonder if I'd smelled it at all. "Do you smell that?"

Both my father and Sophie shook their heads. "Smell what?" my father asked.

"Never mind." I faced my father again. "Do they know who did it?"

"No. The tombstone was toppled but no other damage was done to it or other graves." He shook his head. "They interviewed somebody on the grounds committee of the church who said that the tombstone could not have been lifted out intact except by some kind of construction equipment, but there was no sign of anything despite it being broad daylight."

I felt Sophie staring at me. "Was there anything unusual about the tombstone, Melanie?"

Shrugging, I said, "I don't know. I've never seen it. I went to her funeral, but I left with Dad for Japan right afterward and never saw the tombstone my grandmother selected prior to her death."

"You mean you haven't been to visit since you came back to Charleston?"

Embarrassed, I focused on standing and refluffing the seat cushion. "No. I just . . ." I stopped, then tried again. "It would have reminded me too much about a period of my life that I preferred to pretend never happened."

My father moved toward me. "Like how your mother always told you that your grandmother's house on Legare would one day be yours and then sold it after your grandmother died?"

I looked at him in surprise. "You never said anything to me about that. I never thought you knew. Or cared."

He gave me a half smile. "Oh, I knew. And I cared. But there was nothing I could have done about it. And you made it very clear that you didn't want to talk about it or your mother. Even drunk, I couldn't take your screaming fits. So I just let it go."

Sophie approached and put her arm around my shoulder. "I'm thinking you need to go to the cemetery. I'll come with you if you want."

"Me, too," said my father, although I could see he was uncomfortable. Things had always had to be black or white to him. The shady area between light and darkness that my mother and I inhabited didn't exist for him. I had long since learned to skirt the issue with him, and he developed his own "don't ask, don't tell" policy as far as my sixth sense was concerned.

We are not as we seem. I closed my eyes, trying to block out the words and the distant voice on the telephone. After Jack and I had spent half a year eradicating the ghosts that had haunted my new home, I had hoped that my days of ghost hunting were over. Disembodied voices on a telephone made it obvious that perhaps they weren't. A sliver of apprehension crept up my spine and wedged its way into my false bravado despite my efforts to minimize the implications.

I straightened my shoulders, trying to shake the feeling of unease. "Thank you both, but I think I can handle this. I'll go first thing tomorrow morning to pay my respects and take care of anything that needs to be done to repair the stone so my mother doesn't have to. But then I'm through. That's it. And don't think for one minute that any of this means that I'm going to be forging a relationship with my mother now because I'm not."

I pretended that I didn't notice Sophie and my father exchanging glances with each other and instead marched toward the kitchen, the smell of salt water suddenly heavy in the air.

CHAPTER 3

Since I was a young girl, I'd learned to avoid hospitals, battlefields, and cemeteries. At first I'd thought everybody could hear the cacophony of voices, but it was only after I realized that they were calling my name that I learned how very different I was. I was the only child in elementary school who consistently missed every field trip to historic sites due to sudden onsets of stomach pains and headaches against which my father was powerless. Even back then I knew that revealing I was different would have been social suicide, and thus a lifetime of avoidance and denial was launched. The fact that my mother and I shared this odd gift coupled with my father's insistence that whatever I saw was in my imagination gave me even more reason to pretend otherwise.

I parked my car on Church Street about a block down from St. Philip's cemetery, where my grandmother was buried. Even though I didn't remember exactly where she'd been interred, and the yellow police tape notwithstanding, I would have known approximately where to find her as only those who were born in Charleston were allowed to be buried on the same side of the street as the church. Even famed statesman John C. Calhoun was buried across the street, since he'd been born in Clemson, South Carolina. I remembered my mother gleefully mentioning that his wife, a true Charlestonian, was buried in a separate grave—across the street and nearer the church—as if even in death being a Charlestonian was more important than being Mr. Calhoun's wife.

I heard the babble of voices as I neared the cemetery gates, though I was experienced enough by now to know not to look around to see who was talking. Taking a deep breath, I focused on the sidewalk in front

---

of me and sang the words to ABBA's "Dancing Queen" under my breath to keep from hearing my name called over and over. I knew that if I kept walking—and kept ignoring them—they would eventually stop. My mother once told me that we were beacons of light. It wasn't until after she left that I figured out to whom, but by then I'd only ever seen myself as a moving target, eager not to get hit.

My grandmother's grave was toward the back of the cemetery, near the fence. I remembered now standing here with my mother and father feeling the scratchy starchiness of my new black cotton dress, the high humidity of summer, and the oppressive scent of too many flowers making me sigh in the heat. My father had taken me up in his arms and that's when I'd seen all of the people crowding around the empty grave—not all of them breathing. Most disconcerting of all was that they all were looking at me.

I stopped outside the yellow police tape that surrounded the grave site—my breath blowing fat puffs of steam into the chilly air—and noted the neatly trimmed grass and the white marble tombstone that looked like it had been gently pulled from the sucking earth and laid to rest on the cool grass. There was no disturbance of the nearby grass or graves, and the hole in which it had stood lay a foot in front of it as if to clarify that the stone hadn't just toppled over but had been deliberately placed.

After first glancing around to make sure nobody was watching, I stepped over the yellow tape and walked closer to the stone so I could get a better look. In carved lettering, I read my grandmother's birth and death dates as well as her complete name, Sarah Manigault Prioleau. Then my eyes widened as I read the inscription beneath:

When bricks crumble, the fireplace falls;
When children cry, the mothers call.
When lies are told, the sins are built,
Within the waves, hide all our guilt.

I read the words two more times, trying to make sense of them. Then my gaze shifted back to the woman's name to make sure that I was at the right grave. *Within the waves, hide all our guilt.* I recalled the scent of salt water wafting through my house and drops of ice slipped down my back.

"I don't know what it means, either, if that's any consolation."

I jerked my head around to see my mother standing behind me wearing a black mink coat with matching hat, her gloved hands clutching the neck closed against the bitter cold. *Always the gloves.*

"It's not," I said coolly.

She moved to stand next to me and gazed down toward the stone. "It's odd how spirits choose to manifest themselves, isn't it? She's trying to tell us something."

"You think so?" I asked, using sarcasm to hide the brief shimmer of hope I'd felt when she'd used the word "us."

Her eyes met mine and she smiled. "What I don't know is what we're going to do about it."

I shoved my hands deep inside my pockets as much because of the cold as because I needed to tighten them into fists. "There's no 'we're' about it. I'm going inside now to find out if I need to pay to get it fixed or if they have insurance for this kind of thing."

I made a move to go past her, but she put her hand on my arm. "Mellie, this is serious. I think this is related to my dream, and if it is, then you're in more danger than I thought."

"Then I'll deal with it. Alone. Like I have for thirty-three years." I shook my arm free and stepped over the tape.

"Do you remember the day your grandmother died?"

I stopped, an old memory pushing at my brain like a scar that hadn't faded enough to let you forget what caused it completely. "Yes," I said. "She fell down the stairs." Slowly, I faced my mother. A look of relief passed over her face, and I realized that she hadn't expected me to stay.

She continued. "She was still alive when I found her at the bottom of the steps."

"That's not what the police report said. She tripped on her high heels and fell. She died immediately." I only knew this because of some perverse curiosity that had made me search through my father's papers once when he was on yet another drinking binge. In a childlike rage, I had hoped to find the reason my mother had abandoned me documented somewhere. As if by seeing it in black-and-white, I could find a way to defend myself. But all I'd found were my parents' divorce papers stating the reason as irreconcilable differences and a copy of the police report concerning my grandmother's sudden death.

My mother raised an elegant eyebrow but didn't ask me how I knew. It was like I was a little girl again and she knew all there was to know about me, which always made it that much harder to handle her abandonment. Everything she knew about me wasn't enough to make her stay.

She dipped her head and I could see her struggling for composure. "I held her head in my lap while she died. I heard her last words."

My lips were numb from the cold and something else I didn't want to name. "What did she say?"

Her eyes met mine. "We are not as we seem."

I shivered inside of my coat, the old memory pressing at my brain again. "What does that mean?" My voice was swept away by a gust of wind, and I realized again that my mother didn't need to hear me to understand what I was saying.

She looked past me, toward the toppled gravestone. "I don't know. But there's something in that house. Something evil. A presence in the house that's been there since I was born."

I swallowed. "Is that why you sold it?"

She nodded but didn't meet my eyes.

"Then why do you want to buy the house back? If it's haunted by an evil presence, why?"

My mother didn't answer right away but didn't move her gaze from my face, either. "Because it's our house, Mellie. Because it was in our family for over two hundred years." She paused. "And I'm stronger now. I can fight it now." She closed her mouth tightly, as if she were afraid unguarded words would leak out, and I knew right away that she was hiding something. The nuances of a mother's face are never lost on her children, even long after a child may have wanted to forget.

My hands balled into fists again. "Don't stress yourself on my account, Mother. I have my own house now, so it's immaterial to me what you do with the house on Legare. Just don't try to pretend that you're concerned about my legacy, because we both know that would be a lie."

She took a step in my direction, her breath fanning out toward me like a web. "There's so much you don't understand, Mellie, and I don't expect you to sit down with me and listen while I try to explain it to you. Just know that my dreams and what's happened here and what's written on her gravestone are all related. Your grandmother needs us to stand together on this, to face what's coming."

I looked at her for a long moment, seeing only a stranger. I watched as the wind blew the fur around her face and flattened the winter grass like a giant's footprint and knew there was more to why she was here. But like her reasons for leaving, her reasons for returning were no longer important to me.

"I'm pretty good at facing things alone, Mother. You taught me that, after all. And it would take a lot more than just a riddle on a tombstone and a silly dream to make me spend any time with you at all." I drew my hand out of my pocket to look at my watch, realizing that I couldn't tell the time because my hand was shaking so badly.

I continued, forcing my voice to remain calm. "I'm going inside to talk to the person in charge, and then I'm heading back to the office. If I don't see you before your trip back home—wherever that is—have a nice flight."

She didn't try to stop me this time as I turned on my heel and headed toward the church. I'd almost reached the front doors before she finally spoke. "I'm sorry, Mellie. I'm sorry I had to leave. I know you don't believe that now, but I had to go."

I kept walking, feeling the tears freeze in my eyes.

"I smell the ocean, Mellie. And I know you do, too."

I pulled open the door and stepped inside, the babble of voices rising behind me like the tide. I let the door bang shut behind me but not before the wind blew in the pungent scent of the sea.

The rest of my day didn't go any better. Two of my offers were rejected—one without a counter—and another house I had under contract in Ansonborough failed the inspection. Repair estimates were hovering around ten thousand and the buyers were balking.

I was in a foul mood when I returned to my empty house and the cold turkey potpie Mrs. Houlihan had left for me in the oven. I ended up feeding half of it to the dog, and then, in a moment of desperation, I decided to take him for a walk.

The day had warmed up considerably, and even now—with the sun setting in wintry pinks and oranges on the horizon—the temperature was bearable. I pulled on my coat and gloves and dressed General Lee in the new argyle sweater Nancy Flaherty had knitted for him and headed out the door. I was embarrassed to be seen with him, having never before been offended by dog nudity, but he'd begun shivering uncontrollably when the thermostat hit below sixty. Nancy told me I could either buy him a condo in Florida or I could accept the sweater.

As usual, I allowed General Lee to decide which route we'd take and we headed out at a brisk trot, the dog a couple of feet in front of me, his nose leading the way, pausing now and again to sniff a front step or growl at a stranger. General Lee had taken it upon himself to become my guard dog, attempting to keep strangers at bay until he had a chance to inspect them. Even then, he was picky about whom to make friends with and would continue to growl if they didn't pass his inspection. Unfortunately for him, despite having the heart and soul of a police dog, he appeared about as threatening as an argyle-draped sofa cushion.

I was so busy thinking about counteroffers and inspection reports that I didn't realize where General Lee was taking us until it was too late. He stopped in front of a set of wrought iron gates on Legare Street, and I had to blink twice before I realized where we were. My gaze swung to the house number stenciled in gold on the mailbox attached to the gate and I blinked again: *Thirty-three Legare.*

The square brick Georgian house with the two-tiered portico domi-nated the garden that grew up around it, which had been brightly colored and intricately designed like jewelry for an already-beautiful woman. I remembered having tea in these gardens with my grandmother and I felt the old sadness return.

Eager to leave, I tugged on the leash but General Lee seemed adamant about staying. I was about to pick him up and carry him back home when I realized we weren't alone. Startled, I turned to examine the lone figure standing about ten feet away from me near the fence, her study of the house apparently interrupted by our arrival. As usual, I wasn't wear-ing my glasses—my one nod to vanity—but I was struck by how familiar she looked.

The stranger began to walk toward me, giving me a better chance to see her in the fading light. She was shorter than my own five feet eight inches and slender—what most people would call petite. Her wavy blond hair hung loosely around her shoulders and Burberry overcoat, and I saw as she grew closer that she carried a notepad and pencil.

"Do I know you?" I asked, studying her more closely, trying to place where I'd seen her before.

"Not in person," she said, stepping closer so I could see the long lashes over clear blue eyes.

I froze, finally realizing why she seemed so familiar. "Emily?" I whispered, my throat tight with shock.

She looked at me oddly. "I used to get that a lot." She bent down and scratched General Lee behind his ears, and I belatedly noticed that he hadn't let out a peep and was trying to roll onto his back to allow this stranger to scratch his belly.

I tugged on his leash to bring him closer to me. "Who are you?"

She stood and faced me and I felt the shock course through me again. Sticking her hand out toward me, she said, "I'm Rebecca Edgerton. We spoke briefly on the phone. About your mother."

Absently, I shook her hand, unable to tear my gaze away from her face. And then the word "mother" brought me back to attention. I yanked my hand away. "Oh, the reporter from the newspaper. I remember."

"I thought I might come see the house she grew up in. Start at the beginning of her story."

I continued to stare at her, unable to shake my first impression. "You look so much like . . ." I couldn't say the name again.

"Emily. I know. I've let my hair grow so I guess the resemblance is even stronger now, but when Emily and I worked together at the paper we would get confused for each other all the time. People used to say that when Jack stopped dating me and started dating Emily he wasn't even aware that he'd switched girlfriends." She laughed, the sound broken, pierced like a veil.

I took a deep breath, more relieved than I could explain.

Rebecca's brow wrinkled. "I didn't realize you knew her."

"I, um, I didn't, actually." I thought for a moment, trying to come up with a better way to explain that I knew what a dead woman looked like because I'd seen her ghost. "Jack must have shown me a picture."

26   KAREN WHITE

She nodded. "Oh, well. That explains it then."

There was something in her expression I couldn't read, something unexpected that made me take a step back. "Well, it was nice meeting you." I pulled on the leash, annoyed to notice that my dog had made himself very comfortable by nestling at her feet. "Come on, General Lee. Let's go home and eat dinner." He stared at me blankly, not moving.

Rebecca took the opportunity to close the distance between us. "Since you're here, maybe you could answer a few questions. Nothing too personal, I promise. Just enough to get me started. If I say anything out of line, just tell me and I'll stop."

The dog was looking up at Rebecca with adoring eyes, and I figured it had to be the blond hair. He was male, after all. "I really don't think so. We're estranged, and I'm afraid your story will have a negative tone if you start with me. I'm sure you wouldn't want that."

"I want the truth; that's all. I hope to get enough interviews to make it a balanced article, but I'm beginning to think that I can't write it at all without insight from her only child."

"Unfortunately, you're going to have to. I know very little about my mother. The truth or otherwise. She left my father and me when I was only seven years old."

Rebecca looked down at her notebook and flipped a page. "Yes. I've got that. It was right after your mother's trip to the emergency room. A miscarriage, I believe."

"A what?" I stared at her blankly, not sure I'd heard correctly.

She glanced up at me. "A miscarriage. A serious one. She almost died according to the hospital records. I guess you would have been about six or seven at the time because it was after your parents separated. You and your mother were living here with your grandmother when it happened. I assumed . . ." She shrugged. "I'm sorry. I thought you would have known."

The back of my mouth tasted like rust. I remembered my father showing up at my grandmother's house and my excitement when I thought he was there to take us both home. But he'd left me there and carried my mother to the car in his arms like a baby. Later my grandmother told me that she'd had appendicitis and needed to stay in the hospital for a couple of days but would be fine. And I had believed her despite how thin my mother looked when she returned or how a baby's crying had been added to the litany of sounds I chased but never found in my grandmother's house.

I shook my head. "No. I didn't know." I tried to smile. "They probably thought I was too young to understand how babies were made"—my smile dropped—"or lost. How did you find out?"

She shrugged but her gaze remained intense. "It's part of my job. I just know where to look and who to ask. I saw an old newspaper article in the archives about your grandmother's death, and there was a brief mention of how it followed on the heels of your mother's hospital stay. It didn't say why she was there of course, but I have an anonymous source at the hospital who looked through the records and found out about the miscarriage. All confidential, of course." She paused for a moment. "The information you need is always there if you're willing to be persistent and look hard enough."

I felt we weren't talking about my mother's illness anymore. Suddenly uncomfortable I took a step back. "I really need to get home now. . . ."

She looked disappointed. "I understand. But just one more thing—please. I want to show you a picture. I promise I will only take one more minute of your time." She smiled, and she looked so much like the dead Emily that I paused, giving Rebecca her chance to whip an enlarged photo of my mother at an opera charity event in New York from her oversized purse.

"You look a lot like her."

I didn't say anything. I'd always hated it when people told me that—mostly because it wasn't true but also because I liked to pretend that we weren't even related.

Rebecca held the picture closer to my face. "She's wearing the most beautiful necklace and earrings in this photo. Do you know anything about them?"

I stared down at the photo, at the diamond-and-sapphire collar necklace and matching chandelier earrings. I remembered my grandmother allowing me to play dress-up with them, sometimes using her silk bathrobe as my gown as I paraded up and down the hallways. "Yes," I said. "They were my grandmother's. My mother must have inherited them when my grandmother passed."

"So they're family heirlooms?" Her eyes narrowed slightly.

"I suppose you could call them that. I do know my grandmother said that they had once been her mother's. How much further back they go I have no idea. To be honest, I think they're a bit gaudy and if they were mine, I'd probably sell them."

"Like your mother sold this house."

I jerked my head up to meet her eyes. "I think I've answered enough questions." I yanked hard on the leash this time, forcing General Lee from his reclining position at Rebecca's feet, and began to walk away, pulling the reluctant dog. "Good night, Miss Edgerton. It was nice meeting you."

"You can call me Rebecca."

I continued to walk away. "Fine, but I don't think we'll be seeing each other again. Good night."

I was about to turn the corner when I heard her say, "Don't bet on it."

Pretending not to hear her, I tugged on the leash and pulled General Lee around the corner with me, wondering what it was about Rebecca Edgerton, besides her resemblance to Jack's dead fiancée, that made me so uneasy.

CHAPTER 4

The rest of my week seemed to pass in slow motion. With the high drama at the beginning of the week—marked by my mother's sudden appearance and my grandmother's bid for attention from the grave—I suppose it was inevitable. But even at work time crept by, my usual enthusiasm for my job somewhat muted as if I were being forced to view my life through half-closed eyes.

On Friday morning as I dragged myself into the office, Nancy Flaherty met me at the door, her golf ball earrings swaying in time to her movements. "You look terrible," she said as she took my coat and briefcase.

"Thank you, Nancy. And how are you?"

She draped my coat over her arm, then reached behind her to the receptionist's desk and picked up a steaming mug of coffee before pressing it into my hands. "I'm thinking your grumpiness lately is because you're missing Jack."

"Because I'm what?" My indignation was forced, mostly because I had the sneaking suspicion that she could be right. "Don't be ridiculous. It's been kind of peaceful without him barging into my house to do research at all hours of the day and night," I said, referring to the book he was currently writing about the former residents of the house I'd inherited. "And I don't have to put up with any of his ridiculous observations or silly comments." I took a sip of my coffee, studying it carefully so I wouldn't have to meet Nancy's knowing eyes. I would never admit to her, or anyone, that despite the presence of Mrs. Houlihan, my dad, Sophie, and Chad, the house had seemed a little empty without Jack's overwhelming presence. Even General Lee hadn't been able to fill the void.

I raised my head, narrowing my eyes. "And why are you being so overly nice to me this morning?" I asked, indicating the coffee and my coat, which was still slung over her arm. "What's wrong?"

She pursed her lips as if deciding whether to lie to me or just blurt the truth out. Apparently deciding on the latter, she said, "Mr. Henderson's waiting in your office. He wants to speak with you."

Although Dave Henderson was technically my boss and the owner of the company, he spent most of his time playing golf—which was what accounted for Nancy's continued employment. There were few other employers who could put up with such a marked devotion to the game of golf to the exclusion of just about everything else—including running a business. Dave had been forced into an early retirement by his wife and cardiologist, which produced a collective sigh of relief by every employee of Henderson Realty. The relief was temporary at best, though, seeing as how he made a point of showing up at the most unexpected times, making sure everybody knew he was still the boss and keeping an eye on productivity. Mostly I saw Dave at sales awards dinners and the weekly sales meetings, where he served as main cheerleader and lead butt kicker. But he was rarely in the office on a nice day—even in the freezing cold. If the sun was shining, Dave was on a green.

I put the coffee mug down, feeling suddenly ill, the donuts and latte from Ruth's Bakery that I'd wolfed down earlier threatening to make a reappearance. "Any idea why he wants to see me?"

Nancy gave me a nervous smile. "I'm not sure. But I think it has something to do with Jimmy. They were in his office yesterday and there was a lot of yelling going on."

"Oh, crap," I said, picking up my briefcase and mentally girding my loins. If Dave Henderson was waiting in my office instead of on a green somewhere, it couldn't be good.

I stood outside my closed office door for a full minute, finding my composure, before turning the handle and standing on the threshold with a bright smile. Dave was sitting at my desk, reading the latest edition of the *Post & Courier*. My Day-Timer calendar, which I kept closed on the corner of my desk, was open as if he'd just been going through it. He wore a golf shirt under a warm Windbreaker and khakis, like he'd been yanked off of the sixteenth hole somewhere, and my mood shifted from simple apprehension to sheer terror.

"Good morning, Dave. It's so good to see you." I plastered a smile on my face so he wouldn't know I was lying.

He continued to read the paper without looking up. "Interesting story in today's paper. They're going to raise that sailboat they found off of Sullivan's Island a few weeks ago. The divers they sent down discovered the name of the boat, apparently one that's been missing since the earthquake of 1886. It's in a relatively shallow area and they're thinking they can raise it intact. If not, they'll just salvage what they can." He rattled the paper as he turned the page. "People are almost as excited as they were when they discovered the *Hunley*."

"Interesting," I said, entering my office slowly and putting my purse and briefcase on a chair before sitting down opposite him. I had no idea what he was talking about, since the only thing I used the newspaper for was to examine the real estate listings.

"You are familiar with the *Hunley*, right?"

I forced myself not to roll my eyes at him. One could not be a Charlestonian and not know about the Confederate submarine that had sunk almost one and a half centuries before and had recently been raised to great fanfare. I might not know how many points the Dow average had plummeted in the last weeks, but I knew about the *Hunley*.

I glanced down at my opened calendar and began to feel a little annoyed. I flicked my eyes up, realizing that Dave was watching me.

"You've got a pretty busy schedule this week, Melanie."

Maybe this wasn't such a bad thing after all. I smiled, keeping my lips from quivering. "Yes. I do. Business has been very good, despite the real estate market not being what we'd want it to be right now. I've already met my sales quota for the month and we're only halfway through."

He began folding up the newspaper, making deliberate sharp creases as he folded it smaller and smaller. I began to feel nervous again. He slapped the newspaper on my desk and stood. I stood, too, not wanting to give him the advantage of towering over me. With heels, we were on an even keel.

"But you'd still be able to fit in a new client or two," he said, examining me closely with brown eyes that were rumored to have made grown men cry.

I swallowed. "Of course. I pride myself on being organized and diligent, and I'm more than capable of handling a fairly large workload. You know that, Mr. Henderson."

He put his fists on my desk and leaned toward me, his face flushing a little. "Then why would you send a celebrity client to Jimmy Thornhill instead of taking her on yourself? Especially when she's your own mother?"

I drew myself up to my full height, my anger greedily taking over my apprehension. "Because Jimmy needs the boost of confidence a big sale could give him. My mother knows the house she wants, so it wouldn't stress him very much. She just needs somebody to handle the paperwork for her." I glared at him. "And why should it matter to you? Henderson Realty gets credit for the sale regardless of who handles it."

He came around the desk so that he stood in front of me. "I care when a potential client has to call me personally to ask for another Realtor."

I swallowed, forcing myself to make my voice sound strong. "My mother called you?"

"Yes. We're acquaintances from years ago. She was almost in tears when she called me, wondering why you wouldn't help her."

"And what did you tell her?" My two donuts and latte fell firmly into the pit of my stomach.

He smiled his closing smile—the smile I knew meant that business was over and he'd won. "I told her that you would call her this morning to schedule a showing of the Legare Street property." He straightened. "Unless, of course, you're not strong enough to look past your differences with your mother to clinch this sale. You'd grab the top sales award for the month for sure." He reached over to my credenza and picked up his golf glove.

"Of course, I could let Wendy Wax handle the sale. Her numbers are pretty close to yours, you know."

"But what about Jimmy? He could really use the sale."

Dave shrugged. "Too soft. The Texan who owns the house on Legare is a real tightwad. I've met him a few times at the club. Never buys his round of drinks, if you know what I mean. We need somebody real sharp for this deal. And Wendy can handle it if you're too busy."

I couldn't stand the thought of my coworker's smugness if she handled this deal instead of me. I knew I'd been played but I couldn't stop myself. "No. That's fine. I'll handle it."

He saluted me with his golf glove. "That's the Melanie I know. Well, I'm glad we had this discussion and we're all in agreement here. I'll expect a call from you to let me know the status on the sale."

Without even a good-bye, he left my office, leaving the door open behind him. I sat back down in my chair, my feet tapping nervously. But I wasn't sure if the nerves were from how unfairly I'd just been treated by my boss or from the thought of being alone again with my mother in the house on Legare.

The house was dark except for a single lamp in the downstairs living room when I let myself in after work. I'd stayed at the office longer than I'd planned, researching recent real estate sales on Legare Street as well as information on the current owners to get a better idea of how desperate they were to move. I prided myself on knowing as much as I could so that when I made an offer on a client's behalf, I knew how much leeway we had for negotiations and at what point we'd walk away. I half hoped that my mother would balk at the current asking price, considering it represented a three-hundred-percent increase over the price at which she'd sold it over three decades before.

The only bright spot in my entire afternoon had been the phone tag I'd played with my mother, each of us taking turns leaving messages so that we'd made an appointment to meet the following morning without once having had to speak with each other.

I pushed open the door and heard the dog bark from the kitchen where Mrs. Houlihan usually left him with a soup bone when she went home. Flipping on the lights as I walked into the foyer, I noted the new addition of scaffolding that reached up to the gold-leaf cornices that Sophie was in the middle of having restored. One of the bracing rods of the scaffolding blocked the stairs and would require I flatten myself to crawl under them if I had any desire to actually use the upper floors of my house. Or sleep in my bedroom. I wondered if Sophie had considered that and just as quickly dismissed the thought.

I paused, my keys held in midair above the hall table. The soft tread of footsteps coming toward me from the living room made me clench a key between two fingers to use as a weapon. Of course, in this house there were no guarantees that any unwanted visitors were the living, breathing kind. Although three of the ghosts had recently been exorcised from the house, both General Lee and I still sensed the presence of several others. But we pretty much stayed out of each other's way and tolerated each other because we were all content to be where we were and not at all eager to leave.

The lights flickered and I spun around toward the light switch, seeing only empty space. My lungs seemed to crystallize as I gulped in a breath of frigid air, the temperature suddenly plummeting as the stench of rotting fish permeated the air, making me gag. I let the keys drop to the table, knowing they wouldn't help me. My breath slowed and stuttered, matching the bubbles of fear that ransacked the skin along my spine. *I am stronger than you. I am stronger than you.* My mother's old mantra came back to haunt me, and I almost smiled at the irony.

I took one step toward the living room and stopped, the sudden jangling of the phone on the hall table jarring in the still air of the quiet house. I froze and stared at it, my breath visible now in chilly puffs. I let it ring six times—three more times after it should have been picked up by my answering machine—before lifting the receiver. My frozen fingers felt scalded by the plastic of the phone and I dropped the receiver, the sound of it hitting the wood of the table unnaturally loud. With shaking fingers, I picked it up again, making sure the heat was only in my imagination before I held the phone to my ear.

"Grandmother?" The line was empty, as if the person on the other end were using a phone in the next room. I held the receiver in two hands now to keep it from shaking. I heard no noise, no breathing on the other end—just silence, as if I'd been plunged into a black hole that absorbed all light and sound like a cosmic sponge.

Melanie.

I strained to hear, not sure if I'd heard my name or not. One thing I knew for sure was that whoever had said my name, it hadn't been my grandmother.

Melanie, I heard again, and I pressed the receiver closer to my ear, fighting the impulse to hang up. The voice was soft and airy and most likely female, assuming it was even human.

"Hello? Who is this?"

The black hole began to pop and crackle, erupting something vile and unholy through the telephone line. I held the phone away from me, then slammed it down. But not before I'd heard the voice again. *I am coming for you, Melanie. I am coming for what is mine.*

General Lee barked in the kitchen and began scratching on the door, interspersing his barks with high-pitched whimpers.

The front door opened and I jumped, knocking over the hall table and sending the phone and my keys clattering to the floor. I spun around and saw my mother and Jack standing in the doorway, Jack holding up the house key I'd given him when he was living there with me to help fend off its ghosts. His gaze took in the toppled hall table and the broken phone. "Are you all right?" He stepped forward and placed his hands on my shoulders, looking carefully into my face. "I'm sorry we didn't knock, but your mother insisted that we needed to get to you right away."

"I'm fine," I said, wondering if they could hear the heavy thudding of my heart, which seemed loud enough to rattle the chandelier above me.

"No. You're not," said my mother, whose face was pale and drawn—as if she'd actually spared a moment worrying about me. She shivered, rubbing her hands on her arms. "It's freezing in here," she said, her clear gaze focused on me.

"It's an old house. Old houses are drafty." I shivered despite the fact that the temperature was quickly returning to normal. I pushed Jack away and held out my hand. "And you can give me that key now since you won't be needing it anymore." All three of us looked at my hand. It was shaking so much that it could have sifted flour.

"You need to sit down, Mellie." My mother's concerned expression was almost fooling even me.

"I don't . . ." Before I could finish, my knees buckled and Jack grabbed me just in time.

With his arm supporting me, he led me into the living room and settled me in a chair while giving directions to my mother on where the kitchen was so she could bring me a glass of water.

"What happened?" Jack asked after we'd heard my mother's heels click across the foyer. Jack squatted in front of my chair to look me in the face. "Is he back?"

I shook my head, understanding his meaning. Jack had helped me exorcise a nasty ghost by the name of Joseph Longo that neither one of us wanted to see again. "No. It was female. I'm not sure how I know that; it was more of an impression. And the odor was different. Like . . . fish. Old, rotting fish."

He sat back on his heels. "I guess that would make sense, then."

"What do you mean?" I asked, feeling light-headed again. Slowly, I leaned forward and rested my forehead on my knees.

I felt Jack's hand on the back of my neck, surprisingly tender as he rubbed the base of my skull. "The boat they found off Sullivan's Island— they released the name of it today."

"And?" I felt so sleepy.

"It was called the *Rose*."

He looked at me expectantly, as if the name should ring a bell. I shook my head, too tired to form a sentence.

"For a true Charlestonian, you know very little about your ancestors. Rose was the name of your maternal great-grandmother. The sailboat was owned by your great-great-grandfather and he named it after her."

I sat up straight, suddenly alert, hearing my mother's approaching footsteps. "Are you saying that the boat they're thinking about raising to the surface once belonged to the Prioleaus?" I shuddered, recalling again the stench of rotting fish.

My mother stood in front of me and pressed the glass of water in my hand. I gulped it down, postponing the inevitable. Sooner or later my mother and I would have to talk. I just wasn't ready for it to be sooner.

"Just like my dream," she said softly. "And if they raise the boat, something evil will be released."

I remembered the voice on the phone and my hand began to shake again, the water in the glass sloshing up on the sides. "It already has."

"I thought so," she said, taking the glass from me. She looked contemplative for a moment before speaking again. "Some spirits aren't tied to any particular location; some are attached in some way to a person"—she raised a dark eyebrow—"or a family."

"Great," I said. "Just when I think I've laid all of my ghosts to rest, you bring me more to deal with."

"Sweetheart, it found you without my help."

I didn't know if I was more surprised to agree that she was right or by the endearment, and I felt a small spark of anger. "I've seemed to manage quite a bit without your help."

"Ouch." Jack stepped between us. "Ladies, we have a problem here. And nothing's going to be resolved if we can't form a truce and just get to the facts." He turned to me. "When we arrived, what was going on here? You were obviously scared out of your mind."

I took a deep breath, wondering how in less than a year I'd gone from being in complete denial about my psychic abilities to being able to talk openly about them to a select group of people the way normal people talk about what they had for breakfast. I knew Jack was responsible, but it wasn't always clear to me if I should thank him or blame him.

"I felt a presence. Something horrible and definitely not a benign presence like the other ghosts in this house."

"You hadn't sensed him before?" Jack asked.

I shook my head. "She," I corrected. "And, no, she was definitely new."

"Did she say anything to you?" my mother asked, her voice wary, and again I felt that she knew something—something she didn't want to share.

I nodded, feeling sick again. "The phone rang right before you came. It was—a voice on the other end. It said . . ." I closed my eyes, smelling the rotting fish again, feeling out of breath as if my head were being held underwater. "It said, 'I'm coming for you, Melanie.'" I paused, wondering if I should continue. Slowly, I said, "'I'm coming for what is mine.'"

My mother's hand flew to her throat, and I saw she still wore her gloves. They were her trademark, but only I knew the real reason why she rarely took them off. Jack pulled a chair closer to her and she sat down.

Jack said, "And the voice on the phone definitely wasn't your grandmother's?"

I shook my head. "Definitely not."

We both looked at my mother, whose lips were pressed tightly together. "I don't understand any of this. But I have no doubt that whatever it is will make it very clear to us eventually. Which means Melanie and I need to stay together. To fight it. Two against one is always better odds."

I stood, looking down at my mother, my fear giving strength to thirty years of loss. "Or you could just leave again. None of this would have happened if you hadn't come back."

She stood, too, facing me, and I realized that we were the exact same height. "It's too late."

I didn't like the sound of her voice. Her tone was ominous, holding something back—something that pricked at the back of my brain like an itch that couldn't be scratched.

She continued. "Whatever it is, it's connected to my great-grandfather's sailboat. And if they raise it, which they will, it's going to be bad for us."

I stared into the face that I'd lain awake at night as a child trying to remember so I wouldn't forget it. And now I felt no relief that I hadn't left out a single curve or the exact shade of her eyes. She was a deliberate stranger—someone who chose to be absent from every birthday past my seventh year—and had spent every milestone of my life so far as the ghost whose presence was always visible as the blank spot next to me in photos.

"There's no 'us,' Mother. If I need to exorcise a spirit, I'll get Jack's help. We've done it before. But it will be a cold day in hell if I ever ask for your help."

She raised her eyebrow, but showed no emotion other than surprise. Jack stepped closer to me and put his arm around my shoulders. "Mrs. Prioleau, Ginnette, I don't see things the way that you and Mellie do, but I've seen enough to understand that when either of you senses trouble, I listen. Which is why I agree with you that Mellie shouldn't be alone until we figure this out."

I was about to argue, but he squeezed my shoulders, silencing me. "I think I should move in again, so you won't have to deal with it alone." He grinned the grin that always did funny things to my stomach. "Just like old times."

THE GIRL ON LEGARE STREET 39

I frowned at him but was thankful for the escape he was offering, regardless of how conniving his suggestion was. I allowed his arm to rest on my shoulders and turned to my mother. "That's right. Jack and I have experience with this sort of thing, so don't worry about me on that account. We won't be needing your help."

"Ah," she said, her gaze traveling from me to Jack and then back again. "I see." She reached down and picked up her purse from the floor by her chair. "I guess you've got it all under control, so I'll just leave then." She began walking toward the foyer but stopped and turned around. "Don't forget our appointment tomorrow at nine o'clock. I'll meet you in front of the Legare Street house."

The relief I felt at her departure dissipated and was quickly replaced by dread. "You still want to buy that house? Don't you have a career in New York you need to get back to?"

She smiled a half smile and for the first time I saw my resemblance to her and it saddened me. "I'm retiring, Mellie. It's better to retire when you're at the top of your game so you won't be remembered as a has-been with a failing voice." She glanced around at her surroundings as if finally noticing them. "I love what you've done with the place," she said, her gaze taking in the mismatched furniture and the empty windows.

Annoyed, I said, "I'm in the middle of the restoration. We've moved most of the furniture out until we refinish the floors and repair all of the plaster. Otherwise, it might get ruined."

Her eyebrow arched again as she regarded us. "Good. So you know a lot about renovation and restoration. Just the person I need to help me after I buy my house."

Before I could say anything, she'd turned on her heel. "See you at nine o'clock tomorrow morning."

I listened as the door latch turned, followed by the soft click of the door shutting behind her.

I yanked myself away from Jack. "She's got a lot of nerve. Like I would help her at all unless my boss forced me to."

To my surprise, Jack was trying hard to hold back laughter.

"What's so funny?"

"You. You're just like her, you know. You always have to get the last word in."

I opened my mouth to protest, then remembered my mother's smile and the way she'd said the word "us" and realized that Jack maybe wasn't so wrong after all.

Instead of answering, I began to walk back toward the kitchen. "I'm taking the dog for a walk."

"I'll come with you," he said as he followed behind me.

As we walked toward the kitchen, I said, "I met an old friend of yours the other day."

"Really? Who?"

"Rebecca Edgerton."

"Ah. She said she was going to contact you about the article she's working on about your mother. I told her that you weren't exactly—close."

I pushed open the kitchen door and paused. "Well, that didn't exactly stop her from contacting me."

He stopped in the doorway, and he was near enough that I could smell his cologne. "It's amazing how much she looks like Emily, don't you think?"

"I don't think I ever noticed," he said, brushing past me into the kitchen.

"Hm," I said, not convinced but unwilling to pick a fight. Dealing with my mother was enough friction for one day.

I watched as Jack put the collar on General Lee; then I led the way out the back door. I was glad for Jack's company and relieved that I wouldn't be staying in the house alone, but I was also aware that both he and I knew I'd never admit it to him in a thousand years.

CHAPTER 5

True to his word, Jack spent the night in the third-floor guest room without my having to acknowledge his presence. I did leave fresh sheets and clean towels outside his room to demonstrate that his being there was appreciated if not quite welcome. But even though he was sleeping on a separate floor, I knew he was sleeping under the same roof I was—the way a dog knows you're hiding a treat in your pocket.

I left the house early the next morning to avoid him and because I couldn't sleep anyway. I spent two hours in my office drinking sugared coffee and organizing my office supplies as I waited for nine o'clock. I also made a phone call to Sophie, knowing that the prospect of her getting inside a historic home South of Broad would more than make up for the fact that I woke her from a dead sleep hours before she planned on being ambulatory. She didn't ask me why I wanted her there with me while I showed my mother her childhood home. And that's why Sophie Wallen was the person I liked best in this world.

I arrived first, at eight fifty. I despised tardiness almost as much as bad table manners and unpolished shoes. This was probably a throwback to my years of being raised by a military father, albeit an alcoholic one, who taught me the rules if only so I could make sure he was dressed properly before being propelled out the door in the morning with a strong cup of coffee.

I stood on the sidewalk in front of the gate tapping my foot. I would forgive Sophie for being late; it was as much a part of her personality as her Birkenstocks. But I would only give my mother until five after nine and then I was out of there.

I spotted Sophie's bright green Volkswagen Beetle and waved to her as she found a spot at the curb across the street. I stared as she exited the car, for once not transfixed by what she wore but instead by the rows and rows of tiny braids with multicolored beads that cascaded down the sides and back of her head. While the hairstyle itself wasn't so bad, it made Sophie's tiny head look like a specimen found in a shrunken-head collection I'd once seen in a potential client's personal library.

"What happened?" I asked, waiting for her to approach. "I hope you're at least pressing charges."

She smiled broadly as she stepped up on the sidewalk. "One of my students offered to do it and I let her. Chad loves it."

I raised my eyebrows but was stopped from saying anything else by her look of wonder as she took in the house behind us. "You are the luckiest human being on the planet, I want you to know. First you inherit the Vanderhorst mansion on Tradd through sheer luck, and then your mother shows up to buy your family home—another architectural masterpiece—giving you access to two of the most beautiful and historic residences in Charleston. And to think you used to rent a condo in Mt. Pleasant."

"Did it ever occur to you that I might have actually preferred that condo? I can vaguely recall days when I didn't have to spend all my time, energy, and fingernails scraping paint from ancient plaster. Or schedule my days around various craftsmen. I now spend more time with carpenters and painters than I do with my manicurist and masseuse."

She smiled again, a dreamy expression on her face as she looked up at the three-story Georgian double house whose two-story portico projected over the sidewalk, casting us both in shadow. As if I hadn't spoken, she said, "This house is a classic. It was built around 1756, I think."

I crossed my arms over my chest. "It was 1755, actually. And the two-story portico with the Ionic columns was added in 1826, showing the neoclassical tastes of the owner during a time when the Federal style was all the rage."

Sophie turned to me, her self-satisfied smile even broader. "Maybe there's hope for you, after all. You should probably come talk to one of my restoration classes at the college now that you actually know what you're talking about. To give a perspective on a real restoration. You might even impress them if you throw in that word 'neoclassical' a couple of times."

I snorted but was secretly pleased. I had once been a "tear-down-the-old-dilapidated-building-and-put-up-a-much-needed-parking-garage" kind of girl before becoming a reluctant home owner. Although I wasn't officially an old-house hugger, I was definitely not the same person I'd been before I inherited the house on Tradd Street. I realized now that living in a white-walled, ornamentation-free condo prior to inheriting the house had been a form of self-preservation created by a young girl who'd seen the house in which she and six generations of her family had been born sold to a couple from Texas who'd made their fortune in scrap metal.

"What's with the garden?" Sophie asked as she peered through the garden gate.

"It's hideous, isn't it?" I said, swinging it open. "But wait until you see the interior. The listing on the Internet has a lot of pictures, and all I'm going to say is that I hope those were just really bad photos and don't do it justice. According to the listing agent, the wife didn't use a decorator for most of the house, saying she liked to use her own style."

Sophie frowned, staring at the cement and glass blocks whose only claim to art appeared to be the pedestals they'd been set upon. She paused in front of a rusted metal sculpture that looked remarkably like an old car door from Detroit's better days. "What is this?"

"A car door from a Cadillac Seville. I'd say circa 1977."

We both turned to see my mother in fur coat and leather gloves scrutinizing a garden that no longer resembled the one she and I had tea in with my grandmother. The parterre herb garden was gone, as were the Confederate jasmine vines and the boxwoods, and I could see from the frown lines on my mother's face that she was seeing what wasn't there anymore, too. "This is a disaster, isn't it?"

Sophie stuck her hand out and shook my mother's gloved one. "It's a pleasure to meet you, Ms. Prioleau. I'm Sophie Wallen; I teach historic restoration at the college. The recording of you singing the part of Isolde in *Tristan and Isolde* at the Bayreuth Festival is always on my CD player. I've practically worn through it I've listened to it so much."

My mother actually blushed, her gaze taking in Sophie's braids.

"Thank you. I'm flattered, especially coming from you. I've been studying up on some of the recent restorations in the city and I'm very familiar with your work. Very impressive. You have such an eye for detail and beauty." She glanced over at me. "I'm assuming that's why Mellie has brought you here for the showing?"

Feeling almost nauseous at the fanfest between my mother and Sophie, I stepped between them. "Actually, Sophie's a good friend of mine. I wanted her with me in case I needed a witness."

My mother smiled but didn't say anything. I pointedly glanced at my watch. "It's four minutes after nine and I've got another showing after this one so let's get this over with." The two of them followed as I walked quickly to the marble steps flanked by wrought iron railings.

"I figured you wouldn't want to wait more than five minutes, so I hurried through breakfast to get here." My mother's voice wasn't completely clear of sarcasm.

My cheeks flushed with her accurate assumption and I fumbled for the key in the lockbox. "Some people take their responsibilities seriously. Mine include not being late. If one morning appointment is late, then it makes me late for all of my appointments for the rest of the day. It's not a good way to run a business. Or a life," I added as I took the key from the box and turned the lock to open the front door.

We crowded into the wide center hall that ran the length of the house, the large formal entertaining rooms scattered on either side of the impressive entry. I had resisted setting foot inside the house until I had to, relegating my research solely to what I could find from the Internet and the listing agent. This meant, of course, that I was as surprised as Sophie and my mother.

"Oh," said Sophie, seemingly at a loss for a better word.

I waited for the rush of grief and loss to roll over me like an oncoming tide. Instead, I stared at the room before me, looking for remnants of my grandmother and my life with her. But I saw only a faint likeness—like the ghost image left on your eyelids after the flash from a camera.

We stood gaping at the marble-tiled floor with the faux-zebra shag area rug galloping down the middle of the hall. The elegant egg-and-dart carved cornices had been painted black to offset the fuchsia hue of the walls. Lime green beanbag chairs with legs offered seating to anybody

with enough taste to make their knees go weak upon viewing the psychedelic colors of the hallway.

"She did all of her own decorating," I reminded them.

My mother spun around, taking in the Italian gilt-wood chandelier
that had managed to escape the paint gun and the framed portraits on the
walls that looked like they could have been done by the owner's grandchildren. Or monkeys.

Sophie moved over to a pink lacquer hall table and pulled on the
drawer knob, which responded by falling off in her hand. She delicately
put the knob back on the shiny surface and backed away as if whatever
the table had was contagious.

"What—style would you say this is?" I asked Sophie.

"Early Garage Sale Revival, I believe," my mother responded with a
straight face. I turned away so she wouldn't see my smile or know that
she'd said exactly what I was thinking.

"Wow," said Sophie, who had wandered into one of the formal rooms
that flanked the hall. "I've seen this window from the outside, but it's even
more amazing from the inside."

I hesitated briefly before joining her in the room. This room had
been my favorite—the room I spent the most time in with my grandmother playing cards or reading with my feet tucked up on one of her
priceless antique sofas. If the weather was bad, we'd have our tea in
here and Grandmother Prioleau would allow me to pour, regardless
of her Aubusson rug. It was a room in which I'd felt loved and cared
for—instead of the object of constant friction I was when I was with
my parents.

Most of all, I loved the huge window that had been installed in the
late 1800s. It was an odd window, not really in keeping with the style of
the house or the style of the Victorian period. If anything, it appeared almost contemporary, the two female figures not clearly discernible unless
you knew where to look—and how to look at the glass. Wisteria vines
ran through the window, intersecting at will like a huge road map leading to nowhere. Although its inspiration and meaning had doubtless been
known at one time, both had long since been lost to the past.

I walked over to Sophie so that I stood in the shaft of sunlight that
the window transfixed into a buttery yellow. Turning my face up to the

warmth, I felt my grandmother's presence as if the sun were her hand on my skin.

Sophie clucked her tongue. "It's a good thing that whoever installed this didn't have to face the Board of Architectural Review or he'd never have gotten it approved." She smiled at me. "And for the first time in my life, I can actually say that was a good thing."

My mother's voice interrupted my reverie. "And it's also a good thing that the current owners didn't see the need to change the window to suit their tastes." She pointedly glanced around at the orange shag carpet, wild daisy wallpaper, and mirrored-plate chandelier.

Sophie ran her hand over the hideous wallpaper. "They've covered up all of the beautiful cypress wood paneling that this house is famous for. What were they thinking?" She shook her head, her braids mimicking the movement as if in agreement. "Luckily, they don't seem to have made any structural changes. Just really horrid cosmetic ones. Whipping it back into shape and returning it to its former glory shouldn't be a problem."

"That's good to know," my mother said, and I felt her eyes on me.

Remembering my job and what I was supposed to be doing, I turned to the large doorway surround. "Please note the widened door openings from the hall and the door surrounds that echo the neoclassical shapes of the portico. They were added at the same time as the portico and date back to the 1820s."

"And this mantel," said my mother—who had moved to the end of the room to stand in front of the fireplace—"is molded from a composition using a mold design by Ramage and Ferguson of Scotland. Only the best for our ancestral Prioleaus." She smiled at me.

Furrowing my brows, I said, "I still don't understand why you needed me here. It's not like you've forgotten anything about the house. Wouldn't it have saved us both a lot of time and energy if you'd just made an offer and signed the papers?"

"I suppose it might have been easier," she said, slowly walking around the room and taking in the architectural beauty that had been forced to share company with the garish colors and metallic fabrics that were as out of place in this house as a whore in church. "But then I wouldn't have the chance of seeing how it felt to be in it with you after all these years."

I watched as Sophie casually walked out of the room, her ruffled denim skirt skimming the wood floor behind her. I frowned after her, willing her to return, but I was pretty sure that her exit hadn't been unintentional.

Turning back to my mother, I said, "Well, now that you know, why don't we leave and go back to my office so I can prepare an offer?"

"We haven't finished looking, Mellie. I want to see the kitchen."

I paused, remembering that the back of the house had a completely different feel from the front. As a child, I had resisted venturing past the front rooms alone, noticing how the whispering grew louder there, the brushes against my skin bolder. But there was one presence I remembered vaguely—a warm presence in whose company I felt safe. He was my protector, and I navigated the house in peace as long as he was with me. Until I'd made the mistake of mentioning him to my father, who told me it was all in my imagination and that my visits to my grandmother's would have to be limited if I didn't stop talking about it.

Even more than the fear of not seeing my grandmother, I was afraid that something might really be wrong with me. So I stopped seeking out my imaginary friend and instead stayed in the front rooms, ignoring the whispering of my name that called me to the back of the house.

"I'll stay here," I said.

Sophie appeared in the back hallway that led to the kitchen, rubbing her arms. "Not to ruin a sale or anything, but I think something's wrong with the heat back here. It's like twenty degrees colder than the rest of the house."

I met my mother's eyes, then reluctantly followed her back to the kitchen.

The space had been recently updated and, despite poor color palette and wallpaper choices, the design was solid as were the cherry cabinets and stainless steel appliances.

"My guess would be that she used a decorator in here," said my mother.

Sophie nodded. "I know that for a fact because I remember being consulted on this job by the designer." She pointed to the far corner of the room where a beautiful fireplace with an Adams mantel had once been and where a wall now stood with the mural of a longhorn cow painted on it.

"Oh my gosh," I said. "Even I think that's sacrilege."

Sophie tucked a braid behind her ear. "I told Debbie, the designer, to leave the fireplace and just cover it up without damaging the woodwork. The mantel was kept intact and stored in the attic. But to remove the whole thing really would have been sacrilege. Hiding it was gross stupidity, but happily *reversible* gross stupidity."

My mother walked over to an open door across from the mural. "Let's take these back stairs to see the upper levels."

"No." The word came out before I could stop it. Both Sophie and my mother looked at me, but only Sophie's expression held a question.

"Her grandmother died falling down these stairs," my mother explained. "But look, Mellie. They have hand railings on both sides now, so it's safer."

I knew Sophie should hear the truth and I would tell her; I just couldn't seem to get my jaw to work properly. I had never been on that stairwell without my protector, and I'd known either from him telling me or from sensing it myself that I should never attempt it otherwise. There was something up there at the top of the stairs. Something not of this world. Something evil.

"I'll stay here." I started to back away and felt something gritty on the floor under my shoe. I lifted my heel and saw what appeared to be large grains of salt. Like sea salt.

My mother walked toward me, her eyes searching my face. "You feel it too, don't you? It's always been here." She stopped in front of me. "But it's about to get stronger."

Sophie joined us, but we didn't break eye contact. "What's going on?"

My cell phone rang, making me jump. Thankful for the distraction, I dug into my purse to retrieve it and saw it was Jack's cell number. "I've got to take this. You two go on up and check out the other two floors."

Reluctantly, Sophie followed my mother up the stairs and I shuddered as I watched them go.

"Hello?" I said into the phone.

"Hi, Mellie. It's me, Jack."

"I know. I saw your name on my screen."

I heard the smile in his voice. "So that means you never deleted my numbers from your cell phone."

"My bad," I said, wishing he could see me roll my eyes. "And just because we're speaking again, doesn't mean we have to."

His tone changed. "I know. But I needed to tell you something important before you read it in the newspaper."

I stared at the kitchen floor, seeing what looked like a trail of salt crossing the ceramic tiles. With shortened breaths, I said, "What is it?"

"Are you all right? You sound out of breath."

"I'm fine," I managed. "Just tell me."

"Well, you remember the news reports about the sailboat that was found off of Sullivan's Island and how they discovered it was your great-great-grandfather's boat? And that it had been missing since 1886?"

"Yes." The word was more breath than speech.

"Before attempting to raise it, the salvage company sent divers down to bring anything interesting out of the boat up to the surface." He stopped. "Maybe I should come see you to tell you all this."

"No," I said. "Go ahead and finish."

He paused for a moment. "Well, they found a steamer trunk and brought it up yesterday. Today, they opened it."

I felt nauseous all of a sudden, and had to sit down on the floor. "And?" I prompted.

"They found human remains inside."

I didn't respond. I was on my knees following the trail of salt, realizing too late that the grainy spills resembled footprints. I held my breath as if preparing to dive into water, and stopped when I saw that the trail of salt led to the back stairway.

"Jack?" I whispered. "I think we have a problem." And then I dropped my phone and started to scream.

CHAPTER 6

I wasn't really sure how I ended up in Jack's Queen Street condo. I just remembered sitting on the kitchen floor in my grandmother's house, my screaming stopped by the feeling of not being able to breathe—as if my head were being held underwater. I must have passed out because the next thing I remember was Sophie and my mother helping Jack put me in the passenger side of his car. I seemed to recall flashbulbs going off and two news vans from local stations parked in front of the house, hulking like vultures.

I lay on Jack's leather couch with an ice pack on my forehead, vaguely aware of my surroundings. The elegant and tasteful furnishings of Jack's condo never ceased to amaze me. It was incongruous how a guy like Jack, who had no compunction about putting his feet up on my coffee table or leaving his dirty dishes on top of the television set, would live in a place that looked like it belonged on the cover of *Architectural Digest*. True, there was the genetic component—his parents owned an exclusive antique shop on King Street—but still.

Quiet voices drifted from the kitchen, Jack's and a soft woman's voice. I knew it wasn't Sophie or my mother. I'd heard them tell Jack they would head in the opposite direction from us in case the newspeople were going to follow. I took the ice pack off and lifted my head.

Amelia Trenholm, Jack's mother and one of my mother's oldest and closest friends, walked toward me, her graceful manner and petite figure at home in the elegant surroundings. She sat down on the sofa next to me and placed a warm hand on my temple.

"You're still a little flushed. Are you feeling better?"

I nodded and tried to sit up, but she put a hand on my shoulder and made me lie down again.

"I want you to eat something before you try standing again, all right?"

Jack appeared behind her holding a tray filled with chocolate-covered cream-filled donuts. My stomach grumbled as Mrs. Trenholm wrapped one in a napkin and handed it to me. "Jack went out and got these. He said they were your favorites." Her voice was dubious.

I took a bite and nodded, realizing how famished I was.

She smiled and shook her head. "You're just like your mother. You inherited her metabolism and both of your parents' addiction to sugar. That's really not fair, you know."

I took another bite, too hungry to take exception to her comparing my mother and me.

Mrs. Trenholm pushed my hair back. "Reporters are staked out at your house and your office, too. We finally turned off your cell phone because there were so many calls from the paper and television stations. And David Henderson called three times. The first was to congratulate you on the publicity. The second was to make sure that you had the Henderson Realty SOLD sign in the front garden of the Legare Street house."

"What was the third one?"

Amelia pursed her lips. "I didn't answer it. That's when I turned off the phone."

"Good move," I said, taking another bite of my donut and already feeling better. "But why does anybody care about human remains that have apparently been in a trunk since 1886?"

Jack sat on the rolled arm of the couch behind my head. "Because the Prioleau name is a prominent one. It's not common for it to be mentioned in the same sentence as the word 'murder.' Let's face it: Whoever is in that trunk didn't get there on their own."

I sat up, my head feeling clearer. "But I didn't put them in there."

"No," countered his mother. "But you're one of only two living descendants of someone who might have. They'll want to know if you know anything, and once you tell them that you don't and no new leads are found, they'll go away."

"Do you really think so?" Despite having spent many of my growing-up years elsewhere, I was still a Charlestonian and held to the belief that a lady should only appear in the paper three times in her life: when she is born, when she is married, and when she dies.

"Are you quite sure . . ." Amelia said as she and Jack and exchanged a glance before they both looked back at me.

"What?"

Jack placed a hand on my shoulder. "Mellie, are you sure you don't know anything? We can't discount your mother's premonition and your recent contact with your grandmother. And then what happened today at your grandmother's house? There was something spread all over the floor that your mother said looked a lot like salt but she didn't know how it got there. And there was a puddle of water by the back stairs."

My eyes met Jack's and a shudder of fear raced up my spine. "I swear I don't know anything. I think my mother does, more than she's letting on, but you'll have to ask her." I swallowed thickly, the last bit of donut stuck somewhere in my throat. "I do think it's related to whatever it was in my house that night you and my mother were there. It's the smell—like seawater. My mother smelled it, too."

The doorbell rang, and when Jack opened the door, my mother stood in the threshold, as if summoned.

"How is she?" she asked as Jack helped her out of her coat. She kept her gloves on as she approached me on the couch. Amelia stood and greeted my mother with a kiss on the cheek before Ginnette took her spot next to me. "I was worried about you."

I didn't have the energy to dispute the facts. Instead I said, "I'm fine. I just . . ."

Her gloved hand brushed my arm. "I know. I saw."

I looked into her eyes, seeing for the first time not the mother I resented, but a person who actually understood that the shadows I saw and the voices I'd been hearing all of my life were real. My father's aversion to all things unexplainable had started me on the road to denial and for once I could be allowed to step off that path. Without looking away, I said, "I have a feeling that whatever was there before, the presence at the top of the stairs I remember, was the same—thing—that came yesterday. But if the boat's been underwater for over one hundred years, how was it here before, when I was a little girl?"

My mother looked down at her gloves, then carefully took them off before picking up my hand and holding it. I didn't jerk away and I think that surprised us both. "Yes. You're right. It's been around since I was a girl. But it was only a shadow then, just like it was when you lived there. I think it needed someone with a psychic ability to project itself into our lives, and I think that's why there weren't any more reports of hauntings in the house after we moved out. But now . . ." She shrugged. "I'm afraid that disturbing the remains has brought it back, but in a form that doesn't need someone like us for energy. I think that's what she—or it—was showing us today in the kitchen. And that's why she followed you to your house. I don't think she's going to leave us alone until she gets what she wants. Or we destroy her."

Our eyes met again. "So you believe they're connected. Your dreams, and the ship being raised, and whatever we've always known to be lurking in Grandmother's house—they're connected in some way. To us."

My mother nodded and looked away, but not before I saw her eyes darken.

"What is it?" I asked. "What aren't you telling me?" I squeezed her hand and we both realized at the same time that it was the first time I had touched her since I was seven years old. I withdrew my hand and laid it on the cool leather of the sofa.

"That's all I know about the spirit. I avoided it when I lived in the house. As I know you did." She smiled a little. "Your grandmother probably knew more, and I have a strong suspicion that if we listen closely, we'll hear what she's trying to tell us."

We. I didn't want that one small word to affect me so much. And maybe I didn't have to let it. My mother and I shared a connection through our psychic abilities if nothing else. I was accustomed to working with people in a professional relationship without necessarily liking them. Surely I could do this one small thing—working with my mother to exorcise a spirit. And then, like after signing a contract with a client at a closing, we could go our separate ways.

I sat up straighter and Jack took my napkin. "So you want me to help you get rid of this spirit."

My mother raised her eyebrow, something I was getting used to seeing. "Actually, I would be helping you get rid of it. It seems to be focused on you." She gave an elegant shrug. "And maybe in return you could help me restore the Legare Street house after I buy it. As Sophie said, it's mostly cosmetic so it shouldn't be as exhausting as your own house. But I would appreciate your knowledge and expertise since you already have so much experience."

I felt as if my head were being squeezed in a vise. For a woman who prided herself on her independence, I was somehow finding myself for the second time within a year without many choices.

I thought for a moment, my gaze focused on my mother's hands and aware of Jack and his mother in the background trying to pretend as if they weren't listening to every word. I hadn't known my mother long, but it was long enough to learn that she was a great manipulator—apparently a trait that seemed to run in the blood along with the ability to see dead people.

Trying to keep myself from smiling, I said, "I think I can do that. But I can't take on the restoration of another house all by myself. I'll need some help."

My mother nodded. "Of course. I assumed you'd solicit your friend Sophie and whoever else has been helping with your house. And I can pay for their time, of course. I'll also ask Amelia to help me with the furniture. I'm fairly certain that I won't want to stick with the fraternity house décor that's there now."

This time I did smile as an idea crept its way into my brain—an idea that seemed like perfect retribution for allowing my mother to have gotten her way. "Actually, I wasn't thinking of Sophie but yes, now that you mention it, I will need her help. I was thinking of my father. He restored the garden on Tradd Street. I'm sure he'd love to take this one over, too."

Her own smile faded. "I don't think . . ."

"It's a deal breaker, Mother. Either he gets involved in this or it's a no-go. Your choice. Remember that Jack and I have gotten rid of a nasty ghost before and I'm sure we could do it again. But I don't think you've ever restored a house on your own."

My mother looked over at Amelia Trenholm, whose face remained impassive. Jack excused himself to go get a nonalcoholic beer from the fridge. But I stopped short of giving myself a mental pat on the back for a blow well delivered. Because some part of me desperately wanted her to say yes.

Ginnette turned back to me. "I have a feeling I will live to regret this but I see no other choice. Besides, if he's working in the garden I won't really have to deal with him all that much."

In response, I mimicked her by raising my eyebrow.

"Fine," she said, standing and pulling her gloves on. "If that's the way it needs to be. And now I think we should prepare a little statement for the press to make them go away. Something to the effect that we know nothing, which is true. We can say that whatever happened over one hundred years ago bears no weight whatsoever on today."

Jack held a hand out to me to help me stand and I took it. "Right. And we know how true that is." He put his arm around me and I leaned into him, remembering the ghost of a little boy who'd compelled us to solve a mystery from the past to clear his mother's name.

My mother took note of Jack's arm before looking back at me. "I didn't say it was the truth, only that's what I'd be telling the press." She picked up her purse. "You'll excuse me if I don't shake hands on this deal." After Ginnette kissed Amelia good-bye, Jack opened the door for her. "You'll be hearing from me," she said. "I'm staying at the Charleston Place Hotel on Meeting for now. I'm eager to be back in my house again."

Apprehension skittered through my blood like sand in an hourglass, slowly at first and then more quickly, hurtling me toward some unknown deadline. "I'll call you in the morning to go over the details of your offer."

"Fine. Good night, Mellie."

I looked at Jack for help, unable to respond with the same words I had last uttered to my mother on the night she left all those years ago.

Jack reached for the door, holding it open. "Good night, Ms. Prioleau."

She sent him a warm smile as I groaned inwardly, and then Jack let the door shut softly behind her.

Although it was a Saturday, I was already up, showered, and dressed by six thirty and busy organizing my underwear drawer by color and style when the doorbell rang. It wasn't that I didn't have other things I should have been doing. The paperwork on my mother's offer needed to be completed, there were proposals for two prospective clients, my car needed washing, and General Lee—currently curled up on top of my pillow—needed to be taken to the groomer. But years of therapy had shown me that organizing was my method of regaining control of my life, and my life had flown so far off the rails in the last week that I wasn't sure if I'd ever be able to pull it back.

I peered out of my window, looking for another media van but saw only a red Audi convertible. Despite my mother's predictions, her statement to the press had been like a swat at a nestful of angry hornets. Reporters had been buzzing around me, my office, my house, and my mother, giving me a brief moment of sympathy for Britney Spears.

Pressing my face against the window again, I strained to see further down the block and spotted Jack's Porsche directly behind the Audi. The doorbell rang again and I ran down the stairs, then cautiously walked toward the door. Through the leaded-glass window I could make out the forms of two people, one male and one female. I wasn't sure who the woman was, but the man was unmistakable.

"Jack?" I asked as I pulled the door open. "It's six thirty in the morning."

"Sorry," he said, looking anything but. "I must have left my key in my room. But I knew you'd be awake, probably up alphabetizing your coffee table books or something, and would welcome the interruption."

I opened my mouth to argue but shut it abruptly and not just because of how close to the truth he actually was. My gaze strayed to the blond woman next to him and I stared at her in surprise.

"Mellie, you might remember meeting . . ."

"Rebecca Edgerton," I said coolly. "I remember. She's a reporter, you know."

"Yes," he said, indicating for Rebecca to enter ahead of him. He blew on his hands, then rubbed them together before quickly shutting the door, leaving a chilly reminder of the cold weather outside lingering in the foyer.

I stood and stared at them, waiting for an explanation.

"Why don't we go into the kitchen and I'll make some coffee," Jack said. "Then we can talk."

"I'd love that," said Rebecca. "We've been up all night and I could really use the caffeine."

I shot Jack one of my mother's looks with the raised eyebrow before turning to lead the way back to the kitchen. "All night, hmm?"

"I had my cell phone on, Mellie. All you had to do was call if you needed me."

"We were just catching up," Rebecca interjected. "Jack and I haven't seen each other in a few years, so there was a lot of ground to cover."

"I bet." I went to the pantry and pulled out a large can of coffee. Jack appeared at my elbow and took it from me.

"You go sit down and let me do this." Softly he said, "I don't want you near anything that resembles a weapon."

I did as he suggested, if only not to give Rebecca anything to write about, and pulled out a chair at the kitchen table across from her. General Lee entered the kitchen, then promptly moved to the table and parked himself at Rebecca's feet, tilting his head to make it easier for her to scratch him behind the ears. I glared at him before turning to Rebecca. "So, you and Jack used to date before he met Emily."

Rebecca smiled sweetly. "Yes. And then after Emily—left—we sort of lost touch. I guess the life of a famous writer keeps a person busy."

Jack put a scoop of coffee into the filter. "Oh, that and other things." He slid a glance at me and an unwelcome tingle erupted in my toes. "Which brings me to why we're here." He hit the ON switch on the coffeemaker and joined us at the table. "I think Rebecca can help us."

"Help us?" I asked. "With what?" I stared at Jack, ignoring Rebecca. Out of the corner of my eye I saw her lift General Lee onto her lap, and the little traitor actually licked her cheek.

"Eradicating your mother's house of its ghosts," Rebecca said.

I threw my hands up. "Great, Jack. Why don't you just broadcast the fact that my mother and I belong in a freak show? I have a business reputation to uphold, you know."

Rebecca touched my arm. "He confided in me as a friend, not as a reporter, although I think my connections could help as well."

"We don't need any help, thank you. Jack and I have had some success in this area before, and with my mother's assistance, I think we'll have this problem solved very quickly." I moved away from her, uncomfortable not only with her proximity but with her knowledge of my psychic abilities. It wasn't how I identified myself. Rather, it was more like a genetic quirk such as curly hair or protruding ears. To be known as the woman who can see dead people was humiliating at best.

Jack leaned forward, his eyes serious. "You really think so, Mellie? Everything we've experienced so far has indicated that we're dealing with a whole different ball game. It would appear that this—whatever we want to call it—has been hanging around the house for a long time, waiting for you."

I swallowed. "That could be true. But, as my mother said, the two of us together should be enough to fight it."

He didn't drop his gaze. "Mellie, the two of you once lived in the house with your grandmother and the three of you weren't enough. That's what's worrying me. That"—he narrowed his eyes—"and the thought that your mother isn't telling us everything she knows."

The same thought had been tugging at the back of my brain like a fly buzzing around my ear, but I kept swatting it away. I didn't want to believe there was more to this story. Despite what others might believe, I was afraid of the supernatural. I wasn't afraid of all spirits, of course, but certainly those that made threatening phone calls and physically attacked me. Just because I could see them or communicate with them did not make them my friends, which is why I needed to believe that my mother and I could make it go away and that there wasn't anything else to worry about.

"I don't think . . ." I began.

Rebecca interrupted. "I already told Jack that anything I eventually write about your mother will get her approval first. I understand that knowing about her psychic abilities, as well as yours, is privileged information and I won't betray your trust. This is just one of those opportunities that could really make my career." She regarded me hopefully, and once again I was struck by how familiar she looked—and not just because of her resemblance to Emily.

"Rebecca's a bit psychic as well," Jack added, and I could tell by Rebecca's expression that she hadn't wanted Jack to tell me. But when Jack looked back at me it was apparent that he knew how she felt and wanted me to know anyway.

He continued. "Not to the extent you are, though. She doesn't see dead people, but she's scary good at premonitions."

Silently, I regarded Rebecca and was curious if she'd known about Emily's illness and her subsequent death, but had chosen to keep it from Jack. And I couldn't help but wonder if her reappearance in Jack's life now had more to do with their past romantic involvement than any interest Rebecca might have in my family.

Rebecca splayed her fingers on the wood surface of the table—her skin pale, her fingernails polished a shiny petal pink. They, too, seemed familiar. "It's in my family. My mother, aunt, and grandmother have it, too."

"Rebecca's already started doing research, finding out the names of both family members and close friends to help determine who the person found on the boat might be. Her sources would be a really great asset for you."

I sat back in my chair, watching Jack closely and trying to understand why he so desperately wanted Rebecca to help us. Maybe it had something to do with her strong resemblance to the woman he'd loved and lost. "So what have you discovered so far?"

She smiled smugly. "When they brought up the *Hunley* submarine after one hundred and thirty-six years underwater, there were still skeletal remains as well as viable DNA. They used it to find the crew members' descendants. It might be possible to determine, at the very least, if the person found on the boat is related to you."

Rebecca raised an eyebrow and I almost told her to stop doing that before I realized how irrational I'd sound. She continued. "The difference here is that the *Hunley* crew members were covered in silt, which worked toward their preservation. I think in addition to teeth and hair, they found brain matter, too. The body in the trunk wasn't so well preserved, and with all those years in warm salt water, they'll be lucky to find enough bones to piece together to figure out a definitive sex and age. It won't give you a name, but the information could certainly narrow down the list. That's where I come in." She paused as if waiting to see if I was going to let her continue or stop her absurd assumption that she could help me. Even General Lee had stopped his licking and was looking at me intently to see what I would do.

Rebecca continued. "I can at least narrow the list by researching birth and death dates and their connection to the Prioleau family. I've done so much research on your family that I probably already have the information we need." She smiled at Jack and I wanted to tell her to stop doing that, too. "I'll share everything I find with Jack, who might be able to use it in his next book. You never know"—she looked back at me—"what Jack will decide to write about next. And if this mystery is juicy enough, I can imagine it will be a great follow-up to the Vanderhorst story he's working on now."

"Really?" I asked. It was my turn to raise an eyebrow. "And you two have already talked about this?"

"Not exactly," Jack said.

"Yes," Rebecca said at the same time.

Jack stood and began pouring coffee into our mugs, and I noticed how many sugars and how much cream he put into Rebecca's mug without having to ask her. "What I meant to say is that Rebecca mentioned it to me and I'll certainly keep it in mind." He carried the three mugs over to the table and put them in front of us. "But I'd never write a word without your permission."

I didn't say anything, stalling for time by blowing on my hot coffee. I wasn't crazy about the idea of working with an outsider, but adding another person to the mix might make the whole ordeal go faster. This would mean my mother could live in peace in her house without requiring my presence in her life for very long, I wouldn't have to enter my house in fear that something was waiting for me, and it would keep Jack hanging around for a while longer. Not that I was interested in him romantically, of course. It was just that he knew a lot about furniture placement and could hang a painting straight.

I took a sip from my mug and savored it for a long moment. "We could certainly give it a trial run," I conceded. "See how we work together." I took another sip. "But one last thing . . ."

Rebecca watched me carefully.

"If you need to make any mention of my mother's past penchant for telling fortunes at parties, say that it's 'intuition.' That my mother's what they call 'an intuitive.'"

After a short pause she said, "Fine. I can do that." She drained her mug, then waited for Jack to pull out her chair before she stood, cradling General Lee like a baby before gently putting him on the floor. Instead of running to me, he sat at her feet, and I thought he might even have sent me a defiant look.

I stood, too—without assistance—and pointedly looked at Jack, who seemed to be fixated on Rebecca.

"I'd better go now. Thanks for the coffee," she said to me before turning to Jack. "And thanks for last night. I had fun. I'll give you a call later." She kissed him on the cheek, lingering a little longer than necessary, and I found myself studying the wood grain of the Shaker table.

After Jack helped her into her coat, she stood still for a moment, her expression thoughtful. "Have you been up to the attic yet in your mother's house?"

I shook my head. "It's not her house yet. We're working on it. Why?"

"I think you need to. I believe it's still filled with Prioleau family things and there's something up there you need to see. A portrait, maybe."

"And you know this—how?"

Jack leaned on the table. "She has dreams. Sometimes they make sense, and sometimes they don't."

Rebecca nodded. "That's right. And I saw—something, maybe a painting or photograph, in the attic that I felt in the dream would mean something to you."

I studied her doubtfully. "We'll be doing a few walk-throughs. I'll make sure there's access to the attic and go take a look."

"Great," she said before looking at Jack. "I'm afraid I'll get lost in this big old house. Would you mind walking me out?"

"Not at all," we said in unison, and I couldn't help but smirk at him as we led Rebecca to the front door.

We had made it as far as the front porch when I realized I had another question for her. "That picture, or whatever it is—the one in the attic. What made you think I'd be interested in seeing it?"

She narrowed her eyes a little as she regarded me, turning her head to the right as I remembered seeing Emily do, and I wondered who had copied whom. "Because the subject of the portrait looks exactly like you."

Something cold brushed the back of my neck, and I twisted to look at Jack. But he was staring at Rebecca as if he, too, had seen a ghost.

"Good-bye, again," she said, and she appeared to be lingering as if waiting for Jack to go with her. I picked up General Lee to prevent him from defecting, too.

"Good-bye," I said, reaching for the door and swinging it shut before she could say anything else.

CHAPTER 7

I stood in the light of the stained-glass window in the house on Legare Street with my eyes closed, seeing behind my lids only the beautiful window and remembering the way the room had looked when my grandmother lived here. I stayed there for a long time in the silence, knowing that when I opened my eyes again I'd be assaulted with faux-animal prints, psychedelic colors, and furniture made from plastic.

I had been amazed at how quickly the owners had accepted my mother's offer. We asked to be able to go through the attic before closing to determine if there were any family heirlooms we wanted to keep with the house. When the owner had said it was all old junk and we were welcome to all of it, I knew that we would probably find a treasure trove of antique furniture and priceless art, which was why I was standing now in the house by myself, waiting for my mother and too afraid to venture past the front rooms. I'd thought about waiting on the sidewalk outside, but the temperature had dipped back into the twenties and I disliked being cold even more than I disliked nasty ghosts.

The sound of a footfall came from the foyer and my eyes flickered open. It was a heavy step, like that made from a boot, and I stilled—waiting. I was soon rewarded with the sound of a second booted foot hitting the stairs, and I turned and walked quickly to the foyer to face the sweeping staircase. I knew who it was before I saw him—the specter of my childhood, my imaginary friend and great protector. My father had told me he was a figment of my imagination, and I think at some point I had come to believe him. But in the small corner of my mind where childish hopes cling like cotton candy, I knew he was real.

"Hello," I said into the dust motes that danced like iridescent fairies in the triangle of light from the window over the door. I sensed him rather than saw him, aware of the outline of a tall man leaning against the mahogany banister. I peered at him through the corner of my eye, never directly at him. As a child I'd learned that if I looked directly at him he'd go away, leaving only the trace scent of gunpowder and the lingering thought that maybe my father was right after all.

"It's been a long time," I said, and I felt him smile. Metal clinked against metal, and I pictured his long musket brushing against the large brass buttons of his dark green military jacket. I had the impression of a tricorn hat, large red cuffs on his jacket, and black leather gaiters with shiny buttons marching up the sides. He was back, my protector. Or maybe he'd never left. And I found myself wondering if he ever tired of carrying his musket for over two hundred years.

He began walking down the stairs toward me, his hand outstretched, and I tilted my head slightly, trying to get a better glimpse of him. I paused and felt the oddest sensation of heat warming my cheeks. Although he hadn't changed in the intervening years, I obviously had. Whereas he had once been the invisible playmate of a seven-year-old child, I now saw him as a young and very handsome soldier. I'm sure he must always have been handsome, but seeing him now through the eyes of a thirty-nine-year-old woman, I registered his height, the blond hair that curled out from under his hat, the eyes that seemed almost black but were lit with what I could have sworn was a sparkle of amusement. There was a sadness there, too, a sadness I didn't remember noticing as a child but seemed now to be as much a part of him as the uniform he wore.

He reached the bottom step and I felt his hand brush my arm, but I wasn't afraid. I'd never been afraid when he was there. Still feeling the heat in my cheeks, I raised my hand but hesitated when I heard the sound of one car door slamming shut followed by another. In surprise, I turned my head and looked directly at him, realizing my mistake as soon as I saw him fade like the smoke from an extinguished candle.

The sound of quick footsteps coming up the walkway preceded the front door being thrown open. My mother stood there with her gloved hand on the door handle, her cheeks pink and her eyes a vivid green. They settled on me and she frowned.

"Why is that man here? You said he'd be working in the garden and that I wouldn't have any contact with him. And why . . ." She stopped speaking as her eyes widened and her gaze focused on the spot behind me where the soldier had been.

I turned around and stiffened with surprise. My soldier stood there— in solid form—so clear I could see the beard stubble on his chin and his thick eyelashes. He too seemed surprised, his gaze widening as it settled on me and then moved to my mother. There was recognition in his eyes and in my mother's as he slowly put a leg forward, swept his hat from his head, and gave her a courtly bow before completely disappearing.

My questions stilled on my lips as my father filled the doorway behind my mother, his brows knitted together in annoyance. "And good morning to you, too, Ginnette. We can at least be civil to each other, can't we? Or are you too much of a diva now to be cordial to the father of your only child?"

"Mellie." My mother tried to shut the door behind her but my father stepped forward, blocking it from closing. "Would you please explain to your father that he's supposed to be working outside in the garden and that I have nothing to say to him?"

Still stunned by the solid presence of the soldier and my mind racing with the possibilities of why he would choose this moment to appear, it took me a few moments to process what my parents were saying.

Not willing to wait for my reply, Ginnette faced my father. "I think we said everything that needed to be said thirty-three years ago, and I have no desire to revisit one of the most difficult times in my life. So"— she crossed her arms over her chest and tapped a foot, diva-like—"why don't you go dig a hole in the garden or something so Mellie and I can do what we came here to do?"

To my surprise, my dad smiled one of the smiles I remembered from my girlhood—before our lives had unraveled—a smile that engaged his eyes along with his mouth and had always been reserved for my mother alone. After she left, it had gone too, and I'd imagined it packed away with the boxes in the attic with the rest of the detritus of their marriage that he no longer cared to revisit.

"I think you're more beautiful now than you've ever been, Ginny."

Caught off guard, my mother struggled to retain her anger. Finally she said, "Nobody calls me that anymore. I prefer Ginnette."

He just stood there, smiling. "But I still think of you as the Ginny Prioleau who swept me off my feet and stole my heart. I'm too old now to think of you as anything other than my beautiful Ginny."

I tried not to smile, horrified as I was to relive a similar conversation I'd had with Jack when I'd tried to convince him that he wasn't welcome to call me by the nickname my mother had given me. I was pretty sure that my mother would have as much luck convincing my father as I'd had with Jack.

Her chin quivered and then her cheeks pinkened even more. *Could she be blushing?* "Don't flatter me, James. I'm only two months younger than you so we both know how old that makes me."

Despite her words, she kept peering up at my father through thick eyelashes, and I fought the urge to gag. "Okay, you two. I think I've heard enough." I moved between them and faced my father, my eyes widening to show him my disapproval of his consorting with the enemy. "Dad, why don't you go outside and look around and jot down some ideas and a few ballpark estimates of the cost involved in implementing your proposed changes." I grabbed hold of his elbow and led him to the door. "I'll call you later to discuss."

I opened the door and he stepped out. "Thanks, Dad. Later." He opened his mouth to say something, but I didn't hear what it was because I'd already closed the door.

My mother had regained her composure by the time I turned around. She'd taken off her coat and thrown it on one of the beanbag chairs but still wore her gloves. Leading the way to the stairs, I said, "Let's go up to the attic. Follow me." She didn't ask why we were going the long way around since taking the back stairs would be quicker. She didn't need to.

We climbed the stairs to the third floor, then walked around the up-stairs hall that encircled the stairwell until we made it to the door to the attic stairs. I'd been up here once with my grandmother and remembered it as a place where the unwanted items of a family with pack rat tenden-cies discarded items long past their usefulness. Sort of like a pasture for old horses but not as scenic.

Grandmother had gone in for less than a minute to grab a floor fan for my bedroom and then marched me out before I'd had the chance to remove one dust cover but not before I'd heard the cacophony of voices that always seemed to accompany old things. She'd picked up the fan and then ushered me out before any of the voices recognized me and called me by name.

I stood for a moment with my hand on the doorknob, focusing on the task at hand and turning my thoughts inward to block out anything I didn't want to see or hear. I didn't have to look behind me to know that my mother was doing the same thing. Slowly, I turned the handle and headed up the attic stairs, my mother behind me, her gloved hand sliding up the banister.

Pale gray light filtered through the oval window on the front of the house, gently illuminating the specters of shrouded furniture and piles of miscellanea. I grabbed what looked like a dismembered chair leg and swatted at the collection of spiderwebs that had gathered in the corners before succumbing to age by sagging into the walkways somebody had once designed by pushing back furniture.

I lifted the flashlight I'd stashed in my purse and flipped it on to peer into the dark recesses of the attic space. "The current owners aren't interested in taking anything that's up here, so if you want it just say the word. Otherwise, they're going to hire somebody to dispose of it."

She nodded, her hands held tightly together in front of her. When I was small, I'd asked her why she always wore gloves and she'd told me it was because she was always cold. It wasn't until I was much older when I'd touched a hat in a vintage-clothing shop and seen somebody else's life flash before my eyes that I began to understand. Whereas it only happened on occasion with me, I assumed it must have been often enough to compel my mother to always cover her hands. My father'd had no patience for it, and I remembered him hiding her gloves more than once.

We both turned slowly, taking in what the flashlight could illuminate. There was a large assortment of garage sale–type junk, but there was also an equal amount of furniture and other smaller items like brass fireplace andirons and a stack of paintings against the far wall under the window. I paused by a cradle—completely intact, with a moth-eaten baby blanket still inside. If one were sentimental about one's family history and past, such a thing would probably be valuable intrinsically if not financially. I looked away and walked past it, glad I wasn't one of those misguided people who put the memories of people long gone at the top of their priority lists. These same people spent an inordinate amount of money on old houses for the sheer desire of spending even more money restoring them. I'm not sure how much of this I still believed in but it didn't matter; I had inherited my house and therefore was excluded from my own scorn.

I watched my mother's face soften as she examined the tangible memories of her family's history, and I looked away, doubting the sincerity of her sentimentality. I'd been her daughter, after all, but apparently not valuable enough to keep.

"I'd like to keep all of this. Tell the owners to leave it all intact and I'll sort through it later."

I nodded and turned away, not able to look at her.

"What's that over there?" My mother pointed to a large rectangular frame leaning against the wall next to a wooden hat rack where an old fedora, minus its brim, perched precariously on one of the prongs.

I swung the flashlight to where she pointed but could see only the back of a gilt frame. Walking toward it, I remembered what Rebecca had said to me about there being some sort of portrait in the attic that I needed to see. I paused—feeling suddenly chilled—and I thought I heard somebody whisper my name. "Did you say something?"

My mother's eyes met mine and she shook her head almost imperceptibly. "Focus," she said as we both moved toward the frame.

"Hold this," I said and handed her the flashlight. I reached down and put a hand on either side of the frame, then lifted it before turning it around to lean it back against the wall. "Shine the flashlight on it."

The circle of light danced over the dark oil paint like a spirit orb. I squinted and stepped closer to get a better look, feeling compelled to see something I didn't really want to.

"Dear God." My mother's voice sounded tight and constricted and not really hers at all.

"What is it?" I was still standing too close to see past the glare of the flashlight. I moved back, stepping into a pile of telephone books and knocking them over but I barely noticed. I was too busy staring at the portrait in front of me.

It was a painting of two young girls, about nine and ten years old. They wore clothing of the late nineteenth century, with high necks and straight skirts, and black leather ankle boots. Both had their long brown hair pulled back with satiny bows, and matching bangs that highlighted wide hazel eyes. One was slightly taller than the other, making me think they were sisters very close in age. It was only after scrutinizing their faces closely that I was able to make out subtle differences in their features—the height of their brows, the angle of cheekbones, the shape of their chins.

But it was mostly the light in their eyes, the auras of their personalities that had been captured by the artist that differed the most. The taller girl had a slight smile on her lips that hinted at the held-back laughter of a secret joke. Her eyes were guileless, looking directly out of the painting as if she had nothing to hide.

The other girl was smiling, too, but not with amusement. It was more like the smile of a person who has done something wrong and gotten away with it. Her eyes glittered with a long-held secret—a secret I wasn't sure I wanted to know.

But what was even more arresting than the girls' resemblance to each other was their resemblance to me.

"Who are they?" I asked my mother, my gaze fixed on the portrait.

"I have no idea. I've never seen this painting before. It must always have been in the attic because to my knowledge it has never hung anywhere downstairs. I just . . ." Her fingertips gingerly pressed against her lips.

"I know. They look like me. And you, if you look at the hairline of the taller girl; she's got a widow's peak just like yours. So they must be ancestors, right?"

She nodded. "But not your grandmother, she was born in 1900. Maybe her mother. Although I was pretty sure my grandmother was an only child."

I knelt in front of the portrait, hoping to see it better. Squinting, and wishing I could forget vanity long enough to actually throw my glasses into my purse, I peered closely at the two girls, seeing something new this time, something that seemed to catch the light and nestle into the lacy fabric of the taller girl's blouse. Leaning closer, I saw a small golden locket in the shape of a heart. Moving forward so that my nose was almost pressed to the canvas, I noticed the letter *M* engraved in the gold.

My mother saw what I was looking at and shifted the flashlight over to the shorter girl. "She's wearing one, too." With a look of reproach, she handed me the flashlight before opening her purse and pulling out a pair of stylish reading glasses. After sliding them on, she bent slightly forward. "This one has an R on it." She stepped back, her brow furrowed. "That's really odd," she said. "My grandmother's name was Rose, but I'm positive she didn't have a sister—or any sibling, for that matter. I would say that these girls aren't members of the family at all except for the uncanny resemblance to you."

"Uncanny is one way to describe it," I said, studying the portrait again. My scrutiny moved from the girls to the scene behind them, and again I felt the odd sensation of thinking I should know what I was looking at, but I had no clue. They were standing in the shade of a huge oak tree situated on a rise of land, a large body of water glittering behind them, a stretch of sandy beach just visible in the corner of the portrait. In the distant background, a white antebellum mansion squatted in the center of a row of oaks.

"Do you recognize the house?" I asked, turning to my mother.

Her face had paled, and she appeared as gray and transparent as a photo negative in the dim attic light. "No. But the ocean . . ."

She didn't say any more because she didn't have to. I'd been remembering the sunken sailboat, too—and the human remains found on board. And the trail of salt in the kitchen.

"I know. I thought the same thing. But what's odd is that . . ."

I felt my mother quietly watching me.

I continued. "Yesterday a friend of Jack's, Rebecca Edgerton, told me she'd had a dream about this attic, and how if I looked I'd find a portrait or picture of some kind of someone who resembles me."

"Really?" She cocked an elegant brow. "So this reporter is an acquaintance of Jack's. How interesting. She keeps leaving me messages, you know." Her eyes narrowed slightly. "And she's just a—friend?"

I frowned, wondering why she'd be more concerned about the relationship between Jack and Rebecca than Rebecca's psychic abilities. Of course, to us acknowledging psychic abilities would be on par with the excitement generated by the purchase of a new toothbrush in another household.

"Old friends. They used to date before Rebecca introduced Jack to her friend Emily. What's so weird is how much Rebecca and Emily resemble each other. And I get the feeling that Jack might be attracted to her because of it."

"Ah, yes. Emily, the fiancée. Poor girl. Jack's mother told me how Emily jilted Jack before the wedding without telling him she was sick." She shook her head. "But for Jack to find out later, after she'd died. That's the most tragic part of all." She fixed me with a piercing gaze. "No wonder he's attracted to Rebecca now." She patted my arm. "But don't worry, Mellie. I'm sure what he's after from Rebecca is more of a closure with Emily than any other kind of relationship. He never had his chance to say good-bye, and Rebecca's offering the chance to him now. Like a surrogate of sorts."

I pulled away. "I really couldn't care less, Mother. If you knew me at all, you'd realize that Jack and I are completely wrong for each other. We just don't have that kind of relationship, if you even want to call it that. It's more work related than anything and when he finishes his book and doesn't need to be around my house so much for his research anymore, I doubt I'll ever see him again."

Ignoring her dubious expression, I grabbed the frame with both hands. "If you could open the door for me, I'd like to bring this downstairs to examine it in better light. And I'd like Jack to take a look at it, too. He might recognize the setting."

Smiling to herself, my mother took one last look around the attic before heading toward the door. As I walked by with the painting, she said, "Isn't Jack living with you? You could just bring it home."

I set the painting down, my arms tired. "Firstly, he's not living with me. He's staying with me temporarily, in a guest room, because he's under the false impression that I need him for protection. Secondly, this painting doesn't belong to you yet and removing it from the house would be considered stealing."

"I guess you have a point," she said closing the attic door, then following me down the hall. "But what if the current owners see the painting and decide to keep it?"

We both looked around at the orange shag carpeting and vinyl pinwheel mobiles that hung suspended from the hallway ceiling light fixtures. "They won't," we said simultaneously and continued toward the front stairs.

We were halfway down when I remembered something I'd wanted to ask her. I stopped and faced her, balancing the frame on the step behind me. "Earlier, when you came in, you saw the soldier, too, didn't you?"

I watched her hesitate as something flickered behind her eyes, like a ghost flitting across the room. "Yes," she admitted as she resumed her descent, moving in front of me so I couldn't see her face or read her eyes, and I knew she'd done it on purpose. "I saw him."

I followed her into the foyer, resting the painting against the newel post. "I remember him from when Grandmother lived here."

"Yes. I know." She made a fuss of putting on her coat and buttoning it with her gloved fingers. "He was here when I was a girl, too."

I looked at her with surprise. "You never told me." A flash of anger seared through me as it occurred to me that there was so much more we didn't know about each other. And all because she simply hadn't bothered to be there.

"No. I didn't," she said, her voice soft. She lifted her hand to touch my arm but withdrew it, knowing I'd jerk away again. "I suppose there are many things I never told you, and I'm sorry. But maybe . . ." She gave me a tentative smile. "Maybe we'll have a chance now that I'm back to talk about things. To get to know each other better."

My phone rang, which stopped me from telling her that she had long ago missed her chance at sharing any part of my life. She was simply too late. I felt the prick of tears behind my eyes, and I turned my back on her to answer the phone, ashamed to let her see me cry.

"I have to get this," I said, flipping open my phone.

She waited for a moment and when I didn't turn around, she said, "I'll go now. Let me know the details on the closing."

I nodded and waited for the sound of the door latching behind me, realizing too late that I hadn't thought to ask her why the soldier had appeared so solid to me for the first time, and why I thought it might have had something to do with my mother's arrival.

I closed my phone without checking to see who it was and let my gaze return to the portrait—and found myself staring back at two sets of hazel eyes that were so remarkably similar to each other's and to mine, the subtle differences in shading now apparent in the brighter light. I stepped closer, my own eyes widening as I realized that the taller girl's eyes were slightly tilted up at the corners, a near mirror image of my own.

A small sound began in the eaves of the old house, racing through the plaster and lumber of the ancient frame, the sound a tiny wail at first and then erupting into a baby's helpless cries. I'd heard it before as a young girl, but until I'd spoken with Rebecca, its origins had been as elusive to me as those of my soldier.

I swallowed thickly and turned to the door, recalling one more thing I hadn't known about my mother, then let myself out.

CHAPTER 8

I returned home from the closing on the Legare Street property completely exhausted. The paperwork had been straightforward—I prided myself on having everything organized and laid out so that there was no wasted time—but the personal vibes in the room were both intrusive and uncomfortable. Everyone at the table—except for me—seemed to think a daughter acting as her mother's Realtor was cute and indicated a close bond. Smiling through clenched teeth for an hour turned out to be more exhausting than running a marathon.

I dropped everything in the foyer, not having the energy to bring my stuff all the way inside, then kicked off my shoes, scattering them across the marble tiled floor. "Hello," I called, hearing voices from another part of the house.

"Yo, Melanie! We're in here."

I grinned at hearing Chad Arasi's voice and followed the sound to the dining room. He was the male equivalent of Sophie's bohemian persona, right down to the braid he wore at the back of his head and the environmentally savvy bicycle he used for transportation to and from his job as a professor of music at the College of Charleston. He used words like "dude" and "awesome" and didn't seem to mind Sophie's fashion choices, which was one of the main reasons why I'd been pushing them together since Chad had first moved to Charleston from California and hired me as his Realtor earlier that year.

He now lived with Sophie—platonically—because according to Sophie their zodiac signs would be incompatible in a romantic relationship. That's what she said anyway, but I was pretty sure it had more to do with her independent nature—and her unwillingness to view a romantic relationship as anything but a power struggle. Staring at Sophie and Chad—now in matching Birkenstock sandals and having a lively conversation about the merits of Federal versus Georgian architectural styles—I made a note to redouble my efforts to get them together.

They were standing in the large doorway between the living and dining rooms with the warped pocket doors that had been removed now lying supine on two separate workbenches that had been assembled in the emptied dining room.

"It's the Melster," Chad said, approaching before kissing me on both cheeks. "We were wondering if you'd be bruised and bloodied after the closing." He made a big show of checking me out for injuries. "And seeing you whole makes us wonder if your mother's okay."

I smirked. "Very funny. It was pretty—intense. But it's over. And hopefully, after we get her house 'cleansed,' I shouldn't have to run into her at all." I ignored their shared glance and moved to where the doors lay patiently waiting. "How's it going?"

Chad shook his head. "Too early to tell, really. I'm going to try to find some matching hardwood to make a wedge for both doors to see if that'll work. Maybe shim the bottoms, too. The tracks and all the hardware need to be replaced, which isn't going to be cheap." He smiled brightly. "But Sophie and I agree that it'll look beautiful when we're all done."

I examined the offending doors for a moment. "Or maybe we could just close up the opening and forget it was ever here."

Both Sophie and Chad looked at me with identical expressions of horror and it was hard not to laugh. "Fine, fine. Do what needs to be done." I sighed. The discovery in the house of a hidden cache of diamonds had certainly helped finance the restoration, but sometimes I began to believe that the entire contents of Fort Knox wouldn't be sufficient to fund the job. I envisioned myself working at selling houses well into my nineties just to support myself and this house. I occasionally even had the odd thought that I actually enjoyed restoring the house, but usually only before I received one of the receipts Sophie gave me for materials or labor from the horde of workmen she commissioned for various jobs. Then my thoughts tended to stray more to a flaming match and some kind of accelerant.

I looked around, realizing I hadn't heard the dog barking when I came in. "Where's General Lee?"

Sophie watched my face carefully. "Jack and Rebecca took him for a walk."

"Who?" I wasn't sure if I was more surprised by the fact that Rebecca was walking my dog or that Chad and Sophie would be on a first-name basis with her already.

Chad explained. "The little guy has been locked up in the kitchen all afternoon because Sophie's been here and I guess they felt he could use the exercise."

"They?" I said, still not able to wrap my mind around the fact that Jack and Rebecca might be out walking *my* dog.

Chad tightened his braid. "Well, it was just Jack at first but when he went to leave, Rebecca came, so she went with him."

I nodded, slightly mollified. "What else is going on?" I asked hesitantly, afraid of Sophie's answer. Her answers always managed to cost me at least a thousand dollars and as many hours in sweat equity.

Again I noticed an exchange of glances. Sophie smiled her brightest smile, the one that reminded me of a nurse's right after she tells you it won't hurt a bit but before she jabs the large needle into your arm.

"It's time to talk about redoing the floors. I know I mentioned to you that we could do it room by room to cause you the least amount of inconvenience. But after thinking about it and discussing it with Chad, we realized that doing it that way would probably take two to three times longer and it would be best to just do them all at once."

I looked at them both, waiting for the big needle jab. "Okay. That sounds fine. Just let me know when and I'll take a couple of days off from work to help."

Again, the shared glance and I inadvertently flinched, knowing that the needle was poised and ready.

Chad intervened. "That's totally cool that you can help. Soph here wants everything done by hand so it will take as many people as we can get. But it's, um, going to take more than a couple of days."

"Like three or four?" I suggested helpfully.

"Um, not exactly. We're thinking maybe closer to a month. Or more. It's a big job. We'll have to remove all the existing furniture that's not al-

ready in storage because of the mess from the sanding. And then there'll
be a couple of coats of stain on top of that and then the wax. The smell
can be pretty noxious. . . ." His voice trailed off.

I'd stopped listening after hearing the word "month." "You're saying I
need to move out of my house for an entire month, or maybe more."

They both nodded, uncannily resembling matching bobbleheads.
"Bingo," they said in unison. Looking at each other, they both said, "Jinx!"
and started to laugh.

I was spared from throwing up by the voice behind me. "You can stay
with me."

Recognizing Jack's voice, I turned around to see him and Rebecca,
with General Lee in her arms. I noticed how he didn't squirm to be released when he saw me.

"Don't be ridiculous, Jack. I'll be moving into my house in a week
or so. Since I need Melanie's help with some of the renovations, it would
make sense for her to just move into her old room."

I hadn't noticed my mother at first; she must have come in right after
Jack and Rebecca but early enough to hear Jack's offer.

"I don't . . ." I started.

Sophie practically leapt with enthusiasm. "That's a great idea! That
way you'll be on hand to assist me and your mother with all the—work
that needs to be done on the house."

I knew her pause before the word "work" was intentional, and I appreciated her caution in front of Rebecca. I frowned, knowing that what
she said made sense. But I was more than leery about moving into that
house—and not just because my mother would be living there, too.

"I really don't think . . ." Again I was interrupted, but this time it was
by Jack.

"She's right. It makes perfect sense. You'd be close enough to home
to check on the progress here, plus you'd be on-site to help your mother
with all the, um, work on her house."

Appalled, I searched for my voice and any words strong enough to
dissuade the mob. "I don't want to impose on my mother. A hotel would
be fine. Really."

I felt four sets of accusatory eyes on me. Five, if you included General
Lee.

"You wouldn't be imposing, Mellie. You'd be helping me." My mother schooled her face into an appropriately groveling yet not-too-pathetic expression. "I'm not as young as I used to be, you know, and moving all of my belongings from a different state plus all the upheaval of a renovation just might do me in. And," she added with a note of triumph, "it would give us time to plan your fortieth-birthday party."

Rebecca's eyes widened. "I had no idea you were that old." Her long lashes fluttered as her cheeks reddened. "I'm sorry. That's not what I meant. I meant you don't look that old." She closed her eyes, her face reddening further, but she remained silent, unwilling or unable to dig a deeper hole.

Seeing a chance to change the subject, I said, "Mother, I don't believe you've met Rebecca Edgerton. She's writing a story about you for the *Post & Courier*. Rebecca, this is my mother, Ginnette Prioleau."

My mother held out her gloved hand, her brow raised in true diva fashion. "Oh, yes. I believe we spoke briefly once. And you've left several messages for me since. How nice to meet you in person." She didn't apologize for not returning the messages.

"Likewise," said Rebecca, gingerly taking the proffered hand and looking miserable, considering she'd somehow orchestrated meeting her prey in person.

My mother turned back to me. "Melanie may be turning forty, but she just keeps getting more and more beautiful each year, doesn't she, Jack?" She beamed at Jack.

"Just like the finish on an antique piece of furniture," he said, grinning. "More lovely, and with a little bit of shine."

I scowled at him, not liking being compared to an armoire, and faced my mother. If the comment had come from anybody else besides my mother, I would have hugged her for it. Instead I looked away, but felt all eyes staring at me—waiting for an answer—and I began to feel like someone who'd just told a little kid the truth about Santa Claus.

Jack's arm went around my shoulder and he bent close to my ear, his breath racing like little pinpricks up my bare neck. "Come on, Mellie. It's just for a short time. And I'll be there to rescue you if you need me."

My gaze traveled from my mother to Jack and then back again. Mrs. Trenholm had once told me she thought Jack could charm the blue out of the sky. I wasn't sure if she'd been complimenting her son or warning me. Either way, I believed she was right. Jack Trenholm had an alarming way of getting me to do things I didn't want to do.

I let out a slow breath through clenched teeth. "Fine," I said. "Whatever. I guess I can survive anything for a month."

Sophie shifted uncomfortably in her Birkenstocks and exchanged a surreptitious glance with Chad. "Um, a month is only a guesstimate. There's always the possibility it could take longer. For instance, if it rains a lot the high humidity will delay the drying of the floors between layers of stain and sealant. That's totally out of our control, of course, but it could add to the total time."

"You can stay as long as you need, Mellie. My house is always open to you." My mother smiled gently and I looked away.

I had a sudden vision of me in a barrel heading toward a large waterfall, and there was nothing I could do about it.

I was spared a response by a small squeak from General Lee, and then he came racing in to me from the foyer. I picked him up, checking his small body to make sure he was intact, then walked out of the room toward the foyer where Rebecca had wandered while I'd been strongarmed into moving in with my mother.

She was staring at the portrait of the two girls. I'd brought it to my house for temporary safekeeping while the previous occupants of the Legare Street house moved their belongings. It was leaning against the recently replastered wall of the foyer, and more than once I'd wanted to face it toward the wall to avoid the following gaze of the painting's subjects.

Rebecca looked up as we approached. "Sorry. I must have squeezed him too tightly. It's just . . ." She indicated the painting. "It's—it's just like what I remembered from my dream."

"What is it?" Jack walked closer and put a hand on her arm, and I was annoyed at myself for letting that little bit of contact between them bother me.

Keeping the dog in my arms as a sort of screen between me and the painting, I stepped closer and turned to Jack. "I didn't have a chance to show you what my mother and I found in the attic in the Legare Street house. We don't know who the girls are, but the setting seems familiar and I wanted to see if you recognized either the subjects or the setting."

He shook his head slowly, studying the painting closely. "I definitely see a family resemblance. But then again . . ." He looked up at me and narrowed his eyes and was silent for a moment. "I'm not so sure."

"Look," said Rebecca, pointing to the hidden locket on the taller girl's chest. Her index finger shook and she quickly folded it into her fist as if she didn't want anybody to see.

"They each have one," I said, regarding her closely. "Do you see anything you recognize? Maybe the house?"

It took her a moment to answer. "No. Not at all. It's just that it's so—striking." She squatted to get a better look just as I'd done before, but I doubted it was because her eyesight was deteriorating with age. I guessed that she was about five years younger than I was, and I couldn't help but look down at her hair part to see if she had any grays yet. She didn't.

Jack held up his cell phone and snapped a picture. "I'm going to show this to Yvonne Craig at the historical society. I don't recognize anything in this painting but she might."

I remembered meeting Yvonne when Jack and I had been researching part of my Tradd Street house's past. I'll admit to being a little jealous of her because of the fondness in Jack's voice whenever he said her name and the inordinate amount of time he seemed to spend with her. It wasn't until I'd met her—complete with support hose and walker—that I realized Jack had been leading me on purposely and that Ms. Craig was old enough to be his grandmother.

"Can I go with you?" Rebecca asked, her blue eyes wide.

I'd just been about to ask the same thing but remained silent now. Tagging along with them as a third wheel was about as appealing to me as spending a month living with my mother.

Jack put his phone back into his pocket and glanced at me. I was already preparing a gentle way to decline his offer to accompany them when he said, "You should probably stay here and start packing up your things to take to your mother's. I'll be happy to help you cart it all over when you're ready."

I felt like a balloon that had lost all of its air and then been run over by a truck. Twice. I forced a smile. "I was just about to say the same thing."

Chad and Sophie excused themselves and returned to contemplating the pocket doors as I herded the rest of the group to the front door. "Call me if you find out anything," I said to Jack.

Rebecca handed my mother her business card and after a brief pause my mother accepted it. "Just in case you accidentally deleted my messages on your answering machine," Rebecca said, her eyes not giving anything away. "I'd like to set up a time to interview you."

Ginnette gave an elegant shrug. "I'm afraid that won't be possible anytime soon. I have to fly back to New York to supervise the listing of my apartment and then pack up everything. I'll be sure to call you when everything has settled."

Rebecca's expression grew cool. "I understand. I'll call from time to time just to check your availability."

"Yes, certainly," my mother replied, and it was hard for me not to lift my palms in the air to double high-five her.

Jack and Rebecca left while my mother lingered inside the door.

"I'm not so sure about that Rebecca," she said after they were out of earshot.

"Mother, I really don't care about her and Jack. He's completely free to pursue whomever he wants."

She glanced over to the portrait again. "I wasn't really referring to her and Jack, but I suppose the warning would bode well there, too." She gave me a pointed glance. "I was referring to her interest in our family. She reminds me of a vulture hovering over a foundering ship."

"I think she's harmless. She can dredge up whatever she wants because it has no bearing on me. I have nothing to hide."

Her eyebrow crept up. "Don't you?"

The way she said it, full of resonance and innuendo, I could understand her success on a stage. I faced her fully. "What are you holding back? What is it that you don't want me to know? Do you know something about my past or our family—like whoever that might be they found on the sailboat—that Rebecca could find out? Because if you do, let me know now so I'm prepared."

She shook her head slowly but her eyes never left my face. "I know only as much as you do. Truly. I suppose we'll just have to muddle through and figure this out together."

She looked so convincing, and I might have been convinced if I didn't remind myself of what a brilliant actor she was. What most people don't realize about opera singers is that not only do they have to have a good voice, but they also need to know how to act—if only to translate into actions whatever they happen to be singing in Italian or German or whatever. I wasn't a fan of opera for obvious reasons, but I knew enough about it to be wary when my mother looked me in the eye and denied something.

I remembered the baby's crying from the day before echoing in the empty rooms of the old house and knew there'd been at least one thing she'd kept from me. "Rebecca told me about your miscarriage. I would have thought you'd have mentioned it. I don't want to be taken unawares again."

She lifted her chin but didn't say anything right away. Finally, she said, "There was no opportunity to tell you. You were too young to understand when it happened and I didn't want to upset you."

I felt the rush of hurt and disappointment like spilled milk and broken glass; both were irretrievably gone and much too late to cry over. "Hurt me? And leaving me without as much as a reason why or a good-bye was much less hurtful?"

She looked at me for a long time, and I found I was holding my breath, hoping she would finally tell me what I wanted to hear. Instead, she turned away and breezed through the open door, her fur coat close enough to tickle my nose. She paused but kept her back to me. "We will have to do this together, you know. Even with the help of others, it will come down to just the two of us." She pulled her collar close to her neck. "I'll be gone about a week or so. You can move into my house at any time but I suspect you'll want to wait until I return."

I remained silent as she walked down the steps. She turned her head slightly and looked back at me. "Good-bye," she said.

I didn't answer, knowing that her one word was thirty-three years too late.

CHAPTER 9

I was staring at the computer screen in my office, checking new listings and making notes, when Nancy Flaherty buzzed me on my intercom.

"You have a visitor, Melanie."

I could tell she was smiling and her consonants had gone soft as if they'd fallen out of slack lips onto a pillow. Sighing, I pressed the button to respond. "Jack doesn't have an appointment so he's going to have to wait. Tell him to cool his heels for a while and I'll be out as soon as I'm done here."

"I didn't think I needed an appointment, Mellie, since the two of us are practically living together."

I jerked out of my seat at the sound of Jack's voice in the doorway, flinging my glasses across the room at the same time. Struggling to regain my composure, I said, "You startled me."

With his trademark grin, he sauntered across the office and retrieved my glasses. "I noticed." Returning the glasses to me, he said, "I believe these are yours."

I stared at them as if I'd never seen them before and as if they hadn't been perched on my nose merely seconds before. "Yes. I believe they are." I took them from his outstretched hand and tossed them into my drawer. "They're more of a fashion statement than anything, really. Somebody told me they made me look more professional."

He looked at me with that annoying smirk that was at the same time achingly familiar. "You're a beautiful woman, Mellie. With or without the glasses."

His words had an opposite effect than the one he'd intended. I sat down in my chair, deflated. "What do you want, Jack?"

He sat down across from my desk and stretched out his long legs. "What makes you think I want something?"

"Because you're always nice to me right before you ask me for something."

He looked hurt. "I'm always nice to you."

Technically, that was true. But his being nice always led me to do something I didn't want to be doing. "Spit it out, Jack. The earlier I tell you 'no' the earlier you'll leave so I can get back to work."

"Fine, then. I wanted to know if you'd like to take a road trip today."

"Today?" I looked down anxiously at my desk with my neat to-do list and the stack of pink phone messages I still had to return.

"Yes, today. Right now, actually. It's still early enough that if we left now, I could have you back by your nine o'clock bedtime."

I wasn't sure if it was the mention of my bedtime that made his eyes sparkle or the prospect of taking a road trip. Remembering his easy dismissal of me the previous day when he took Rebecca to visit Yvonne at the historical archives, my mind started preparing my refusal when my mouth asked, "Where to?"

"Ulmer."

"Ulmer?" The name wasn't familiar. "Ulmer as in your long-lost uncle Ulmer?"

He smirked, unveiling a dimple that had a completely unwarranted and unwanted effect on my blood pressure. "No. I meant Ulmer as in Ulmer, South Carolina. Or right outside it, anyway. It's about a two-hour drive from Charleston on State Route 321."

I frowned, remembering past road trips I'd made with USC college friends to their parents' old family hunting lodges or restored farmhouses. They were second homes and used for family gatherings and holidays where friends with nowhere else to go were always welcomed and sometimes pitied.

"Isn't 321 the road that cuts through a bunch of swamps where the only signs of human habitation are billboards that advertise deer corn and bait worms?"

"The very one."

"Then why do we want to go there?" I realized too late that I'd used the word "we" instead of "you" and that I was already hooked—ready to be reeled in and thrown on deck.

A smug smile crossed his face. "To go see a two-hundred-year-old plantation that has old family portraits still hanging on the wall that I thought we should look at."

My computer screen flipped to the screen saver—a rolling marquee that read: WASTED TIME IS LOST SALES!—which reminded me how long I'd been idle. Irritated, I asked, "Why would I want to go see somebody else's old family portraits? And do they really expect any tourists that far out in the middle of nowhere?"

"Actually, it's not open to the public. It's a private home and still owned by the family that purchased the house back in the 1930s from the descendants of the builder. And I'm suggesting going there because when I showed Yvonne the picture of the portrait of the two girls you found in your mother's attic, she said I needed to go there."

Intrigued, I sat up. "Why?"

"Well, she didn't have a picture of it anywhere in the archives, but she's been inside the house several times to catalog its contents and re-members the portrait. It's of a young girl—and she's wearing a necklace that Yvonne thinks is very similar to the one worn by the girls in your painting."

"How similar?" I asked slowly.

"Similar enough to think it would be worthwhile to drop everything and take a road trip to the nether regions of South Carolina."

I looked down at my desk again and all of the work I still had wait-ing for me, the marquee's scroll sliding past the screen with an accusatory glare. "I'm not sure if I . . ."

"Mellie?"

My eyes met his and I noticed how the dark blue sweater under his leather jacket matched his eyes. "Yes?" I said hesitantly.

"Have you ever played hooky before?"

I shook my head.

Jack sighed. "I didn't think so. I'm going to go get your coat while you clean up here, and I'll meet you out front."

He left before I could argue, or maybe I waited too long to argue.

Whatever was the case, I didn't feel right letting him wait up front all day so I dutifully cleaned up my desk, switched off my computer, and left my office, coming back once to retrieve my glasses and toss them into my purse.

We took Jack's Porsche because he said it would get us there faster. I only agreed after he assured me it had the requisite airbags and ABS. After denying my request to stop at a fast-food restaurant to get fries and a shake to eat in the car—although he promised we'd stop someplace on the way as long as I didn't actually bring any food into the car—we headed west on Interstate 26.

I refrained from looking at the speedometer and commenting on how fast he was going in exchange for being in control of the radio. I found an oldies station that was playing an hour of ABBA and leaned back into my leather seat thinking that life couldn't get much better.

We chatted during the commercial breaks about his parents and the restoration of my house and the progress on his current manuscript that involved him spending so much time in my attic going through the previous owner's papers. He skillfully skirted any mention of my mother and I was thankful for that until I began to question his motives for being so nice to me. I was about to ask him out loud when his cell phone rang.

He hit a button on his dash to answer it and I heard the caller's voice broadcast into the car. "Hi, Jackie. Where are you? I'm sitting outside your condo with a bag of ribs from Sticky Fingers and a bottle of wine."

I recognized Rebecca's voice and turned to look out my side window as he picked up his Bluetooth and put it to his ear so I could only hear his side of the conversation.

"I'm actually on the way to Ulmer right now. I wanted to see that painting Yvonne told us about for myself. I'll be home by nine."

I noticed how he'd omitted mentioning that he wasn't alone. I closed my eyes and listened to the lyrics of "Waterloo" while pretending to block out Jack's half of the conversation.

"I'm disappointed, too," he was saying quietly but not quietly enough that I couldn't still hear him over the purr of the car's engine. "Can I take a rain check for tomorrow? Great. I'll see you then." He took his Bluetooth off his ear and tossed it into the console.

I felt him looking at me, and I was beginning to think he assumed I was sleeping when he said, "Sorry about that. It was Rebecca. She was wondering where I was," he added unnecessarily.

I nodded sleepily. "I know." I was silent for a moment. "I still can't get over how much she looks like Emily."

Jack continued to stare at the road in front of us. "Others have mentioned that before but I don't think I'd really ever noticed it."

I felt a perverse need to press on despite Jack's obvious desire not to. "They're practically twins. As a matter of fact, when I first met Rebecca, I thought it *was* Emily and that she'd come back."

He turned to consider me before concentrating on his driving again. "Emily's definitely gone. I feel it."

I didn't have any doubts either but I let Jack contemplate the knowledge alone. Still, Rebecca's intrusion into my life wouldn't allow me to drop the subject completely. "I can't help but wonder if your attraction to Rebecca could be because she does look so much like Emily. Like she's playing a role for you, to give you the chance to say good-bye to Emily that you didn't have before."

"That's ridiculous. Don't you think I can tell the difference between two different women? And what makes you think I'm attracted to her? We're just old friends, getting reacquainted with each other."

I snorted. "You're male. She's blond. And she's definitely interested, *Jackie*. Need I say more?"

"Do I detect a hint of jealousy, Mellie?"

Before I could deny it, he swerved off the highway onto a little dirt side road that had a sign that read: SWEET POTATOES—$5 GALLON BUCKET. A field of high sandy rows were dotted with the orange skin of the potatoes, glowing like meteors in the winter sunlight.

I grabbed on to the door handle to keep myself from falling into the driver's seat if only because Jack would have enjoyed that too much. "What are you doing?"

"Don't you like sweet potatoes?"

I frowned at him. "I'm from the South. It's illegal to be a Southerner and not like sweet potatoes."

He grinned the grin that always had the unfortunate response of raising my internal temperature several degrees. "Is it? I didn't know. It's a good thing I love them, then. And I make a mean sweet potato bread."

He pulled sharply into a dirt clearing where an elderly woman sat in her pickup truck, buckets piled with potatoes as large as suckling pigs in the truck bed.

I turned back to Jack. "You make bread? From scratch?"

Putting the car in park, he took the key from the ignition. "Somebody gave us a bread maker as a wedding gift and told me to keep it even when it became apparent there would be no wedding. What else was I going to do with it?"

I thought of several things including returning it to the store, but I remained silent as I watched him exit the car. His words had been flippant, but I'd sensed the thin veil of grief that still hovered over him like a sigh. How long did it take a person to get over a broken heart? And what happened if you never did?

It didn't take very long for the woman in the truck to begin batting her eyelashes at Jack as he spoke, his arm draped on the door surround as he leaned toward her. Eventually, he slid out his wallet and handed her a five before lifting a bucket from the truck. He came to my side of the car and paused, staring in at me.

I opened my door. "Do you need something?"

Jack eyed his minuscule trunk and nonexistent backseat. "Yeah. A place to put these."

I followed his gaze to the floor in front of me. "Please don't tell me you want me to stick the bucket between my legs for the rest of the trip." I sighed, recognizing the inevitability of the situation but not willing to give in too easily.

"I'll make you a loaf of sweet potato bread," he offered helpfully.

"Deal," I said, hoisting the bucket and situating it between my feet on the floor of the car. "If the tires start to deflate, we can throw them out the window one by one like ballast."

Jack slid behind the wheel. "Don't you dare. I've got just enough to make a few loaves of bread and a pie for Rebecca. She loves sweet potato pie."

I looked down at the offending spuds, no longer seeing them as just an inconvenience but more as an affront. Maybe if we stopped to look at the scenery they could be accidentally left behind.

"So, how long did you date Rebecca?" The question was out of my mouth before I could call it back.

He seemed amused. "Long enough to know that she likes sweet potato pie."

Chagrined, I sat back in my seat. "But not long enough not to have your head turned when somebody new appeared on the scene."

He knew I was talking about Emily, but he didn't take the bait and instead raised the volume on the radio. "I know this will be hard for you, but try not to bruise the potatoes by clenching your legs so tightly together."

"That's not funny," I said as he sped off with a wave to the woman in the truck.

"It wasn't meant to be. I was simply concerned about the potatoes."

"Sure you were," I said as I turned away and watched as the sun dipped behind darkening clouds and the first splat of rain hit the windshield.

Mimosa Hall was little more than a large farmhouse with a covered porch and white clapboard siding that seemed to glow in the gray of the pouring rain.

"What time was our appointment?" I asked as Jack pulled into a gravel drive and shut off the ignition.

"What appointment?"

"To see the house, obviously. Please don't tell me that we just drove two hours to get here and we might not even be able to get in the house."

"Where's your sense of adventure?" he asked, watching the rain drum against the windshield and judging the distance between the car and the house.

"It's not adventure I hate, it's wasting my time." I tried to hoist the bucket of potatoes to free my legs but couldn't position myself to do it.

"Allow me," said Jack, and he leaned forward to lift it, apparently taking his time and readjusting his grip several times before finally succeeding in dislodging it from its prison between my legs and balancing it on the console. "I'm going to race to the door and knock on it. If everything's fine, I'll motion for you to follow." He handed me the bucket. "Stick this on the seat when I leave."

I kept my ideas of where I'd like to stick it quiet and watched as he ran up to the door. It was painted black and large gaslight lanterns on either side of the door were lit, piercing the gloom. I watched as Jack knocked twice and then waited before the door slowly opened and an older man, with a stocky build, ruddy complexion, and wearing a hunter's flannel shirt, peered out at Jack through thick glasses.

They spoke for a moment and instead of Jack motioning for me to come, he followed the man inside, closing the door behind them. Annoyed beyond belief, I wrapped my coat around me, then threw open the car door and began running to the porch. Unfortunately, my legs were more cramped from holding the bucket in place than I had thought and my motor coordination—never very good at the best of times—failed me completely and I tripped, landing in a deep puddle that seemed to have been recently carved by a large truck wheel. My shins, what was left of them, stung in the icy water. I blinked heavily, my eyes tingling with pain, as more icy rivulets wound their way inside my coat, soaking my dress through to my skin.

The rain seemed to stop suddenly, but I could still hear it thumping against something hard. I opened my eyes to find Jack standing over me with a blue-and-white-striped golf umbrella, waterfalls of water spilling around the edges like a jester's hat.

"What are you doing?" he asked calmly.

I was still on my hands and knees. I looked up in annoyance. "I'm studying the effects of raindrops on puddles." I lifted a hand and he hauled me to a standing position. "You were supposed to motion for me to follow you."

He squinted at my drowned-rat appearance. "I thought borrowing an umbrella and coming to get you would be a better idea."

My teeth were chattering now and all I could do was nod. With one arm around my shoulders and the other holding the umbrella, he steered me toward the house. "I'm sure Mr. McGowan will give you a towel. Or two," he added after giving me a second glance.

The older man, presumably Mr. McGowan, held the front door open for us. Jack tossed the umbrella onto the porch floor and ushered me inside. I stood on a braided wool rug, shivering as Jack made the introductions, but I wasn't really listening. I was trying to hear past the sound of water dripping off me and onto the wood floors. It was just a whisper, unintelligible, but with a certain urgency I recognized. I closed my eyes to hear better and a shudder tripped through me as the voice crept closer and whispered in my ear. *Melanie.*

My eyes flew open to find Jack and Mr. McGowan staring at me expectantly. The top of an old sea captain's chest that was used as a bench in the foyer was opened, revealing stacks of neatly folded blankets and towels. "Yes, thank you," I said, hoping I'd guessed correctly at the question. Jack poked me in the back. "Nice to meet you," I added hastily.

Mr. McGowan ambled to the chest and pulled out a large beach towel. "We always keep these handy for the grandkids. They love to go playing in the creek out back." He pronounced it "crick" and I tried to smile, but it stopped midway when I became aware of the sudden and pungent odor of rotting fish.

I tried to tell Jack as he helped me out of my sodden coat and placed the towel around my shoulders, but my teeth were clenched too tightly together to keep from chattering—and not all of it because of the cold.

I slipped out of my waterlogged and now completely ruined pumps and was led into a warm living area furnished with antique farmhouse furniture in yellowed pine and scuffed oak. Soft checkered rugs anchored the comfortable sitting area that surrounded a crackling fireplace. I would have felt more relaxed if I didn't feel someone watching me from behind, close enough that I could feel the cold breath on my neck. *I am stronger than you,* I whispered to myself, and Jack looked at me oddly.

Jack turned to our host. "It's very nice of you to let us in to see the painting, Mr. McGowan. We don't mean to put you out."

Mr. McGowan waved his hand dismissively. "I love getting visitors. With my wife gone to visit her sister in Atlanta, I was feeling lonely." He winked. "Plus I hate drinking alone." He opened an armoire on the far side of the room, with shelves of glasses and bottles crammed inside. "I converted this myself to give me a little 'man space.'" He winked again, but this time it was directed at Jack. He held up a bottle of brandy. "It's a little early, but I figure the lady here could use a bit to warm up."

"Not for me, thanks. I'm driving," said Jack. "But I'm sure Mellie would like some. She's shaking like a mouse at a cat convention."

I scowled at him before turning to Mr. McGowan. Forcing my mouth open, I said, "I don't drink hard liquor, but thank you." I felt a little sanctimonious saying that, knowing that although I was the daughter of an alcoholic, Jack had been in the trenches himself.

Mr. McGowan pulled two glasses from the cabinet and began pouring. "This is the best thing for you when you're as cold as you appear to be. Trust me. Just a few sips and you'll feel as if you're sunbathing on a beach."

I was cold inside my bones, and my extremities were gradually growing numb. With an encouraging nod from Jack, I said, "All right. Just a little, please."

He poured a generous portion into two double old-fashioned glasses and handed one to me. "Thank you," I said, trying to hold the glass steady so its contents wouldn't slosh up over the sides. I took a healthy sip, nearly gagging as the heat trickled down my throat and filled my nose with steam. I coughed, my eyes watering, but it did the trick. Immediately, I felt my core begin to thaw and greedily took another sip to hurry along the process. I couldn't fight the presence that seemed to be hovering over me if I was frozen solid.

"Can we see the painting?" I asked, moving forward, and somehow missed a step. It wasn't as if I couldn't see where to put my foot on the floor; it was more like the floor wasn't staying where it should be.

Mr. McGowan topped off my glass before leading us into the dining room. The smell of rotten fish was stronger in there, and I took another deep sip of my brandy to fortify myself. I was already feeling warmer and more confident, and only a little bit shaky on my feet. I looked up at Jack to see if he'd noticed anything, but he was focused on the painting between the two front windows.

This portrait, while obviously painted by a different artist than the portrait of the two girls, was eerily similar. The subject of the painting, another young girl who appeared to be a little older than the girls in the first painting, was staring out of the canvas. She was long and lean and standing by an upholstered chair in an indistinct room. Her face and expression were unremarkable, although her coloring, the shape of her mouth, and the way her eyes tilted up at the corners made me think of the taller girl in the other painting. There was nothing memorable about this painting at all except for the heart-shaped locket around her neck, which bore the inscribed initial *A*.

I remembered the glasses I'd left behind in my purse in the car and cursed under my breath. At least I'd thought it was under my breath until I saw both Jack and Mr. McGowan look at me oddly. "Sorry," I murmured, the word quickly followed by a little hiccup. "Excuse me," I said, my hand over my mouth as I swallowed back a second one before taking another gulp of my brandy. I was completely warm now and would have forgotten all about falling in the puddle if my wet hair wasn't stuck to my face and my stockinged feet didn't squish with each step I took.

I was relaxed, too, in a way I rarely let myself be. So relaxed that when I felt the cold finger touch the back of my arm, I didn't jerk away. It was as if I almost believed that I could be stronger than it was.

Jack stepped closer to the painting and flipped open his phone to examine the picture he'd taken the previous day. "The locket appears to be identical to the other two. Right down to the font used for the engraving and the design that goes around the heart-shaped face." He turned to Mr. McGowan. "What do you know about this painting?"

The older man took a sip of his brandy. "Not much. It was here when my father purchased the house back in the thirties. The family that lived here for about a hundred and fifty years before we bought it was originally from somewhere up north. New England, I recall. My wife discovered that from a box of letters she found in the attic. Big family, too. According to the letters, they were always asking for relatives to come down to visit, or to come help them with the farm. Must have been a wealthy family, too, because they sent a lot of money up north. Came across tough times during the Depression, though, which is how my family came to own the property."

I stood and stared at the girl's hands while nursing my brandy and wondered hazily what seemed so familiar about them. I knew there were questions I should be asking, but my tongue seemed to be nestled into a corner of my mouth where it didn't want to be disturbed. Jack kept glancing at me as if wondering why I was so silent, but I held my wobbling finger to my lips to show him that I had to be quiet, if only to hear my name whispered again into my ear by the same voice I'd heard before. Each time I heard it, I took another sip of brandy until even my fear disappeared into a locked box for which I'd conveniently lost the key.

Jack put his arm around my shoulders but I didn't have the energy to protest, especially since I realized I'd been leaning and most likely would have keeled over if it hadn't been for Jack keeping me vertical. "Do you remember the family's name?"

Mr. McGowan shook his head. "Not offhand. My wife might know. Or we could certainly find out by going through the letters again. Either way, you'll have to wait until she gets back next week. She has a filing system that I'm not allowed near." He chuckled. "You know how some women are. She files everything. Even my socks are filed in alphabetical order by color."

"How very odd," said Jack. "Must be difficult to live with sometimes."

I went to elbow him in the ribs, but my elbow missed and I struck air instead, causing me to twist to the left in an odd and outdated dance move. Jack put his arm around my shoulders again and pulled me so close that I couldn't move and didn't really need to work that hard to stand up. He leaned into my ear and whispered, "That's what happens when you listen to too much ABBA."

My left hand was trapped and I couldn't swat at him, so I took another sip of brandy instead.

I tried to focus my eyes again on the floating picture in front of me, trying to see whatever it was I was supposed to. In the calm part of my brain that was numbed by the brandy and nicely insulated from my fear, I knew that the thing whispering my name wanted to hurt me and the reason why had something to do with the portrait in front of me.

I turned to Jack to ask him to take a picture but couldn't remember the exact words I needed. Lifting my index finger from my brandy glass, I made a motion of clicking the shutter button. Catching on quickly, he dug into his pocket and pulled out the digital camera I'd given him to hold. After first leading me to a wall to lean against, he took several pictures from different angles, including one close-up of the artist's signature.

After pocketing the camera and peeling me off of the wall, he turned to Mr. McGowan. "You've been very generous with your time, sir, so we won't take up any more of it." He offered his hand and they shook. "And if it's all right with you, I'd like to call your wife when she returns to see what she might know."

Our host led us back into the foyer. "Oh, she'd love it. She fancies herself a bit of a genealogist and loves to talk about it. Just make sure you have a nice comfortable seat first before you dial the number." He chuckled and then thumped Jack on the back and I heard the whoosh of air coming from his lungs.

As we stood inside the front door I smiled my good-bye to Mr. Mc-Gowan, not sure I could pry my tongue from the roof of my mouth. Jack took the beach towel off of my shoulders, then pried the brandy glass out of my hand before handing them back to our host.

The old man opened the door and stuck his head outside. "Looks like it's stopped raining, so you won't get wet getting back to the car. Just watch out for puddles."

Jack smiled. "Thanks again, Mr. McGowan."

"You're most welcome, young man." He pointed to me and winked conspiratorially. "And she's a keeper, that one. Nice and quiet."

Before I could set the facts straight, Jack retrieved our shoes, then hurriedly hustled me out of the house and down the porch steps. He stuffed me into the car, then buckled my seat belt, struggling to reach around me as I attempted to snuggle with the bucket of potatoes he'd put in my lap. As soon as he was finished, I rested my head on top of a large spud and closed my eyes, aware of Jack putting his coat over me and tucking in the edges.

I must have slept the entire trip home because the next thing I realized I was being thrown over Jack's shoulder like a sack of potatoes and carried up the stairs of my house—having no idea how he'd managed to get both of us around Sophie's scaffolding at the bottom of the staircase. I grunted, trying to show him that I was aware that he was manhandling me without mentioning that I didn't mind the placement of his hand on my rear end.

He pulled the bedclothes off of my bed, then slipped me gently onto the mattress and I fell back, ready to sink into blissful sleep again.

I felt him sliding my shoes off. "You can't go to sleep yet," Jack said. "Your clothes are still wet. You need to take them off."

"That's the oldest line in the book," I mumbled, burying my face in the pillow.

I felt myself being dragged up by my arm. "And I'll admit to having used it myself more than once, but this time I'm actually serious. Hang on."

He left the bed to go into my adjoining bathroom, and I took the opportunity to flop back down on the mattress.

He returned, holding my thick flannel nightgown and a pair of wool ski socks. "I found these behind the door and something tells me this is what you wear to bed." He thrust them at me. "Put these on. I'll turn my head, but let me know if you need any help."

I snorted, a little louder than I'd intended, and somehow managed to remove my dress and underclothes with surprisingly little damage to them or any furniture and slipped on my nightgown, leaving Jack the job of putting on my socks because every time I leaned forward to do it I fell over. Then I lay back in my bed and allowed Jack to pull the covers up to my chin.

He went into the bathroom again and returned with two aspirin, a glass of water, and the wastebasket, which he put by the side of the bed. "You might need this later." He pushed my hair out of my face and made me take the aspirin. I hazily recalled doing the same thing for my father, and I felt a wave of shame.

"I'm sorry," I muttered, staring at him with blurry eyes and feeling like I wanted to cry.

"Don't be. It happens. And I'm glad it's me here to take care of you so don't worry about it."

After placing the glass on a coaster on my bedside table and watching me collapse back onto my pillow, he said, "I'll be in the guest room with General Lee. I'll leave our doors open, so if you need me you can just shout."

I was about to slip into unconsciousness again when I remembered something I needed to tell him. I grabbed him by the arm to prevent him from leaving. "It was there today. At the house with the painting."

"What was there?"

"That—spirit. The one that's always been in my mother's house. The one I felt in my mother's kitchen when I went there the first time." I lowered my voice, just in case somebody else might be listening. "I think it followed me."

He gave me a questioning look. "I didn't know it worked that way. Don't ghosts haunt houses or buildings?"

I shook my head vigorously on the pillow, feeling my cheeks jostling from the exertion. "They can do whatever they want to. But there's one thing I'm pretty sure of." I pulled on both of his arms to get him to lean closer to me. "It wanted to hurt me."

His face was close enough to mine that I could smell his cologne and the shampoo he used to wash his hair. I closed my eyes and breathed deeply, enjoying the effect it had on all of my extremities. I opened my eyes again to find his dark blue ones very close to mine. Feeling like a giddy schoolgirl again, I said, "You want to know a secret?"

His eyes flashed with amusement—and with something else I wasn't sure he wanted me to see.

I reached up to whisper in his ear. "I like you. I like you a whole lot, but I'm never going to let you know that." I hiccupped in his ear before I fell back onto the pillow. I had the sneaking suspicion that it might actually have been a burp, but Jack was kind enough not to mention it. "That's because Sophie once told me to stay away from men who are emotionally unbelievable."

The corner of his mouth quirked up. "I think that would be 'emotionally unavailable,' Mellie." His voice was soft with a hint of amusement, and I wondered in what was left of my brain if I'd said anything that he might use against me later.

I'd already lost the train of our conversation. Not letting him pull back, I said, "I need you to do a favor for me."

I watched as his eyes drifted down to my lips before dragging them back up. "What is it?" he asked softly.

"Don't let my mother throw me that fortieth-birthday party."

Jack gently dislodged a strand of hair from my mouth. "Why not, Mellie? I think she's trying to find a way to connect with you. And throwing you a party is her way of doing it." He paused and I felt his warm weight on the edge of the mattress next to me. "Would it be so difficult for you to let her?"

I shook my head, trying to make him understand the thing that was so clear to me. "Because then everybody would know that I'm old. That I'm a dried-up husk of a woman whose biological clock is running on daylight saving time without a battery." I stifled another hiccup. "Fifty years ago I'd be called somebody's eccentric spinster aunt and I'd have to sit on my front porch all day and spit at people who walked by." I shook my head again briskly, trying to clear it. "I could just wash my face until I can't breathe." I looked at his blank expression and realized that I hadn't understood what I just said, either.

His lips trembled a little. "Mellie. Firstly, you don't have any nieces or nephews so you can't be called anybody's aunt. Secondly, you're a beautiful, intelligent, and vibrant woman who doesn't look a day over thirty, which is a miracle I can attest to because I've seen what you eat. You should be proud of who you are and what you've accomplished, regardless of your age." He paused for a moment. "I know your relationship with your mother is difficult right now. But she's reaching out to you. Maybe you should give her a chance."

I blinked slowly, fighting sleep. "What did you say?"

He took a deep breath. "I said lots. Which part are you asking about?"

"The part where you said I was beautiful."

"Oh, yeah," he said. "That part." He chuckled and my whole body vibrated with it. "I said you were beautiful, vibrant, and intelligent. And I might add that if you were also sober and knew we were having this conversation, you would probably have to kill me."

I smiled smugly. "You think I'm beautiful." I frowned, trying to grab a thought that kept floating away. "Aren't you supposed to kiss me now?" I moved up to touch my lips to his but he pulled back.

Gently, he disengaged my fingers from his arms. "Mellie, trust me. It's not that I don't want to. It's just that I don't make a habit of kissing women who are barely conscious. I like them to be fully awake so they remember it in the morning." He stood and retucked my covers, then surprised me by leaning over and kissing me on my forehead. Then he moved his lips to my ear and whispered, "Just for the record that was almost kiss number three."

I listened as his footsteps crossed the floor. Before he reached the door, I said, "Number four, but I'm not counting."

I fell asleep listening to him laugh while he walked down the hall toward the guest room, his footsteps lulling me into a dreamless sleep.

CHAPTER 10

All through my shower the following morning, bits of conversation kept sifting through my consciousness, like recalling a dream. If only it *could* have been a dream. With dreams, you're the only witness and you're free to do whatever your subconscious tells you. You willingly do it in the privacy of your own mind. Unfortunately, judging from the humiliating fragments that kept jumbling inside my brain, everything I'd said and done the previous day had had an audience. I pressed my forehead against the cold tile of the shower to try and stop it from throbbing and wondered if it were possible to fake my own death and move to another continent.

Moving quietly so as not to awaken Jack in the guest room and actually have to look him in the face, I threw a few essentials into a suitcase and crept down the stairs and through the back door after giving a quick greeting to Mrs. Houlihan and General Lee in the kitchen. I had no intention of moving into my mother's house before she returned from New York, but I'd hired a cleaning crew to scrub the house from top to bottom after the previous owners had moved out and I needed to be there to let them in. And if I brought a few things over each time I went to the house on Legare, I wouldn't have to ask Jack for help. It was my plan to never actually have to speak with him again.

I parked on the street in front of my mother's house to allow the cleaning people access to the driveway when they arrived and sat for a few minutes to wait for my head to clear and my stomach to stop churning, realizing my unease wasn't completely due to the previous day's excess.

With a fortifying breath, I pulled my bag out of the backseat and made my way inside the house. Despite the DayGlo paint colors on the walls and moldings, the house didn't appear as awful as it had on my previous visits because of the absence of the hideous furniture and accessories.

I spun in a slow circle, seeing with my newly trained eyes the classic architecture and perfect symmetry of the foyer superimposed on my memories of my grandmother's house and the happy days I'd spent here as a child. But the clash of colors on the walls brought me quickly out of my reverie and I felt the odd need to reassure the old house that help was on the way. I'd already scheduled an appointment with Sophie to walk through each room to decide on historically accurate color schemes and any reverse remodeling that needed to be done. I wasn't as sold on the "historically accurate" part as Sophie was, but I did know that any type of color scheme was an improvement to the existing circus-like hues.

Fishing through my purse, I found two more aspirin. I knew from experience with my father's hangovers that if I stayed ahead of the headache, I had a much better chance of hanging on to the contents of my stomach. Dropping my purse and bag by the front door, I paused. The kitchen wasn't far from the foyer, but I was alone and in no mood to face whatever it was that lurked in the house and whose presence I sensed even now.

"Hello?" I called out, feeling silly, but wanting to alert my soldier that I was there. I listened to the silence, waiting to hear a clang of metal against metal or his booted footfall. I heard nothing, but neither did I hear my name being called by the menacing voice I'd experienced once before and had no desire to experience again.

Feeling somewhat reassured, I made my way quickly to the kitchen in search of tap water to wash down the aspirin, hesitating briefly in the entrance to make sure the door to the back stairs was closed, just as I'd done as a child.

I was leaning over the sink with my hands cupped like a bowl when I sensed a presence behind me. Swallowing my aspirin quickly, I spun around in time to see my soldier casually leaning against the wall by the door leading to the back stairs, his booted legs crossed at the ankles. He began to fade until I averted my eyes.

"Good morning," I said out loud, not remembering if we'd ever really had a conversation when I was a child.

You have grown into a beautiful woman since I saw you last.

The words had not been spoken out loud, but I heard them inside my head as if they had been. His words were heavily accented, and I smiled in recognition.

I felt myself flushing as I leaned back against the sink, aware again of how tall he was, and how his blond hair seemed to gleam from the sunlight streaming through the plantation shutters on the windows. "What's your name?" I asked, feeling foolish, but not because I was speaking out loud to a phantom. I felt foolish because I should have known his name and didn't, despite remembering him from the long-ago years of my childhood.

He bowed and I heard his boot heels click together. *Is it not enough that I know yours?*

I shook my head. "No. If we're to be friends, it's only fair if we know each other's names."

I felt his eyes on me but I didn't turn to look, sure I would see a sparkle of amusement in them. *Maybe we are not meant to be—friends.*

"Melanie?"

The soldier disappeared as quickly as if a light switch had been flicked off at the sound of my father's voice.

My father came into the kitchen and looked around. "Who were you talking to?"

"No one," I said. "Maybe you heard the radio from a passing car."

"Uh-huh," was all he said. He finally got a good glimpse of my face and bloodshot eyes. "What happened to you? You look like you've been pulled the wrong way through a hedge."

"Thanks, Daddy. I'd rather not talk about it, okay? I drank too much, I know I shouldn't have, and I doubt I'll ever willingly do it again. Trust me." I winced again, remembering snatches of my conversation with Jack.

He pressed his lips together as if forcing himself to reserve comment. "Is your mother here?"

Glad of the change in subject, I said, "No. She's in New York tying up some loose ends."

He actually looked disappointed. I crossed my arms over my chest. "Why? I got the impression that she wasn't interested in seeing you again."

He walked toward me and shrugged, then stuck his hand in his pocket. "Maybe so. But I have something here that she might be interested in seeing." He pulled out a small zippered plastic bag with something balled up at the bottom of it. "I know your mother has sent her lawyers to deal with the salvage company responsible for discovering your great-great-grandfather's sailboat, but I thought a personal visit might get us a little closer to the action. I figured if anybody should be near the site, it should be me since the media doesn't have any idea who I am—yet."

I stared at the bag, not wanting to touch it. "Are you allowed to have that?" I looked up. "There's also the matter of human remains being found on board. I doubt the authorities would want anything removed from the scene until they've had a chance to look at it." I didn't really care. Old things and their histories had never held much interest for me. All I knew was that I didn't want anything to do with whatever was in the bag and I needed to try and persuade him to return it.

He raised both eyebrows, succeeding in appearing as innocent as a puppy. "They already have." Clearing his throat, he held the bag out to me. "The captain's an old army buddy of mine and thought this should be yours. They've already run all the tests they can and taken all the pictures they need. My friend figured it would be better off with you than in some government vault for the next fifty years."

I stared at the bag while my father held it out to me, waiting me out. He'd been out of the military for a long time, but I underestimated his endurance and his willingness to wait until he saw the right opportunity and went in for the kill. "If you don't take it, I'll have to give it to your mother."

He'd known, of course, the one thing to say. I took the bag, the once-clear sides now cloudy from so much handling.

"Go on. Open it."

The top pulled apart easily and I could now see a tarnished gold chain, its luster dulled by years beneath the salty water of the ocean. Gingerly, I lifted it out of the bag, my hand stilling as I spotted the heart-shaped locket dangling from it.

"It's beautiful, isn't it?" he asked.

"It is," I said, touching the flat gold locket but sensing nothing except the cold quiet at the bottom of the ocean. Relief rushed through me that I hadn't been able to see anything else and my fingers closed over it. "Where was it found?"

"Inside the trunk. With the remains."

The locket slipped out of my hands, landing on a black marble tile, the chain extended like a spider lying in wait.

"What's wrong?" he asked, stooping to pick it up.

"Come here," I said, then led the way into the downstairs drawing room where I'd placed the portrait of the girls after bringing it from the Tradd Street house following the closing. I stopped short in the threshold, feeling disoriented—like being on an escalator that suddenly begins to move in the opposite direction. I stared at the painting, my breath suspended. When I'd moved it into the room, I'd placed it facing against the wall. But now the portrait of the two girls faced out toward the room, the eyes of the shorter girl glaring out at me with what seemed to be a menacing grin in the dim corner of the room. I blinked, thinking it must be a trick of the light.

My father walked closer to the portrait, the locket dripping through his fingers. "It's identical. Isn't it? It's a little hard to tell because this one's so dark, but look at this edging. And here." He used his thumb to brush hard against the front of the locket, then took out an eyeglass cloth from his back pocket and rubbed it back and forth over the gold. "I thought so. It has an engraved initial, too."

He held it up, and the stink of rotting fish reached me at the same moment I noticed the initial *M* rising out of the grime on the locket like a dead thing from the grave. "It could be the same one. Couldn't it?"

I nodded, swallowing thickly and wanting desperately to run out of the room. But how could I do that in front of a person who'd never believe me? For the first time in my adult life, I wished my mother were there.

"It's an *M*—for Melanie," he said, and before I realized what he was trying to do, he was standing behind me and fastening the locket around my neck. I froze, unable to move as if a great weight were pressing on my shoulders, holding my feet to the floor. The chain felt warm on my neck as if the heat from another's skin had touched it first. I smelled salt and ocean air and the pervading stench of spoiled fish. I resisted the urge to gag, but not because of the necklace; the necklace felt as if it belonged on my neck,

and not just because of the initial. And when I ran my fingers over the large
M I had the distinct feeling that whatever rotting presence we'd resurrected
from the bottom of the ocean didn't want me to have it.

"Someone's at the door," my father said, and I realized he was repeating himself and that I hadn't heard him the first time.

I blinked at him. "The door," he said again. "Would you like me to
go get it?"

Eager to leave the room, I backed out, waiting until the last moment
to turn my back on the portrait. I threw the door open and found Rebecca Edgerton grinning widely on the other side.

"Good morning," she chirped, and I wondered absently if she'd ever
been a cheerleader. I knew if I'd asked Jack he'd be able to tell me along
with a list of all of her injuries and where any scars might be located.

"Hello," I answered, peering behind her to make sure she was alone.
I had no intention of speaking with Jack in the foreseeable millennium,
and I especially didn't want it to happen in front of Rebecca. "Jack's not
here." I stood in the doorway, blocking her access.

"I know," she said, her smile now forced. "I already spoke with him
and he told me I could find you here."

"How nice of him. So what brings you out so early?" I blinked hard.
The sharp sun that angled through the doorway was like a dazzling dag-
ger to my bleary and swollen eyes, but my vision was clear enough to see
Rebecca's immaculate appearance and freshly manicured fingers. I hid
my own behind my back, still trying to flake off the paint that had ad-
hered to my nails much more effectively than to the fat cherubs anchored
in marble pear trees on the fireplace surround in my tiny library.

Rebecca looked behind her, then shivered in her pink cashmere coat.
"Do you think I could come in? It's a personal thing that I'm sure you
wouldn't want anybody else hearing. Besides, it's freezing out here."

Reluctantly, I opened the door wider so she could enter. As she took
her coat off, she examined her surroundings, her fingers stalling on the last
button as she caught sight of the heating vents that had been painted black-
and-white to match the zebra rug that I couldn't even bring myself to give
to Goodwill for fear they'd be insulted. Besides, with all the painting we
were planning on doing, it could come in handy as a drop cloth.

Seeing the question in her eyes, I hastily added, "I had nothing to do with the décor and neither did my family. We'll be working with Sophie Wallen to return everything to colors actually found in nature."

She continued spinning, as if trying to get a 360-degree view of the foyer and its kaleidoscope of colors. "This is practically profane," she said, and I was surprised to hear the anger in her voice. "Some people would die to have the honor to live in a historic home like this, and to think that someone would . . ." Her hands indicated the fuchsia walls. "It defies logic."

"And good taste," I muttered and saw her lips curve up in a smile. I watched her for a moment longer, captured by a fleeting glimpse of something familiar that was too brief to recognize.

"Who is it, Melanie?"

"My dad's here," I explained to Rebecca, leading the way into the drawing room.

He stood in front of the portrait of the girls as if mesmerized, his back to us. "I see something of your mother and you in the taller one," he said. "But the shorter one." He shook his head. "There's a strong physical resemblance, but there's . . . something else about her. Something that makes me feel as if they're not sisters. Cousins maybe?"

I stopped behind him. "Dad? This is Rebecca Edgerton, the reporter who's doing the story on Mother."

He faced her and held out his hand to shake. "It's a pleasure to finally meet you. Jack told me all about you."

I looked at Rebecca, who seemed to be as surprised as I was. "Really?" we said in unison.

My dad frowned as he looked from one of us to the other. "Mostly because of your connection with Emily."

"Oh," we said again in unison, but Rebecca sounded disappointed.

Rebecca shook his hand. "Well, it's a pleasure to meet you, Colonel Middleton."

"You've done your research," he said, acknowledging her use of his correct rank. In the past, when he was still drinking and people in bars would look at his insignia and medals and call him General, he wouldn't correct them.

"It's my job, sir. I've been working on this story about your ex-wife for some time now. You'd be surprised at the information I've discovered."

His eyes flickered over to mine in an unasked question before they returned to Rebecca. "Oh, you'd be surprised how many hidden skeletons we have in our family. Not that we'd share them with you, of course."

"Really? And I think you'd be surprised how enterprising my methods can be when it comes to digging up family secrets. Not that I'd share them with you, of course."

To my indignation, my father laughed before beaming at Rebecca in admiration. "Well, I can certainly see why Jack still talks about you."

Eager to see her leave, I said, "I've got an appointment, so if there's something you came to tell me . . . ?"

Her gaze was chilly as it rested on me. "Yes, sorry. I received a call this morning from one of my sources at the coroner's office with a pretty good scoop. I've already written my story and filed it with the paper with instructions not to run it until I spoke with you first."

"So if we don't like what you have to say, you won't run the story?" I tried to keep the belligerence out of my voice but I couldn't help it. There was something about Rebecca Edgerton that reminded me of biting into cold ice cream.

"No. I'm only doing this out of courtesy because of your connection with Jack."

I crossed my arms so that my hands wouldn't find themselves around her neck. "Then you'd better hurry up and tell us so you can get that story printed."

Without preamble, she said, "They've received the preliminary results of the examination on the human remains found in the sailboat." She paused for effect. "It's definitely a female and they estimate she was about twenty years old at the time of her death."

"That certainly tells us nothing," I said, keeping my arms crossed.

"Oh, there's more." Her eyes brightened like a child's on Christmas morning. "The top portion of the skull was largely intact, but shows signs of trauma—as if the head sustained an injury by a blow or a fall. That could have been the cause of death."

I let my arms drop. "Well, then. Go ahead and print it. The media can't possibly want to ask me about a homicide that occurred a hundred years before I was born. And personally, I couldn't care less. It's old news, in other words."

Rebecca bristled, apparently at my lack of amazement at her researching prowess. "Well, I guess that's all the information I have to tell you." She pursed her lips. "I'll be going, then. Nice to meet you, Colonel. . . ."

Her voice trailed away as a ray of yellowy light struck the stained-glass window. At the same moment, heavy clouds broke away in front of the sun and opened the sky like a door. "That's—incredible," she said, her gaze focused on the window with its hidden figures and secret meanings.

I wanted to stop her, to pull her away from it and explain that it was my window and the best part of my childhood—the one thing from the past I had allowed myself to cherish the way some people cherished old things—and I wasn't in the mood to share it, least of all with her.

"This is really unusual for a house this old," she said, walking nearer.

My hands balled themselves into little fists, my fingernails digging into my palms. "It's not original to the house," I said as my father stepped between Rebecca and me.

Rebecca pulled a notepad out of her purse and began to write. "It looks like it might be late nineteenth century." She faced me. "Am I right?"

I gave her a grudging nod. "You seem to know a lot about old houses."

She studied me for a moment, then shrugged. "You pick things up when you're in this business, I guess." She returned to jotting notes onto her pad. "Do you know who had it installed?"

"No, I'm afraid I don't. Why would you want to know?"

She didn't bother to look at me as she wrote, but I sensed that despite her tone, nothing she said to me was offhand. "You never know what will work in a story, what sorts of little tidbits would make it more interesting."

I turned to face the window again, surreptitiously tucking the locket back into my blouse, feeling the surprising heat of it on my bare skin, sensing again that somebody had just let it go from a tightly held fist. "Really?" I said.

"Really. It's what makes a good journalist." She put her pad back into her purse. "I've taken up enough of your time, so I'll let you go. When I see Jack, I'm going to ask him to go see if Yvonne Craig might know something. She's a real wealth of information about Charleston and its history, you know."

"I've heard that somewhere." My dad shot me a warning glance for my sarcasm. It was one thing he'd never tolerated from me and something I'd learned to utilize only when he was out of earshot. I began walking toward the front door. "Thanks for stopping by. Can't imagine that the news would create much of a media frenzy, but then again Britney Spears' decision to go pantyless made front-page news. Go figure."

Rebecca paused by the front door. "Be that as it may, it will be news for some. The Prioleaus have their reputation to maintain and I suppose the discovery of a body, regardless of how old, might be a trifle inconvenient, if not downright embarrassing."

Her eyes were bright and clear as they regarded me, and not for the first time I felt a twinge of unease. There was something more to Rebecca Edgerton than she was letting on, something more than her connection with Jack or her pursuit of my mother's story. I moved my hand to my neck to make sure the locket was well hidden inside my blouse, not entirely sure why I would choose to hide it from her.

She frowned slightly. "Do you smell that? I could swear it smells like . . . gunpowder. Yes, that's it. It reminds me of the smell that hangs over battlefields when they do the battle reenactments."

I pretended to sniff the air, although there was no need; I'd sensed the presence of my soldier from the moment we'd stepped into the foyer. "No, I don't smell anything," I said, opening the door wider so she'd take the hint and just leave.

She smiled. "Well, then. It must be a wood fire in somebody's chimney. Thanks again, Melanie, and nice to meet you, Colonel," she added over my shoulder. Returning her attention to me, she said, "And when you see Jack tell him to call me on my cell. He has the number."

"Sure," I said, smiling and waiting for my face to crack. It wasn't until she was at the bottom of the steps that it occurred to me she was the first person besides my grandmother, my mother, and me who had ever sensed the soldier's presence. I stared after her as she made her way down the walk toward the gate, and as I started to close the front door I became aware that the skin where the locket lay on my chest had become uncomfortably hot.

CHAPTER 11

I'd just closed the last of my suitcases when I heard Jack call from downstairs. "Mellie? Are you here? I hope so because the front door is wide open."

Crap. I'd left the door open so I could shuttle my personal belongings from the house to the car in preparation for my move to the house on Legare Street. "Crap," I said out loud as I yanked the suitcase from the bed and let it fall to the floor. General Lee pawed eagerly at the closed bedroom door at the sound of Jack's voice. I scooped him up and whispered in his ear, "Jack is not our friend, remember? He eats little dogs for breakfast."

His ears perked up and his eyes widened, but he turned toward the door again in anticipation of Jack's arrival.

"Mellie!" Jack called again.

I opened the door a crack, listening as Jack's footsteps faded toward the kitchen in the back of the house. Using the opportunity, I grabbed the suitcase with my free hand and headed toward the stairs. I was on the bottom tread when I heard Jack walking back from the kitchen. I ducked into the dining room, then looked furtively around me for a place to hide. All of the window treatments and furniture had been removed in anticipation of the floor stripping that was scheduled to start as soon as I moved out, leaving nothing to hide behind.

I eyed the butler's pantry, the door partially obscured in the room's wall paneling. Dropping the suitcase, I pried open the door and slipped inside just as I heard Jack's voice in the dining room. Belatedly, I recalled the suitcase I'd left behind.

Jack rapped on the door. "Mellie? Are you in there?"

I was hoping that if I didn't answer he'd go away. Any thoughtful, kind, and considerate gentleman would.

Without asking again, Jack opened the door and peered inside at the darkness—and me standing inside holding the dog.

"There you are," I said to General Lee as I pushed past Jack into the living room. "I have no idea how he got in there."

Jack's lips twitched, but some element of self-preservation held him back from laughing outright. "You're not avoiding me, are you?"

"Avoiding you? Of course not. Why would I do that?"

He shrugged, folding his arms across his chest, his eyes alit with an alarming sparkle. "I have no idea. It's just that ever since we took our road trip to Mimosa Hall you haven't answered any of my phone calls and you haven't been home when I've stopped by."

I focused on scratching General Lee behind the ears. "I've been busy. I had to put all of the furniture in storage, get all of the kitchen stuff on Mrs. Houlihan's list together so she can operate in my mother's kitchen, and then get myself packed up to go to Legare Street. It's been time consuming."

Jack rubbed his jaw, the sparkle in his eyes not diminishing. "Well, that's a relief. I was thinking it had to do with me putting you to bed when you were half conscious."

I felt the blood rush to my cheeks. "Why? Did I say anything? Anything that might make you think less of me?"

"Oh, no. Not at all. Actually, I was thinking you were avoiding me because you were embarrassed that I know what you sleep in at night. It was pretty horrifying, you know. All that flannel."

The relief made my toes tingle. Maybe the snatches of conversation that kept floating in my brain really had been a dream. I put General Lee on the floor. "It's not like you haven't seen worse," I said, referring to sharing a bathroom with me after he'd moved in the first time so I wouldn't be alone in the old house. There'd been more than one occasion when I'd neglected to remove my drying lingerie from the shower.

"That's debatable." Jack bent down to pet the dog, then eyed the suitcase. "Can I help you load your car?"

"All done," I said, glancing at my watch. "And with five minutes to spare. Your mother's meeting me over at the Legare Street house to talk about furniture, so I've got to run."

"I know. She told me. That's how I figured I'd find you here."

Without asking, he picked up my suitcase and motioned for me to walk in front of him, General Lee tagging along behind us. "So what did you need to talk with me about that you couldn't leave on voice mail?"

I walked into the foyer and opened the front door for him.

"Mrs. McGowan is back home and she gave me a call. Thought you might be interested in our conversation."

I felt a little shiver of apprehension tease my spine, remembering the voice that had whispered my name, recalling my fear even through the haze of brandy. "What did she say?"

"She said that she makes the best blueberry cobbler and invited me to come try some next time I'm in her neck of the woods."

I rolled my eyes. No woman, even one who'd never laid eyes on Jack, was immune to his charms. It was nauseating, really. "Did she say anything else?"

"Yep. That the name of the New England family that owned the house before the McGowans was the Crandall family from Darien, Connecticut."

I waited for him to say something more. "And?"

"That's all. Does the name ring a bell with you?"

"Not at all." We reached my car and I moved to the driver's side to push the trunk release, then waited while Jack added my suitcase to the rest of the bags inside. He frowned at them before shutting the trunk.

"She did say that she'd go through the old letters again and see if she can find out anything else. She does remember some kind of family tragedy from sometime in the latter half of the 1800s. Couldn't remember exactly what. But she's going to go back and look, see what she can find out, then let me know. Maybe I'll go down for a visit and some blueberry cobbler."

"You do that," I said as I slid into the driver's seat. I caught a movement near the old oak tree and I startled, remembering the woman and the child who had once haunted that section of the garden. But the person pointing a camera at me and crouched behind the Confederate roses was definitely not a ghost.

Jack followed my gaze and saw the photographer, too. "You go on ahead. I'll take care of this guy. I'll catch up with you later."

"Thanks," I said, meaning it. The media attention since the raising of the *Rose* had died down considerably during the ensuing weeks, but every once in a while an overeager photographer or journalist could be found waiting to catch me off guard. It was really no more than a nuisance, but I bristled at the attention. I read each headline with dread, waiting for the words "psychic Realtor" or "spook-seeing agent" attached to any of the articles or photographs. Luckily, everything had been focused on the sailboat and the human remains found on board, and my career was intact. For now.

"And could you please put General Lee in the kitchen?"

Jack picked up the dog, then saluted me before heading toward the garden.

I put the car into gear, then drove the short blocks over to Legare. I spotted Amelia's Mercedes in front of the house and saw that she'd opened the gates to the narrow driveway at the side of the house—a premium in this South of Broad neighborhood.

After parking the car, I walked to the front of the house and found Jack's mother sitting on a square plastic block that might have been an intentional seat, surveying the wreckage of the garden.

She looked up at me and smiled distractedly. "Hello, dear." She indicated the wasteland around her. "There really aren't words to describe this, are there?"

"No, there really aren't. At least not ones I'd use in polite company. Not to worry, though. I've asked my father to turn his magic on this garden, just like he did for me on Tradd Street. He's almost done with repairing the damage the police made when they dug up the fountain. I have every faith that he'll make this one even more spectacular."

Amelia raised both eyebrows. "And your mother is okay with your father being so close?"

"She didn't have a choice. If she wants me to help her, my father is part of the package."

She smiled as she stood, brushing off the back of her skirt. "I suppose that's fair, then."

I led the way to the wide front steps, inordinately relieved that I wasn't alone. Not that the diminutive Mrs. Trenholm could offer any kind of substantial barrier between me and whatever it was that waited in this house. Still, I found comfort in another living, breathing presence.

I pulled out my key chain—every key neatly labeled with a different-colored dot of fingernail polish—and pulled out the Scarlet Woman key. I paused before sticking it into the lock. "I have to warn you, Amelia, it's a little horrifying."

"After seeing the garden, I think I'm prepared," she said, straightening her shoulders.

I pushed open the door and we walked slowly into the foyer. We stood still in the quiet house as I listened for voices and Amelia took in the circus-like colors and the dearth of furnishings.

She spoke first. "I feel like I've been immersed in a Salvador Dalí painting. And that's not really a good thing. I shudder to think what it looked like with their furniture. Your mother hinted at how bad it was, but even my imagination wasn't this good. . . ." Her voice trailed away as she took in the zebra-striped shag rug.

Closing the door behind us, I said, "Thankfully, the previous owners took all of their furniture with them. They did leave behind everything in the attic, which appears to be old Prioleau family artifacts, but not a lot of furniture. I'm fairly sure my mother didn't take it with her when she sold the house, so I'm left wondering what happened to it all."

Amelia didn't answer at first. Instead, she walked ahead of me into the drawing room with the large stained-glass window and looked at it for a long moment as if searching for the right words. She turned around with a soft expression on her face. Gently, she said, "The house was sold completely furnished. Your mother felt it best."

I waited for her to elaborate, to explain how my mother could have thought that selling the family home wasn't enough—that she'd needed to include all the furnishings, too, to complete her betrayal. But Amelia remained silent, her eyes kind.

"Of course she did," I said, my voice harsher than I'd meant it to be, the hurt as fresh as it had been the first day I'd become motherless. "Come on," I said, my voice lighter. "Let's walk through and we'll go over what kind of furniture we're going to need."

I made to move away, but Amelia held me back with a gentle touch on my arm. "The owners auctioned off the furniture not long after they purchased the house. I know because I was here and acquired several high-end antiques, which I subsequently sold to various collectors."

I stared at her for a moment, working to keep the hope out of my voice. "Do you have records showing who the buyers were?"

"I have records of every piece of furniture we've ever sold since we opened the store. I'll be more than happy to pull out the information. Then you and your mother can discuss if it's something you want, and I'll be happy to contact the current owners. Nothing's guaranteed, of course, but if I explain that we're attempting to return the furniture to its original home, they might be persuaded to sell."

I'd stopped listening after she said "you and your mother." Refurbishing this house wasn't about my mother and what she wanted. I'd begun to think of it as my chance to get back a little of what had been taken from me. She'd already hired Amelia to procure furniture; she didn't have to know where it came from. Smiling, I said, "I'll be happy to take care of it. I'm sure my mother would want as many original pieces as possible."

"I understand," she said, and I knew she did and she wasn't going to refute my words. "The good news is that one of the pieces I'd sold after the auction was recently reacquired. It's at the store now."

"What is it?"

"It's a lady's writing desk. It's made of mahogany, and has beautiful carvings on the Queen Anne legs."

My mouth went a little dry. "I think I know it. My grandmother had a desk like that in her sitting room." My mind went back over the years to a memory of me sitting at my grandmother's feet, brushing my fingers against the wood carvings of fish and seaweed carved into the wood of the legs.

Swallowing back the memory, I turned to Amelia. "How did it happen that it came back to you?"

Amelia began to walk around the perimeter of the room, frowning at the wallpapered walls covered with daisies and the garage sale chandelier. She used a manicured nail to flick at the high-lacquered violet paint on a window frame before turning to face me. "The buyers kept it for only about six months before they contacted me to find out if I'd like to buy it back." She crossed her arms elegantly across her chest. "They said it had 'strange vibes.' That the temperature of the room where they'd placed it always seemed to be about ten degrees colder than the rest of the house."

I stilled, unable to form a response.

She continued. "It's been in the shop ever since. It's a beautiful piece and gets a lot of interest, but potential buyers tend to shy away from it at the last moment. I'll give you a nice price so I can make room for something else that will sell."

"Yes," I said, my voice sticky, "I'm definitely interested."

"Wonderful." She walked toward me and took both of my hands in hers. "I know none of this is easy for you. But it will be okay in the end. I promise you. I've known your mother for a very long time, and even if I don't understand her motives, I know she makes all of her decisions from a good heart." She squeezed my hands as I tried to pull them away. "She loves you, Melanie. You should never doubt that."

She let go of my hands and I pulled away. "We'll have to agree to disagree on that point, Amelia." I held out my arm, indicating for her to move in front of me. "Let's go look at the rest of the house to give you an idea of all that's needed."

She patted my arm as she walked by, but I looked away, seeing again a little girl who'd awakened one morning to find her mother gone.

I closed the door behind Amelia an hour later, wondering again how such a kind and intelligent woman could have given birth to Jack Trenholm. I'd only met his father briefly, so I was left to assume that the answer might lie in that end of the gene pool.

Preoccupied with my conversation with Amelia and thoughts of my mother, I didn't remember to be afraid as I began to walk toward the kitchen to call Jack and find out where he was. He'd promised to help me move in, after all, and I was dreading dragging all the stuff from my car into the house after having done it all by myself in reverse just a few hours before.

As I reached for my purse, I heard my name. *Melanie.* I straightened slowly, realizing I could see my breath in the suddenly chilly kitchen. I turned around, clutching my cell phone to my chest.

Go away, Melanie. This is my house.

I trembled, more afraid than even I wanted to admit. *I am stronger than you*, I said to myself, repeating my mother's mantra. I wanted to ask who it was, but I knew that to engage it in conversation would give it strength I wasn't sure I wanted to witness. *I am stronger than you*, I repeated, beginning to back out of the room.

Your mother does not want you, either. That is why she went away. Something cold and sharp brushed against my cheek and I cried out, feeling something sticky drip down my skin. I touched my fingers to my face, then brought my hand in front of me to see what it was. My hand was shaking so badly it took me a moment to see the blood staining my fingertips.

I recalled the wet footprints in the kitchen and belatedly realized that whatever or whoever it was, was no longer bound to the back staircase or the back rooms. It was venturing farther than it had in the past as if something was giving it strength. Something or someone.

I tried to move but I was held in place, as if my feet were encased in cement blocks. I looked around desperately, trying to determine from what direction the next attack would come. That's when I heard another voice, a familiar one that sent palpable relief surging through me. The presence left me immediately, but the temperature in the room remained cold, my breath coming out in fast little puffs.

My knees betrayed me by buckling, and I sank down onto the kitchen floor before I embarrassed myself by falling.

Melanie.

From the corner of my eye, I spotted my protector leaning against the stove, one booted ankle crossed over the other.

"Thank you," I said out loud, more glad to see him than I could express.

You are hurt.

"Yes. Something scratched me. Who was it?"

He didn't answer. Instead I heard him walk toward me, his heels striking the kitchen floor tiles. I didn't look up as he stopped next to me.

You are very brave, my beautiful Melanie. A very attractive combination.

I was aware of his German accent, and of how solid he felt next to me. I was also aware that he'd avoided answering my question.

Close your eyes, Melanie.

I shook my head. "No."

I will not hurt you. I am your friend. Close your eyes and I will make you better.

After hesitating again for a moment, I closed my eyes. I felt him lean down next to me and use gentle fingers to move the hair away from my injured cheek, followed by the distinct sensation of lips brushing mine. Warmth pressed through to me, sending electric sparks directly into my bloodstream. My eyes flickered open in surprise and he vanished. Bringing my fingers to my cheek, I realized that my cheek had healed.

"Mellie?"

It was Jack. I twisted around and saw him standing in the kitchen doorway. "The front door was unlocked, so I let myself in. What are you doing on the floor?"

"I, um, I—I was waiting for you. No chairs," I said, indicating the obvious. I wasn't sure why I didn't tell Jack the truth. It wasn't that I didn't think Jack wouldn't believe me. I think it had more to do with the random thought of wanting to keep my protector all to myself.

He looked at me oddly. "Are you alone?"

"Of course," I answered a little too quickly.

"Because I thought I heard you talking."

I struggled to my feet, my knees still feeling weak. "I was. To myself." I held up my cell phone. "I was leaving my to-do list on my voice mail."

He continued to stare at me oddly.

"What?" I asked.

"Well, you're flushed and your eyes are sparkling. Maybe your to-do lists have that effect on you, but if you were anybody else, I'd say that you'd just been soundly kissed. Or more."

Realizing that was pretty much the way I was feeling, I brushed past him. "You really need to get your mind out of the gutter, Jack."

He followed me out of the kitchen. "Hold up, Mellie. I was about to give you a compliment."

Suspicious, I slowed down and turned to look at him.

He smiled, his blue eyes doing their thing again. "I was going to say that when you look like that, you don't look like a—how did you put it?—'dried-out husk of a woman.'"

Oh, God. So those scraps of conversation I thought had been completely in my head hadn't been. I thought briefly of throwing my cell phone at him, but I knew Jack wasn't worth the trouble of getting a new one. "You lied to me. You said I didn't say anything embarrassing when I was drunk."

"No, I said that you didn't say anything that would make me think less of you. Giving in to your innermost fears about turning forty was sort of sweet, actually. I think we may have bonded."

I held up my hand to get him to stop speaking. "Enough. I don't want to hear another word about it. Instead, do you think you could make yourself useful and help me bring my things in from the car? Just pile everything in the foyer because I don't know where I'm going to be sleeping yet."

Without waiting for him to answer, I yanked the front door open and headed down the steps, taking gulps of the cold air to try and cool myself down.

"Is it okay if I still think you're beautiful?" he called after me.

I didn't answer, remembering instead the kiss on my lips, and how my protector had made me forget for a few moments what the other voice had said: *Your mother does not want you, either. That is why she went away.* I turned around to make sure Jack was following, then made my way to unload the car for my return to the house on Legare Street.

CHAPTER 12

Juggling my donuts and coffee, I backed into the door to Henderson Realty, the wind buffeting my coat and hair so I could barely see. The door was whipped out of my hand and as I struggled to grab it, a small feminine hand reached around and held it open for me so that I could enter the building.

I turned with a smile to thank my rescuer, but felt my smile faltering when I recognized Rebecca Edgerton.

"Good morning, Melanie," she said, her face and perky attitude more than I could usually handle first thing in the morning. "I know it's awfully early, but Jack told me that you're an early bird just like me so I figured this might be the best time to catch you."

Nancy came from behind the receptionist's desk to help us with our coats. I tried not to stare when I realized she was dressed in head-to-toe argyle. I knew she went through golf withdrawal when the weather didn't cooperate with her plans to play, and I figured this was her way of dealing with the grief.

"Thanks, Nancy. This is Rebecca Edgerton, a reporter at the newspaper. She's an old friend of Jack's."

I wished I hadn't said that last part when I watched Nancy's smile broaden. "Oh, a friend of Jack's! How nice. I haven't seen him in a while. How's he doing?"

"He's doing great, actually. He's heading to the airport later this morning to pick up Melanie's mother."

"He is?" I asked, shocked that she'd know this tidbit of information but I wouldn't.

"Yes. She called Jack a few days ago to set it all up. Seems that she's done with all of her business in New York and she's ready to move in to her house."

I felt sick, not sure if it was because I'd been left out of my mother's plans or because her return meant that tonight would be my first night in the Legare Street house. Sophie was growing impatient waiting to start on the floors, but I'd explained that I wasn't spending a single night in my mother's house alone. Frowning, I said, "I wonder why she didn't call me."

Both Nancy and Rebecca looked at me. Finally, Rebecca said, "Probably because she wasn't sure you'd answer."

I opened my mouth to protest, then closed it, knowing she was most likely correct. Instead I turned to Nancy. "Could you please hold my calls and bring some coffee for Rebecca?"

"Sure, no problem. Do you like cream and sugar, Rebecca?"

"Lots of sugar and real cream, if you have it. I can never have enough sugar!" She let out a little laugh until she realized that both Nancy and I were looking at her oddly.

"No problem," Nancy said, raising her eyebrows at my bag of donuts and latte with extra sugar. "I get that a lot around here."

I led the way back to my office and motioned for Rebecca to follow. I set my coffee and donuts on my desk and sat down, indicating the chair opposite for Rebecca. She sat while I flicked on my computer and opened up my appointment calendar, placing my BlackBerry next to it so I could reconcile my schedule. I knew it was overkill, but after first getting my BlackBerry, I would lie awake at night worrying about missing appointments because I'd lost my BlackBerry and my backup on my laptop had disappeared. Better safe than sorry had been my motto since I learned at an early age that I needed to set two alarms for my dad so he could get up in time for work.

I looked up and saw Rebecca eyeing my donut bag with the grease spots on the bottom of it. I opened up my second drawer and dropped the bag inside before she had the chance to ask me to share with her.

"So, what brings you here first thing in the morning?" I asked, trying to sound interested.

She slapped her hands on her knees. "Well, two things, actually. Firstly, Jack and I were having so much fun at dinner last night that I forgot to ask him if you two discovered anything at Mimosa Hall." Her blue eyes widened as she waited for my response, but I sensed more than just casual interest.

"The trip itself to Ulmer was pretty uneventful," I said slowly, skipping over the sweet potatoes, icy water puddle, and brandy. "But inside the house, we did see a portrait of a girl wearing a locket that looked pretty identical to the one worn by the girls in the portrait we found in the Legare Street attic."

"Really? How interesting. Did you take pictures?"

"Jack did. We haven't had a chance to compare them yet. I stuck the portrait back in the attic because I have painters coming to the house this week and Jack and I keep missing each other." I kept the part about the menacing voice to myself, not willing to share that bit of information with Rebecca. I still wasn't sure that I trusted her—and that everything I said wouldn't end up as fodder in a newspaper exposé one day.

"Did it have an initial on it like the ones in the portrait?" Rebecca leaned forward, almost imperceptibly.

I frowned, trying to remember beyond the haze of the brandy. "Yes. Actually, it did. The letter *A*."

I watched as her already-pale face turned a shade whiter. "An *A*? Are you sure?"

"Definitely. No doubt about that. I believe Jack took a close-up so you can ask him when you see him again." I tried unsuccessfully to keep the snide tone from my voice. I looked at her closely. "Are you feeling all right?"

She nodded, but her smile was shaky. "I didn't sleep well last night."

She didn't explain and I wasn't interested in a blow-by-blow account. Still, she looked as if she might keel over in her chair. With a heavy sigh, I pulled the donuts out of my drawer. "Maybe you should eat something."

Her eyes brightened as she spotted the grease-spotted bag. "Thank you. I think that might help."

I spread two napkins on my desk, placing a donut on top of one before sliding it over to her. "Careful with the powdered sugar. It gets everywhere."

Nancy entered my office with the coffee and set two mugs down on the desk. Before I could reach for my personal mug—the one with "I'm

#1" on one side and a magic ink image of a house that was replaced with the word "SOLD" on the other whenever hot liquid was poured inside—Rebecca picked it up and took a sip. I stared at the remaining mug with golf balls splattered all over it and slid it toward me so Rebecca wouldn't take that, too.

Nancy eyed the donuts. "Something big must be going on here because I've never seen Melanie share her donuts with anybody. People fear for their fingers if they get too close."

I sent her a withering glance. "Rebecca wasn't feeling well. Figured a sugar rush could help."

We both watched as Rebecca took a huge bite out of her donut, then quickly polished off the rest of it with a second bite. She smiled at us while chewing, then took another sip from my mug before speaking.

"Sorry. I guess I was hungry."

Nancy watched as I edged my donut closer to me and quickly took a bite of it to stake my claim. I even thought about licking it, just in case. "I bought cinnamon rolls for the office," Nancy said. "I could bring a couple of them in if you're still hungry."

Rebecca perked up even more. "Oh, yes. Please. If it's not too much trouble, that is." Her smile widened and a speck of powdered sugar fell from her lower lip.

Nancy's questioning look was quickly replaced by a polite smile. "I'll go get those rolls for you and be right back."

"Thanks," Rebecca called to Nancy's departing back. "And when you have a minute, I want to know where you got those argyle pants. They look great."

Nancy shot back an appreciative grin before heading toward the break room.

Rebecca turned back to me. "Where were we? Oh, yes. We were talking about my not sleeping last night."

I shoved half of my donut into my mouth so I couldn't say what I really wanted to and instead just nodded politely.

"I had another dream. About you, believe it or not." She smiled tentatively and I noticed that she had more powdered sugar on her chin. "You were with a man, and I had the strong impression that there was something—between you. Like you were lovers."

THE GIRL ON LEGARE STREET 123

"Really?" I nonchalantly picked up my mug and took a sip.

"It wasn't Jack."

I thought I saw a gleam of satisfaction in her eyes. "Well, that's a re-lief," I said through a surprising stab of disappointment. I took another sip of coffee.

"Actually, he was blond. And he spoke English but with a heavy accent."

My leg had begun to bounce on my knee and I lowered my hand to get it to stop. "That's weird," I said, trying not to show any interest. "What were we doing?"

Rebecca squirmed a little in her seat. "Um, well, not that I saw any-thing specifically, but I got the strongest feeling that the two of you had been—intimate."

I coughed, spitting up coffee. I jerked to a stand and grabbed a napkin from the donut bag to wipe my chin and desk. I wanted to ask her if the man was wearing a Revolutionary War uniform but that would give too much away. Instead, I said, "That's pretty disturbing, seeing as how I'm not dating anybody right now."

"Oh, I didn't say that you were dating him."

Our eyes met and she sent me a half smile full of innuendo. "Any idea who he is?" she asked.

"Not at all," I said without looking away. I sat back down. "Any idea who you think he might be?"

Rebecca shook her head. "Not exactly, although I know that you were in the kitchen in the house on Legare Street. And he kept pointing at a fireplace that I don't remember seeing when I was there."

"Interesting," I said. "Because there used to be a fireplace in the kitchen, but the previous owners plastered over it."

She raised an eyebrow. "Well, then. Maybe whoever he is wants you to restore it."

"Maybe," I said. "He's probably some dead historical preservationist who's appalled by what the house looks like now. Believe me. Even I might be tempted to rise from the dead if somebody did that to my house."

Nancy reentered the office with two plates, each with a cinnamon roll and fork, and placed one in front of each of us. Rebecca was already reaching for her fork before Nancy even made it back to the door.

Rebecca smiled and dabbed at the corners of her mouth with a napkin. "Speaking of old houses, I was wondering if you recalled the name of the current owner at Mimosa Hall. Thought it might ring a bell and help us tie the girls in the portraits together."

"The last name is McGowan, but they weren't the original owners. Jack told me that the McGowans bought the house from the Crandall family during the Depression. Mrs. McGowan—who was out of town when we stopped by—is going through her attic to look for more information, but she remembers some sort of tragedy in the last half of the 1800s that affected the family. She said she'd let Jack know when she finds out."

Rebecca's hand froze in midair as she held her napkin up to her face. "Crandall? Are you sure?"

"Yes, that's definitely what Jack told me. Why, do you know of them?"

She seemed to studiously relax. "It's just that, well, Crandall doesn't sound like a local name, that's all."

"No, they were from Connecticut. According to Jack's research with Yvonne, the Crandalls were always having family come visit from up north."

"Interesting," she said, her voice tight. "Maybe researching the family is something I could do. Help figure out at least who the girl with the *A* locket is, which may or may not lead us to the identity of the two girls in your portrait."

"Great," I said, moving my calendar and BlackBerry closer to me to give Rebecca the hint that I needed to get back to work.

Surprisingly astute, she stood. "I'll let you get back to work, then. Thanks for the donut and the cinnamon roll—can't think of a better way to start my day."

I frowned, recalling having said the exact same thing more than once. "Thanks for stopping by. Let me know if you find out anything about the girl in the portrait."

"Will do." She slung her purse over her shoulder. "Oh, and I almost forgot about the second thing I wanted to ask you about."

I looked up at her, my BlackBerry poised and ready in my hand. "Yes?"

"It's a favor, actually. Every year, the historical society presents a Christmas tour of homes and I suggested that we include your mother's house on the tour this year. It's a rather late addition, but I thought it should be included."

I stared at her in horror. "You can't be serious. It's like the inside of a frat house on a psychedelic trip, and there's no way we can decorate in time for the tour. . . ."

Rebecca cut me off with a wave of her hand. "That's the point. I thought we could make the Legare Street house the first on the tour to show people what happens when the historical aspects of these homes are ignored, then follow with the rest of the homes of the tour, which shows the other end of the spectrum."

I shook my head. "My mother would never agree. . . ."

Rebecca cut me off again. "Actually, she already has. I spoke with her while she was in New York and she thought it a great idea."

I frowned. "She answered your phone call?"

Rebecca had the decency to look abashed. "Actually, I borrowed Jack's phone when he was taking out the trash. She didn't know it was me."

I frowned again, wondering if I should be more appalled by Rebecca's subterfuge or the fact that my mother had agreed to open her house for a home tour. "She said yes?"

"Yes. It's a great fund-raiser for the historical society, and she thought it would be a great way to reintroduce herself to Charleston. She's already promised them that the house will be included on next year's tour as a sort of 'before and after' home. She also said that you would be more than happy to act as tour guide for the house."

"She did?" My surprise easily slipped into anger. "Wasn't that generous of her."

Rebecca nodded. "I said the same thing. She said that now you're such a pro on restoration, you could give the tour explaining your plans for the house."

I was shaking my head. "No. I won't do it. Sorry. I'm not an expert, nor do I pretend to be. Ask Sophie."

Rebecca looked crestfallen. "But Jack already said you'd be happy to do it and you're already on the roster."

I dropped my BlackBerry on the desk. "Jack?"

"Yes. He's already working on your Civil War–era costumes. He thought the two of you could do it together." Her face brightened a bit. "Photographers from the *Post & Courier* and *Charleston* magazine will be there. I would think it would be good for business to get your face and name out there."

She'd hit the right target, of course, as I'm sure she'd planned. While I was silently weighing the pros and cons of dressing up and leading a tour in a house I hated versus the exposure for my business, Rebecca saw her opportunity to escape and started edging her way to the door. Before I could say anything else, she had reached the doorway. "I can tell you're busy. I'll send you more details as we get closer. Thanks again." With a little wave, she left, leaving a trail of expensive perfume behind.

I stood on the steps in front of the Legare Street house, unsure if I should knock or let myself in. It was the home of a stranger, after all, and the rules of engagement were new to me.

The overnight bag containing the last remnants of the possessions I would need for the next few months or so—my cosmetics, hair products, flannel nightgown and slippers, as well as several worksheets I'd made to accelerate the work schedule and decrease the time I'd have to spend in the house—was slung over my shoulder as I stood contemplating the door. I looked back at my car and General Lee, who sat in the back in his car seat, and his reassuring gaze gave me a boost of moral support.

An unfamiliar white Cadillac sedan was parked in the driveway and Jack's Porsche, thankfully, was missing. According to Rebecca, he would have brought my mother to her house nearly three hours earlier. It was plenty of time, according to my own calculations, for him to bring in her luggage, attempt to be charming, and leave, which was why I'd waited until five o'clock to make an appearance. I glanced nervously at the early-evening sky before raising my hand to give a tentative knock.

As I waited, I practiced a bland, unemotional expression with which to greet my mother and held it for a long three minutes before I began the process all over again, starting with three louder knocks.

My face began to hurt after another three minutes, so I very reluctantly dropped my hand to the doorknob, hesitating only a moment before turning it. I was surprised to find it unlocked and wondered if my mother had forgotten to lock it or, from experience, if something else might be involved.

Slowly, I pushed open the door, the shock of the carnival-like interior not having dwindled since the last time my senses were assaulted by it. But somewhere, behind the garish colors and tasteless accents, I smelled the familiar scent of these old houses: of polished wood, antique fabrics, and the soft breath of people long since gone but whose presence lingered still. Accompanied always, of course, by the sound of an alarming amount of money being sucked out the door. Despite my growing appreciation for the historic grand dames south of Broad Street, there were still moments—usually after another brutal session of scraping paint from hand-carved moldings or sanding through a century's worth of varnish—when I would wistfully imagine a wrecking ball solving all of the restoration woes in one fell swoop.

I stepped into the empty foyer, my attention turned to the closed door leading into the drawing room. The subdued rhythm of murmuring voices drifted toward me, and I was reminded of a similar scene from when I was a girl. Dropping my bag, I allowed anger to push me forward. I didn't pause at the closed door but instead flung it open, my thoughts confirmed when I saw my mother and another woman facing each other in two Windsor chairs. The chairs looked suspiciously like two from my house on Tradd Street that Sophie said she'd find a temporary home for while my floors were being restored. My mother, without gloves, held the hands of the other woman, their palms faceup, my mother's eyes open and turned toward the ceiling, which I noticed for the first time had inexplicably been wallpapered with purple stars and clouds.

A rush of cold air enveloped me as my mother's empty gaze shifted toward me, like a moth seeking flame. The lights flickered and dimmed as I stood in the doorway, the strings of plastic beads that hung over the front-facing windows beginning to sway as what felt like a force field around my mother pushed at me like a padded fist. But instead of repelling me, it seemed to be reaching out to me, sucking me toward it. I gripped the doorway, the wood weeping with moisture under my palms, threatening my grip. I looked up again at the hideous ceiling toward the mirrored chandelier with its thirty or more small rounded bulbs and watched as the lights brightened to a startling intensity before one by one each bulb shattered like stars plummeting to earth.

The two women dropped their hands and covered their heads.

"Go!"

I startled, not recognizing the deep voice as my mother's until she repeated herself. "Get out!" she said, louder. "Quickly. It's not safe in here!"

Stumbling, I backed out of the room, feeling the force around me begin to diminish, like a child's fingers being pulled one by one from her mother's skirts.

I collapsed on top of the pile of my belongings, too exhausted to stand or keep moving. I sat there, breathing heavily, until my mother and her companion emerged from the parlor.

My mother immediately crossed the room and took my hands, the feel of her skin on mine as foreign to me as another language. I tried to pull away but she held tightly.

"You felt it, didn't you?"

I didn't answer, my eyes traveling to the woman standing behind her wringing her hands and looking as if she wanted nothing more than to leave.

I faced my mother again. "You were giving a reading, weren't you? You know Daddy doesn't like you to do that."

A spark of amusement lit her eyes for a moment. "But this is my house. He has no say in what I choose to do." She squeezed my hands and peered into my eyes. "Are you all right?"

I nodded and to my relief she let go of my hands and stood. Indicating her companion, she said, "This is Gloria Elmore, an old friend of mine. She wanted to talk to her son."

I didn't need to ask if the son was dead; I'd seen him standing beside his mother right before the chandelier exploded, his gaping head wound confirming my suspicion that he was no longer among the living.

I stood, too, and greeted Mrs. Elmore, wondering if she'd been one of the many friends of my mother's who used to crowd around her at parties and private readings when I was a small child—and whose presence in our lives fueled the tension between my parents.

I waited while my mother led Mrs. Elmore to the door amid apologies and vague explanations of overloaded fuse boxes. The back of my neck tingled as the unmistakable scent of gunpowder filled my nostrils. I glanced around the foyer for my soldier but didn't see him, not sure from whom he was hiding.

The door had barely closed behind Mrs. Elmore before I rounded on my mother. "What are you thinking? You've been back not even a day and you're already intent on making us laughingstocks in this town. Do you not care that I have a professional reputation to uphold and that your sideshow antics might hurt me?" I held up my hand. "Oh, wait. Never mind. Hurting me has never held you back, so why would I expect it to now? You just go ahead and destroy the life that I've worked so hard to build. The part that wasn't destroyed when you walked out on me and Daddy."

I began to march toward the door for a dramatic exit but stopped when I realized that I had nowhere else to go. I could hear the smile in my mother's voice when she spoke as if she realized it, too.

"This is who we are, Mellie. It's our gift. And we can choose to hide it from the world or we can choose to help others with it. Either way, it's not going away."

I felt exhausted all of a sudden, having known the truth of her words since the first time my father shouted at me to stop talking to people he said weren't there. It was the thing that had bonded my mother and me together, and I'd spent years trying to untie the knots. Unfortunately, as I had learned as a small child, wanting something badly didn't always mean you'd get it.

My eyes met hers. "Why are you here? Why have you really come back?"

She looked as tired as I felt. She paused for a moment before speaking. Softly, she said, "For you. Everything I've ever done has been for you."

"You have an odd way of showing it," I said, the anger in my voice gone, the words full of resignation. A flash of light from the parlor caught my attention and my mother and I both turned toward the doorway. I started to move toward it but my mother's hand held me back.

"It's nothing," she said. "Just Mrs. Elmore's son saying good-bye."

Confused, I looked at her. She'd spoken with enough departed spirits when I lived with her to know that the type of phenomenon we'd just witnessed wasn't usual or expected. Something had changed. "But nothing happened until I entered the room."

She glanced away from me to the pile of bags and moved to pick up my small cosmetics case. "I do think it had something to do with the wiring. I'm sure you can give me a recommendation for a good electrician." She smiled. "Come on, let's get you settled."

I was too old to allow my mother's and my past to rule my life, and the best way to handle the situation was not to contradict her regardless of how wrong I knew her to be. I picked up my overnight bag. "I need to get General Lee out of the car. But first let me know what room you want me to take. Nothing in the back of the house, please."

Her eyes lit with amusement again. "You and I are in the two front bedrooms, the ones that connect through the dressing room. The walls are painted lime green, and I promise those will be the first we paint. Can't see starting each day with a migraine." She paused for a moment. "There's also a, um, er, ceiling mural in your bedroom depicting what I think might be a scene from Nero's last days. You might want to sleep on your side until we can get that fixed."

I looked at her with alarm but she'd already turned toward the stairs. She was halfway up the staircase before she spoke again. "We need to talk about your fortieth-birthday party. I was thinking Hibernian Hall or White Point Gardens with lots of fireworks. Or the yacht club, but I'd always thought you'd have your wedding reception there, so I'd like to hold out on that one. Regardless, we'll need to do something with your hair. I was thinking highlights to frame your face. Maybe we should ask Jack what he thinks."

It was unclear if she was referring to my birthday party or my hair; either way, I'd rather ask a sneaker-clad, camera-laden tourist, or General Lee for that matter, than ask Jack's advice on anything. I didn't think I could take his smug satisfaction that I would defer to him on any matter more consequential than furniture placement.

I made a face at my mother's retreating back, unable to find words to respond. Each footstep as I climbed the stairs was leaden—weighed down with thirty-three years' worth of unasked questions. I stared at her back and her bare hands avoiding the banister and wondered why after all this time Ginnette Prioleau Middleton had suddenly decided to become my mother. Or why the thought didn't upset me as much as it should have.

CHAPTER 13

I awoke the next morning to General Lee shivering next to me—our breath visible in cloudy puffs above our heads. The sheets and blankets were lying in puddles around the bed and all four windows were wide open, long vermilion drapes fluttering like moths inside the room. Gathering the little dog to my chest, I struggled to close the windows, then returned to the bed for another twenty minutes, this time with covers, until we were both thawed enough to venture out again.

I wasn't afraid. Not of these ghosts, anyway. I'd known them since childhood and realized they were simply making their presence known to me. I'd even surprised myself by falling asleep quickly the night before, not caring to dwell on the measure of comfort I'd felt at the proximity of the connecting door to my mother's room. I'd attempted to read—a university press publication about the origins of the Historic Charleston Foundation loaned to me by Sophie to give me a deeper appreciation for historical homes and the efforts to restore them for our collective posterity—but I'd fallen asleep after the first page. It wasn't that the book was poorly written or the subject all that uninteresting; it was only that I lived historical home restoration every day and had the nubby fingernails to prove it. There was no reason to relive my misery in bedtime reading.

I took a quick shower in the adjoining bathroom, trying to ignore the mirrored ceilings and walls and the red-velvet-upholstered window treatments that seemed more suitable for a bordello. Keeping my back to the shower spray so I could see the door, I loofahed, exfoliated, shaved, soaped, shampooed, and conditioned with at least one eye open the entire time. After slathering myself with lotion, I hurriedly dressed, then headed downstairs—General Lee following closely.

The sound of murmuring voices, one male and one female, led me to the kitchen. I recognized my mother's voice and what sounded like her giggling. With faster steps I made it to the louvered saloon-style doors to the kitchen and pushed them open.

My parents, each holding steaming mugs of coffee with a large plate of donuts on the table between them, sat very close and were looking at each other as if they were teenagers at a sock hop. A bouquet of fresh pink roses sat on the counter next to what appeared to be a stack of photographs. They looked up at the same time with matching expressions of guilt and horror as if just caught in the act of consorting with the enemy.

My mother stood abruptly, sloshing coffee from her mug, and that's when I noticed the red silk negligee, nearly transparent, that barely covered the matching teddy she wore underneath. I opened my mouth to offer to fetch my terry-cloth robe but stopped, somehow reluctant to advertise the fact that my mother wore sexier lingerie than I did. And looked better in it, too. Although both of us had the long and lean Prioleau genes, she'd somehow managed to snag a rogue gene from an unknown limb of the family tree and ended up with breasts. I, on the other hand, had worn training bras through high school and most of college for encouragement purposes only, and even now could probably go braless without anyone noticing.

"Morning," I said. Then, to prevent myself from saying the only other word that came to mind— "Ew"—I crossed to the kitchen counter where the coffeemaker and a clean mug were sitting, poured myself a cup, then took General Lee outside to relieve himself. When we came back in, General Lee immediately went to the food bowl that somebody— probably my dad—had already filled and I faced my parents.

"Good morning, Mellie. Your father stopped by to bring us donuts from Ruth's Bakery. It was our favorite, remember? I used to take you there as a little girl."

I closed my eyes, the steam from my coffee dampening my face. I hadn't remembered, of course. I doubt I would have been going there all these years if I had. But I'd always wondered if the reason I kept going back had less to do with the wonderful donuts and coffee I got there, and more to do with searching for something I'd lost but could never name.

Opening my eyes again, I turned around to face them. "No. I can't say I remember." Never one to resist sugar, I approached the table without looking at either one of them and took a glazed donut.

"I love your suit, Mellie," my mother said, eyeing me critically. "You should have the skirt shortened, though. You've got fabulous legs and you shouldn't be ashamed to show them a little."

Swallowing the donut that was sticking in my throat, I said, "In my profession, Mother, I need to be taken seriously and dressing like a hooker isn't a good way to accomplish that." I stared pointedly at her revealing outfit.

I took another bite from my donut, surprised my mother hadn't risen to the bait and said something about frumpy almost forty-year-olds remaining single. I looked back at her and saw that she was staring at my neck.

"What is that?"

Confused, I placed my coffee mug on the table and reached up to the open-neck collar of my jacket and felt the gold heart-shaped locket with the initial *M*. I wasn't sure why I wore it. It was in bad need of a thorough cleaning and I didn't even like it that much. It was more like a compulsion that made me keep it around my neck as a sort of talisman, I supposed. For what, I wasn't sure.

My father stood, too. "I gave that to her, Ginny. We found it on the boat and figured it belonged with Melanie instead of in a plastic bag somewhere. They'd already documented it and tested it so it's not like I was tampering with evidence or anything."

My mother didn't appear to be listening. "It's like the one in the portrait."

I nodded, and our eyes met.

She raised her hand, then lowered it slowly. Speaking softly, out of my father's hearing range, she asked, "Why didn't you show this to me before?"

The answer was easy. "Because I know what it does to you."

She raised an eyebrow. "I wouldn't have thought you cared."

I paused, considering her words. I had thought about asking her to hold the locket, to see if it would tell her anything, but I knew what some objects did to her. I remembered days when she was feverish and unable to eat, days when the visions and voices wouldn't leave her alone because she'd handled something with a powerful message. It's why she wore the gloves, after all. Still, I wasn't sure if I hadn't asked because I thought it would harm her, or if I was afraid that she'd tell me no.

I slid a glance to my father, who was pretending he wasn't trying to listen. "There are other ways to determine the identity of the women in the portrait," I said.

She took a step toward me and put a hand on my arm before I could step back. "But don't you see? That's why I'm here. We need to do this together." She squeezed my arm slightly. "And I would do anything for you. Anything. Because you're my daughter, Mellie."

She said the last part as if it explained everything, as if it filled in all the empty nooks and crannies of my childhood like melted butter on a muffin. It surprised me enough that I hardly noticed when she stepped closer and raised her bare hand, clasping the locket in her fist.

At first, it didn't appear that anything was happening. Then her hand began to shake as if electricity was coursing through her body. Her eyes rolled back, her eyelashes fluttering, and her other hand came up to grasp her arm as if to keep it still. Her mouth opened, but she seemed unable to speak, or maybe her own words were being silenced by something unseen. Then, in a voice that wasn't hers in words as thick and heavy as black tar, she said, "Give it back." She licked her lips, and I saw that they were cracked and peeling now, like someone who'd been swimming in the ocean for a long time. Slowly, the voice said, "It's mine. It's all mine."

Before I could respond or react, my mother pulled away, dropping the locket as if it had burned her. It scalded my skin where it settled, and I watched while my mother flexed and unflexed her fist.

"Are you all right?" I asked.

"Yes. Yes, I'm fine," she said as she walked across the kitchen to the sink and began pouring water over her hand.

My father had stood, and was staring at my mother. "What the hell was that?"

Neither of us answered, either because we didn't know the answer or because even if we did, it wouldn't matter if we told him or not; he still wouldn't believe us.

"Who was it?" I asked my mother, my voice tight.

She shook her head as she leaned on the counter, trying to catch her breath. "I'm not sure." She shook her head again, as if trying to clear it, then met my eyes with hers. Hers were wide and reddened, and for a moment it was not my mother's eyes that stared back at me. She blinked hard before speaking. "But I do know that you shouldn't be wearing that locket. It's bad, Mellie. It belonged to—her." She clenched her eyes shut for a moment. "No, that's not right. It did—but then it didn't."

"That doesn't make any sense." I grabbed the locket, unsure of my attachment to it, but not wanting to lose it, either, and felt only cold metal. I felt sick to my stomach, smelling again the odors of stagnant seawater and rotting fish. I wanted to bolt from the room, to deny that this was happening, but I was stuck watching a scene from a horror film whose ending I could only guess.

"We are not as we seem, remember? Maybe it's all connected." My mother's gaze didn't waver as I struggled to say something glib, to make the memory of the voice go away, to pretend that I couldn't see and smell things that weren't there.

"What the hell is going on here?" my father demanded again.

My mother and I just stared at each other in mutual understanding, while my father looked on. It had always been that way with the three of us, and I wasn't really surprised to see that nothing had changed in the intervening years.

She closed her eyes for a moment, then swallowed before walking toward my father. "Don't say another word. This is beyond your understanding and your ability to see things that aren't black-and-white. I will not have this argument again with you, so leave it be."

My father looked at me for support or argument—I wasn't sure which—but I could only turn away. I felt like a child again, unable to choose sides between two teams I loved equally.

Pulling her shoulders back and trying to look as regal as a person who was wearing less than a yard of flimsy material could, my mother said, "I'm leaving now so you can tell Melanie what you told me earlier and then discuss your plans for the garden. Melanie will be in charge of that, so you won't need to deal with me at all. I'm sure we can all agree that's for the best." She started to leave, then turned back to my father, and I wondered if he'd heard her voice shake, too. "And I've told you before, don't call me Ginny. My name is Ginnette."

She took another donut and wrapped it in a napkin before making her grand exit through the saloon doors, trying to disguise her unsteady steps, the sound of her high-heeled slippers fading away as they tapped down the hall.

I stared after her for a long moment, wondering when it had happened that my mother had changed from stranger to ally.

I held up my hand, anticipating what my father planned to say. "Don't say it because I don't want to hear it. Let's just agree to disagree so that we can discuss the garden."

His gaze shifted to the locket around my neck and then back to my face. He looked wounded, but there was nothing I could do about that. Trying to get him to understand our ability to see things he couldn't was a lot like trying to get permission to build a skyscraper in downtown Charleston. "Fine, if that's the way you want it. But all this hocus-pocus . . ."

"Daddy," I interrupted.

"Right." He scooped up the photographs on the counter, then held out a chair for me and I sat at the Shaker table, another remnant I recognized from my house on Tradd Street. I made a mental note to have a little chat with Sophie. I took a deep breath, trying to calm myself after hearing that voice. It wasn't something one easily forgot or pushed aside.

My father sat down next to me and began shuffling the pictures in his hand. He fixed me with a clear-eyed stare that I was still getting used to. I could smell his cologne, and I wondered how long it would be before I stopped expecting the odor of stale beer and sour whiskey that accompanied all of my childhood memories of him.

After a deep breath, he said, "They completed the forensics tests on the remains yesterday and they're releasing the news to the press later today."

I stiffened, my leg bouncing erratically under the table.

My dad continued. "The authorities will be in touch to make it official, but my buddy told me that I was allowed to tell you and your mother the results ahead of time as long as you kept it to yourselves."

"Of course," I said, my lips dry.

"They determined that the body was definitely that of a female of approximately five feet two inches tall. And that she was between twenty and twenty-four years old at the time of her death."

I closed my eyes briefly, remembering the voice, knowing he was right. I managed to stay calm. "Anything else?"

He nodded, still flipping through the photographs. That was another thing I'd noticed since he'd been going to AA; his hands were always moving as if attempting to keep them so busy that they wouldn't notice the absence of a bottle or glass clutched in them.

"You already know about the skull injury, but they also found some sort of genetic anomaly in the hip. He explained it in some kind of medical jargon, but it's basically a joint issue that can be surgically taken care of today, but back then you would have just lived with a limp."

I leaned forward. "A limp? Nobody in the Prioleau family has ever limped as far as I know—or had surgery to correct it. I can double-check that with Mother. And with Rebecca. She's apparently done a lot of research into our family. Maybe she's found something, too."

He nodded, his hands still flipping through the photographs. "I'm hoping whoever it was is unrelated to you so this whole thing goes away quicker."

I met his eyes but could only nod. He wouldn't want to know that nothing would go away until my mother and I could make her go away. Or until I decided to leave the house on Legare to its ghosts.

I put my hands on his, stilling them. "Can I see the pictures?"

"Sure," he said, sliding them over to me. "I remembered there were pictures of the garden taken when your grandmother lived here in the sixties and early seventies. I had a box of photos that I took from the house after your grandmother died, and I figured they might be in there." He tapped the photo on top. "I was right. These pictures will be a great blueprint for me to use to restore the garden to the way it was."

I began to sift through them, each photograph a memory of the best part of my childhood. There were shots of the herb parterre garden and the climbing Confederate jasmine that clung to the front gates, and the ornamental brick walkways edged with precise boxwoods whose scent always reminded me of home.

But there were pictures, too, of a much younger me sipping tea from real china cups on a wrought iron table, my grandmother sitting next to me on the bench and smiling into the camera. And I noticed how much the adult me now resembled her and it made me smile. I stopped before one photograph of me laughing in front of a statue my grandmother had bought in Italy—and that I had found uproariously funny because the little boy was naked. But the thing that caught my attention most was the diamond-and-sapphire necklace and earrings I wore. I'm sure they were worth a lot of money, but my grandmother never hesitated to let me wear them during one of our tea parties. I remembered, too, how Rebecca had asked me about them and how she'd seen my mother wearing them in a newspaper photo.

"You laughed a lot as a little girl." His gaze searched mine.

I stared at the picture recalling the time before my mother left, of afternoons spent in my grandmother's garden, and of early mornings whiled away tucked between my parents in their large bed while they shared the newspaper and drank coffee.

"Yes," I said slowly. "I did." I didn't want to meet his eyes, afraid he'd see the little girl again—and compare her to me.

"It wasn't such a bad childhood, was it? Despite—things?"

I raised my gaze to meet his, remembering, too, the traveling I'd done with my father when I'd gone to live with him, of seeing the pyramids of Egypt, the Taj Mahal, the Eiffel Tower, and the Thames River. I'd liked traveling with him; I'd found it easier to forget my mother when we were in exotic places, and my father had always made it a point not to drink until he'd put me to sleep at night. In those dusty hot places, I could pretend that I was someone else.

"No, Daddy. It wasn't all bad. I have good memories, too."

His expression of relief made me want to cry, and I had to look away.

My dad pointed at one of the photos. "There must have been something wrong with the camera because every single one of these photographs has the same white spots on them. Never in the same place, but always there."

I looked to where his finger pointed to a cluster of white balls of light flitting over my left shoulder. Slowly, I flipped through the remaining photographs, noticing the same light splotches on all of the pictures.

I didn't bother to point out to my father that the photographs had been taken by different cameras—some with a Polaroid, others with a 35 millimeter camera. I had a pretty good idea what had caused the blotches, but I wasn't about to get into another argument with him.

I paused at the last photograph of my grandmother and me. We were in the garden at the side of the house where the beautiful stained-glass window was. I was smiling into the camera with the kind of cheesy smile that only young children can get away with, but my grandmother was facing the window, pointing at it. My gaze traveled to where she pointed and I paused, bringing the photograph closer to my face and wishing I'd worn my glasses.

It must have been about midday because the sun was shining full force on the window. But something about the way the sun hit the glass transformed it into an image I'd never seen before. I'd always marveled at how the stained-glass looked different inside than it did outside. I'd noticed the same thing in churches with large stained-glass windows. But this looked like an entirely different glass layer had been placed on the back of the window, created in such a way as to only show the image in a certain angle of light.

What was so astounding in this image was that it no longer even resembled the one on the inside glass. Instead of random lines and patterns, it appeared to be some kind of aerial impression of a place foreign to me, yet complete with shoreline, trees, and the unmistakable columns of a Greek Revival house. But superimposed over the left quadrant of the image and overlapping the shoreline, was an odd representation of an angel's head with long, flowing hair and large wings that swept behind the head and came to a precise point. The figure was slightly tilted, so that the point of the wings swept over the water, but its tip was seemingly buried in the land.

I turned the photograph around to show my dad. "Did you notice this one?"

He reached into his pocket for his bifocals—apparently hidden from my mother, although upon my last calculation they were nearly the same age—and perched them on his nose.

"Now, then, isn't that interesting? It's a completely different image, isn't it?"

"Most definitely. I wonder why."

He handed the photograph back to me and snorted. "Those Prioleaus—always ones for puzzles. Your own mother made me solve a riddle to figure out her answer to my marriage proposal."

"Which was yes," I said, unable to stop my grin.

"Yeah, it was." He rested his chin in his hand and stared at me, but I didn't think he was seeing me at all.

"You're right about the puzzles. There's one on Grandmother Sarah's tombstone that I can't quite figure out, although to be honest I haven't given it that much thought. Nothing like a mother reappearing in one's life again to reorganize one's life. Anyway, I don't think Jack's seen it yet but he needs to. He's good at solving puzzles, but don't tell him I said that."

"Don't tell me that you said what?"

My father and I turned in unison to the saloon doors that Jack was holding open to allow Sophie and Chad, their arms laden with what appeared to be fabric and decorator books, into the kitchen.

My father stood and took the pile from Sophie's arms and placed them on the table before taking the ones from Jack's free hand and doing the same. Chad's armful slammed down on the counter and he looked at us apologetically.

"Dude," he said, apparently to my dad, who fisted his right hand like Chad's and pressed his knuckles against Chad's.

"Dude," my father repeated without a trace of sarcasm, "what's with the entourage?"

"Can't fit all Sophie's stuff in her Beetle or on my Schwinn, so Jack offered to use his pickup truck."

I raised my eyebrows as I slipped the photographs into my jacket pocket to study again later. "Jack has a pickup truck?"

Jack grinned. "I am a born-and-bred South Carolinian male who can shoot straight, treat his mama nice, and could once hold his liquor. I do believe it's against the law in the great state of South Carolina for a guy like me not to own a pickup truck." His grin widened as he looked at me, making the temperature in the room do funny things. "So, what did you not want me to know?"

"That you're good at solving puzzles," my dad said.

"That you're annoying and intrusive," I said at the same time.

Both men sent me a reproachful look before my dad said, "Melanie was telling me about how the Prioleaus have always been into puzzles. I believe my mother-in-law, Melanie's grandmother, even had a room here at the house where she kept all sorts of puzzles and cipher books and that sort of thing. Anyway, Melanie mentioned the rhyme on her grandmother's grave and how she hasn't been able to make heads or tails of it." He gave me a sidelong glance. "She mentioned you might be able to shed some light on it."

With a deferential tone, Jack said, "I'd be more than happy to accompany Mellie to the cemetery to see if I can help. I have been known to solve a puzzle or two."

"Melanie doesn't like to go in cemeteries, Jack," Sophie interjected.

I turned to Sophie, noticing her getup for the first time. "What are you wearing?" I asked, almost afraid to hear the answer.

She twirled for my inspection. "Isn't it great? A student of mine is from Nepal and she gave me this sari thinking I might like it. A friend had given it to her and it didn't suit her style."

I could see why, but I didn't mention it to Sophie. It was tie-dyed in hues not normally seen in the natural world with weird splashes of rhinestones that looked like someone had vomited them out and not bothered to clean up. Alone, it was an eyesore; mixed with a striped chenille turtleneck, paint-splattered sweats, rainbow-striped toe socks, and Birkenstocks, it was something from which nightmares are made.

"You look amazing, Soph," Chad said with such a sparkle in his eyes that I almost had to look away. Then he glanced at me and winked, and I knew without a doubt that Chad didn't care what Sophie looked like on the outside because to him she was the most beautiful woman in the world and nothing she wore could ever change that.

I caught Jack's gaze and realized with a start that he was thinking the same thing, and I felt myself coloring. It wasn't because he knew my thoughts or even that he might have caught a wistfulness in my eyes; it was because despite a brash exterior and irreverent quips, Jack Trenholm knew what true love was and could recognize it in other people. Even though I'd come to learn how deeply he'd loved his late fiancée, his behavior usually made it very easy to forget that he had any depth of feeling. I realized I'd felt much better when I thought of him as simply shallow and crass.

I cleared my throat. "You're right, Sophie. I don't like cemeteries. But if Jack's not too afraid, he can go by himself."

"It's not being in the cemetery alone that frightens me; it's the possibility that Mellie might get me into a dark corner, so it might be better if I do go alone." He flashed a smile at me, making me wonder exactly what all I'd said and done the night I was drunk. In a serious tone, he said, "I'll bring my camera and snap a few pictures. That way we can blow them up and separate the words and play with them a bit to see if there might be a hidden meaning in it."

The thought to do that had never occurred to me, and I looked at Jack with grudging admiration.

Eager to change the subject, I walked over to the books that Sophie and Chad had brought in. "What are all these?"

"Fabric swatches and paint samples," explained Sophie. "All of the colors have already been approved by the Board of Architectural Review. I know they can only control the exterior colors, but I know that you, under my expert tutelage, will want to do a thorough restoration and use only those colors that might have been used when the house was first built."

I flipped through several cardboard strips of paint chips, surprised to find that I actually liked the jewel-like hues of Persian blue and mustardy yellows—until I noticed that written on the back of each card were what looked like recipes using things like iron oxide, ocher, milk, and what appeared to be actual berries.

"What's this?" I asked, holding up a paint chip of a pale green and flipping it over. "You don't expect us to actually make the paint, right?" I smiled, to let her know that I was in on the joke.

She looked offended. "Of course. Otherwise it wouldn't be historically accurate, would it?"

I blinked several times, waiting for her to smile to let me know she wasn't serious. When she continued with a straight face, I slowly put down the paint chip. "I'll, um, go over these with my mother and let you know." I knew there had to be at least one paint company that made historically accurate colors in a good old-fashioned factory and that didn't involve me actually scraping rust from pipes or collecting berries in a field somewhere.

Jack picked up another paint sample and studied it for a moment. "I'm glad you're changing the color scheme. Every time I walk into the foyer, I want to bark like a circus seal."

"Don't let me stop you," I said, my voice trailing away. A movement out the kitchen window caught my attention, and I turned my gaze to the street, where I spotted Rebecca's little red Audi convertible pulling up to the curb. At about the same time, I heard my mother's footsteps approaching from the hallway.

I grabbed Jack's arm. "You know, I'm thinking I need to see the gravestone again, anyway. Let's go to the cemetery now and take some pictures. If you don't have your camera, we'll stop by your apartment and get it first."

I didn't wait for a response, and was glad he didn't show any resistance as I dragged him toward the back door. "Bye, Daddy. Good to see you, Chad and Sophie—I'll let you know what Mother and I decide on the paint."

Sophie raised her hand. "You'll need to decide pretty quickly so we can display your choices for the Christmas home tour next weekend. And don't forget your costume fitting on Wednesday . . ."

I gave a brief wave and had pulled Jack through the door and closed it before my mother made it into the kitchen.

"I think I like it when you're rough," Jack said.

I frowned and jerked my hand away from his arm. "I don't have my purse, so we'll have to take your car."

"Where are we going?"

We turned in unison to see a dimpling Rebecca standing on the back brick walkway. Some perverse sixth sense must have sent her to the back door instead of the front.

Jack stepped forward and kissed her on the cheek in greeting. "Good morning, Rebecca. You look beautiful, as always."

She pinkened, which only made her look prettier and perkier in her pink cashmere coat. "Thank you, Jack." She turned from his embrace. "And good morning to you, Melanie." She turned back to Jack. "Where are you heading?"

"To St. Philip's to see Melanie's grandmother's gravestone. There's some odd wording on it, and I thought we might be able to figure something out together. But three brains are always better than two, so why don't you come along?"

I thought I might have to use my fingers to force a smile but managed without them. "That's a great idea, Jack. Let's all go together."

Jack led us to his car and opened up the passenger door. Rebecca stepped forward first and I thought she was going to do the right thing by crawling into the minuscule backseat, but my hopes plummeted when I saw her move the front seat forward and step back for me to cram my tall frame into the back.

With my knees tucked under my chin, we headed down Legare Street, and I found myself wondering once again how my tidy, orderly life had gone the way of hoop skirts and cars with long tail fins. I tried to remember a time when my dysfunctional family was out of sight and out of mind, and my only concerns were my monthly sales figures and making reasonable payments on my low-maintenance condo.

Now I owned an enormous historic and hugely expensive house, my parents were both back in my life and wanting to parent me thirty years too late, and I had a sinking feeling that Jack Trenholm was intent on becoming a permanent fixture in my life. Some people would have considered that last part icing on their cupcake; I saw it only as a bunion on my life that rubbed whenever I wore shoes.

I leaned my head back and closed my eyes as we headed toward Church Street, trying to count my blessings as my grandmother Prioleau had taught me to do all those years ago, but instead I only managed to feel like a cornfield awaiting a swarm of locusts.

CHAPTER 14

I opened my eyes as we took a left off Broad onto Church, unwilling to miss the beautiful vista of the church that was built in the middle of the street, forcing the road to go around it so everyone could admire the three Tuscan porticoes that fronted the three Church Street facades. Sophie told me that the church had been built butting out in the middle of the street because of English tradition and that this vista was the most photographed in all of Charleston. I told her that I doubted the latter only to be contrary; but I accepted the former having had it drummed into me since birth that England would always be the standard against which everything Charlestonians did was compared.

Despite the fact it was a week before Christmas, the temperature had turned warmer, hovering around the midsixties. I hadn't had time to grab a jacket or sweater, which wouldn't have been a problem if we'd been heading anywhere besides a cemetery. As usual, a spot at the curb opened up as Jack approached and he neatly slipped into the space.

Rebecca waited patiently for Jack to come to her side of the car and help her out. They stood talking quietly on the sidewalk while I waited for somebody to at least move the front seat up. With an impatient snort, I unlatched the seat lock and struggled to release myself from the back-seat, tangling my ankle around the dangling front seat belt and plunging forward onto the sidewalk.

I would have fallen on my face if I hadn't been caught up into the arms of a male passerby with a soft cashmere coat and strong hands.

"Melanie?"

My face was so close to his that I almost couldn't focus. "Marc?"

Marc Longo kissed my cheek and smiled, revealing white teeth in a darkly handsome face that reminded me all over again why I'd fallen for him. That had been right before I'd found out that he was more interested in the Confederate diamonds hidden in my house than in any of my charms.

"I've missed you," he said, and I almost believed the sincerity in his eyes. "You haven't returned any of my phone calls or letters. We left things between us—unresolved."

I pulled away, taking a step back. "I've missed you, too," I admitted, although it was only partly true. I missed the way he'd made me feel—young, beautiful, and vibrant. He would have never made me sit in the backseat of his car. Sensing Jack and Rebecca watching us, I smiled warmly at him, and then gave him a quick peck on the cheek.

"Does this mean I'm forgiven?" His dark eyes searched mine and I began to believe that maybe he did care something for me. He had no more reason to feign affection for me, after all. Unless his next words were to ask me for a loan.

"Only partly," I said, knowing I had Jack's full attention now. "Your behavior wasn't exactly stellar. But if you call me again, I promise to take the call and give you a chance to redeem yourself. I'll tell Nancy not to hang up on you."

"Good," he said. "She's pretty tough. She should be part of our national defense."

I smiled up at him, wondering what it would be like to be alone with him again after all he'd put me through. But we'd had good times together, too, and I figured I owed him at least one chance to atone for his sins. If it cost him a nice meal at Blossom, then so be it.

"Hello, Matt." Jack stepped between us, but he didn't offer his hand to shake. "How's the jaw?" He was referring to the last time the two had met, when Jack had felt the need to somehow restore my honor with the fist he planted on Marc's face.

"Better, thank you. I don't blame you for what you did. Melanie is a woman worth fighting for, and I'll admit I deserved it." He smiled down at me, and placed his arm over my shoulder. "And now she's agreed that she's going to at least give me a chance to try and redeem myself."

"I don't think Melanie—" Jack was interrupted by Rebecca poking her hand between them.

"Marc Longo? I interviewed you last year about your winery for *Charleston* magazine. I understand you just had a fabulous crop and the winery is doing a phenomenal business now. Congratulations."

Marc took her small hand between both of his and kissed her on each cheek while Jack and I looked on with similar expressions of disbelief.

"Of course I remember. Rebecca, isn't it? I could never forget such a lovely face." They smiled at each other in mutual admiration and I thought I felt my stomach turn. "You must come and do a follow-up piece about my latest project."

"And what might that be?" Her tone was professional and restrained, but I could have sworn that she batted her eyelashes at him.

"I'm writing a book. Already have an agent and some interest from a few of the big New York publishers."

"Really?" Jack interjected. "Is it a children's book with lots of pictures?"

Jack's tone had changed from mere annoyance to something else, leaving me to wonder if he was threatened by Marc's foray into his territory.

Ignoring Jack, Marc continued. "I'll treat you to lunch at our new restaurant. We were able to convince a French Laundry chef from Napa to come work for us, and I promise you it will be a treat you won't soon forget."

Rebecca smiled, revealing dimples on either side of her mouth. "I'd love to. I'll give your secretary a call next week to set something up."

"Wonderful." Marc looked back at Jack. "I have no idea what you're doing with two such beautiful women, but I'm quite sure you don't deserve it." With a mock bow, he said, "Ladies, it's been a pleasure and I'll speak with you both soon." Then he turned on his heel and left.

Jack faced me. "Surely you're not going to have dinner with the guy. He doesn't have the most stellar of reputations, or have you already forgotten?"

He looked genuinely angry, and I was flattered for a moment until I remembered the ride I'd just endured in the back of his Porsche. "My personal life is absolutely no concern of yours and I'd appreciate it if you'd keep your opinions to yourself."

I began walking to the wrought iron gate that led into St. Philip's cemetery. "Come on. Let's get this over with. Don't forget your camera.

It's in the backseat. I think it left a permanent impression on the back of my thigh."

I strode into the cemetery, feeling the immediate chill and hearing the din of voices that seemed to crowd me like buzzing flies. I paused by a marker and read the inscription on the weathered stone as I waited for Rebecca and Jack to catch up. FOR NOW WE SEE THROUGH A GLASS DARKLY, BUT THEN FACE TO FACE. NOW I KNOW IN PART, BUT THEN SHALL I KNOW, EVEN AS ALSO I AM KNOWN. I CORINTHIANS 13:12.

A shiver coursed through me as the flicker of a shadow caught my attention from the corner of my eye. A whirring sound began in my head, almost as if it was deliberately blocking another sound. I twirled around, trying to catch sight of whatever it was that I had seen, feeling danger and sanctuary almost simultaneously. Confused, I stopped, focusing on the sound and hearing a faint voice above the din, the words like tiny bells. *Be careful, Melanie.*

"Grandmother?" The sound of crunching leaves underfoot made me twirl, my startled gasp drowned by the pealing bells of St. Philip's.

Rebecca and Jack approached, her manicured hand tucked neatly into the crook of his arm. I made a mental note to solicit her help manually peeling paint from a ceiling medallion with her bare fingers. Feeling better with that mental image, I managed to smile, overlooking Jack's expression of concern. "This way," I said as I led them to my grandmother's grave.

Thankfully, the stone had been replaced to its original spot, and the yellow tape removed. "Here," I said, indicating the odd verse on the marker.

Jack read it aloud:

When bricks crumble, the fireplace falls;
When children cry, the mothers call.
When lies are told, the sins are built,
Within the waves, hide all our guilt.

I waited for him to say something else, then realized they were both staring at me. I'd been humming ABBA's "Waterloo" to block out the sound of my name being called over and over. "Sorry," I said.

Jack raised his camera and began snapping pictures of not just the headstone, but the entire grave and its surroundings. Rebecca pulled a notepad out of her purse and was taking notes. "She died in 1975 but had this verse planned in advance."

"Yes," I said. "I never saw it though, and neither did my mother before we moved away. We've only just seen it and have no idea what any of it is about."

Her clear blue eyes regarded me calmly. "Well, obviously, the waves have something to do with the sunken *Rose*, don't you think? And seeing as how the *Rose* disappeared during the earthquake of 1886, I would have to assume that the line about bricks crumbling would be related to that."

Jack looked at Rebecca as if she'd just discovered sliced bread. "You're brilliant, Rebecca."

She brightened, then tilted her face to him like a pink daisy turning toward the sun. I made another mental note to get her to help with outdoor tasks, too, to splash dark splotches of freckles across her little nose and throw a few wrinkles on her forehead.

They both turned to look at me and I realized that I might have been humming "Take a Chance on Me" a little too loudly. "Sorry," I said again, trying to study the words I should have paid more attention to the first time I'd seen them. I thought Rebecca was probably right, considering what we knew now about the sunken ship, but I was just a little perturbed that I hadn't been the one to figure it out first. "I'd like to study it a little further before I jump to any conclusions," I added, trying to keep a smug tone from my voice. "And try to figure out what lies and sins she might be referring to."

We continued to study the marker as Jack took more pictures. And I studied Jack and Rebecca surreptitiously, trying to see if they were hearing anything out of the ordinary, too, since the voices had now reached earsplitting levels. I resisted the impulse to press my hands over my ears, and focused instead on trying to hear the one voice I thought had been my grandmother's. *Look closely, Melanie.*

I glanced at Rebecca to see if she'd spoken, but she was busily jotting something down in her notebook. I leaned in closer to see if we might have missed something, and that's when I noticed the engraved decorative edge that wound its way around the circumference of the marker, lassoing the words.

"Look," I said, pointing to the line. "It looks familiar, doesn't it?"

They both turned to stare where I was pointing.

"Not to me," Rebecca said dismissively before returning to her notebook.

Jack continued to look at it, then snapped a few more pictures. "It's not familiar to me, but it still might be to you. Think hard, Mellie, where you might have seen it before."

I clenched my eyes and began humming again, blocking out all sights and sounds, the memory of where I'd seen those markings hovering close like a scent. I shivered again and tried to shove my hands into my pockets, but my right hand was blocked by something inside.

I looked down in confusion, not remembering putting anything there, then stuck my fingers inside and gingerly pulled out the photographs my dad had given me earlier that morning. I glanced down at the one on top, the photo of my grandmother staring at the outside drawing room window as the sun illuminated its secrets. "I found it," I said, holding up the picture for Jack to see. "Here." I pointed to what appeared to be a vine encompassing the image that was depicted in the stained glass.

Jack held the photograph next to the grave marker to compare. "It's definitely the same. And from what I know of your grandmother, I doubt it's a coincidence."

"There aren't any coincidences, remember?" I said, reminding him of his oft-used phrase that had turned out to be largely true.

I was rewarded with a wink. "So you do listen to me." He turned back to the photo. "But where is this?"

Rebecca came and stood next to him to view the picture. "It's taken from the garden outside the Legare Street house."

Jack and I both stared at her and she shrugged. "While I was doing my research on your mother I spent a lot of time studying the garden, which is how I recognized it. Despite the, um, aesthetic changes made by the previous owners."

I turned back to Jack. "You can only see this picture when you're standing outside and the sun is hitting it in a particular way. The window isn't original to the house, but was installed sometime in the late 1800s."

"Which means that whatever the secret in the window is, it might somehow be related to the sailboat." Jack lowered his camera. "And your grandmother wanted to make sure that somebody found out what it was."

Rebecca glanced at her watch before shoving her notebook back into her purse. "My mother drove in today from Summerville to do some shopping and I'm meeting her for lunch over on King Street, so I've got to run. I'll have my mother run me by Legare Street later to pick up my car. Then I'm going to see what I can dig up regarding the window. Who ordered it, who made it, that kind of thing. There's a chance that the original paperwork might still exist. I'll let you know what I find out. In the meantime, you can work on the tombstone rhyme." She blew a kiss at Jack. "I'll call you later, Jackie. Bye, Melanie." With a brief wave, she turned and crossed the street, then turned to shout. "Don't forget your costume fittings! I texted you both the address." She waved again, then began to walk away, her pink coat quickly disappearing from view.

"I've got to run, too," I said. "I've got a house showing at one o'clock, but I've got some paperwork and phone calls I want to take care of first."

"Mellie, I'm sure you're hungry. Let's grab a bite. My treat. I'll even let you sit in the front seat."

I stared at him indignantly. "I didn't mind sitting in the back."

"Right. I was afraid the back of Rebecca's head might melt on my seat from your stare. Come on. What do you say? I'll have you at your showing in plenty of time. And we can work on the rhyme, see if we can figure anything out. We can do Hominy Grill on Rutledge. I could go for some of their shrimp and grits."

A chilly breeze stirred the leaves behind me, pushing at me like a hand on my back. The voices had died down, as if they were listening to my conversation, waiting for my response. "I really have too much to do. I thought I'd see what leftovers Mrs. Houlihan left in the fridge to eat on the way over to the office."

The light in Jack's eyes shifted as he stepped forward, making me nervous. "Do you ever do anything just because you want to, Mellie? Or because you think it might be fun?"

I stepped back, not liking how close he was standing. "Of course I do. I just think that fun, like everything else, needs to be scheduled so it doesn't interfere with more important things. And right now, I need to make sure I'm not late for my next appointment." I stared pointedly at his car. "I'd appreciate it if you'd drive me home, but I could walk if it's too much trouble."

He took a step closer so that our noses were almost touching but I didn't step back this time, wanting to stand my ground. Softly, he said, "You had a terrible childhood. I get it. And you certainly deserve a lot of praise for turning out as well as you did, and even for forging a new relationship with your father."

"Please stop," I said, my voice struggling for conviction. Somewhere in my brain, I heard Sophie's voice telling me that I needed to find somebody to let go with, to allow them in to see what she referred to as the "kinder, gentler Melanie Middleton." But I couldn't help but think that if I ever allowed myself to let it all go with Jack, I might never find myself again. Or worse, I'd find myself back where I'd started, as a scared and angry little girl abandoned by the two people who were supposed to love her best.

Jack's thumbs gently rubbed at my jaw. Ignoring my request, he continued. "Somewhere along the way, you forgot how to have fun. One day, Melanie Middleton, I'm going to take you out of your little box and we're going to have a little fun together. And you're going to like it so much that you're going to thank me."

My breath was coming in little gasps now, mostly from indignation but I couldn't deny the little tremor of anticipation, either. I stiffened my shoulders. "You already tried that, remember? I missed a whole day of work so you could take me to the backwoods of Timbuktu and get me drunk. What part of that was supposed to be fun?"

He grinned his killer grin and stepped back. "You weren't supposed to get drunk, but yeah, I had a good time." He chuckled to himself, then walked to his car and opened up the passenger door for me.

"What's so funny?" I asked, hesitating briefly before stepping into the front seat. I was relieved that he'd stopped touching me, but worried, too.

He chuckled again. "Nothing." He shut my door and went around the car to get into the driver's side.

"Then what are you laughing at?" I racked my brain again, wondering what I might have said to him when I wasn't sober enough to remember—anything that might be used against me. I had a fuzzy impression of me burping in his ear, but I quickly dismissed it as being too improbable.

He started the engine and turned to face me, his eyes sparkling, which made my blood do that stupid swishing thing. "You. You're almost forty years old and you still haven't grown up."

I turned away, annoyed and angry. "Is that so? And you think you're the one to fix me."

He pulled the car away from the curb. "Well, it sure as hell isn't Marc Longo."

Surprised at the vehemence in his tone, I sat back in my seat as we sped forward on Church Street, looping around the church that intruded into the roadway. "Where are you taking me?"

"To Legare Street, like you asked. Because you have so much work to do."

I looked away—not seeing the passing scenery as it flickered by—and wondered why I was so disappointed.

It was full dark by the time I returned to the house on Legare Street later that night, exhausted from hours spent showing a couple from Poughkeepsie houses in the Colonial Lake neighborhood. They'd complained about how old everything was, and how high the real estate prices were despite all of the fixing up they'd be required to do, and it was all I could do to not tell them that if they wanted new, cookie-cutter, and move-in ready, they should be considering a move to the Atlanta suburbs instead.

I'd managed to convince them to look at newer construction in Daniel Island and had spent the last three hours in my office making appointments for the following day.

I hesitated on the steps leading up to the front door, noticing that the front lights were off. I didn't want to step into that shadowy place, where I couldn't see what might be hiding in the corners. I dug into my purse and pulled out my mini emergency kit and took out the small flashlight

I'd never had a need for until now. I shone it into the corners, then approached the door, key held ready.

I stuck the key in and was about to turn the knob when I glanced up at one of the sidelights by the door and froze, the air around me suddenly brittle. The face of a girl stared back at me through the wavy panes of glass, the eyes dark and glittering, the space between us filled with an almost palpable hatred. The air seemed to shimmer with it, warming my face through the bitter night air. My hand shook, the key rattling in the lock as my eyes met hers.

I am stronger than you. I wasn't sure if I'd spoken the words out loud or to myself, and I had the distinct impression that the words would have no effect on this spirit. I felt the knob turn under my hand and I resisted, not wanting to be face-to-face with whoever the girl was, knowing that my strength alone wouldn't be enough.

The knob turned again, harder this time, and I felt myself losing my grip as the door swung inward. I stifled a small scream as I recognized Sophie in her endearingly familiar Birkenstocks and wild hair.

"I could have sworn I turned the front lights on," she said, moving to the light switch and flipping them on. "And you've got to have the thermostat looked at. I swear it's thirty below in . . ."

Her last words came out in a puff of air as I threw myself at her, clutching tightly to her sari as my gaze darted to the lit corners of the vast hallway.

"Whoa, Melanie. It's good to see you, too." She held me at arm's length and peered into my face, small frown lines appearing between her eyebrows. "What happened to you? It looks like you've seen a . . ." Her voice petered away as her eyes widened.

I kicked the door shut with my foot and nodded. "She was right here. One of the girls from the portrait—only she looked to be a bit older. The shorter one wearing the locket with an *R* on it." I reached inside my jacket and pulled out the locket with the *M* engraved across the face. "The one that looks like this."

Sophie raised an eyebrow as she stared at it. "Where did that come from?"

"The sailboat." I fluttered my hand in front of her to stop the recriminations that were already bubbling up to her lips. "They've already photographed it and documented it. The guy on the salvage team is an old friend of my father's and figured that since it essentially belonged to me, I should have it."

Sophie tightened her lips around her teeth, making her look more like a professor than her outfits ever could. "And you're going to give it back now."

"Believe me. I can't give it back fast enough. The previous owner has been asking for it."

Her eyes widened again, but she knew better than to ask. "Any idea who she is, yet?"

I shook my head. "Not yet. We're working on it. So far everything points to my great-grandmother, Rose. But she was an only child, which doesn't explain who the other girl in the portrait is. The one wearing the *M* necklace. Nor does it explain why she seems to dislike me so much."

I put my briefcase down and took my coat off while a clock, stuck onto the front of a lacquered piece of driftwood and inadvertently left on the wall in the parlor by the previous owners, began to strike the hour. I looked back at Sophie. "It's eight o'clock. Why are you still here? And where is my mother?"

"Your father took her out to dinner, to discuss the garden, as she kept explaining to me even though I didn't ask. I'm still here because she didn't want you to be alone in the house and asked if I'd stay here until she got back."

I was still stuck on the first part of her explanation and didn't have time to analyze the second. I noticed Sophie's dry eyes and nose for the first time. "Where's General Lee?"

"In your room. I explained to your mother about my allergies and she was very understanding. The little guy wouldn't use the back stairs, though. Kept barking at them with his tail between his legs, so your mother took him up the front stairs."

"Makes sense," I said. "I'm starving. I hope Mrs. Houlihan left me something good." I began walking back toward the kitchen, but turned around when I realized Sophie wasn't following me. "Is there anything else?"

"Yes, actually, there is. A truck from Trenholm's Antiques dropped off a desk today. Your mother recognized it as having belonged to your grandmother and had them put it in your grandmother's sitting room."

"Great. I wasn't expecting it so soon, but I'm glad it's here already." When Sophie remained where she was without moving to follow me, I took a step toward her. "Is anything wrong with it?"

"Nothing's wrong, exactly. Just weird—and I can't believe I'm using that word after I've hung around you for so long." She smiled apologetically at me, a thick beaded braid falling from its haphazard placement on top of her head.

"Yes?" I prompted.

"Well, right when it was being delivered, the house phone rang and I answered it. It was Rebecca. She asked me if we'd had a new piece of furniture brought into the house recently, and I told her about the desk. She got really excited and said she'd had a dream about something hidden inside of it, like a book or something, and she wanted to come over right away to see if she could find it."

"What did you tell her?"

"That I'd found a secret compartment already. All those old desks had them, so it wasn't that big of a stretch. But I told her there was nothing in it."

"Dang." My shoulders sagged. "I guess that's one clue we're not going to be able to use." I ground the heels of my hands into my eyes. "I'm so exhausted. I just want this over with. I want to find out who this girl is and get rid of her so I can go back to my life."

I peered back at Sophie, who was watching me with a satisfied grin on her face. "I didn't say that I told her the truth."

"Soph!" I said with surprise as she brought out what appeared to be a tattered leather-bound book from a drooping pocket in her sweatpants. "Why didn't you tell her?"

She shrugged. "Because I don't trust her. I saw her at the library today at the college, in the special-collections section on the third floor. I was looking for some historic photos of the interior of this house and saw her with her nose buried in a book, taking notes. She was real careful to cover up what she'd been writing, and tried to be evasive when I asked her what she was doing. Knowing she couldn't stop me without causing a scene, I flipped up the cover of the book she'd been looking at and saw that it was a pictorial history of Louis Tiffany windows from 1878 to 1933." She stared at me pointedly. "Rebecca finally let on that she was looking for information on the drawing room window, but hadn't found anything useful yet."

"But you didn't believe her?"

"I'm not sure. But I didn't tell her what I'd found in the desk because I wanted you to see it first. It was your grandmother's desk, after all."

Sophie placed the brown leather book in my proffered hand and I flipped it open to reveal lined pages filled with small, neat cursive writing. "It looks like a journal," I said as I sat down on the bottom step to get a better look. Sophie sat down next to me. I surprised her by putting my arm around her shoulders and hugging her. "You're a good friend, Soph. Even though I no longer know what fingernails are supposed to look like, I still think you're the best, best friend ever."

She snorted, then elbowed me in the side. "You'd still turn me in for a *What Not to Wear* episode and you know it."

I elbowed her back. "Yeah. But you'd end up thanking me for it."

She shook her head, her beaded braids dancing around her face. "I doubt it." Opening up the cover of the journal, she said, "There aren't any names in here that I can see; everything's written in the first person with only a few initials thrown in. It's as if the writer was afraid somebody might find it and read it."

I flipped through some of the pages. "How old do you think it is?"

"Hard to tell exactly, but from the quality of the paper, and the type of ink on the pages, and even the good condition of the leather cover, I'd say between one hundred and one hundred and fifty years old. You'll have to take it to an expert to be sure, but I think I'm pretty close."

My stomach rumbled, reminding me that I hadn't eaten yet, and I was about to say something about making the journal wait until after we'd eaten when two words on a page caught my attention: "Hessian soldier."

Wishing I had my glasses with me, I squinted and brought the book up to my face to see better, and read the words out loud. "My Hessian soldier watches over me and I know that while he is here, I am protected. I don't think she can see him, but I think she suspects something. We are so close in age and should have much in common, but I find that I can never truly relax when I'm in her company. It's as if she watches me always, like a cat at a mouse hole, waiting for me to be less vigilant."

The sickly sweet odor of gunpowder trickled in the air in front of me and I looked up, careful not to look directly at the specter of the soldier.

"We're not alone, are we?" asked Sophie, rubbing her arms where I could see gooseflesh prickling her skin.

I shook my head. "No." I turned my face closer to the soldier. "Who were you protecting?"

He didn't answer, and I could tell that he was uncomfortable, as if I'd discovered part of his secret. Impatient for an answer, I turned toward him, remembering too late not to look at him. With a shimmer in the air, he was gone just as quietly and as quickly as he had appeared.

CHAPTER 15

I awoke with a start—disoriented—and realizing somebody had been calling my name. General Lee was spread out on the pillow next to me, snoring quietly, the headlights from a passing car spearing shafts of light across the wallpapered walls and hideous ceiling mural before throwing me back into complete darkness again.

Searching for my glasses on the nightstand, I stuck them in front of my face to read the glowing numbers on the clock by my bed: three thirteen a.m. I groaned, then listened again, wondering if I'd just been dreaming. I'd surprised myself by falling asleep quickly for the second night in a row, despite the jarring experience of witnessing my father trying to kiss my mother good night at the front door. Luckily, I'd heard them from the kitchen where Sophie had been watching me work on a new spreadsheet for the Legare house restoration, so I was able to throw the door open before any permanent damage was done.

Melanie.

I sat up, fully awake now, and the sickly sweet scent of gunpowder was heavy in the room. As my eyes adjusted to the darkness, I made out the dark shadow of a man in a tricorn hat by the door. I blinked, studying it so hard that I barely noticed the door opening with a soft creak, a blast of warm air from the hallway making me realize how cold my room was.

Follow me, Melanie.

I knew not to be afraid, but I was reluctant to follow him out into the darkened house. I sensed him waiting for me, though, and realized he would wait for as long as it took me to get out of bed and follow him.

I slid off the tall bed that had been moved from my mother's apartment in New York and was one of the few things of good taste that now resided in the house. I gripped one of its thick mahogany posts as I put my fuzzy slippers on, then grabbed my terry-cloth robe and followed the soldier out into the hallway.

Since the streetlamps didn't reach this far into the interior of the house, it was dark and I found myself following his scent down the front stairs and into the kitchen. I paused for a moment outside the saloon doors, remembering the wet footprints and feeling my first fissure of fear.

Do not be afraid, Melanie. I am here.

Swallowing thickly, I pushed the doors open and stepped into the kitchen. Keeping my back to the door, I slid over to the light switch and flipped it on. The recessed lights glowed dully overhead for a brief moment before sputtering out one by one, as if something else in the room was zapping all of their energy.

I smelled his scent again, reassured that he was still there. "What do you want?" I asked.

Come here.

I scanned the dim kitchen, pools of shallow light from the streetlamps dripping onto the dark wood cabinets and countertops. I stopped at the wall mural of the longhorn cow and saw my soldier leaning against what was once an Adams mantel but was now just empty air. After taking a deep breath, I headed toward him, careful to avoid running into the kitchen table. I stopped in front of him, not looking directly at his face, but instead concentrating on how clearly I could see his hand as it rested on the invisible mantel, the glow of a streetlight illuminating the fine blond hairs on the backs of his fingers.

"What is it?" I whispered, not really sure why I was being quiet. My mother couldn't have heard us up in her bedroom. But the entire time I was aware of the dark door on the other side of the kitchen that led up the back stairs.

It is in there.

"What is?"

What you seek.

I studied the solid wall for a moment, not understanding. "I don't know what you mean."

Within the waves, hide all our guilt.

I strained my eyes to see his face better in the dark, but all was in shadow. "That's on my grandmother's gravestone. What does it mean?"

I heard him sigh and then, almost imperceptibly, I felt a soft brush of fingers against my jawline, soft enough to be mistaken for a trickle of air. My breath caught with the icy heat of his touch, and I wanted to step away and stay at the same time. In the years I'd known him as a young girl, he'd never touched me, and I wondered what had changed to embolden him now that I'd returned to this house.

You are so beautiful, Melanie.

Months of fending off Jack gave me the strength I needed to keep hold of my senses. "Who are you? What's your name? What guilt is hidden beneath the waves?"

He touched me again, and I was sure it was to make me stop asking questions. He stood in front of me now, both hands feathering light strokes on my neck. I kept my gaze on the wood floor, resisting the temptation to give in to the sensation of ice and heat teasing my skin.

"Who were you trying to protect?" I asked, my voice shaky, but determined to find answers.

His fingers stopped, and I thought I could hear him breathe, or maybe it was the house breathing, a silent, palpable beat of unknown origin.

"Who were you trying to protect?" I asked again, feeling him leave me before the words had completely escaped from my mouth.

The lights flickered on brightly above me, accompanied by the sound of the swinging doors, and I spun around to find my mother standing inside the kitchen doorway, thankfully wearing a short robe that covered most of her skin.

"He was here, wasn't he?"

I knew better than to pretend I didn't know whom she was talking about. "Yes. He woke me up and brought me down here." I pointed to the wall behind me. "He said that what I seek is in here. And he quoted the last line on Grandmother's gravestone: Within the waves, hide all our guilt."

She frowned, then stepped closer. "You're—flushed. And your eyes are really bright." Her eyes widened. "Did he touch you?"

I nodded, and felt myself blushing, remembering how good it had felt. "Yes. He did it before, a few days ago. He didn't hurt me."

She shook her head, then sat down at the table. "No. He wouldn't."

I sat down opposite. "What do you mean?"

A small smile lifted her lips. "He's a gentleman."

I chewed on my lip, realizing with surprised relief that my mother was the only person I could discuss this with. "Sophie found a journal in Grandmother's desk. But I don't think it was hers. Sophie thinks it's at least one hundred years old, possibly older."

My mother raised an eyebrow as she waited for me to continue.

"I haven't had a chance to read through it yet, but when I was flipping through the pages, I came to an entry about a Hessian soldier. And how the journal writer felt he was there to protect her." I held my mother's gaze for a moment. "It looks like he's been here for a long time, protecting people."

She shook her head. "Not just people. Women." She frowned again. "But the fact that he can touch you now . . ." She bit her lower lip, as if to prevent herself from going on.

"Tell me." My voice was harsher than I'd meant it to be, but I'd lived for so long with unanswered questions that I didn't think I could live with one more.

"It means you're stronger. That you're a brighter beacon now than you've ever been." Her fingers drummed restlessly on the table. "It will be easier for those lost souls seeking the light to find you now. You'll need to be prepared."

"But what has that got to do with his touching me?" I glanced down at my exposed forearms, seeing the goose bumps prickling the skin.

My mother leaned forward. "That they can feed off your strength to make themselves stronger. And not just for those that mean us no harm."

I shivered, remembering what had happened when I'd been in the kitchen by myself. "When you were in New York, there was—an incident. The girl from the boat, she was in here. She scratched me. But the soldier came and made her go away."

Her hand cupped my cheek, her thumb gently rubbing my skin as her brow furrowed with worry. I didn't flinch or pull away. "Why now, though? What's changed?"

She dropped her hand, then slid the sugar bowl toward her and began to spin it in circles, her gaze focused on it. "You're older, your abilities stronger whether or not you want them to be and regardless of whether you've been actively using them."

I knew she wasn't done, so I remained silent, waiting.

"And because I'm here. The two of us together are like a bonfire in the darkness. Things won't stay quiet for long."

"That's what we want, though, right? Because then we can make them go away."

She swallowed, then nodded, swirling the sugar bowl in tight circles. "That's the way it usually works."

I put my hand on hers to still it. "What aren't you telling me?"

She looked at me, and I saw such sadness in her eyes that I didn't pull my hand back right away. "Why do you think I'm not telling you everything?"

I sat back in my chair, placing my hands in my lap, my eyes locked on hers. "Because I remember, from the time before you left. The way you looked at me. The way you answered my questions with questions or answered me by changing the subject. It made me feel as if it was Christmastime, and you'd hidden presents all over the house so I couldn't find them. Only, it wasn't Christmas, was it?"

She dropped her gaze for a moment. "I've told you what I know, Mellie. I don't know who the girl is, but I suspect she's been here for a very long time, before I was born, even. And I know your German soldier. He was here when I was a child, but I don't know who he is, either. Only that he seems to be here to protect. That's all I know." She smiled a secretive smile. "And he never touched me."

We stared at each other for a long time until my mother looked away, her gaze falling on the stack of photographs I'd left on the table. She began thumbing through them, pausing over each one. She stopped at the one of my grandmother and the window.

"You can see what a beacon you were back when you were a child." She tapped a photo with a long red-painted fingernail, pointing to a cluster of white spots my father had thought meant a defective camera. "It could be the combined presence of your grandmother, too, but they're all gathered around you." She leaned her elbows on the table. "It's a gift, Mellie. A gift you can use to help others, if you choose. But it shouldn't be a burden, or something you're ashamed of."

I crossed my arms over my chest. "Maybe for somebody like you. You're an opera singer, an artistic person. People expect you to be eccentric. But I'm a Realtor. Clients generally don't want to buy houses from somebody who sees and talks with dead people. I agreed to help you get rid of this spirit, but as soon as we're done, I'm back to pretending I don't see them or hear them."

My mother smiled softly, her face reminding me so much of my childhood that it hurt to look at her. I concentrated on the sugar bowl as she spoke. "I'm glad we're doing this together, Mellie. I won't lie and tell you I haven't been looking forward to it, hoping that maybe somehow it will bring us together. That maybe you'll learn that this gift we share is our bond."

I jerked to a stand, but my anger was muted, like a fist wrapped in soft velvet. "A long time ago I would have welcomed a bond between us. But I've spent most of my life trying to separate myself from you, and I'm too old and too tired to go back to another place and time." I shook my head. "I don't know why you left, or even if those reasons should mean anything to me now. But I'm proud of who I've become, without your help and despite what you did to me. So no, Mother. The main reason I don't want to accept this 'thing' you call a gift is because it is the one thing we do have in common. And believe me, there is nothing I've ever wanted to have in common with you."

I turned around before she could recognize what I'd said for the lie it was, but not before I'd seen the slight upturn of her lips as if she knew it anyway.

∞

I sucked in my breath as Sophie stood behind me, stuck a knee in the lower part of my back, and pulled on the corset strings. I thought I was going to pass out from lack of oxygen as spots danced across my field of vision.

"Why on earth do I need to wear this thing? It's bad enough you've got me looking like Scarlett O'Hara on the way to Twelve Oaks, but how authentic do I really need to be?"

Sophie collapsed on the bed, panting with exertion. "It's not for authenticity. It's to give you cleavage and to make the male tourists who march through here tonight give an extra donation to the historical society."

I caught sight of myself in the cheval mirror—another rescue from the Tradd Street house—and nearly didn't recognize myself. She was right. Pushing up all of my insides above the waistline had actually given the false impression of real breasts, if only my lungs hadn't been squashed against my rib cage allowing only small puffs of air to be inhaled at one time.

I pirouetted, admiring the navy blue silk gown with white lace encircling the off-the-shoulder décolletage and decorating the wrists. There was something to be said about the enhanced hourglass figure of 1860s fashions, but one day spent in a Charleston July without air-conditioning would send me running for a pair of shorts and padded bikini top.

"I think your mother's sapphires add a nice touch."

My hands went up to the heirloom necklace. My mother had brought the necklace and earrings to me in a black jeweled box as a sort of peace offering as I was getting dressed. I was about to refuse when she reminded me that they'd been my grandmother's, and that she would have wanted me to wear them, too.

Sophie continued. "I'm not sure if that locket goes with them, though. It sort of looks out of place."

"Yeah, you're probably right. It's just that . . ." I paused, trying to put into words the odd sensation I had that the locket belonged with the sapphires, and how hesitant I became whenever I tried to take it off. "I think it works. Besides, you're the last person in the world I want to take fashion advice from."

Sophie just blinked at me as if she didn't understand what I was talking about.

I turned around and met her gaze. "Remind me again why I'm doing this?"

"Because photographers from *Charleston* magazine, the *Post & Courier*, and *Southern Living* will be on the tour tonight, so that your face, name, and business information will be splashed all over the place, giving you more exposure than you ever dreamed of. You're also doing it because it will bring in money for the historical society, which furthers the cause dearest to our hearts: historic restoration in our favorite city."

I approached the bed and turned around to sit, stopping midway as I learned that it wasn't as simple as it should have been. I tried flipping the hoop forward, then backward, and ended up lifting it up to my waist and exposing myself before I managed a half-sitting, half-standing position.

Sophie's face was expressionless. "Perhaps you shouldn't do that in public."

"Why am I the only one in costume? Even Rebecca gets to wear normal clothes."

"That's because Rebecca doesn't have a claim to two fabulous houses in the historic district and you do. I think it irks her, too."

"What do you mean?"

"Oh, I don't know. Little comments here and there. Like how you don't know how lucky you are, how some people would kill to be in your position, and how you're completely unappreciative of what's been handed to you on a silver platter. Makes me think the green-eyed monster of jealousy is sitting on her shoulder and sticking a tongue out at you."

I grimaced. "I've definitely got to assign that girl to some heavy-duty paint stripping and introduce her to some of my bills, show her my fingernails, even. That might bring her down to my reality."

Sophie turned to me, her hands on her narrow hips. "Are you really so oblivious, Melanie? Have I not taught you anything regarding the real reasons behind historical preservation?"

I stared back at her. "Is that a rhetorical question?"

She frowned. "I hope you understand how all the work you've done has been for the entire global community. If we tear down everything old to make room for newer, more impersonal structures, we've lost a part of our past, a thing of beauty and meaning. Gone forever."

I slid off the bed and began rearranging my skirts. "Just like my plaster-free hair, manicures, and investment portfolio." I turned toward the mirror before she could see the smile that would tell her I knew exactly what she was talking about. I was just afraid to say it in front of Sophie because then I was likely to end up restoring yet another house.

There was a brief knock on the door and then Mrs. Houlihan stuck her head around the corner. She winked at me when she saw me in the dress. "You look gorgeous, Miss Melanie. Fit for a barbecue at Twelve Oaks."

I rolled my eyes, then tried to hitch up my bodice a little further to cover up a bit more of the vast expanse of exposed skin. "Exactly what I was afraid of."

"Just wanted to let you know that I've placed the punch and glasses on a tray in the front parlor. And Mr. Jack is here and I was wondering where you'd like me to put him."

I opened my mouth to give a few suggestions but Sophie interrupted me. "Tell him we'll be right down. The tour is scheduled to start in ten minutes."

"And don't you worry about General Lee. I've got him a nice soup bone to keep him happy." Mrs. Houlihan winked at me again, then disappeared behind the door. We listened as her heavy tread disappeared down the hallway. Sophie moved toward the door. "I'm going to go check on your mother. She's in charge of herding so that you don't have to worry about the stray tourist who heads in the wrong direction."

"What about Rebecca? I thought she was supposed to be here, too."

Sophie smirked. "I pulled some strings and had her reassigned to the Old City Jail over on the corner of Magazine and Franklin. She gets to direct people to the toilet facilities. Although she did threaten to stop by later on."

"How did you pull that off? I thought she was in charge of the whole thing tonight."

Sophie clasped her hands behind her back, attempting to look innocent. "Oh, when she asked for my help in getting volunteer tour guides from the college, the axis of power shifted in my direction."

I put my hand up and high-fived her. "One last question: What if I have to go to the bathroom?"

She wrinkled her nose as she pretended to consider the question for a moment. "Do your best to hold it. If that fails, ask Mrs. Houlihan for a pot."

"Gee, thanks. You know, I liked you better when you weren't pining for a guy. You were a lot nicer then."

"What do you mean?"

"Oh, come on, Soph. You and Chad. You're like Raggedy Ann and Andy, practically stitched together with the same thread. You've used the stupidest excuse in the book—what was it, incompatible astrology signs?—to keep him away from you because of some misplaced sense of feminism and independence. But you're practically attached at the hip and living together, for crying out loud. Would you just admit that you're both crazy about each other so we can all move on and you can start being nice again?"

She stared at me for a long moment, her face completely expressionless. One could never tell how Sophie felt because her emotions were so even-keeled. But I could see her exposed toes in her Birkenstocks, and watched as she curled them tightly.

"How about we reach a compromise? I'll start taking your relationship advice when you start taking my fashion advice. Because from where I'm standing, neither one of us is really qualified on either subject. And if you really want to analyze a weird relationship, yours and Jack's would be better suited to put under a microscope. You're both so hot for each other the temperature rises about twenty degrees whenever you're in the same room together. But you're both either too stubborn, ignorant, or mentally challenged to figure out what to do about it." She drew a deep breath. "So when you've worked out whatever it is that's between you and Jack, then come talk to me about Chad."

I looked at her, dumbfounded. The last time I'd seen her so agitated was when I told her I was knocking out a wall to extend the master suite in the Tradd Street house. "Ouch," was all I managed to say, but I wasn't even sure if she was right or wrong about Jack and me.

She turned to leave the room. "I'll see you downstairs."

After a few deep breaths, I shook my dress in place, then managed to squeeze myself through the doorway and make it to the top of the stairs without tripping or knocking anything over. It was a very good thing that most of the house was empty, with only fabric and paint swatches displayed on easels in the main rooms of the house for the anticipated visitors.

The house smelled of narcissus and citrus, courtesy of my father's decorating prowess. Lined up on the stairs were potted narcissus, swaddled in burlap and tied with red twine, their sweet aroma floating in the hall like a cloud. The nine fireplace mantels—minus the one in the kitchen that was currently being stored in the attic—were covered in pine swags my father had gathered himself and artfully arranged with pinecones and various citrus fruits of all colors and sizes. In all of my years growing up with him, it had never occurred to me to think that inside my rough-hewn military officer father lay an inner Martha Stewart.

A loud wolf whistle brought my attention to the bottom of the stairs. I spotted Jack, in full Confederate uniform complete with plumed hat and gleaming saber, leaning on the newel post and doing a pretty good impersonation of his estimable ancestor George Trenholm, Southern blockade runner and model for the literary character of Rhett Butler. Having grown up in a military family where I saw uniforms every day, I'd never thought much about the supposed attraction of men in uniform. But the sight of Jack Trenholm in Confederate gray was certainly more than enough to make me change my mind.

"Nice dress," he said. His gaze traveled over the gown, then rested on the sapphires around my neck before settling on my face.

I shrugged nonchalantly. "Just something I found in my closet."

His grin broadened as he spread out his arms. "Yeah. Me, too."

Doing my best to pretend to ignore him, I clutched the banister and carefully made my way to the bottom step. I eyed the three yellow stripes on his sleeve. "Only a sergeant, Jack? I thought you'd at least be a general."

He swept his hat from his head, took my hand, and then kissed the back of it, sending a small hot flash up my arm. "Didn't want to appear too farb."

"Farb?"

"It's a term we use in reenacting: far be it from reality. It's a deroga-tory term aimed at anybody whose costuming is less than authentic or ridiculously inappropriate."

"You're a reenactor?"

"Yes, ma'am. The First South Carolina Cavalry. And, yes, along with my pickup truck, I'm also a card-carrying member of the NRA. You know, Mellie, considering what close friends we are, I'm hurt that you seem to know so little about me."

"Close?" I asked, extricating my hand from his grasp.

"Well, we could be closer if you'd ever let me past the worksheets and the BlackBerry. Closest I ever came was when you were three sheets to the wind, but that's not how I'd recommend getting to know each other better. Although your attempts were admirable, even a bit amusing."

I narrowed my eyes. "I thought you said . . ."

I was interrupted by Sophie and my mother emerging from my mother's room. As they came down the staircase, Jack bowed, then took turns kissing their hands. "Ladies," he drawled. "How fortunate I am to be surrounded by such loveliness."

Sophie snorted, then continued on into the front parlor. My mother, looking elegant and half her age in a black velvet sheath dress, tapped him on the arm with a gloved hand. "Now, Jack." I was surprised to see that her face was serious. "I need you to stay with Mellie at all times. Do you understand?"

"Mother, I really don't think that's necessary . . ."

She turned to me, her eyes straying to the locket nestled among the sapphires. "I thought you were going to return that."

I nodded. "I plan to. I just—haven't done it yet."

Her eyes met mine for just a moment before facing Jack again. "I'll be greeting people at the door and showing them where the refreshments are, so I'll feel better knowing that you're with her."

Jack's serious expression matched my mother's, and I had the horrifying thought that the two of them had been talking about me in my absence. "I will."

"Mother, the house will be filled with people. Surely . . ." My words trailed away as I caught the scent of gunpowder.

"Good. He's here. I feel better now."

I felt him behind me, but I didn't turn around. Something felt different, though, his presence more solid. And I had the impression that if I turned around and looked in his face, he'd still be there.

"Who?" asked Jack, his gaze wandering the empty foyer.

"An old friend," my mother said.

We looked at each other and I found it oddly satisfying not to have to explain myself—to look into somebody else's eyes and know that not only did they already understand, but that what I could see and hear was as normal as breathing.

The door knocker sounded on the front door and Sophie emerged from the parlor. "Okay, everybody, get into your positions. The first tour is here, so let's make it worth their ticket price."

My mother joined Sophie; then Jack lifted his arm and I placed my hand on it, still aware of the soldier behind me—and of another presence, too, that was neither warm nor welcoming. Jack began to lead me away from the staircase, but I hesitated, the need to turn around too strong. I turned my head, looking straight at the apparition, and he remained solid. He appeared to be real, until I realized that I was staring at the zebra rug through him.

He lifted his hat to me and cocked his head in the direction of the kitchen, as if asking me to follow, then slowly walked down the remaining steps and into the hallway. He stopped once and looked behind him to see if I was following, then continued on his way, disappearing into the kitchen, the saloon doors swinging in his wake, followed shortly by the sound of General Lee barking.

Jack followed my gaze, watching the saloon doors swing. Slowly, my eyes met his. "You sure know how to add to an evening's entertainment, Mellie." He frowned. "Should I be scared?"

"No." I shivered, feeling another set of eyes on us. "Not of him, anyway."

The front door opened and a group of about twenty people poured into the foyer, their voices echoing off the floor and empty walls. Jack and I smiled and stepped forward to greet them, and all the time I was aware of somebody watching me, as if waiting for her chance to catch me alone again. Jack squeezed my hand and I looked up into his blue eyes, making me wonder not for the first time just which one might be the most dangerous.

CHAPTER 16

The evening seemed interminable. Although I did find people's reactions to the current color palette of the house amusing, and took some pride and satisfaction in showing them our plans for the restoration, I couldn't shake the feeling that I was being watched the entire time—and that a battle was brewing somewhere in the depths of the great house. I imagined during lulls of conversation that I could hear the house breathe—a soft pulse that emanated from the very walls and reverberated under my skin.

The kitchen hadn't been included in the tour since, with the exception of resurrecting the fireplace and mantel, it had not only already been restored and modernized, but didn't resemble a painting accident. Still, every time we'd walked near it, I'd glanced back at the closed doors and felt that the soldier was still inside, waiting for me.

The last guest had just left and I was sliding my grateful feet out of my shoes when the front door opened again. I was about to tell whoever it was that the tour was over but closed my mouth when I recognized Rebecca. She didn't look as perky as she usually did, probably as a result of explaining where the ladies' room was once too often, but she dimpled when she spotted Jack.

She approached him and gave him a kiss on his cheek before greeting everyone else with a perfunctory glance. "I'm sorry to stop by so late but I knew you'd all still be here. I wanted to thank everybody for participating and to let you know that it looks like we raised almost double what we raised last year." She beamed, as if all the success firmly rested on her petite shoulders. "I also wanted to tell everyone that I've made a little progress on finding the origins of the window in the drawing room." She paused for effect. "I ran into Sophie at the College of Charleston library, and I didn't want to spoil the surprise before I had anything conclusive."

Sophie and I exchanged a glance.

Rebecca gripped her hands together. "I discovered that the window was designed by an apprentice of Louis Tiffany's, an Irishman by the name of John Nolan, who set up shop here in Charleston in 1880. His shop is long gone, but there's a chance that his business records might have survived in archives somewhere. I figured we could ask Yvonne for help in finding . . ."

Her voice trailed away and I realized that she was staring at me. Although she'd only given me a cursory glance when she walked in, she must have just noticed the dress and jewelry.

Slowly, she walked toward me. "Your . . . jewelry. It's beautiful."

"Thank you," I said warily. "My mother let me wear them."

"Yes. I believe I once showed you a photo of your mother wearing them." She faced my mother. "They're heirlooms, I believe."

My mother nodded, then moved to stand next to me. For some reason, I found comfort in that.

Rebecca continued. "Do you know the history behind them?"

My mother shook her head. "All I know is that they were my mother's, and that her mother gave them to her. I have no idea where they came from originally."

"And the locket?" Rebecca asked. "Is that a family heirloom, too?"

I'd forgotten I was wearing it, and my hand went to my neck where I grasped the cold metal heart. "No. It was found on the *Rose* when they were salvaging it."

She raised an eyebrow.

"Don't worry. I, it's going back. I just . . . haven't returned it yet. But I will." I added the last part to convince myself more than anything.

"It's just like the lockets in the portrait, isn't it?" Rebecca stepped closer, close enough that I could smell the mint she must have popped into her mouth before she entered the house—and something else that was vaguely familiar. With a start, I realized that we both used the same shampoo.

My hoop skirt prevented her from getting closer, and I relaxed a little. "It does seem that way."

Rebecca's eyes seemed transfixed on the locket. "Do you mind if I examine it more closely?"

I only paused for a moment. "Sure." Jack stepped up behind me and unclasped the chain from around my neck, his fingers lingering a little longer than necessary, at least long enough to change the temperature in the room.

He surprised me by holding on to the chain while Rebecca looked at the locket, as if he weren't willing to let it go. Rebecca flipped it over in her palm and I found myself studying her hands again, wondering why they seemed so familiar.

Slowly, she looked up, her gaze focusing on the sapphires around my neck and hanging from my ears before she met my eyes. "Any idea who this belonged to?"

I shook my head. "It has an *M* just like the one in the portrait. Mother has started sifting through things in the attic to see if we can find a jewelry box or really anything where the *R* locket might be, but we haven't found anything so far. In the meantime, I've made an appointment at the historical society library for next week to see what Yvonne and I can find hanging on my family tree." I spoke lightly, trying to dispel Rebecca's sudden seriousness. It made me nervous, as if she knew a cliff loomed behind me but was allowing me to remain ignorant of impending danger.

"Let me know what you find out," she said. "I'd suggest meeting with Yvonne together, but my schedule is just so crazy, tons of research for my 'favorite Charlestonians' series. I have an appointment with Yvonne next Monday, but it's only for half an hour. Hardly enough time as it is." She flipped the locket over one more time. "I assume you've already opened it."

I nodded. "It's empty."

Rebecca tugged on the locket, but Jack didn't relinquish his hold on the chain. Pursing her lips, she let go, and Jack quickly pooled the chain and locket in his own hand. "Before you return this, Mellie, I'd like to have an old family friend take a look at it. He's done some work for my parents. He's a jeweler who specializes in estate jewelry. He can clean it up, see if there's anything we might have missed. The corrosion is caused by other metals used with the gold, and it could be hiding finer engravings." He looked up at me with a wry smile. "Or, since this is Mellie's family we're probably talking about, some secret code or puzzle."

Rebecca's lips pursed tighter. Then she seemed to forcibly relax them and mold them into a smile. "That's a great idea, Jack. Maybe I can go with you."

"Maybe," Jack said, and I wondered if he was being purposefully non-committal. I caught my mother's eye and she raised her eyebrows in silent agreement. I felt myself smiling and turned away.

Jack closed his fist over the necklace. "I brought a change of clothes, so if you ladies will excuse me for a moment . . ." He gave us a mock bow and a smile that would have done Rhett Butler proud, then headed toward the staircase, all three of us turning to watch him walk away. I faced my mother, giving her an accusatory stare as she began to fumble with her gloves.

"I suppose we should start cleaning up the parlor, and bringing the dirty glasses to the kitchen." She led the way to the parlor, with Rebecca and Sophie following.

"I'll be right with you," I said, hoping they'd assume I was heading toward a bathroom. I waited until they disappeared into the drawing room, then moved to the kitchen. I paused outside the darkened room, wondering why Mrs. Houlihan would have turned out the lights when she left.

Gingerly, I pushed open one of the doors to stick my hand inside, then jumped back with a cry held in my throat as General Lee threw himself through the open space, then ran faster than I'd ever seen him move to the foyer and up the stairs, the sound of his paws frantically searching for purchase on the zebra-striped runner.

I stuck my hand inside the door again, found the light switch, and flipped it to the ON position, but nothing happened. I swallowed, recalling all the cheap horror films I'd seen in my life—the ones where the stupid girl enters the dark room anyway—and hesitated.

Melanie.

My soldier was there, as I'd known he would be, but he wasn't in solid form. Instead, I sensed a darkening shadow against the fireplace wall, a wavering of air, and I wondered what had made him change again.

Come here.

I sensed a tone of desperation in his voice that was new to me. I tried the light switch again. "No."

Within the waves, hide all our guilt. The answer is over here, Melanie.

I tried the switch one more time, but the room remained dark.

You know you are safe with me.

I turned back toward the hallway, hearing my mother's voice and Rebecca's laugh. It irked me that she'd been able to figure out so much already, and I'd done nothing but make an appointment to study my own family tree. I turned back to the kitchen, blocked out the inner moviegoer voice that shouted, *Don't go into the dark room, stupid,* and pushed through the doors, feeling the chilly air as it hit the bare skin on my shoulders.

As before, I walked slowly and carefully toward the wall with the longhorn cow mural, noting with some relief that the door to the back stairs was closed. The silk of my gown swished like little whispers in the dark, and I was acutely aware of how the fabric felt against my skin. I saw that he was leaning against the invisible mantel again, his hat tucked under his arm.

"What do you want with me in the dark?" I asked, avoiding looking at his face.

I heard an unfamiliar sound and realized he was chuckling. My face flamed with the realization that men over the ages hadn't really evolved that much.

"I'm leaving." I faced the door.

Stay. I can help you if you will allow me.

Turning back around, I said, "Then tell me what I need to know. What's behind the wall?"

What you seek.

I held back a scream of frustration. "Can't you tell me? I don't even know what I'm looking for."

So impatient, Melanie. You were not like that as a child. What made you change?

I was so surprised by his words that I barely noticed that his hands were touching my face again, the odd icy-hot feeling tiptoeing along my skin.

I tried to step away, but the fireplace wall pressed against my back. "Who are you?" I closed my eyes to resist the temptation to look him in the face. I didn't want him to leave, at least not before I had some questions answered.

I told you before. A friend.

"Then tell me your name. We can't be friends if you know my name but I don't know yours."

It is dangerous for you to know.

I almost opened my eyes then. My mother had told me the same thing, years ago. To know a spirit's name gave them power over you, but only if you deliberately summoned them, calling them by name. A medium had to be fairly sure she was strong enough—and in control—before beckoning a spirit from whatever place he'd been lingering.

His fingers slid behind my neck, then through my hair, loosening the pins and pulling out the chignon that Sophie had worked on for an hour. I fought hard to find my voice, wondering in the remaining sane part of my brain how his touch could feel so good. The idea that he was purposefully distracting me from my questions flitted past my jumbled thoughts. "And you're a protector, too. But you've been a protector before, haven't you? To my mother, and the girl who wrote the diary. Who was she?" I forced out, aware suddenly that he was pulling my face forward.

You look like her.

"Who? The girl who wrote the journal?"

No. My love.

I wanted to ask him who she was, but soft lips feathered a kiss against mine, shocking me into silence as I gave in to the sensation of ice melting into warm syrup. I opened my lips slightly in a halfhearted protest and he pressed against me harder. I tasted ocean breezes and hot sand. I felt drunk with feeling, remembering the last time I'd felt that way. In a house fire on Tradd Street I'd been almost dead from smoke inhalation, and Jack had placed his mouth against mine and brought me back to life with his own breath. That light-headedness and sense of reawakening coursed through me now, and thinking of Jack made me melt into this stranger's kiss, opening my mouth and pressing harder against his.

He pulled away and I realized that he must have heard the approaching footsteps, too. *My name is Wilhelm.*

Surprised, I opened my eyes and looked at him directly. And in the moment before he vanished completely, I saw his blue eyes cloud with fear and a blast of unease flooded my senses. I had inadvertently sent him away, and I knew from experience he would have to build up his strength before he could reappear. My eyes were fully adjusted to the dark now, and I slowly moved my gaze around the room, stopping abruptly at the door to the back stairs that was now gaping wide open.

The smell of rotting fish hit me right before the icy air, freezing my voice in my throat.

Melanie.

The voice was the same one I'd heard my mother speaking, and that I'd heard at the McGowans' plantation house. I frantically searched the room to find the source of the voice, but all I saw was blackness dappled with outside shadows projected on the walls from the streetlamps.

I began sidestepping along the wall, knowing I'd eventually reach the door—and just hoping I could move fast enough.

Melanie.

The word was spoken against my ear, and I stopped, my feet unwilling or unable to move.

Give it back.

The words seemed to grow louder instead of fading, my eardrums aching from the sound of them. Cold fingers fumbled at my neck, and I felt the clasp snap as the locket was snatched away from me.

It is mine! the voice screeched. I slid down the wall to a squat, pressing my hands against my ringing ears.

The icy fingers were at my neck again, but this time they were pressing against the flesh there, squeezing the breath out of me. I struck out at empty air and tried to shout for help, but the word came out as a gasp of air. Spots danced in front of me as the fingers dug into my neck, my throat burning, my eyes blinded with light. I tried to call out one more time, realizing as I began to slip into unconsciousness that the word I was trying to say was *Jack.*

And then I was breathing on my own and seeing brightness because the kitchen lights were on. Then Jack was kneeling next to me, his face pale, and his eyes full of worry.

"Are you all right?" He moved the hair out of my face and examined my eyes closely.

I nodded slightly, afraid that if I moved too much, he'd stop touching me.

"Damn," he said through clenched teeth. "I promised your mother that I wouldn't let you out of my sight. I'm sorry."

I thought of something flip to say, but forgot what it was when I realized how scared he really was for me.

"What happened?" he asked, helping me as I struggled to stand. "Are you all right? Do you need a doctor?"

I shook my head, unwilling to field questions from medical personnel and briefly imagining their reactions if I answered them truthfully. "No. I'm fine." My gaze shifted to the back stairs. "Close that door." My throat was raw and achy as I spoke, the words like sandpaper against stone.

He closed the door, then returned to my side before gathering me in his arms and holding me until I'd stopped shaking. When he released me, he kept his hands on my arms as if he were afraid to let me go.

"Were you in here by yourself? I thought I heard voices."

My hand went to my lips, and I remembered Wilhelm. But I hesitated to speak, almost as if doing so would be a betrayal of some sort. To whom, I wasn't sure.

Jack's gaze fell to my mouth, still swollen from the kiss, and his eyes narrowed. "Was it Marc Longo? Was he here?"

I shook my head, disoriented but still aware enough to feel gratified that Jack could be jealous. "No. It was her—the girl from the boat. I know it was her because I—smelled her."

His blue gaze dropped to my neck and I watched as they widened with shock. "She tried to choke you." Gently, he touched the place where I'd felt the icy fingers, taking some of the sting away.

It wasn't a question, but I nodded anyway. "She tore off the locket, too." I swallowed again, my throat hurting. "She said it was hers."

His brows furrowed. "Who is she?"

"I don't know. I don't understand what any of it means."

Jack continued to stroke my neck, his fingers moving down to my shoulders, tracing my collarbone. I couldn't help but think about the anger in his voice when he'd asked if Marc had been here, and a little tremor electrified my spine.

His voice was soft, his breath warm on my face. "We'll figure it out. We work pretty well together, don't we?"

I nodded dumbly as we stared at each other, my sense of caution muted. I struggled hard to find it, knowing I was no match for Jack Trenholm without it.

"But if we're going to continue to work together, you've got to stop trying to get yourself killed, all right? I feel responsible for you, and I have no idea why." He was looking right at me, but I had a feeling that he wasn't speaking to me anymore.

I needed to move away from him, but for the second time that night my feet refused to obey me. I fought for control, trying to ignore my stubborn feet and Jack's fingers. I cleared my throat, searching for a subject on neutral ground. "Why didn't you let Rebecca have the locket? When she wanted to look at it, you wouldn't let it out of your grasp."

He shrugged, his eyes focused on mine and I tried not to notice how blue they were at night. "I didn't like the way she was looking at it. Like it belonged to her." He paused. "I have a feeling that she's envious of you."

I remembered Sophie telling me the same thing. "Because I have access to two historic albatrosses?"

I waited to hear him laugh, but he was silent for a moment, and I felt fear again for the second time that night. But this wasn't the type of fear you felt when the breath was being choked out of you; this was the kind of fear you felt when you thought you were about to lose everything.

"No," he said softly. "At least that's only part of it." He was standing so close still, yet I didn't ask him to move away.

"Then why?" I persisted.

"Because she thinks that you and I are an item." His warm breath dusted the bare skin on my shoulders and I saw that he was leaning closer. All I had to do was tilt my face and our lips would touch. But I held back, focusing instead on the millions of reasons why kissing Jack Trenholm was a bad idea, the least of which being his ability to make me lose control. And being in control was the only thing I'd learned that I could truly count on.

I swallowed, hoping he couldn't hear it in the quiet room, then forced a flippant smile. "Right. Like I would fall for a conceited, shallow-hearted womanizer. She must not think very much of me."

His eyes hardened, but his smile didn't falter. "Right. Because you're really known for your high standards in men. Like Marc Longo. That was a great call on your part."

I tried to push away, but Jack kept his firm grip on my shoulders. "There must be something seriously wrong with you, Mellie, for you to jump into bed with a guy whose motives are clearly not in your best interests. And then you agree to have lunch with him even after you discover what a real shit he is." Something flickered behind his eyes. If it had been anyone else besides Jack, I would have said it was hurt. "You're either a masochist, or you're really, really afraid of thawing that ice ball in your chest that used to be a heart." He leaned closer. "What are you afraid of, Mellie? Forgetting who you are or where you've been for just a moment? Could it really be that bad?"

I turned my head, too exhausted to try and pull away again. "Leave me alone. You don't know the first thing about me, or about women. You're in pictures all over the Internet with a different beautiful woman in every one." I turned my head and met his quizzical gaze. "Yes. I Googled you—so what? It just goes to show that you're incapable of appreciating a woman for anything other than how she looks on your arm. I guess when they figure out you're a . . . a"—I rolled my eyes, never having been one to come up with a good put-down when I needed one—"a toad-faced idiot, you've already moved on to the next woman. Emily must have been a saint." I bit my lip, wishing I could call back the entire tirade, especially the last part. But I was scared—scared of being this close to him, scared of my feelings for him—and I was desperate to push him as far away from me as I could.

His eyes were like blue ice, and for the first time since I'd met him, I was reminded that he was a military man—a trained soldier who could be very, very dangerous. I swallowed, waiting for him to continue.

Jack's voice was very controlled when he spoke. "A toad-faced idiot? How very erudite, Melanie. I've been called many things, but I can honestly say that's the first time I've ever been called that." His gaze dropped to my lips again before returning to meet my gaze. "So, who else was here with you besides the girl from the boat?"

I didn't answer, knowing that to tell him the truth was to open myself up to a new barrage of Jack's opinions, most of which I knew to be true.

"Was it your soldier, Mellie? Your protector? Your mother told me about him, you know."

My hand went to my lips, remembering the kiss, remembering how I'd thought of Jack, feeling relieved at the anger that flooded through me at the memory. I pulled back from where Jack's fingers stroked my cheek, clinging to the hard-won control that governed my life. I had seen the dark room of a life lived in chaos, had felt my feet poking over the ledge, and I never wanted to get that close again.

"Rebecca knows about him, too," Jack continued. His hands moved to my shoulders, but I remained still, not wanting to show him how his touch affected me.

"Rebecca?" I was finding it difficult to follow the conversation, distracted by the brush of his thumb on my collarbone. I wanted him to stop. Needed him to stop. But my tongue was useless, and I found myself creeping too close to the precipice.

"She told me that she keeps seeing the two of you in her dreams."

I swallowed heavily. "How fascinating. Don't you two have more interesting things to discuss than me? Like what shade of pink she should wear? Or why you dumped her for Emily or why Rebecca is back in your life?" I felt physically sick at the words pouring out of my mouth, but I couldn't stop them. I felt like a cornered animal, and I did the only thing I knew to protect myself.

He raised an eyebrow, but spoke as if I hadn't said anything. "I guess he's your ideal lover, isn't he? He's the safest relationship you could ever hope for. I mean, you can't get too involved or be too committed if he's already dead, can you?"

I put my palms on his chest and pushed him, forcing him to take a step back. "You're one to talk, Jack. You're doing the same thing with Rebecca."

For a moment, Jack looked almost dangerous. "How so?" he asked slowly.

"You're only attracted to Rebecca because she reminds you of Emily. But she'll never be Emily, so you're safe. No real relationship can come of it because she'll never be the one you really want."

He stared at me for a long time without moving, and while I didn't feel fear, I definitely felt nervous. "Ouch." He straightened, but didn't take his eyes from my face. "Thank you for that insightful observation, Melanie. I wasn't aware that you held a degree in psychiatry as well as rigid scheduling. But thanks for letting me know what a pain in the ass I must be to you. I promise not to offend you with my presence any longer."

Jack turned and headed toward the door, pausing before he opened it. Without looking back at me, he said, "You're wrong, you know." He didn't move, nor did he speak, and for a moment I thought he wouldn't continue. Then he said, "Maybe my attraction to Rebecca isn't because she reminds me of Emily." He turned his head and our eyes met. "Maybe it's because she reminds me of you."

He pushed open the doors and strode through them, the heels of his boots echoing on the marble floors. I pressed my hands against my chest, fighting the need to cry and to call him back, to at least reassure myself that any damage caused by careless words wasn't permanent. Instead, I did neither, my pride creating a huge chasm between Jack and me. I couldn't quite forgive him for what he'd said about me and my soldier, mostly because I feared that he might be right.

I quickly headed to the door—eager not to be left alone again in the kitchen—but I stopped when I heard him shout back, "And that was almost kiss number five. Not that you're counting, of course."

I placed my hands on my cheeks, eager to cool them from the flush that was already rising up from my neck, and my eyes caught sight of reflected light under the kitchen table. I knew what it was, and approached it carefully, afraid that whoever had snatched it from my neck might be looking for it. I gathered it up from the floor and stood, then held the cold metal of the locket in my hand for a long time, staring at the broken clasp, trying to figure out what she'd meant when she said that it belonged to her—and wishing that Jack was still there to tell me.

CHAPTER 17

I sat curled up in the lime green beanbag chair—inadvertently left in an empty bedroom by the previous owners—and blinked my eyes at the journal I'd been reading for over two hours. My eyes felt gritty and strained from reading the compressed script, the penmanship beautiful but filled with flourishes that made it very difficult to decipher.

The handwriting was definitely that of a female and she seemed to be in her mid- to late teens. Although most of what I'd read so far was comprised of the everyday life of a Charleston resident in the latter half of the nineteenth century, I was enthralled. I'd never been a fan of history, about things that had happened in the past that nobody remembered anymore, but this was different. It was a lot like communicating with a ghost, except in this instance I finally got to hear what they were thinking.

Most telling of all was the writer's description of the house. It was definitely thirty-three Legare, with its two-tiered portico and stained-glass window, which, according to the writer, "dominated the downstairs drawing room, and created a lot of nasty head shakes from neighbors as it was being installed." I'd smiled to myself at that one, wondering if some of those neighbors were charter members of the first Board of Architectural Review—or whatever it would have been called back then.

I paid close attention to her description of the window, noting how closely it resembled the window of my childhood.

The window is large and what some would refer to as unattractive, yet it holds a strange fascination for R. I recognized the image of two girls in it first, which made her angry, and then I was forced to pretend that she had been the one to discover it as she relayed the story to Father.

My protector appears enthralled as well, and I have found him staring at it many times. I ask him what he sees but all he will do is tap four times on the window, which will startle R or whoever else is in the room at the time. And when I look up he is always tapping at the same place, at the top right corner, which appears empty from this side of the window.

I see my soldier almost every day. He says he is my protector. He hears me when I speak to him, so yesterday I found the courage to ask him why he is always near. He said because he saved my life when I was a baby, and he was grateful for having been given the chance to redeem himself for a past mistake. He goes away whenever I ask him more questions about what mistake he made. He also disappears whenever I look right at him, as if I am stronger than he is and I overpower him somehow.

I was in the downstairs drawing room this morning, admiring the window, when he appeared. R rushed into the room, unannounced, demanding to know to whom I had been speaking. I was astonished to learn that she could not see him at all since he is so real to me. I have seen spirits since I was a little girl, and I was almost a young woman before I discovered that not everybody does. It is my secret, and I have told no one including R. But still, since R is four years older than I and has thus lived in this house for four more years, I would have thought that she would have come to know him. I must ask him why.

I made some notes in my notepad, then flipped open my phone to call Jack before slowly closing it. I hadn't seen or spoken to Jack for two weeks, ever since the night of the house tour. After a couple of days of silence, I'd figured out that he was avoiding me, but it had taken me nearly the full two weeks to finally stop calling and leaving messages. I somehow thought that because I was pretending that none of what happened actually had, he could, too, and we could go on as before. Sophie had called this my self-denial; I chose to refer to it as self-preservation.

I hadn't even heard from him at Christmas. My mother, father, and I were invited to his parents' house for Christmas dinner, but Amelia and

John Trenholm were obviously embarrassed when they'd had to explain that Jack was spending Christmas with Rebecca's family in Summerville. At least I was spared the agony of watching my parents pretend to ignore each other, as my father declined the invitation. He said he would rather spend his day off going over plans for his garden, and had actually sounded excited about the prospect.

The final blow had come when Amelia gave me a wrapped present from under the tree. I'd been excited until I realized that the attached tag read: MERRY CHRISTMAS FROM JACK AND REBECCA, in her handwriting. Inside was a salon-quality blow-dryer with a note explaining it was a replacement for the one I'd destroyed by using it to melt wallpaper glue in order to remove it from the cypress walls of the Legare Street drawing room.

Sighing, I placed the phone back on the table, whatever I'd wanted to tell Jack forgotten.

The situation was, essentially, what I'd longed for, but I couldn't help feeling as if I'd lost something valuable long before I'd discovered its worth.

I listened to my mother in the connecting dressing room. We'd managed to paint over the purple-and-brown faux-leopard wall treatment in a warm ivory tone so she could officially move into the master bedroom. Her clothes—four crates' worth—had arrived the day before, and like Sophie at a yard sale Ginnette had dug right in and set about organizing her closet.

She'd instructed me to stay in my room, within shouting distance. I'd told her about what had happened in the kitchen the night of the tour, and ever since she'd been reluctant to let me out of her sight. I didn't want to admit that she was right, that the spirits in the house did seem to be getting stronger, or at least more insistent. We needed to bide our time, she said, until we were strong enough to fight. When I asked her when that would be, I hadn't liked the look in her eyes when she'd told me simply, "You'll know." I'd spent every night since lying awake until I thought she would be asleep, then slowly cracking open the connecting door between our rooms. She never asked, and I never said anything, the boundary between us softer yet still unyielding.

I'd initially started out my morning by helping my mother organize her closet, but I'd wasted too much time trying on some of the beautiful clothes. I had nice clothes, too, but they were all for business and function. My mother's wardrobe was something out of *Dynasty*—with jeweled buttons, puffed sleeves, and heavenly fabrics. Although her tops tended to have extra material in the chest area, everything else fit as if they'd been made for me. I wondered at what age I'd grown to be her size, and if she would have let me borrow her clothes. Our eyes met, and I knew she'd been thinking the same thing. For a moment, I was a little girl again, listening as she told me how sometimes people had to do the right thing even if it meant letting go of the one thing they loved most in the world. And for the first time, I almost believed her.

She eventually sent me back to my room to read the journal, and that's where I'd been ever since. I stared down at the leather-bound book, then stood before walking over to the connecting door. I paused with my hand raised, ready to knock, lowering then raising my hand again two more times before I gave in and knocked.

My mother opened the door. Her usually perfect chignon was lop-sided and half hanging down her face, and I noticed that she had changed clothes to something that might actually have been velour sweatpants and a matching jacket. But it wasn't until my gaze had taken in her feet that realization dawned on me.

"When was Sophie here?" I demanded.

She looked surprised. "While you were at work. How did you know?"

"The Birkenstocks."

She pointed her toe and twisted her foot back and forth to give me a better view. "Sophie and I happen to wear the same size, and she thought it might be easier for me to wear these while unloading and lugging things up the stairs. And you know what, she was right! They are actually quite comfortable. She loaned me the warm-up suit, too."

Before I could think of something to say that didn't involve the words "intervention" or "psychologist," we turned our heads toward the sound of heavy footsteps in the hallway. Chad appeared at the door, two arm-loads of clothing in each arm. "Yo, Dudette." He smiled broadly, his teeth shining brightly in his perpetually tanned face. He turned to my mother. "Yo, Miss Ginnette, here's the last load."

"Hi, Chad." I placed the journal on a side table, then stepped forward to take some of the clothes from his arms. As I placed them carefully onto the existing pile on the bed, I asked, "And why, exactly, aren't we letting a moving company do this?"

A shocked expression covered my mother's face. "I don't let just anybody touch my clothing. I'm very particular about my things."

I eyed her outfit again, and muttered under my breath, "Apparently not anymore." Turning to Chad, I asked, "How did you get roped into this?"

My mother, with a long sequined gown folded over her arm, interjected, "Because your father was working in the garden and was about to volunteer when Chad showed up. It was the perfect solution."

I wondered why Chad would be at the Legare Street house. "Did you need something from me, Chad? Everything all right back at my house?"

"Everything's fine. We're almost through with the stripping of the second floor and I'm about to tackle the staircase. Jack's been helping a lot, too, with removing all the baseboards. He's developed what he's calling the 'Melanie Middleton method' of numbering all the pieces so we know where they go when it's time to put them back. I even showed him how to use a spreadsheet to keep track of it all."

I wasn't sure if I should be flattered or annoyed. If Jack was involved, I'd bet on the latter. "Jack's been helping?"

"Yeah. He's been spending a lot of time with the papers in the attic doing research for his book, but he comes and helps us when he wants to take a break."

The news of Jack's being at my house and interacting with my friends stung. It made me feel like the only kid without a Valentine's Day card. It was especially painful because I was fairly sure that one of the main reasons why he was there was because he knew that I wouldn't be. I kept going over his parting words to me the night of the tour. *Maybe it's because she reminds me of you.* I'd planned on ignoring them, and never bringing them up again between us. But it seemed that I needn't have bothered thinking about them at all. He'd apparently taken to heart the things I'd said to him in anger, and I should have been thrilled that he wasn't interfering in my life anymore. Only, I wasn't.

"Great," I said, and my mother slid a glance toward me as if she recognized that my tone of voice and what I was saying were out of sync. Just like a mother who'd been around her child all of her life would do. Or maybe it was just one of those skills that mothers picked up in the first few years and never quite forgot.

I forced a smile. "Tell him I said hello. And, um, tell him that they're tearing out the plaster covering the kitchen fireplace tomorrow. He might want to be here to see what's behind it."

Chad looked at me oddly. "Sure will. But he said he was going back to his condo to try and get some writing done, so I don't know when I'll see him next." He shoved his hands in his jeans pockets and stood there, staring at the dentil molding as if he'd never seen anything like it before. I waited for him to leave, but he continued to stand where he was without saying anything.

"Is there something else?"

He looked back at me as if remembering I was there and shuffled his feet. My mother ducked discreetly into the closet. "I need your help."

"With what?"

He looked down at his sandal-clad feet—with socks in deference to the season—and shuffled them again. I watched as his face shifted from easy and open to almost tortured. I touched his arm in alarm. "Is there something wrong with the house?" I had visions of hordes of termites camping out in the mahogany stairwell of the Tradd Street house. Or maybe one of the rare glass sidelights by the front door had cracked in the cold weather. Even worse, I pictured myself writing yet another check out with lots of zeros for a repair that couldn't be postponed. I felt sick to my stomach waiting for him to answer, not pausing to consider how odd that I could be so concerned about something I'd once referred to as a goiter on my neck and, more kindly, a pile of lumber.

"No. The house is fine," he said in his slow, California manner. "It's just . . ."

I waited, resisting the impulse to pull at his shirt collar to yank the words in quicker succession from his mouth. "What?"

"I need to borrow an electric floor sander."

I blinked at him in both relief and amazement. "You need a floor sander," I repeated. It looked like he might cry, and I groaned inwardly, hoping he wasn't about to pull my mother from the closet so we could have a group hug.

His face wrinkled a bit as he spoke. "It's just that I don't think I can hand-sand one more square inch of floor in your house. It's like I'm being punished for some bad karma or something." He looked directly into my eyes and I could have sworn I saw tears. "Sophie's doing a field study with one of her classes all week, so I'm pretty much alone at the house to do more sanding. I figured . . ." He stopped, unable to continue.

"You figured that if she wasn't there to see, you could get some sanding out of the way with the electric sander."

Chad nodded and I squeezed his arm, trying not to smile. "No problem. It's being stored temporarily outside in the garden shed for lack of a better place for it. It's yours for as long as you need it."

His eyes were worried. "And you won't . . ."

"My lips are sealed."

He nodded with relief, his eyes closed for a moment. "I don't care what Jack says, Melanie. I think you're one of the nicest people I know. And you're really not *that* uptight once people get to know you."

Before I could say anything, Chad enveloped me in a tight hug, his organic wool sweater scratching my cheek. "I wanted to let you know that I'm having mine and Sophie's star charts read by a professional astrologer."

"Really? I thought that Sophie was the only one who bought in to that stuff."

"She is." He looked down at his feet. "But I'm thinking that this whole 'incompatible signs' thing is just a cover. She's so independent, you know? And I think it's just an excuse to keep her independence and keep me at a distance. But together . . ." He smiled and looked away for a moment. "It's like she's the sun and I'm the moon and it takes both of us to make a whole day."

I stared at him, not sure if he was being eloquent or just speaking in tongues. I decided to cut to the chase. "Do you love her, Chad?"

He nodded, and I was relieved that he hadn't tried to put his feelings into words again.

"Good. Because even a blind man could see that the two of you were made for each other." I pushed him toward the door. "So go do whatever you have to do to show her how much you care for her and want to be with her. And I won't tell a soul about the sander. Promise."

He looked at me gratefully as I propelled him out of the room. "Ciao, Miss Ginnette, catch you later."

My mother stuck her head out from the closet. "Good-bye, Chad."

After Chad left, my mother turned to me. "Was there something you needed, Mellie?"

I looked around for where I'd placed the journal, having forgotten why I'd come in there in the first place. I held the book in my hands, suddenly shy and unsure how to approach her.

"I've been reading the journal we found in Grandmother's desk. I don't know who the writer is, yet, but I know she lived in this house with another girl whose name begins with an R. I get the feeling that they're sisters, but the writer doesn't come right out and say it." I glanced up at my mother to gauge her reaction to my next words. "She mentions a protector who she can see and talk to, but R can't see him."

I knew what I needed her to do, but still I hesitated.

"I've been thinking about what's been going on in the house. We've both seen the soldier, but he's not—foggy anymore. And a couple of times he didn't disappear when I looked him in the face."

She nodded, her brows furrowed. "And the other spirit, the girl, she likes to appear when you're alone. Like you're on an even playing field when it's just the two of you." My mother sat down on the bed and a skirt slipped to the floor, but she didn't move to pick it up. "Except for that time in the kitchen when I touched the locket, she hasn't appeared when the two of us are together. Like she knows that together we're too powerful. If we find out her name, if we know who she is and why she's here to harm you, we can exorcise her. She will work very hard to make sure we don't figure that out."

She pointed to the journal. "You want me to hold it, don't you?"

I hesitated a moment before nodding. "I was hoping you might be able to tell me more than what's written within the covers."

She eyed the journal, then looked back at me. "It kills me a little each time."

"I know. That's why I haven't asked you."

For a moment, I thought she was going to refuse, and I felt the old anger resurface. Instead, she held her hands out. "But I would gladly do this a hundred times if I thought it might spare you even a moment of danger." Slowly, she opened her palm so that it was facing me, and there—in faded pink where the burn was healing—was the imprint of the locket.

I sucked in a breath of air. "You didn't tell me." It was a stupid thing to say, and I shook my head.

She sat down on the edge of the bed. "Give me the journal, Mellie. I want to help if I can."

I hesitated, and she reached for it. "Give me the journal."

I swallowed, then placed the book in her hands and she took it, gripping it tightly. The response was almost immediate. Her eyes closed as her hand began to shake. I put my hand over hers only because I didn't know what else to do, and her skin felt cold and wet like snow. Her mouth moved, but nothing came out, a drowning woman searching for air.

I felt real fear then—fear of whatever force was causing this, and fear for my mother. Clothes slipped off the bed in a small avalanche as she continued to grip the book, her head shaking back and forth.

"Mother!" I shouted, wanting to make her stop. She continued to shake uncontrollably. "Mother!" I called out again and this time she responded by jerking her arm back and hurling the book across the room. It hit the freshly painted wall, denting the plaster, before it landed on the hardwood floor.

My mother stared at me, her chest rising and falling rapidly and her eyes blinking slowly.

"What is it?" I asked, almost afraid to know. "What did you see?"

Shakily, she stood and put her hands on my shoulders, whether to steady me or her I wasn't sure.

"What did you see?" I asked again.

Her eyes were clear as she answered and it took me a moment to recognize the single word that came out of her mouth.

She dropped her hands and said it again, just to make sure I'd heard, and I watched her lips move as if in slow motion as she formed the one word. "Rebecca."

CHAPTER 18

I paused on the outdoor steps, hearing the staccato snipping of manual hedge cutters. Until about a year ago, I'd had no idea what hedge cutters were or what they sounded like, and I still wasn't sure if my new-found knowledge was a good thing or not.

My hands shook as I turned the key to lock the front door, having not yet completely recovered from watching what happened when my mother touched the journal. She seemed disoriented, but insisted it was only because she needed to take a nap and nothing more. I wanted to reschedule my appointment with Yvonne so I could stay with her, but she wouldn't hear of it.

I followed the sound to the side of the house where my grandmother's garden had once been the pride of Legare Street. Most of the former residents' cement blobs and hulking metal monoliths had been removed. I'd instructed for them to be tossed in a Dumpster but instead listened to Amelia Trenholm when she convinced me to get them appraised first.

Shocked as I was by their apparent value, I happily took the money from an independent art dealer and purchased a Queen Anne console table and bookcase for the upstairs sitting room, and still had money left over to convert my bathroom from a bordello to something that more resembled a spa.

My father stood with his back to me, pruning back two large crepe myrtles that had once been no taller than my six-year-old self. He stepped back when he saw me, and lowered the clippers. "Who knows the last time somebody did any cleaning up in this garden? Seems to me those people just let everything go wild."

"Maybe they did it as a distraction so people wouldn't mind the inside so much."

He smiled at me, his eyes bright, and it occurred to me how new it was to see him smile, and how hard he had to have worked to have something to smile about.

"Come here," he said, motioning for me to follow before leading me to the edge of the house. "Look what I found." He moved aside tall grass that hadn't yet fallen to the hedge clippers and revealed my grandmother's prized Miss Charleston camellias. Despite being neglected and overgrown, large deep red semidouble blooms resembling the puffed-out cheeks of cherubs clung stubbornly to their stems. These camellias had been Grandmother's favorites, but not just for their beauty and scent. She loved them because of how brave they were to bloom brightly in the winter months when everything else slept.

"I can't wait to clean this grass out and let those flowers go to town. I've got some pretty amazing plans for this garden, a sort of mix between old and new design. I'm even going to resurrect your grandmother's famous knot garden." He grinned broadly and I couldn't help but grin back, his enthusiasm contagious.

"Daddy . . ." I began, and he tilted his head toward me, waiting for me to continue. Speaking of my feelings came unnaturally to me. I'd spent a lifetime pretending I didn't hurt, and making believe that I didn't require affection or the give-and-take of any close relationship. And somehow along the way, I'd forgotten how to show him how much he meant to me.

"Daddy," I started again. "You've done a great job."

He met my gaze, and I wondered if he was noticing that my eyes were just like his. He nodded tightly, both of us knowing that I wasn't talking about the garden, yet each aware of how much I needed to pretend that we were. "Thanks, Peanut."

I grimaced and rolled my eyes, warmed by the use of my old nickname. I studied him for a moment. "You know, Daddy, I'd be happy to help you find a house. It's silly in this market to rent when you could get something pretty decent right now." I thought of the cramped one-bedroom, one-bathroom apartment in North Charleston where he'd lived ever since he retired. Initially, he'd told me it was only until he got settled, but that had been more than five years ago.

He squinted at me in the sunlight. "Yeah, I've thought about it. I think I'm going to wait on it a bit, though. Try to limit any more life changes for the time being."

I nodded, understanding. "Just let me know. I'll do it without a fee, of course."

"I would hope so," he said, pretending to be offended. Then it was his turn to study me. He seemed to be struggling with words, as if unsure how to string them together in a way that wouldn't make me run. Finally, he said, "I wish you could find a way to forgive your mother. She tried to reach you all those years, and I wouldn't let her. You've forgiven me. Why can't you do the same for her?"

Sadness welled up from inside of me, surprising me only because of the absence of anger. I shook my head, wondering when the anger had gone. Maybe it had been when my mother had touched the journal, knowing it would hurt her but doing it anyway because she thought it might help me. I swallowed. "She left, Daddy. You didn't."

He didn't look away and I had trouble holding his gaze. I turned to leave, then stopped. "Can you do me a favor?" I asked.

"Anything. What?"

I smiled to myself, noticing how he'd agreed to help me without knowing what I was going to ask. "I need to go see Yvonne, but Mother isn't feeling well and is lying down. I didn't want to leave her, but she insisted that she was okay. I'd feel better knowing that you're keeping an eye on her while I'm gone."

He put down the clippers and began peeling off his gardening gloves. "What happened?"

"You don't want to know."

His lips tightened over his teeth. "Some of that hocus-pocus upset her?"

I pressed the collar of my coat up to my neck, feeling chilled in the cool air. "Don't go there, Dad."

"But . . ."

"Please, Daddy. And if you're going to go up there to upset her more, then just stay out here. I would have thought after forty years, you might have opened your mind a tad. Stepped out of your box a little. It's not like Mother and I have been making this stuff up all this time just to annoy you. Maybe if you'd stop to think for a moment, you might discover that life isn't all just black-and-white."

We stared at each other for a long moment, both of us surprised that I'd spoken at all, much less defended my mother and admitted to being psychic all in the same breath.

"Fine," he said. "I won't say or do anything to upset her."

I nodded, recognizing his don't ask, don't tell policy as the truce it was. "Thank you," I said. "And don't . . ." I paused, trying to find a better way to say it, then gave up. "Don't leave her by herself."

He looked at me from beneath lowered brows and I saw him struggling not to argue with me. "I'll stay with her."

"Great. I'll be back around five."

As I watched my father enter the house, I felt a little like I was leaving a lion to watch over a lamb. But I knew he'd take care of her, and protect her if she needed it. Whoever had been haunting me had yet to include my mother, but if I'd learned anything about dead people it was that they were a lot like the living, breathing kind; they didn't always behave like you expected them to.

I walked out of the garden to the sidewalk, then turned around as I realized that the sun was in the right spot. Facing the stained-glass window again, I squinted in the bright reflected light. As I studied it closely, I saw how it was really an optical illusion, like one of those pictures of two completely different images. One image was visible right away, but the second one only became obvious after you stared at it for a long time. At first glance it appeared to be random splotches of color and sticklike markings, but as I squinted at it in the sunlight, the image of the map that I'd seen in the photo appeared: the large house, the body of water with the odd angel's head, the figures standing in the lawn. But what I noticed now were all the fine lines that became visible when the sun hit the window, embellishments to the original image that couldn't be seen without the sun's help.

Squinting, and wishing I had my glasses with me, I tried to make out why the border of odd lines and marks had been added, what function they served, and couldn't determine anything. I needed to talk with Rebecca, to see if she'd had any luck turning up any of the paperwork on the window, but I was hesitant to call her. My mother's vision of her while holding the journal had shocked us both, prompting more questions and even fewer answers. Besides, I remembered Rebecca telling me that she had other work deadlines and wouldn't be able to see Yvonne until the following week.

I unsnapped my phone from its place inside my purse and used the telephoto button to take a close-up picture of the window before carefully placing the phone back where it belonged. Then I pushed open the gate and walked out to the sidewalk, going over my mental notes of all the things I needed to discuss with Yvonne. I paused for a moment, tilting my head to hear better, sure I'd heard the sound of a crying baby. It had been soft at first, so soft that I thought I hadn't really heard it. But there it was again, coming from inside the house, and it was louder now. I faced the front door, expecting to see a baby there, but the steps were empty.

The crying softened to a quiet mewling, and I wanted to believe it was just the noise of a lost kitten in the grass. But I recognized the sound from the time following my mother's stay in the hospital when I was a little girl, and how it had awakened me at night until I'd told my mother. The sound went away, at least for that night, and I remembered sleeping well for the first time in a long while. Then the next day my mother was gone and my father took me from the house for what I thought would be forever, and for a long time wished that it had been.

I forced myself to walk away and not look back, sensing that somebody or something was watching me. I reached for my phone as I'd done dozens of times before to call Jack and tell him what had happened, but my hand stopped halfway to my purse. When I reached my car, it rang as if conjured, and I ended up emptying my purse on the hood to find it before I realized it was neatly clipped to the inside pocket where it always was.

I took it out and flipped it open, my anticipation clouded when I saw the name Marc Longo on the screen. We'd been playing phone tag for weeks, trying to set up lunch, but he'd been out of town, and I'd been less than enthusiastic about promptly returning his calls. But now my thoughts turned to Jack, and how he didn't appear to want to have anything to do with me anymore—not that I really blamed him after what I'd said to him—and I realized how desperately lonely I was. And, as Jack had pointed out, a relationship with a ghost didn't count as a relationship.

After a deep breath, I flipped open the phone on the fifth ring and spoke, wishing as I did that it wasn't Jack's face I saw.

∽

I drove the short blocks to the Fireproof Building on Meeting Street where the South Carolina Historical Society library is located. Lacking the Jack Trenholm touch for finding curb parking directly in front of wherever he was heading, I found parking three blocks away, then walked back with five minutes to spare before my appointment with Yvonne.

I ascended the circular stone stairwell, remembering coming here before with Jack while trying to find out more about the Confederate diamonds hidden in my Tradd Street house. Yvonne was an octogenarian with a sharp mind and even sharper wit who knew just about every source in the archives at the historical society. And if she didn't know it personally, then she could tell you where to find it.

Yvonne sat at a table in the reading room, a box of folders and a stack of books on a corner of the table. She smiled when she saw me and stood, never one to let her arthritis get the best of her. She wore a pink cashmere sweater set over a pink tweed skirt and she smelled of roses as I leaned down to kiss her cheek.

"Jack's not with me," I said, not really understanding my need to explain.

"I know. He took me to dinner last night at S.N.O.B. and we had a nice heart-to-heart."

"Oh," I said, trying to sound disinterested but wanting her to feel obliged to tell me everything.

"He's been working very hard on his book," she continued. "He was actually here this morning with that blond reporter from the *Post & Courier*. Rebecca somebody. I was surprised that you weren't with them since they were looking for information on the Prioleau house on Legare."

"They were here today? I thought her appointment with you was for next Monday." I remembered Rebecca telling me that she was busy doing research for another "famous Charlestonian" article and wouldn't be able to see Yvonne until the following week. "Did she have to change it?"

Yvonne shook her head. "No. Her appointment was for today, at ten o'clock sharp."

She sat down and indicated the chair next to hers. I'd already unloaded my coat and scarf in the locker room so I had nothing to fiddle with while I tried to figure out a way to tactfully ask her what she'd found for them.

"I kept the records out just in case you wanted to see them, too."

I looked at her, grateful. "Thank you." I waited for her to pull three pieces of paper from one of the folders. One appeared to be a handwritten order from a John Nolan & Sons on Market Street, and another was a receipt from the same business. But it was the third piece of paper that caught my attention. It was larger than the other two, and it appeared to be a vellum-type paper. On it was a miniature replica of the stained-glass window at my mother's house.

I pulled my phone out of my purse and flipped it open to the picture I'd taken earlier of the window. "Look," I said, showing Yvonne. "I took this picture right before I came here."

She looked at it closely before I held it up to the drawing next to it. "It's almost identical, isn't it?"

We sat in silence for several minutes, comparing the two pictures, our heads turning back and forth like spectators at a tennis match.

"The differences are pretty subtle, aren't they? At first glance you don't notice the changes, but after you become familiar with one or the other, you start to notice the differences. It's like one of those games in puzzle books my grandmother used to give me to play with while she watched her soaps. What looks like the same picture appears on opposite pages and you circle the differences." I looked at Yvonne. "If any other family besides my own was behind this, I'd say it was coincidence. But the Prioleaus are known for their love of puzzles."

"Which makes you believe that this was done on purpose."

"Absolutely."

"And I think you're right. I'm only surprised that Jack hasn't noticed it, too. It's really out of character for him to miss something like this. He must be distracted." She gave me a pointed look.

"Can I make a copy of all these?"

Yvonne smiled. "I already did. Jack asked for copies, too, so I made extra just in case you wanted your own set."

"Thanks, Yvonne. I owe you dinner," I said, recalling how Jack always took Yvonne to the nicest eateries in town as repayment for going above and beyond her duties as a research librarian. It didn't escape my notice that I was probably receiving the same level of treatment due to my association with Jack. It was disconcerting, but I was going to take advantage of it while I could.

I looked at the picture on my phone again, then back at the drawing. Tapping my fingers on the wooden tabletop, I thought back to what my grandmother had taught me about applying logic to puzzles and problems. She'd shown me how to unravel a puzzle like a thread, creating an alternate beginning and end, examining the new strands in unexpected ways, like starting at the end instead of the beginning.

My fingers stopped in midair, then came to rest on the table in front of me. I slid the receipt over to look at it again. "Do you know, or do you have any kind of records that would show, what happened to the shop after John Nolan died or moved away? Like deeds or that kind of thing?"

Her eyes sparkled. "You're beginning to sound like Jack. Plucking random ideas from out of nowhere and convincing others to help him hunt unicorns."

She was smiling but I wasn't sure that was a compliment. "Is that a good thing?"

She almost looked offended. "Of course. Our Jack is very successful at what he does. He'll question the color of the sky if he thinks there's a possibility that everybody might be wrong about an accepted knowledge. Well, except for that Alamo fiasco, but there are still some experts who say he was right," she said, referring to his canceled book contract because of its public debunking on national television. "So, what unicorns are you hunting?"

I had to think for a moment to figure out what she meant. "Oh, right. Well, see, the changes were made to the window after the original order was placed." I turned the description page toward her. "There isn't an angel head on the original order, and this odd line design that goes around the entire window was added, too. And no people, see?" I pointed to the people standing beneath the oak tree near the house in the picture on my cell phone. I squinted, trying to see the details more clearly.

"You need glasses, dear. Squinting will give you wrinkles."

"I have glasses. I just always forget to bring them with me."

She blinked slowly behind her own wide-framed glasses. "Despite evidence to the contrary, Jack is much more attracted to what's in here"—she pointed to her forehead—"than anything else. In other words, he wouldn't find glasses a turnoff at all."

It was my turn to blink slowly at her. "I'm not trying to impress Jack Trenholm, if that's what you're getting at, Yvonne. He's just not my type."

She was silent for a moment. "I didn't know such a woman existed."

"Excuse me?"

"You heard me." She cleared her throat. "Now show me what else you found." She looked down at the map and I could have sworn I saw her roll her eyes.

Trying not to squint, I held the drawing closer to my face, then looked at the picture on my phone. "The window was installed in 1871, meaning the changes could have been made anytime after that."

"Or maybe the changes were made during the design process and simply not recorded."

I nodded, happy to have her play devil's advocate. It reminded me of my childhood, working on mind teasers with my grandmother where I'd question and she'd answer with another question until I'd figured it out for myself. I had a flash of my mother, in what my grandmother called the puzzle room in her house, laughing and hugging me because I'd figured out a difficult one. It saddened me to think of it, too easily reminded of how very few memories of my mother I had.

Yvonne was watching me closely as I answered. "True, which is why I want to make sure that we've looked through all the existing records from the window maker, just in case there was some written record of any changes."

"But what if the requested changes were made verbally?"

I smiled, enjoying the way our minds worked together. "Then there won't be any records to find. But that can't be helped. Which brings me to my request about searching for deeds on the window maker's business."

"Assuming that a son didn't inherit, and an ongoing concern was valuable enough that an astute businessman would consider purchasing the business, and attaching his own name to the storefront."

"Bingo."

She folded her hands primly in front of her. "It's a long shot, of course, but I like your creative thinking."

"I guess that's better than calling it a crapshoot, but I'll take it. So, do you have access to that sort of information?"

"I do. I've got some other projects that I'm working on at the moment, but I see no reason why I can't squeeze it in between. Give me a couple of days and I'll give you a call whether or not I find something. I'll admit I'm intrigued, although I must say it's a bit more far-fetched than most of my requests."

"Welcome to my world," I muttered. Smiling, I said, "That's great. Thank you." I glanced over to the stack of large books on the corner. "Any luck with the family tree?"

Yvonne stood and took a book off of the top of the stack. "You, Miss Middleton, have been blessed with an old Charleston name. There is certainly no shortage of family histories and genealogies; the hardest part was narrowing down your branch of the Prioleau family tree."

She slid a piece of paper out of the middle of the book and flipped it open to the marked page. "This book is a personal history of the Manigault-Prioleau branch, done in the early 1940s by a distant relation, most likely trying to prove his own bloodline, but a great source, anyway."

I leaned close to the page she indicated, mindful of summoning wrinkles and trying not to involve my forehead or brows while I squinted. I followed her pink-tinted and neatly clipped nail as she indicated names on the hand-drawn tree.

"I'm not sure how far you want to go back, but this one goes back to the early 1700s, when the earliest members of your family were farmers on Johns Island."

"Johns Island? I just always assumed they'd lived in the Legare Street house."

"No." She pulled the second book from the stack and opened it to another marked page. "According to this history, written by another relative in 1898, they didn't purchase the house on Legare until 1783."

I glanced over at the book. "So they weren't the original owners?"

She shook her head. "No. Apparently, your great-great-great-great-great-grandfather came into his fortune around the time of the Revolutionary War and made enough to purchase the house. They still owned the property on Johns Island, and had apparently acquired enough wealth and land to become one of the largest sea-island cotton plantations on Johns Island. It's around that time that they decided they were important enough to name their farm and called it Belle Meade."

"I recall the name of the plantation. My grandmother took me there. It's part of a golf community now. But for the rest, I had no idea. I really know very little about my family history."

Yvonne pursed her lips. "Don't say that too loud. You might be asked to leave the city and relinquish your last name." She winked.

Laughing, I asked, "Could I get photocopies of that part of the book? I might as well educate myself while I have the chance."

Yvonne slid a new manila folder from the side of the desk. "I already did, thinking you might want to read more. It's in here with the rest of the photocopies."

I looked at her in surprise. "You're amazing, Yvonne. Really."

She grinned broadly, her perfect dentures gleaming. "I've heard that more than once. I guess that's why they pay me the big bucks."

I laughed again. "I'll let you get dessert and something to go when I take you out, all right?"

"I'd hoped you were going to say that." She moved away the second book so that I was staring at the family tree again.

I glanced briefly at the generations preceding the Civil War, and focused on my great-great-grandfather's generation. I looked at birth, marriage, and death dates, seeing nothing new or surprising. Leonard Prioleau had married Cecilia Allston in 1855, and their only daughter, Rose, was born in 1866. Rose Allston Prioleau married Charles Manigault in 1890 and died in 1946. She gave birth to my grandmother, Sarah Allston Manigault, in 1900. The only interesting item of information was that

Sarah apparently married a distant relation whose last name was Prioleau, bringing the family name back to the Legare Street house until Sarah's daughter, my mother Ginnette, married James Middleton.

"I was hoping I'd find a mention of Rose having a sister, but there's nothing on the family tree." I looked back at Rose's name. "Having just one child, a daughter, seems to be a family trait." I recalled the sound of a baby's crying, and what Rebecca had told me about my mother's miscarriage, and wondered if my life would have been different if I'd had a younger brother or sister. If that would have been enough to get my mother to stay.

"That it does. And since your mother wasn't born until 1945, it would seem that she was a bit of an afterthought. I suppose you're lucky that the house is still in your family, considering there were no males to inherit for at least three generations."

"I suppose," I said, feeling an odd sense of panic at the thought of the house not being mine. Then again, it hadn't been mine for a very long time, and I'd grown used to saying that it didn't matter anymore. "Can I . . . ?" I began.

Yvonne tapped the manila folder. "The copy's already in here. I also made copies of any pictures I found of anybody on your family tree while I was researching, in case you wanted to put faces with any of the names."

"That will be more than helpful, thank you." I looked at my watch. "I've got a showing in half an hour, so I have to leave now." I stood and began stacking the books, then picked up the folder with my copies. "Thank you, Yvonne. I'll call you later to set up our dinner."

"I'll look forward to it." She stood, too, then smoothed down her skirt. "And tell Jack that I said hello."

"I'm, well, I'm not sure when I'll be speaking with him again."

She regarded me silently, her eyes nonjudging. "I think he's fooled you into believing he's—what was it he said you called him?—'a conceited, shallow-hearted womanizer'?"

My cheeks flamed. "He told you I said that?"

"And more. But that's just a mask he wears to protect himself, and I think you know that. He was hurt deeply when Emily left. Even now that he knows the truth, it still hurts. He's a man who doesn't give his heart easily, but when he does, he gives it completely. And he's definitely not emotionally unavailable or a 'toad-faced idiot.'"

I touched my face, feeling the heat. "I didn't really say that, did I?"

"Something to that effect, I believe. But not to worry, dear. That's not why he's upset with you." She moved around the table to where I stood. "He's upset because you're right about his attraction to Rebecca."

I raised an eyebrow. "He said that?"

She raised a corner of her mouth in a half smile. "Of course not. He's a male, so he probably hasn't even figured that out himself. But that's not the only reason, either."

I waited for her to continue, getting nervous at the sparkle in her eyes. "What's the other reason?"

"He's upset because I think he might be more than a little bit in love with you, and he feels guilty because of Emily."

"Because of Emily? But she's dead."

"Yes. But think about it from Jack's perspective. She left him when he was planning to spend the rest of his life with her. For a man such as Jack to make that kind of commitment, he would have really been in love. But there was no good-bye for him, no closure. Even though he knows she's gone, somewhere in his mind he feels that they're still engaged to be married, and that having feelings for you is almost like cheating."

I knew my cheeks couldn't get any redder, so I didn't bother to look away. Instead, I asked, "How do you know all of this?"

"I'm eighty-nine years old, dear, but I'm not dead."

"Well, then. I'll have to remember that. And I don't think you're right, Yvonne. I'd know."

She looked at me dubiously as I slid my chair back under the table. I paused, a niggling thought dancing beyond my field of vision, like a stray thread from a tapestry. I faced Yvonne.

"You've been so helpful that I almost hate to ask you for one more thing, but I just had another thought."

"It'll cost you another meal, and it won't be cheap." She smiled sweetly.

"Deal." I leaned forward. "The house that you sent Jack and me to, Mimosa Hall in Ulmer, the original family name was Crandall. Jack told me that they'd lost everything in the Depression and sold it to the current owner's family. Could you find out what you can about the original family? Family tree, letters, that sort of thing? Mrs. McGowan, the current owner, has a bunch of letters and documents in her attic and Jack is planning another trip down there to go through them, but I'd really like to know more now. There was something about that portrait. . . ." I shuddered, remembering the cold breath on my neck—and the voice in my ear. "Anyway," I continued, "Mrs. McGowan told Jack that some sort of tragedy occurred in the latter half of the nineteenth century, and I'm curious to learn what that was."

"Crandall?" She took the pen she wore on a chain around her neck and scribbled something down on a notepad she'd left on the table. "Will do. I'll let you know what I find when I call you back about the window."

"Thanks." On impulse, I leaned over and hugged her, then kissed her on the cheek. "You really are amazing."

Her eyes sparkled as she leaned a little closer to me. "Do you want to know something I'm even better at than research?"

I glanced around at the few people who were at other tables in the reading room, some of them looking up from the books and staring at us. I leaned closer. "What?"

"Matchmaking. I've never been wrong. And I'll tell you right now that Rebecca what's-her-name is not the gal for our Jack."

I stepped back, not really wanting to hear her opinion as to who just might be the "right gal." "Thank you, Yvonne, but Jack's love life is really none of my business."

She let out a loud and uncharacteristic laugh, then quieted quickly when more people raised their heads.

Eager to leave, I said, "Thanks again, I'll talk with you soon."

She said good-bye, and I left as quickly as I could, before she could say anything else that closely mirrored my own thoughts.

CHAPTER 19

The plumber, the decorator (recommended by Amelia Trenholm), and a demolition crew were scheduled to be at the house at nine, so I figured I had a couple of hours to try and speak to Jack. I told myself that my need to see Jack had everything to do with finding more answers to all the questions that kept piling up and nothing at all to do with the fact that I might actually be missing him. Or that the memory of the last time I'd seen him and the things we'd said—not to mention the almost kiss—was haunting me more than any ghost ever had.

He still hadn't returned any of my phone calls, so I figured the best way would be to just show up on his doorstep. It would be more painful for me if he refused to see me, but I had to at least try.

Gripping my briefcase, which held the folder of photocopied materials Yvonne had given me and the journal, I pressed the buzzer to the downstairs door of Jack's converted warehouse loft, and waited for a moment, listening as a lone car rattled by on Queen Street.

I hardly recognized the scratchy voice on the intercom. "Go away, Mellie."

"How did you know it was me?" I looked around for a camera but didn't see one.

"Because nobody else I know would be stupid enough to ring my bell before ten o'clock in the morning."

That stung, but I was determined not to let it show. "It's important and you haven't returned any of my phone calls."

He sighed heavily into the intercom and I frowned at it, trying to translate.

"Couldn't this have waited until lunchtime? I had a late night."

I frowned at the little white buttons in front of me. "I've got contractors coming to the house at nine, and I'm having lunch with Marc Longo at noon, and then I have office hours starting at three o'clock. This was the only time I could fit you into my schedule."

I thought I heard him chuckle but I wasn't sure. "So, can I come up?"

Following a brief pause, he said, "All right. But be forewarned. I just got out of bed and I sleep naked."

I tried to quell the rush of heat that took over me like an alien force, making me feel like a sheltered teenager on her first date. "Could you please throw something on?" But the words were spoken to empty air. I heard a buzz, then a click, and I pushed the door open, which allowed me access to the foyer. I rode up in the elevator to the top floor, using the time to try and compose myself and stop thinking of Jack naked.

The door was open when I reached his condo. I stuck my head in and called his name twice before entering and closing the door behind me. "Jack," I called again as I walked into the large space. It was still the exquisitely furnished renovated warehouse space I remembered, with exceptional but unpretentious artwork on the walls and tasteful objets d'art on low tables and shelves.

But the place was a mess, with old newspapers, pizza boxes, and mail stacked haphazardly throughout the space, making my fingers itch to start straightening things. The scent of cigarette smoke hung heavy in the air, and when I went to the bar in the kitchen to drop my coat and keys, I noticed several overflowing ashtrays. Unable to stop myself, I scooped them off the granite bar and emptied them in the trash bin under the sink.

"If I handed you a vacuum cleaner, would you take a spin around the place?"

I jumped at the sound of Jack's voice and started to shout at him when my tongue suddenly found itself wedged in my throat. Jack appeared as if he'd been struggling through the desert for a week, with a dark beard sprouting on his cheeks and chin. As impervious to his charms as I tried to be, I couldn't help but admit that Jack Trenholm was a gorgeous man. But now he was completely devastating. My eyes slowly moved down from the new facial hair to his shirtless and very bare chest, down the flat stomach, and then to the blue jeans with the top button conveniently left unlatched. My gaze finally dropped to the floor, where I noted he was barefoot.

I ripped my eyes back to his face, where I was greeted by his familiar smirk, making me drop my gaze to eye level, which brought me in close proximity to his shirtless chest. I unwedged my tongue and blurted out the first thing that came to me. "Your feet are naked." I let the words sink in for a moment before I realized what I'd actually said. "Bare, I mean."

"Thank you, Captain Obvious."

I swallowed thickly, keeping my eyes firmly focused above the collarbone. "It's pretty cold outside. You should probably be wearing a shirt."

He reached down to what appeared to be one of several dirty laundry mounds scattered throughout the living room, and plucked a white T-shirt from the top. His sidelong glance took in my flushed cheeks and damp forehead and he raised his eyebrows at me, but he didn't make a characteristic snide comment like I expected him to.

"I wouldn't want to catch cold. That's for sure," he said as he slid the T-shirt over his head while I stole a last glance at his bare chest and washboard abs. "Sorry about the mess. The cleaning lady doesn't come until tomorrow. And I wasn't expecting visitors."

Ignoring him, I walked into the large living space, noticing the fire in the gas fireplace for the first time, and seeing another overflowing ashtray on the coffee table. "I didn't know you smoked."

"I don't. I actually find it a disgusting habit."

I waved my hand in front of my face. "So do I. So who's been smoking in here?" I was pretty sure Rebecca didn't smoke, but I held my breath anyway, waiting for his answer.

"Me," he said, picking up a full pack and staring at it for a moment before flinging it across the room. It hit the mantel of the brick fireplace, knocking over a framed photograph.

Instinctively, I walked to the fireplace and picked up the frame to return it to its spot on the mantel, relieved to find it was a picture of his parents and not of Emily. I actually thought it was sweet that he'd have his parents' photograph in his condo, and wondered what they'd think if they knew he was smoking.

I faced him. "So why are you doing it?" I asked, indicating the ashtray.

"Because I can't drink a beer."

"Oh," I said, because I understood, and because I couldn't think of anything better to say. I remembered my father going through packs of gum, leaving their foil wrappings all over the house during his many efforts to stop drinking—as if the act of putting something in his mouth besides alcohol could fool his brain into thinking he was numbed enough to face his life.

We regarded each other as I felt the warmth of the fire at my back. I had the errant thought that it would be so much nicer if it were a real fireplace, which was odd, really, because I used to always advise clients to convert their wood-burning fireplaces to gas to circumvent the hassle of dealing with hauling wood and disposing of ashes. It had never occurred to me that the crackle of a warm fireplace lost a lot of its warmth without the smell of burning wood.

"What's going on here, Jack?" I asked as the first fissure of worry surreptitiously crept into the spot where I kept my heart.

"What makes you think something's going on?"

My eyes scanned the piles of laundry, dirty dishes, and ashtrays. Knowing that sarcasm was his native tongue, I said, "Gee, I don't know." Putting my hands on my hips, I asked him again. "Really, Jack, what's going on here?"

Regarding me steadily, he said, "Oh, nothing much. It's just that after having been firmly put in my place by a woman—a Realtor, no less—my editor's not returning phone calls from either me or my agent. No news is always bad news in the publishing world and I think my book deal is going to fall through. Again."

The Jack I knew wouldn't succumb so easily to imagined bad news. I also knew from experience that what he needed was the truth. "I'm sorry. That must be rough. But you need to go to a meeting, Jack."

He sat down on the black leather sofa and patted the seat next to him. "I know. I've already called your dad and we're going together tonight."

"Good," I said, not moving.

He again patted the seat next to him. "Come on and sit. I promise I won't bite."

Swallowing back any protests, I did as he asked but tried to sit as far away from him as possible. My strategy backfired as his weight caused me to slide from my side of the cushion to his.

"Why are you here, Mellie? To insult me some more? I think I caught the gist of how you really feel about me the last time I saw you."

"Look, I'm really sorry about that. I was just taken off guard by a couple of ghosts, that's all. I was scared. Of the ghosts," I added quickly.

He raised a cocky eyebrow, which just made me straighten my shoulders. "But you said you would help me with this investigation." I went ahead and swallowed my pride. "And there's really nobody else who's any good at this except for you."

His eyebrow didn't lower, but he managed to look as surprised as I was that I would admit to that.

I continued. "I figured we could still be like coworkers, working on a project together. Our personal lives don't have to be involved at all." I paused when it appeared that I hadn't been convincing enough. "And if you think this whole investigation is worth writing a book about, I'm sure I could talk my parents into agreeing."

This time he did lower his eyebrow. "Let me hear you say it."

"Say what?"

"Say, 'I need your help, Jack, because I can't do this on my own.'"

"But . . ."

He interrupted me. "Say it, or there's no deal."

Knowing I didn't have a choice, I repeated, "I need your help, Jack, because I can't do this on my own."

With one swipe of his arm, he slid everything from the coffee table—ashtray, pizza box, and unopened mail—onto the floor before sitting back, his hands on his knees. "Fine then. Show me what you've got."

Without waiting for him to change his mind, I slid my briefcase from my shoulder and set it on the coffee table before methodically removing the journal and the folder Yvonne had given me. "This is the journal Sophie found in my grandmother's desk. The one we got from your mother's store. I've read through most of it, although I can't say it's really shed any light on anything because the writer—obviously a girl—only uses initials and never any names. But the journal is definitely from the same era as the portrait of the two girls, and the writer refers to a girl named

R. I've stopped assuming it was my great-grandmother Rose because R seems to be a little hellion, even to the extent of being suspected in the disappearance of the writer's beloved cat."

"And how, exactly, would that mean that R can't be your great-grandmother?"

I tried to keep my indignation under control. "Because I'm—we're—my family isn't like that."

"Right. You're known instead as great animal lovers." I knew he was referring to the fact that I'd been trying to off-load General Lee ever since I'd inherited the little fluff ball less than a year before. Not that I was actively trying anymore, but every once in a while I'd make a big show out of offering him to somebody I knew would never say yes.

"It's not just that." I turned to the page I'd read about the ghost that R couldn't see. "Look right here. The journal writer can see the soldier's ghost, but R can't. My mother remembers her mother telling her that my great-grandmother Rose had a strong sixth sense. It's sort of like a genetic trait like eyes that tilt up at the corners or brown hair."

He took the journal from my hands and began to leaf through it, pausing for periods to read complete entries. "Here's an interesting one." He sat up straight and cleared his throat.

C has called twice this week, and I am not sure what to make of it. He says he is here to see R, but then always finds an excuse to include me on carriage rides or to a play or even just to sit in the parlor. People have always assumed that R and I are closely related since our features are so similar. Perhaps C is merely trying to learn our differences so as not to make an embarrassing mistake in the future. On his last visit he went so far as to mention that when R and I are sitting down we could almost be mistaken for twins.

I suppose because R is older, it is expected that she should be courted first, but I fear C is raising expectations in her. It is not her heartbreak that I fear; it is the repercussions others have to live with if she is disappointed. She has made it very clear to me that she has her cap set on him and while I refrained from saying that she threatened me if things do not work out between them, I fear that she will find some way to make me suffer for it.

Jack looked up from the journal. "Sounds a little ominous." He drummed his fingers on the pages for a moment. "Maybe they're sisters, and it's nothing more than sibling rivalry."

"I don't get that feeling from reading the journal entries. And they definitely wouldn't be Prioleaus, because there are no sisters anywhere on the family tree for the last eight generations." I shook my head. "Guessing isn't going to get us anywhere. Yvonne photocopied pages from a family history. I'm going to create a mini-spreadsheet and write down all the names I come across in alphabetical order. That way, we'll have an organized list of family members, as well as all of those females with an *M* and *R* for their first initials."

Jack seemed to be struggling not to smile. "What's so funny?" I asked.

"Nothing. You're just so cute when you're being anal."

I bristled. "Well, that's one way of looking at it, I guess. But I'm a great organizer, and I think if you follow some of my techniques you might even find them useful when you're researching one of your books."

His face darkened for a moment. To change the subject, I said, "There's something else about the journal you should know." I swallowed, wondering how much of the story to tell him before finally settling on the whole thing. "My mother—you've probably noticed how she always wears gloves."

He nodded. "My mother explained it to me. How her psychic ability seems to mostly manifest itself through handling objects, either voluntarily or involuntarily."

I couldn't resist a smile. "Thank you for making that sound so scientific. I heard my father once describe it as 'throwing fits because she doesn't like the feel of something' and 'female histrionics' among other things."

"Don't be so hard on him, Mellie. He's a military man. Seeing things in any way besides black-and-white could mean the difference between life and death. His training is in his blood, and it would take something pretty significant to make him change his mind. Watching you and your mother converse with thin air probably isn't going to do it."

I leaned toward him. "Then why are you so accepting of all this? You're a military guy, too."

He grinned a true grin for the first time since I'd been there, and I relaxed a little. "So you've been Googling me again."

"Nice try. It's on your last book jacket."

"Oh, right." He frowned for a moment. "I guess maybe it's because I wasn't career military, like your dad. And maybe it's because of all the stuff I saw happening in your house. Things flying through the air, doors locking when they weren't supposed to. Phone calls coming from nowhere. In writing, we refer to it as a 'suspension of disbelief.' I simply chose to go with that rather than question my own sanity."

"Great. Well, hold on to that thought because I have something new to throw at you. My mother held the journal yesterday. I wasn't sure about giving it to her, but she insisted. It makes her physically sick to touch some things, which is why I didn't want her to, but in the end I'm glad she did."

He moved closer until our knees were touching, and I was surprised when he quickly moved his leg out of the way. "Why, what happened?"

"She went into a sort of—trance. It looked like she was trying to speak, but only one word came out." I watched him closely, wondering what his reaction would be. Slowly and deliberately I said, "Rebecca."

He didn't say anything right away, his expression unreadable. Then, "Rebecca? Rebecca Edgerton? She's sure?"

I nodded. "She has no idea why. Sometimes, a spirit uses an object as a portal of communication with somebody who's sensitive—like my mother. The message isn't about the book; it's about whatever image is projected. That's what the writer was trying to communicate with my mother."

His stubble bristled as he rubbed it with his palm. "Did you ask Rebecca about it?"

"No. She doesn't even know about the journal yet."

He raised an eyebrow in question.

"Sophie neglected to tell Rebecca when she discovered it, and it just hasn't come up since." I looked away, not wanting to tell him the real reason was because neither Sophie nor I completely trusted Rebecca.

"But you're going to, right?"

"I guess I'll have to. She wanted to be there for the wall demolition, so she'll be at the house later and I'll tell her then. Maybe she'll have something to add."

He stood, then offered his hand to help me stand. After hesitating for a moment, I took it. I expected him to hold it longer—or to pull me closer—but he let go of it quickly. "Come here," he said, leading me to the partitioned area of the space that he used for his office.

The mahogany partner's desk was littered with paper and empty Coke cans, his Mac computer nearly buried in the mess. The couch was unrecognizable in its new incarnation as a laundry basket. "I like what you've done with the place," I said.

"Thanks," he replied with a tight grin. As he'd done with the coffee table, he shoved everything off the couch onto the floor. "Have a seat."

He moved to the desk and began shuffling through papers. "Contrary to popular belief, I do occasionally work. While working on my final draft of the Confederate diamond story—which, by the way, I've tentatively entitled *The House on Tradd Street*—and waiting for my editor to call me back, I've been reading through some of the material Yvonne gave me."

"Yvonne told me you'd been to see her with Rebecca. I could have sworn that Rebecca told me that her appointment with Yvonne wasn't until next week."

He glanced at me for a moment, but didn't say anything before returning his attention to the mounds of paper on his desk. Finally, he pulled out a folder very similar to mine and came to sit next to me on the couch. "I know better than to ask you how much you know of your family's history, so I'll just start right off by educating you."

I gave him a smug look. "I happen to know that my ancestors started out as farmers on Johns Island before moving on to growing sea-island cotton."

His smug look matched my own. "Yvonne told you that, didn't she?"

"Maybe. Maybe not."

"Uh-huh. Then you may also know that the location of their former cotton plantation was on Bohicket Creek, which leads right to the Edisto River, then out to the ocean."

"Fascinating."

His eyes flickered up at me and I realized that his casual tone was only meant to keep me off my guard. "It certainly is. Especially when the source of your ancestors' income is called into question."

"They were farmers. You just said that."

"They started out as farmers and then seemed to have had a sudden reversal of fortune that led them to become very successful cotton growers in addition to purchasing the house on Legare. It wasn't cheap, even by 1700s standards."

"So what are you suggesting?"

He shuffled through some of the papers in his hands. "Actually, as much as I'd like to take credit for this, I have to give credit where credit is due. I got this from the family history compiled by a Robert Ravenel Prioleau, some distant relative of yours from what I can tell. It certainly explains why multiple copies of the book weren't made and distributed. I'm actually surprised that they allowed a single copy to survive."

"What do you mean?" I asked, wondering if the whole Prioleau clan had been burned at the stake for witchcraft because they could see dead people, then somebody sued for defamation of character. But this was the eighteenth century we were talking about, not the twenty-first.

He turned his blue gaze on me full force. "They were wreckers, Mellie. Your illustrious ancestors started out as wreckers. Slightly higher on the food chain than pirates, but much lower than the leisurely planter class they assimilated into once they'd made enough money to stop plundering ships."

"Excuse me? What on earth is a wrecker?"

Jack shook his head. "Mellie, Mellie, your knowledge of local history is horrible. I should send a letter to your high school and have them revoke your diploma." He leaned an elbow against the back of the couch, which had the unfortunate effect of tightening his T-shirt against his chest. I tried to focus on his eyes but found that just as difficult.

"A wrecker, Mellie, is a person who uses offshore lights that mimic those of a lighthouse to entice ships into unsafe waters. When the ship founders, the wreckers scavenge the cargo. Or, sometimes, wreckers would simply scavenge ships following a storm, letting Mother Nature do their dirty work."

"What about the passengers and crew? What would happen to them?"

"Most of the time, they'd be left to drown. Any survivors would most likely be killed so as to prevent witnesses from talking. Much worse than just making somebody's pet cat disappear, isn't it?"

My eyes widened. "That's—despicable. I don't—no. That can't be right. That just can't be my family. Besides, what kind of proof do you have?"

"Careful, Mellie, or people will start thinking you care about bloodlines and all that. As for proof, well, I would guess there really isn't any definitive proof unless we can find mention somewhere of someone on your family tree winding up on the wrong side of a gallows. But this Robert Prioleau implies that it's no mere coincidence that reports of missing cargo ships along the coastline near Johns Island coincide with an upturn in your family's financial position."

I stood. "It's an interesting hypothesis, sure, but I'm not banking on it. Besides, what does it have to do with anything? You're talking 1700s. The *Rose* was about one hundred and fifty years afterward."

Jack stood, too, and stuck his hands in the back pockets of his jeans. "True. But remember the picture hidden in the outside of the window of your house? There's the ocean, and a plantation house, among other things. It started me thinking, that's all."

I was silent for a moment, thinking, too. "Because there's no such thing as a coincidence," I said slowly, using his oft-repeated adage.

He raised his eyebrow again, but something was gone from his eyes. I realized that for the first time since I'd met Jack Trenholm, he wasn't hiding behind his usual guise of happy-go-lucky guy and it saddened me. I didn't seriously think that I'd had anything to do with it, though, and assumed that as soon as he heard from his editor he'd be back to true form. In the meantime, maybe thinking about the next book and helping me solve the mystery of what was lingering in my mother's house was what he needed to raise his spirits.

I began to walk to the door. "So are you coming? They're demolishing the wall in the kitchen today. No more longhorn cow."

Jack studied me for a moment before answering, and I began to think that I'd been wrong. "No. I don't think so. Rebecca will be there, and she can tell me what I missed. If anything."

I was surprised at how much it hurt hearing his words. I forced a smile. "My soldier keeps telling me that what I seek is behind the wall."

His expression was unreadable. "Tell Rebecca to take pictures."

I started to tell him what Yvonne had told me, about his guilt about Emily and his supposed feelings for me, but I stopped, not sure even I was ready for that topic of conversation. His aloofness was what I wanted, and if I kept telling myself that, maybe I could even begin to believe it, too. "The journal," I said instead, remembering I'd left the book on the coffee table.

Jack left to retrieve it, then handed it to me while standing as far away from me as he could without being rude. I reached for the book and he let go before I realized I didn't have a good grasp on it. It flipped in the air between us, landing on the right top corner before coming to rest on the hardwood floor next to Jack's feet.

He moved to get it but I held up my hand. "I got it." I bent to retrieve it, noticing the bent back corner before opening it up to the back page to assess the damage.

"Look," I said, holding it up for Jack to get a better view.

He took a step closer and I watched a smile climb up his face. "What have we got here?"

On the back page, behind the paper binding that had been glued to the back cover, the edge of what appeared to be a heavy-stock card poked up through the loosened edge.

"You've got nails, Mellie. Pull it out."

I grabbed the corner of the card between my thumbnail and forefinger and pulled it up easily, figuring it had just been stuck inside after the glued edge had been worried open.

I stared at the block-printed words for a long moment before finally flipping it over and showing it to Jack.

"It looks like an old-fashioned calling card." Slowly, he read the words out loud. "Meredith Prioleau. Thirty-three Legare Street." Our eyes met above the card, and for a moment he was the old Jack. With the familiar sparkle in his eyes, he said, "I think we just found our M."

CHAPTER 20

I reached the house on Legare right after the demolition crew and the plumber, Rich Kobylt, a familiar face from all the work he'd done in the Tradd Street house. The decorator had called on my way back from Jack's to let me know she'd been delayed.

My mother had led everyone into the kitchen, where she was serving them coffee and donuts from Ruth's Bakery. I placed my purse, briefcase, and Yvonne's folder on the table before pointing to my watch when I got my mother's attention to remind her of the tight schedule, but she pretended she didn't understand.

Rich turned to me, powdered sugar on his lips. "Good morning, Miz Middleton. I appreciate you recommending me to your mother for this job."

"You're welcome, Rich. You did a wonderful job in my house so it was easy to recommend you. And I appreciate your punctuality." I shot a glance at my mother to see if she was listening.

Rich turned serious. "If you don't mind, Miz Middleton, I'd like to have a word with you in private."

Worried that he might tell me that refurbishing the red-velvet-walled bathroom of my nightmares couldn't be done, I led him into the hallway. "What is it?"

He seemed a little embarrassed and did a lot of fiddling with the tools on his belt. "Well, you remember that little problem I had at your Tradd Street house?"

I raised my eyebrows, hoping it wasn't what I was thinking.

"About the ghosts?" he prompted.

"Ah, yeah. Right." It never ceased to surprise me when I ran into other people like myself. Being psychic was apparently an equal-opportunity offender.

"Um, this house isn't haunted, too, is it?"

"Why do you ask?"

He frowned as he looked down at me. "I thought I saw a young woman in an upstairs window when I opened the front gate. She didn't look happy to see me."

"It could have been my housekeeper, Mrs. Houlihan," I lied, knowing that she was driving General Lee to my father's apartment to keep him out of the way while the workmen were in the house.

"Could be," he said, sounding less than convinced. He pulled a gold chain with a large crucifix out from his collar. "I wore this, just in case."

I tried very hard not to laugh. "Well, there certainly aren't any vampires. And if you see any ghosts, try not to let it slow you down."

He was still frowning as we both realized I hadn't answered his question. We were distracted by my mother's laugh in the kitchen and turned in that direction.

"Your mama sure is a pretty woman. Y'all look more like sisters."

I stared hard at him, wondering if I should ask him to clarify if I looked older or my mother looked younger. Either way, I wasn't taking it as a compliment. "Thank you, Rich, for that observation," I said as I walked away from the kitchen. "Why don't I go ahead and show you the bathroom I want to demo? If you could get all the water sources turned off so I can send the guys upstairs when they're done in the kitchen, that would be great."

"You don't need to show me, Miz Middleton. Your beautiful mama already showed me, so I'll just mosey my way on upstairs."

"Thanks, Rich," I said, averting my eyes as he headed up the stairs, exposing the ubiquitous plumber's rear cleavage.

I returned to the kitchen at the same time Rebecca arrived through the back door. She made a beeline for the donuts as the workmen gave her admiring glances.

"I've got a bunch of stuff to show you, Melanie, when you have a moment," she said as she patted the satchel slung over her shoulder and took a bite out of the last cream-filled donut—my favorite.

"Excuse me, ladies," one of the workmen said as he lifted the donut plate off of the table to place a drop cloth. "It's going to get pretty dusty in here when we cut through the drywall." His smile broadened when he looked at Rebecca, then let it slip when he caught my expression. "Are you sure you don't want us to save that picture of the cow?"

"No," my mother and I said in unison. We looked at each other for a moment before I turned away, lifting my things from the table as he finished with the drop cloth.

My mother said, "Mellie, I need to go and run some errands. Will you be all right here without me?"

Her face seemed drawn, the skin tight around her eyes and lips. "I'll be fine. But are you feeling all right to go?"

She raised an elegant eyebrow. "And you'd offer to go with me if I weren't?"

I flushed, then blurted out, "No. I'd call Daddy to do it."

She smiled as she slid her coat off a kitchen chair. "Not to worry, then. I already have."

She said her good-byes to the workmen and Rebecca, then left, leaving me to wonder again what had happened all those years ago that made my mother leave not just me, but her marriage behind as well.

Rebecca and I stood back and watched as the men used sledgehammers and saws to break through the wall, obliterating the longhorn cow for good. Rebecca took photographs while I waited impatiently for them to remove all drywall and expose what lay behind it. When Rebecca got tired of taking pictures, she pulled out a chair from the kitchen table and sat, then began jerking her foot up and down as she waited. I frowned at her until I realized I was tapping my foot to the same rhythm.

I wasn't sure what Rebecca was hoping to find, and I had given up guessing. *Within the waves, hide all our guilt.* That's what Wilhelm had told me, and that behind the wall lay what I sought. I wanted to find at least one answer to all the questions, to find one thing that would move me forward to my goal of once again leading a quiet, productive life without the intrusion of family members, workmen, or ghosts.

I looked up when the hammering stopped. "Are you done already?" I was surprised. I'd figured that something that ugly would take a long time to remove, but it had been less than an hour.

The foreman approached and took off his hard hat before wiping his forehead with his sleeve. The air was thick with dust and sweat—and something else that I should have recognized. "Yes, ma'am. We've taken off all of the drywall and exposed the original brick fireplace."

I stepped forward to see the fireplace, original to the house. It was deep, and the back bricks were blackened with use and age. I studied the darkened bricks, looking for whatever Wilhelm had wanted me to see.

"You need to break through the bricks."

We all turned to Rebecca.

The foreman, with drywall dust forming a raccoon pattern on his face from his goggles, wrinkled his forehead. "Well, ma'am, there's no need for that. The fireplace is completely functional, just needs a little cleaning . . ."

"Break through the bricks," she repeated as if the man hadn't spoken. She walked to the side of the fireplace, where a bank of polished cherry cabinets and granite countertops now stood. "There were shelves here, and a hidden door that led behind the fireplace." Rebecca looked at me. "I would think it would be cheaper to break through the bricks than these custom cabinets."

I nodded, not needing to question where she got her information from, but hoping she was right. "Go ahead," I said to the foreman. "Just try to do a little bit first, maybe just a couple of bricks, to see if there's anything behind there. And if there is, we can move on to plan B."

With a little more argument, I finally persuaded him to break through the bricks. Rebecca and I stood back as he hoisted a hammer, aimed it at what appeared to be a brick surrounded by crumbling mortar, and let it go. As a testament to old workmanship, the brick didn't give in, but the mortar shifted, giving the foreman room to use a screwdriver to dig out enough mortar to give him a fingerhold at the side of the brick. With a little more scraping, he removed two bricks, giving me a vantage point to whatever lay within.

I stepped forward. "Can I borrow a flashlight?"

One of the other workmen handed me one, and after flipping it on, I shone it through the opening and looked. The room behind the fireplace was windowless and bare, the air stale and stagnant, and the trace scent of gunpowder and salt water crept through the opening. The beam of the flashlight hit on brick walls and a dirt floor before finally coming to rest on a large nautical chest sitting in front of the far wall. *Your illustrious ancestors started out as wreckers.* I remembered Jack's words as I stared at the chest, half wanting to close up the fireplace and forget what I'd seen.

Instead, I turned to the foreman. "Take as much brick away as you can. Enough for a person to fit through." I worried my lip for a moment, trying to think of what Sophie was going to say when she saw the fireplace. "Maybe you can remove a brick at a time to contain the damage."

"Oh, great, an old-house hugger," one of the workmen muttered under his breath.

The foreman shot him a warning glance. "I understand, Miz Middleton. We'll take it nice and slow and do it one brick at a time." He scratched the back of his neck. "And just so you understand that the price I quoted you for the job didn't include this type of work, so there's gonna have to be some adjustments."

I sighed inwardly, having already had way too much exposure to building contractors during the Tradd Street restoration. "I understand. Just do what you need to do to give us access to what's behind without damaging too much of the original fireplace."

Rebecca took my elbow and gently dragged me away. "It's a room, isn't it? With a sea captain's chest."

I looked at her and nodded. "Another dream?"

"Yes." She glanced back at the fireplace. "It's going to take a while. Let's go in the other room so we can compare notes."

With one last look at the workmen, I allowed Rebecca to lead me back to the foyer. Since the majority of the house was unfurnished until we could decide on paint colors and get the interior painted, we sat on the bottom step.

As Rebecca began to take things out of her satchel, I said, "I visited with Yvonne yesterday afternoon. She said that you and Jack were there earlier in the morning. But I could have sworn that you told me your appointment was next week."

She continued to focus on her satchel, peering into the dark depths. "No, it was always scheduled for yesterday. You must have heard incorrectly."

I didn't point out to her that I'd put it on my BlackBerry so I wouldn't forget to ask her what she'd discovered afterward. I thought about pointing out how it seemed she'd planned to get there first to find out what she could so that she might or might not pass the information on to me. But then I thought of the journal and how I hadn't told her about it yet, and closed my mouth. A secret kept was sometimes as good as a secret shared.

She put the satchel down at our feet. "Not to worry, though. I actually didn't end up finding a lot out with Yvonne, anyway. She made all of these photocopies but kept giving them to Jack instead of me. He said I could look at them afterward, but I like to have my own materials to go through on my own time. Besides, when Jack and I get together, he rarely wants to work." She giggled without looking at me as she sorted her folders.

I pretended that her words hadn't felt like a paper cut dipped in vinegar and instead eyed the stack of folders on her lap. "Looks like you made out all right, anyway."

"These aren't from the historical society." She placed her hands over the stack, and I thought again how familiar they looked. "I got them through the archives at the paper. Remember when they first found the human remains on the boat and I told you I could help narrow down the list of possible candidates? Well, I borrowed the Prioleau family tree from Jack's folder and wrote down all the names on a spreadsheet I made, then I spent a lot of time with the microfiche machines to see if I could find any newspaper articles or photographs of any of the family members. Since we know the gender, approximate age, and height of the person, I thought it might shed some light on who we were looking for."

I looked at her closely. "I'm dying to see what you found, but I have to ask you how you think this might help with the article you're writing about my mother."

She seemed confused for a moment before managing to look insulted. "As any good journalist could tell you, I need to have a good grasp of my subject—her family's history, her past, her present—before I can write the first word. Your mother, and her family, is fascinating to a lot of Charlestonians, myself included, and I want to make sure that I do her story justice. I'm sure you've noticed that I don't skimp on details in any of the other citizen profiles I've already done in the series."

I stared at her blankly. "I'm sorry, but I don't read the paper. I take out the real estate listings and trash the rest. No time," I said weakly.

"I see," she said, although it was clear that she didn't. "Speaking of which, though, I could use a face-to-face interview with your mother, and I was hoping you'd work as an intermediary to set something up."

"She's still not taking your calls?"

"Still." Rebecca smiled, but it appeared as if she might be gritting her teeth. "I was hoping that if she saw us working together, she might be more willing to speak with me."

"Why would you think that? Believe me. I have no influence over her at all."

This time, Rebecca's smile was genuine. "You have a lot more influence than you think. I see the way she defers to your opinion, or waits until you speak. I think she means it to protect you."

"To . . . ?" I couldn't even finish the sentence.

"Really, Melanie, for somebody who sees so much, you see so little of the things right in front of your face." She took a deep breath and before I could stop her from continuing, she said, "I used to think that your mother was trying to protect you from public opinion should news of your psychic gift be made public. But it's something more. It's—I don't know—more personal than that. It's beyond motherly love, even. It's as if you share a bond that most people only dream about."

I wanted to protest, to use my old excuses about how she couldn't have cared very much because she left me, but the picture I had of the mother who'd abandoned me no longer fit the image of the woman who'd reentered my life almost four months before. She wasn't who I thought she should be. She was warm, had a sense of humor, and wanted to throw me a birthday party, albeit thirty-three years too late. Fitting the old image into the new was like trying to fit into somebody else's shoes—foreign, tight, and uncomfortable. But no matter how hard I tried to make the images fit, nothing could ever change the fact that she'd apparently not wanted to be my mother until now.

I focused on the folders again, eager to change the subject. "What did you find in the archives?"

"I'm not really sure. Definitely not anything conclusive. However, I did notice something in all the pictures." She knelt on the marble floor and began to lay out photocopied photographs and portraits. "I'm going to put these down like a family tree to make them easier to identify."

I got down on my hands and knees and began helping her by spreading them out and lining them up evenly—not that I really needed to; Rebecca was probably even more obsessed with order and structure than I was, lining up each generation with an almost laserlike precision. Even I was impressed.

When she'd finished laying them out, she sat back to admire her work. "What do you see?"

"Well, you're missing a lot, but I might be able to help you."

I opened Yvonne's folder, remembering that she'd told me she'd included copies of any picture or portrait she found of anybody on my family tree. I pulled them out, then filled in some of the missing spots on Rebecca's impromptu floor chart, stacking any duplicates.

When I was finished, Rebecca repeated, "So what do you see?"

I stared at the sea of faces, all of them vaguely familiar. Some of the slots didn't have a picture attached to them, but it was easy to spot the family resemblance in the remaining pictures. I saw eyes that could have been hazel and some that appeared green, and I thought I recognized the shape of my nose on several women and a few of the men, going back as far as the 1780s. I noticed, too, that almost all of them wore glasses or some type of eyewear, except for the younger women, which made me aware that I was squinting again in an attempt to see better. I wondered vaguely if vanity might also be a genetic trait.

"I see a lot of people that look a lot like me. Is that what I'm supposed to see?"

Rebecca rolled her eyes. "Look again. It's pretty obvious. Look at the people in the top half of the family tree, and compare them to the last four generations."

I looked at the chart again, and frowned. Finally, I said, "I still don't see it, but I did notice that you have a few pictures of Rose. But they're all of her as an infant or small child so I can't really compare her to the girl in the portrait."

"I know. I searched for her name first, but these are the only pictures I could find of her, which is odd because her name appeared in the newspaper quite a bit as an adult. I found out that following the 1886 earthquake, she traveled through Europe with family friends who lived in England. When she returned, she married her fiancé—who'd been waiting for her since she left—and they traveled all over the world. They really only lived in the house when their daughter, Sarah, was born, and even then Rose tended to be a bit of a recluse. She was quite the philanthropist, though, and gave away an extraordinary amount of money to charity. But I cannot find a single picture of her past early childhood. It would seem she might have been a little camera shy." She pointed to the pictures again. "Come on, Mellie. Look again and tell me what else you see."

I leaned forward, scrutinizing the pictures more, until noses, eyes, and chins seemed to blur together. It wasn't until I'd sat up and looked again that I saw what I thought Rebecca was talking about. My gaze traveled across the family tree, then down to the last four generations. I looked up at Rebecca and met her eyes.

Triumphantly, I said, "Nine out of ten of the people in the pictures we have in the top half of the tree have walking canes. Even the two younger women. And all of them are short, and a little on the plump side." I traced my finger along the marble floor between the pictures, coming to a stop beside my great-grandmother Rose. "All we can tell about Rose is that she was a fat baby, but if you look here at my grandmother Sarah, and my mother, they're all suddenly tall and slender." Rebecca had placed my college graduation photo, a picture of me with permed hair and padded shoulders that I wanted to forget, at the bottom of the chart. But even behind the ridiculous eighties hair and clothing, there was no doubt that I was related to Ginnette and Sarah Prioleau.

"Do we have a picture of Charles, Rose's husband?"

Rebecca shook her head. "Not that I could find. I was hoping that maybe you or your mother might find old photo albums or photographs as you go through the attic."

"We haven't made many inroads into that project, but I'll let you know what we find."

Rebecca studied the pictures again. "Charles must have been tall and slender to explain the rest of you."

I sat back, too, thinking. "The remains found in the boat had a congenital hip defect. Maybe that would explain the walking aids."

Rebecca looked at me with grudging respect. "Good one. I hadn't put those two things together, but I think it makes sense."

She began picking up the photocopies and I helped her, taking care to keep them in order. I felt guilty; she'd freely shared this information with me, yet for no real reason I could think of, I'd withheld the journal from her. Despite misgivings, I realized I needed to be forthcoming, too.

I cleared my throat. "I forgot to tell you. Sophie found a journal hidden in my grandmother's old desk. The writer is unknown, but the book dates back to the late 1800s when my great-grandmother Rose would have been in her late teens or early twenties."

I reached for my purse and pulled the journal out to show it to Rebecca—who was looking at it oddly—and I wondered if she was remembering asking me about it before and how I'd told her that I hadn't found anything.

I continued. "The writer's identity is a mystery, but she refers to another girl about her age whose first initial is *R*, which makes me believe that it can't be Rose because she didn't have any sisters, and the two girls in the journal are definitely living under the same roof. But I can't help but think that the girls in the portrait with the *M* and *R* lockets are most likely the girls in the journal. But who they are, and how the *M* locket was found with the body on our boat, is a mystery."

I looked up from the journal to see that most of the color had drained from Rebecca's cheeks. Her eyes met mine and for the first time since I'd met her, I felt something besides dislike for her. "What's wrong?"

"It's her, isn't it? The girl in the boat. And here in the house. She's here now, watching you. Watching us."

"What do you mean?" I grabbed her arm, feeling how cold it was.

"Your mother. Keep this book away from her. It's—dangerous to her."

"I know. She already touched it. But she's fine now."

She shook her head and closed her eyes. "No, no. I had a dream. She can't touch it again." She opened her eyes. "Promise me."

"I don't think . . ."

"Keep it away from her." Her voice was harsh, and she seemed to realize it, too. She put a hand on my arm. "When I was a girl, I used to have these premonitions all the time, and they were always right. But then I realized that other kids didn't do the same thing, and they thought I was weird, or crazy, or whatever. I was ostracized because of it. I changed schools, and learned how to stop dreaming, much how I expect you learned not to see the things you could." Her lips curled up in a small smile. "The things kids do to fit in." She shook her head. "Anyway, since the first time I met you, outside on the sidewalk before your mother bought the house, I've been having dreams. I don't remember all of them, but they all seem to center around you and your family. And I've been right one hundred percent of the time."

She regarded me steadily, and I thought she wanted to say more. After a moment, I said, "So what do you think it means?"

"I don't know. I'm sure you don't always understand things you hear and see, either. It's a gift, but not an easy one, is it?"

I studied her for a long moment, recalling how my mother had seen her when she'd held the journal and I wanted to tell that to Rebecca now. But I held back, remembering that Sophie didn't trust her. And I still had my own misgivings, which I kept telling myself had nothing to do with Rebecca's relationship with Jack. Despite our shared confidences, I was still convinced that her intrusion into my life wasn't coincidental, and that even her explanation of writing a story about my mother seemed contrived.

Instead I said, "Let me read you an entry from the journal for a little more insight. Notice what it says about R." I flipped through the pages until I found the entry I was looking for.

Father took us out sailing again this morning. He was in the Confederate Navy in his younger days, and I think he is a sailor at heart because he loves nothing more than to be out on the waves, filling his sails to make the boat move as fast as the wind will allow. He has always encouraged R to sail, and to love it as much as he does because, I suppose, she is the eldest. But she has no affinity for it at all, and it might be because of her physical affliction. She hides it well so no one, not even her suitor, knows about it, but I see her at the end of the day when her limp is pronounced from the physical exhaustion that is required to mask it when she walks without assistance. I know not to mention it, even in sympathy or in an effort to assist her, because she looks at me with such venom that I feel guilty at having two perfectly formed and healthy legs.

I love to sail, and I have become quite proficient, and Father takes a lot of pride in me for that. But I find myself pretending that I would rather be on terra firma. It is easier to miss doing something I love than to deal with R.'s wrath that I have succeeded at something that she cannot—and I am not necessarily referring to the ability to sail.

When I finished reading, I looked up at Rebecca. A small pucker had formed between her eyebrows. "This R sounds like a real charmer, doesn't she?"

"I know. Which is why I keep saying she can't be related to me at all. But then again, Jack seems convinced that my ancestors were wreckers, too, so God only knows what other skeletons my family tree might be hiding."

She only nodded, her gaze intense as if she were committing my words to memory.

I turned back to the journal. "And this morning, when I was showing the journal to Jack, we found a calling card that we believe belonged to the writer of the journal." I flipped to the back page, frowning when I saw that the card had slipped back inside the little pocket in which it had been hidden. I was trying to stick my pinkie under the flap when the foreman appeared from the kitchen.

"Excuse me, ladies, but we've made a hole big enough for somebody to pass through. I've already been inside to check to make sure it's structurally sound and it looks good."

The journal forgotten, I slid it onto the step and we both stood, then followed the foreman back to the kitchen. As I walked toward the opening, one of the workmen handed me a flashlight. I glanced back at Rebecca to see her watching me intently.

"Total clearance is only about five and a half feet," said the foreman, pointedly eyeing my four-inch heels. "They were a lot shorter back in the day."

"Apparently," I muttered as I reluctantly slid out of my high-heeled pumps. Then I stepped through the bricks, my stockinged feet touching the cool, hard-packed earth as I breathed in two-hundred-year-old air.

"Can I come in, too?" I looked back through the hole to see Rebecca backlit from the kitchen light.

My first instinct was to tell her no, and I wasn't sure why. Despite our recently shared information, I wasn't quite ready to make her a full partner.

"Just a minute," I said. "There's a really low ceiling, a lot of cobwebs, and not much else. It might not be worth your while. . . ."

I stopped when I saw her foot come through the opening followed by her head and then the rest of her body. She smiled her perky cheerleader smile. "I'm sorry. I couldn't hear you. What were you saying?"

I wanted to be furious, but I couldn't. I even felt a little admiration for her bravado, if only because she'd done exactly what I would have if our situations had been reversed.

"I was saying how dark it was in here and how you should bring your own flashlight."

I heard a click, then saw her holding a flashlight under her chin, hollowing her eyes out and making them appear as black holes. I turned away. "Keep your head down, the ceiling's really low. There's nothing much in here besides the trunk." I gave a cursory sweep of my flashlight over the brick walls, then up to the darkened oak beams that spanned the ceiling in three-foot intervals, with one beam cutting through the middle like the spine in the bleached-out bones of a whale carcass. I allowed the light to touch on them briefly, eager to focus on the trunk. I was slowly lowering the arc of light when Rebecca spoke.

"Hang on. Shine your light up there again." She flicked her flashlight over to the side of the beam on the farthest side of the room, near the wall. "It looks like something's scratched into the side."

We both shone our flashlights at the same spot as we walked in tandem to get a better view, then paused in silence as we read the words. *Wilhelm Hoffmann 1782. Gefangener des Herzens.* We looked at each other. "It's German," I said.

She nodded. "Do you know what it means?"

"No." I shifted, feeling a breath of icy cold stealing up my spine.

"Neither do I. It makes sense that it's German, though."

I stared at her, wondering how she knew. "What makes you think so?"

It was her turn to stare back at me. "You need to brush up on your history, Melanie. In December 1782, the British forces abandoned the city to return to England following the end of the war. A lot of the

Hessian mercenaries deserted, not being particularly loyal to the British Army. A few were lucky to be hidden by Americans." She gave a little shrug. "It meant freedom for some, but for others they simply traded in their uniforms for lives of servitude to their supposed rescuers, who demanded payment for their efforts." Absently, she traced the words with a finger. "It wouldn't surprise me to learn that your Prioleau ancestors, if they really were wreckers, sent him to work on the coast. Much less risky for the family members if he's caught, you know?"

The story of the Hessians seemed vaguely familiar to me, something I had once read in a long-ago history class. I looked back at the carved words. Each letter was made with straight strokes as if etched with a sharpened stick, or maybe even an eating utensil, and I committed them to memory. I thought, too, about what Rebecca had said about the fate of some of the deserters, and I hoped she was wrong about Wilhelm.

Then I turned my attention back to the sea trunk, the wood worn on the front by the empty loop where a padlock might have once been, the brass fittings dulled with age.

I placed my hand on the lid, hoping to feel something—or at least a warning about the contents and to prepare myself. But I felt only cool, varnished wood. Tucking my flashlight under my chin, I tried to pry open the lid but only managed to lift it an inch or so before my grip slipped.

Placing my flashlight on the ground and shining it at the chest, I turned to Rebecca. "Put your flashlight down and help me open this." I glanced at her slim arms and hoped the two of us would be enough. Whatever was in the trunk, I was fairly sure I didn't want the workmen to see it and possibly broadcast the news wherever they could find a willing listener.

Rebecca did as I asked and returned to stand next to me, facing the trunk. "I'm going to count to three, and when I say 'three,' lift the lid."

She nodded, and I began to count. "One, two, three!"

I felt the weight of the lid pressing down on us, the unexpected odor of rotting fish suddenly permeating the small space. I heard Rebecca gag, but she didn't let go of the lid. A cold hand brushed my neck and I shivered, almost letting my fingers slip, but I held on and with a renewed fervor, I strained harder.

I sensed the soldier standing nearby. I felt him as a child is aware of his shadow—stealthy and dark, twisting beyond your sight whichever direction you turn. And then suddenly it seemed as if a third set of hands had joined ours and the lid flew back so fast that it crashed into the wall behind it.

"Everything all right in there?" The foreman stuck his head through the opening.

"We're fine," I said, waving him away. We stood with our hands on the inside of the open lid, waiting to catch our breaths.

One of the flashlights began to sputter, then died, casting deep shadows in the room. Without saying anything, I slowly backed away from the chest, retrieved the remaining flashlight, and then shone it into the yawning black mouth of the empty chest and waited for what I saw to register in my mind.

"It's empty," Rebecca said, her voice muffled as if she were speaking underwater.

I handed her the flashlight and began to tap along the inside and the outside of the chest the way Jack had shown me once, listening for a place that sounded different from the rest—a hidden compartment or bottom used to conceal valuables. The sound was thick and solid all the way around, but I did it twice just to make sure. I straightened, feeling more disappointed than I could explain. "It's definitely empty."

A soft hand stroked my cheek and I glanced up to see Wilhelm, his hat neatly tucked under an arm, his ever-present musket held firmly against his body. The only thing that surprised me about his being there was that he wasn't looking at me; he was focused on Rebecca.

I heard her gasp and I watched as if in slow motion the flashlight tumbled out of her hand. And in the second before the flashlight hit the hard dirt floor and went out, I saw Rebecca's face and realized that she had seen him, too.

CHAPTER 21

I met Marc Longo for lunch on East Bay Street at Blossom—one of my favorite restaurants in a city known for its eateries. I'd chosen to meet him there instead of his picking me up at the house so I'd have the option of leaving whenever I wanted.

Marc and I had a short history, one that ended when I discovered he'd been romancing me solely to find the diamonds hidden in my house. To Marc's credit, he admitted that his attraction to me started that way, but had turned into something else. I wasn't sure if I really believed him, or even why I'd agreed to have lunch with him; all I knew was that he wasn't Jack, and Marc was a suitable distraction for my bruised ego and empty social calendar.

He stood when I approached the table, and kissed me on the cheek. He smelled good, and looked even better, although he was thinner and less muscular than Jack, and he lacked Jack's ability to make you smile even when he wasn't. I mentally chided myself for comparing them, and threw my arms around Marc to make it up to him.

He seemed pleasantly surprised at my greeting, then pulled his chair closer to mine after seating me. "I have to admit, Melanie, that I didn't really expect you to show up today, considering . . ."

I let his voice trail away and smiled. "I thought I owed you at least the opportunity to explain."

Marc took my hand and held it to his lips. "And that's what makes you a true lady, Melanie. Beautiful, smart, and compassionate—an irresistible combination."

I felt myself blushing. Despite our past, I was still fairly confident that

Marc's compliments were real, whereas with Jack I was sometimes left wondering if he had less than altruistic motives for saying something nice. I closed my eyes, castigating myself for comparing Marc to Jack again.

The waiter appeared at the table with a bottle of champagne and a carafe of orange juice. Marc smiled. "I hope you don't mind. I took the liberty of ordering us mimosas." The waiter filled two glasses with a mixture of both and then Marc raised his glass to me. "To forgiveness, and to new beginnings." I clicked my glass with his, took a sweet, bubbly swallow, and smiled back at him, determined to enjoy my lunch.

The waiter returned and we ordered, and I resisted the urge to ask him what was on the dessert menu. When he'd disappeared with our orders, Marc refilled our glasses.

"Melanie, I do mean it when I say I'd like another chance. There are no excuses for my past behavior. Yes, I was desperate, but that was no excuse. I want you to believe that I had—have—feelings for you. I hated myself for lying to you."

I studied the crisp white tablecloth before glancing up at him again. "I accept your apology. It will take me a while to trust you again, but we can start over, if that's what you'd like."

He smiled, and I realized again what a very handsome man he was. He raised his glass and drank. "I'll make it up to you. I promise."

I raised my glass, too. "To new beginnings," I repeated, and took a sip before leaning back in my seat. "So, tell me about this book you're working on. I have to admit that I'm a little surprised; you don't seem the authorly type, if there is such a thing."

He feigned insult. "Maybe I should grow a paunch and start wearing tweed jackets with suede patches on the elbows."

I laughed because that was exactly how I thought a male author should look, and I usually found myself resenting Jack for not fitting the stereotype. I looked down at my bread plate, chastising myself for thinking of Jack again.

"Seriously, though, I'm intrigued. You're a successful businessman; when did the writing bug hit?"

He paused while the waiter placed our plates in front of us before continuing. "Oh, I suppose I've always had the dream of becoming a published author. Then recently I had an inspiration and wrote out an outline and a couple of chapters. A friend of mine knows somebody in the publishing world in New York and sent it in. Two months later, I had an agent and a month after that a bidding war between two different publishers netted me a nice publishing contract."

"That's really amazing. I'd imagine that would make a lot of authors jealous; I don't think it's supposed to work that way. Tell me what it's about."

He shook his head. "It's a little hush-hush right now. Apparently, another writer at another house is working on a similar book so we're rushing to get mine out first. Not to steal anybody else's thunder, of course, but there's no room for an also-ran in this case. As my agent said, I've got to be first or it won't be worth publishing."

We began to eat, savoring our dishes and making comments about the excellence of the food and service. I watched him as he spoke, smiling at his enthusiasm for his new endeavor, and was more than impressed that he'd found a new passion instead of resting on the laurels of his business successes. I studied him with a new appreciation, noticing how thick and brown his hair was, how he had excellent taste in clothes, and how nice he looked when he smiled at me. The only thing wrong with him was that he didn't have blue eyes and he wasn't Jack.

Clearing my head, I focused on what Marc was saying, realizing he'd asked me a question.

"Excuse me?" I asked.

"I was asking if you and Rebecca Edgerton were good friends. I assumed you were when I ran into you at St. Philip's."

I took the last bite of my ricotta gnocchi, chewing slowly as I formulated an answer. "No, not really. She's more a friend of Jack's. She's working on a story for the paper about my mother, Ginnette Prioleau."

"Well, that explains a lot."

"What do you mean?"

Marc signaled for the waiter and ordered the chef's special dessert for one without asking what it was. He even got a thumbs-up from me when he didn't ask for two forks. When the waiter left, he continued. "I took her to lunch last week, prepared to tell her all about my winery and the new restaurant, which I will bring you to the next time, I promise. Instead, she seemed more intent on asking me about my connection to you and your family. She seemed almost—obsessed with your genealogy. I began to think that she's one of those people who believes that studying one's ancestry is an alternative religion. You see that a lot in this city."

A milk chocolate crème brûlée was placed in front of me, but I waited to dig in until Marc had his coffee. "That is a bit odd, but it makes sense. She's writing about my mother, but as she explained to me, knowing my mother's family and their collective past will help her know her subject better."

As I polished off the last bite of crème brûlée, Marc said, "Rebecca and I were actually scheduled to have coffee later to go over her article, but she canceled about an hour ago. Said she had to drive out to Ulmer on urgent business."

For the first time in my life, I was unable to swallow a piece of dessert. I started coughing, and had to drink a nearly full glass of water before I felt I could breathe again. "Ulmer?" I asked. "Ulmer, South Carolina?"

"Yes. Something to do with her research."

"She didn't say what it was about?" I dabbed at the corners of my mouth with my napkin.

"No. And she made it pretty clear that it wasn't something she was prepared to talk about, either. All I know is that she said she'd be back too late to meet with me today but asked for a rain check."

I slid back my chair. "I'm sorry, Marc, but I have to go. Thank you for lunch, and I hope we can do this again soon."

He stood, too, a worried look on his face. "I hope I haven't offended you by something I said. And that you've accepted my apology."

I walked toward him and took both of his hands in mine, sensing his sincerity. "No, you haven't said anything. I just remembered something I have to do. But, yes, I forgive you, and I hope you'll call me soon."

He looked relieved and when he kissed me on my cheek, I only thought of Jack a little bit.

≫

I sat down with a groan on the dining room floor in my house on Tradd Street, feeling as if sawdust covered every square inch of my hair, clothing, grandmother's pearls, and teeth. I glanced at my watch, counting every second until four o'clock when Sophie would leave to go teach a class and Chad and I could bring the electric sander out.

I closed my eyes, giving in to the physical exhaustion, fueled by the frustration of getting nowhere fast. As soon as I'd left Blossom, I'd called Rebecca on her cell number at least ten times, and reached her voice mail each time. I figured that she'd either forgotten to turn on her phone, or she wasn't answering for a reason. Just in case, I called and left messages at both her home phone and her office.

I then futilely tried to reach Jack and Yvonne with the same results. In complete desperation—because I couldn't think of another reason why I might do so—I called my mother, who'd calmly suggested I work off some of my stress with a piece of sandpaper. At the time it had seemed like a good idea.

I must have fallen asleep because I didn't realize my phone was ringing until the third or fourth ring. I dug it out of my pocket and flipped it open a second before it switched to voice mail. "Hello?"

"Hello, Melanie? This is Yvonne Craig at the historical society library, returning your call."

I sat up straight, remembering the octogenarian's perfect posture. "Hello, Yvonne. Thanks for calling me back." I found myself holding my breath, wondering if I'd finally have something to work on instead of just another question.

"Well, I would have gotten back to you sooner, except that Rebecca Edgerton has been bombarding me with requests for her 'famous Charleston citizens of the last fifty years' project. I'd normally stick her at the end of the line except that Jack called on her behalf and told me it would be a personal favor to him if I moved her up to the front."

"Did he now?" I felt something thick and heavy in my gut.

"Actually, she was here a little earlier, which is why I couldn't take your call."

"She was?"

"Yes. She was here looking for more photographs of your great-grandmother Rose, as well as your mother."

"Oh." I frowned, wondering why Rebecca wouldn't have told me what she'd planned to do. Granted, she was a little shaken when she'd left the house after the incident in the hidden room, but I would have thought she'd at least mention it since it involved my family and me. "I understand," I continued. "I was calling to find out if you'd had any luck with tracking down the window order, and the Crandall family tree."

I could hear the smile in Yvonne's words when she answered. "Yes, actually, on both counts. I've made copies and put them in a folder for you."

I stopped myself from pumping my fist in the air. "That's wonderful. I can be there in fifteen minutes to pick them up."

"No need for that. Rebecca explained that the two of you were working together, so I gave the folder to her. I didn't want to, but she was insistent and promised she'd deliver it personally."

"Really?" I said, trying to still the panic rising up in me. "Did she mention when she might be dropping them by?"

"She didn't really say, but she led me to assume that she was bringing the folder directly to you. Didn't you get it?"

I forced a smile into my voice. "Not that I know of. But I wasn't home earlier, so she might have left it in the mailbox or something. Don't worry. I'm sure it's here somewhere."

"I'm sure it is. Although I will say that I'm a little annoyed with Miss Edgerton. The book with the Crandall family tree and history was discovered missing after she left and I'm wondering if she might have accidentally taken it with her. I've tried calling her but I haven't been able to get ahold of her yet. If you reach her before I do, would you please ask her about it? I'm sure it was an accident, but still."

With a sinking feeling, I said, "I'll be sure to ask her, Yvonne."

"If it's of any help, I do remember the information regarding the window changes. Another librarian obtained the copy of the Crandall family tree, so I'm afraid I'm completely useless with that source of information."

"That's fine. I'll see it when I get it. But what did you find out about the window?"

"You were right, Melanie. The glass maker who originally installed the window, John Nolan, sold his business in 1900 to another Irishman, Patrick something-or-other—my memory's not *that* good—and it stayed in his family until the 1950s, when the demand for artistic glass dried up and the business folded."

I tried to stifle my impatience. "That's all very interesting, Yvonne, but . . ."

"I know, sorry. I get lost in the details sometimes. But anyway, I found two ledgers of purchase orders for the new company; the first one from the twenties and the second one from the forties."

"And?" My foot tapped furiously on the floor.

"You'll never believe who placed the order to change the window."

"Try me," I said through gritted teeth.

"The name on the purchase order was Sarah Manigault Prioleau."

My mind went blank for a moment. I'd been so sure she'd say Rose's name that when she said Sarah I was disoriented. "Sarah? Are you sure?"

"Quite sure. I've a memory that's sharper than most people half my age."

"I know. I didn't mean it as an insult. I'm just—surprised. Sarah was my grandmother, and I knew her. Yet she never told me anything about the window."

Yvonne was silent for a moment. "Or maybe she did. You've mentioned how she was fond of puzzles. Maybe you just weren't aware at the time."

I thought of all the times my grandmother and I had spent in the room with the sunlight streaming through the window, and sitting outside in the garden on the reverse side. But I'd been so young then; anything she might have said had long since been forgotten. Maybe simple exposure to the window was her way of implanting it in my memory.

"Maybe," I said uncertainly.

"There was a sketch with the purchase order, and I made a copy of that, too. Although you've already noticed all of the changes from the original order."

"And it's in the folder you gave Rebecca."

"Yes. I do hope I didn't do the wrong thing."

"No, Yvonne. You've been nothing but helpful. One more question, though. Do you remember when the window was changed?"

"Of course." Again, she sounded wounded, as if I somehow doubted her mental capacities and I made a mental note to be more careful with my questions in future. "I'm usually not as good with dates as I am with names, but I remember the year because it was the year I got married: 1947."

I closed my eyes, trying to recall the dates on the family tree that I'd seen recently. My eyes popped open. "That was the year after Rose died."

"Hunting unicorns again, Melanie?" I heard the smile in Yvonne's voice.

"I'm thinking there might have been a deathbed confession of some sort, and this was my grandmother's way of recording it for future generations. She did love her puzzles."

"That's very good, Melanie. And exactly what Jack said, too."

"You've seen Jack?"

"No. He called me this morning. Wanted me to check to see if I had anything—birth records, death records, marriage certificate, anything, really—on a Meredith Prioleau."

Before, I would have been angry that Jack's mind had been quicker than mine in figuring out the next step. But now all I could feel was an odd relief that Jack hadn't completely forgotten about me or abandoned the search. I frowned when it occurred to me that he might not be doing the research for me at all. I grasped the phone tighter. "He beat me to the punch. That was the next thing I was going to ask you. Have you had a chance to look, yet?"

"Just preliminary files so far. And I've found absolutely nothing. Any idea who she might be?"

"None. But I have a feeling she may be a contemporary of Rose's. Maybe a distant cousin?"

"That at least gives me a time period to work with. I'll call you on your cell phone as soon as I learn something." She paused for a moment. "And do try to think of anything your grandmother might have said to you, something that maybe didn't make sense to you back then but might now. I knew your grandmother, you know. Not well, so I suppose I knew more of her than anything else. But it was well known that she had a sharp mind and a sharper sense of humor, and loved mysteries, and riddles, and pranks more than anything. She was also secretly hated by a lot of the women in town because of how she remained whiplike thin yet ate like a pack mule."

I smiled, remembering my grandmother and how we used to fight over the biggest piece of chocolate cake. "I will, Yvonne. And thank you."

I hung up the phone just as I heard high heels coming from the foyer.

"In here," I called, expecting to see Rebecca and more than a little bit relieved. When my mother appeared from around the corner, I must have gasped in surprise.

"Are you all right, Mellie? You look like you've just seen a ghost." Her eyes twinkled, belying the seriousness of her question.

I stood, pocketing my cell phone. "Very funny, Mother. And no, I haven't seen anything. I think the large number of people working in the house during the days keeps them at bay. Were you looking for me?"

"Yes, actually." She leaned forward and before I could step back, she'd plucked a clump of sawdust from my hair and held it up. "I don't think gray is your color, dear."

Before I could stop myself, I smiled, amazed how natural it had felt to have my mother teasing me and making jokes the way mothers were supposed to. At least how other mothers did.

I backed away, feeling self-conscious now as I raked my fingers through my hair. "So what did you need?" I asked, careful to keep my voice neutral. The open hostility had passed if for no other reason than I found it exhausting to keep it up while we lived in close quarters. It might also have had something to do with the fact that my mother had held the journal to help me, regardless of what effect it might have on her. As much as I wanted to, I couldn't forget it.

Small lines formed between her eyebrows. "Rebecca came by the house a little while ago."

I straightened. "Did she leave a folder for me?"

She shook her head. "No. Actually, I think she took something."

"What? There's nothing of any value in the house right now except for a few pieces of heavy furniture." I thought of the sapphire necklace and earrings, but after the incident in the kitchen, I'd had them stored in a safety-deposit box at my bank. I'd figured it was in my best interests to keep them out of the house.

"The journal. I didn't realize it was gone at first. When I came downstairs, I felt a cold draft and found General Lee outside and the kitchen door open. As I went to retrieve the dog, I saw Rebecca getting into her car. I called for her, but she either didn't hear me or pretended not to. Regardless, she got in her car and drove away.

"It wasn't until I got to the kitchen that I remembered you'd left the journal on the kitchen table. And it wasn't there anymore. I checked on the counters and everywhere else to see if it could have been moved, but it was gone."

I started breathing heavily as anger and worry bonded together in a gathering snowball. I wasn't sure which part to be more upset about: that she'd stolen the journal or that she'd left General Lee outside in the cold. "Are you sure it was Rebecca?"

My mother gave me a hard glare. "Blond hair, pink coat, perky steps?"

"Right." I flipped open my phone and hit redial again, trying to reach Rebecca on her cell. I flipped it closed when I reached her voice mail. Then I tried Jack's cell and home number, with the same results.

"Do you know what she's up to?" my mother asked.

"No clue," I said, sliding down the wall and landing in a pile of sawdust, but I didn't care. I was overwhelmed by questions with no answers, and the only person I knew of who could help me figure them out wasn't taking my phone calls.

To my surprise, my mother sat down, too, albeit more elegantly and managing to avoid the piles of sawdust stacked around the room like a minefield. "So what are you going to do about it?"

I shrugged. "Nothing, I guess. I just have no idea what direction to move in next."

"So you're giving up? Just like that? That's not the Melanie Middleton I've heard about."

I turned my head to glare at her. "And you would have heard a lot up there in New York or whatever corner of the world you were."

Her soft smile didn't falter. "Actually, yes. I always had the Charleston paper forwarded to me wherever I was. I have a scrapbook of every sale you've ever made, every article about all your sales awards, and every ad, with some questionable choices in hairstyle, I might add. But I have them all. A mother's brag book, I guess you'd call it."

I looked down at my sawdust-encrusted hands, not knowing what to say.

Softly, she said, "So the Melanie Middleton I thought I knew was tenacious and didn't quit. It seems to me you should think of this whole thing as a listing with multiple offers, and you're going to get a huge commission if your client gets the bid."

Despite myself, I smiled. "Yeah, well, in that scenario I'd know what I was doing. I'm pretty much branching out into new territory here. We have portraits of girls with matching lockets but with initials we can't trace, a ghost who hates me and wants to hurt me, a dead soldier who apparently wants to date me, a hidden room with an empty chest, a window in which Grandmother Sarah stuck a clue that I can't figure out, and a dead body in a boat that once belonged to my family. And I don't have a single thought as to how all of that might be related and/or how any of it might help me figure out how to exorcise the bad spirit who's been in this house since you were a little girl."

My mother was staring at me intently. "What did you say about your grandmother and the window?"

"Oh, right. I just received a phone call from Yvonne at the historical society library. She found a work order dating from 1947, the year after your grandmother Rose died, with Sarah's name on the purchase order. She was the one who made the changes to the window: the addition of the decorative line framing the picture in the window, the angel's head, and the addition of the people. Jack's found some evidence that would suggest that our forebears were wreckers, but again there's no solid proof of anything, although the picture in the window shows a beach and ocean."

A slow smile spread over my mother's face. "Your grandmother Sarah did leave a clue, Mellie."

I frowned at her, not following.

"On her tombstone, remember?" She closed her eyes and recited the words slowly:

> When bricks crumble, the fireplace falls;
> When children cry, the mothers call.
> When lies are told, the sins are built,
> Within the waves, hide all our guilt.

I sat up a little. "Rebecca figured that the bricks crumbling are related to the Charleston earthquake in 1886, and because the sailboat *Rose* disappeared the same year, she thought the last line was about the boat. But I was the one who noticed that the lines framing the tombstone matched the design on the back of the window at your house, which brings me back to where I started. Yvonne—she's been helping with a lot of the research—had a folder for me with some information regarding Grandmother's purchase order for the window as well as a family tree for the Crandall family."

"The Crandall family?"

"Yes. Their house in Ulmer has a portrait of a girl around the same period with an identical locket worn by the girls in our portrait. Jack and I were trying to find the identity of the girl in that portrait, hoping it might shed some light on the other two."

"And what about the window order? What were you trying to find out?"

"I'm not sure. I was hoping that seeing in Grandmother's own words what she was changing might help me figure out what she was trying to tell us."

My mother leaned toward me. "But we've already seen her own words. On the tombstone." Her eyes lit up, exaggerating her resemblance to my grandmother, and also reminding me that she was a Prioleau, too. "You're forgetting a piece of this puzzle, the writer of the journal. It seems to me that her name is an answer to a question we haven't thought to ask yet." Standing, she began to walk around the room, managing to avoid the sawdust piles. "Let's assume Rebecca was right and the first line is about the earthquake. Let's assume, too, that she's right about the last line." She held up a finger on one gloved hand. "So here we have an unidentified body, although she's found with a locket with the initial *M* on it." She held up a finger on her other hand. "And here we have a name with no history: Meredith Prioleau. Have you asked Yvonne for any of the casualty lists from the earthquake?"

I had only a vague memory of studying the earthquake that had rocked the city almost one hundred years before I was born. I was proud to be able to point out the earthquake rods that were drilled into the sides of most of the historic buildings in the city to prospective buyers. But this was the first time I'd really thought about the incident in terms of casualties. Hesitantly, I asked, "Were there casualties?"

My mother stopped her walking and stared down at me before sighing heavily. "About two thousand buildings were destroyed at a cost of about six million dollars at the time, and around one hundred people were killed. They're not sure of the exact numbers because records were destroyed and record keeping wasn't what it is today. Some bodies were never recovered."

"Oh, right. I knew that."

My mother frowned at me. "Regardless, it's something that hasn't been explored yet and it's a place we can start without Rebecca. Or Jack." She waved a gloved hand at my reproachful look. "Oh, I'm not blind, Mellie. I know he hasn't been coming around or calling, and I'm not about to point fingers or blame anyone. Not yet, anyway. But I do think it's time you stopped feeling sorry for yourself and move forward. Besides, nobody buys into the 'poor me' thing you've got going."

She began to rustle around for something in her purse.

I swiped angrily at the sawdust that stuck to my eyelashes. "You have some nerve . . . ," I began.

"You're much too beautiful, talented, and successful for that to work anymore. Time to face the fact that you turned out pretty remarkable despite how much your parents screwed up." She began to walk away. "Let's go. We have work to do."

"But . . ." I tried to formulate a rebuttal to anything she'd said, but she'd managed to insert something nice and I couldn't. I jogged after her, grabbing my coat from the banister. "Where are we going?"

"To find Rebecca. Do you know where she is?"

"In Ulmer."

This made her stop. "Do you know how to get there?"

I stopped, too, almost running into her. "I've been there once, with Jack. I think I remember the way. But it's about a two-hour drive."

She glanced at her watch. "Fine. I'll drive, then, and get us there in half the time."

I wanted to tell her no, to let her know that everything still wasn't okay and that I had missed her for every day of the thirty-three years she'd been away. But she'd said the word "we," and I found myself wanting to believe in second chances and starting over.

I slid into the passenger side of her brand-new sedan and leaned back into the leather seats, contemplating again how very much my life had changed in the relatively short time since I'd had the strange and unexpected inheritance of a historic home on Tradd Street.

CHAPTER 22

We rode mostly in silence. I was quiet because I knew if I said something, I'd be likely to break the tentative truce we had. I figured my mother was being silent for the same reason. She'd started out by asking me questions about my childhood, about dance lessons and best friends, but my clipped answers had probably hinted to her that she was approaching forbidden territory. To mask the silence, I'd found a satellite station playing all ABBA, but my mother quickly changed it to a classical station and we'd left it at that.

I called Yvonne on my cell to ask her about the earthquake casualty lists and she promised to make it a priority and call me back as soon as she found—or didn't find—anything, then returned to navigating our way to Ulmer from memory, making only one false turn.

I called the McGowans, too, but I reached only an answering machine. I left a message, explaining who I was and that I was on my way to see them. My eyes started drifting closed, lulled by the sound of the tires against asphalt, but I was jolted awake by my mother's voice.

"You do realize that a lot of operas are written in German, correct?"

I stared at her, wondering where this line of conversation was leading. "I'll take your word for it."

She grimaced and didn't look at me as she spoke. "I suppose that means you're not a fan of opera."

I didn't answer, not yet ready to tell her how when I was small, and my father wasn't watching, I'd flip channels in the hope of finding her singing somewhere in the world, and that in all of the years of flipping channels, I'd only seen her twice; but I'd never stopped hoping.

"I've been waiting for you to ask me what *Gefangener des Herzens* means."

I sat up straight, fully awake now. I'd completely forgotten that I'd even told her about it. "I've been meaning to plug it into Babel Fish, but it keeps getting pushed farther and farther down on my to-do list. I figured Daddy would know and I'd ask him when he came to trim back Grandmother's camellias tomorrow."

She turned to look at me. "What makes you think that your father would know?"

I shrugged. "Despite being less than reliable, he was the only go-to person I had while growing up, and he always seemed to have an answer."

A corner of her mouth turned upward. "That may be, but I doubt he knows what it means."

"So, are you going to tell me?" I said, sounding slightly peeved and feeling protective of my father.

"It means 'prisoner of the heart.'"

I rubbed the words over in my mind, like a thumb against a coin. "That's interesting. Rebecca thinks he might have been a Hessian soldier who deserted the British Army following the end of the Revolution. He may have been kept there unwillingly, but I wonder what the other part means."

"You can ask him, you know."

I didn't answer right away. Summoning spirits had been something my mother had done, but something I shied away from. I'd never wanted to call attention to my psychic ability, and had even hoped for a long time that if I ignored it, it would go away. Although I'd asked Wilhelm questions before, he'd avoided answering them, and I wondered if it was because I hadn't initiated the contact. "He always seems to find me first."

"We're running out of time, Mellie. I feel her in the house everywhere, not just in the back. We need to find out as much as we can now. But one thing you must be aware of before you summon Wilhelm: When you call him by name, you make him stronger."

I studied her profile for a long moment—the smooth curve of her chin and her long neck, the tight skin belying her age—then looked away. I'd wanted to ask her if she knew about Wilhelm from experience, and what else she knew but wasn't telling me. But the moment passed, the lure of a peaceful truce and companionship with my mother too strong to give up so soon. I let the questions go, allowing myself to be lulled into a half sleep.

As the miles slipped behind the car, I began to feel more and more unsettled, my skin prickling as if someone were blowing cold air on the nape of my neck. I twitched in my seat, and my mother glanced over at me before returning her attention to the road.

When we turned onto the long gravel drive leading up to Mimosa Hall, my mother turned to me. "Do you feel it, too?"

I nodded, again feeling the unfamiliar relief that I didn't need to explain anything to her—or hide anything. "My skin's burning with it," I confessed.

"Mine, too.

I looked at her with surprise. "I would never have guessed." She edged the car to the side of a large pothole. "That's because I've lived with it longer than you have. My mother showed me how to hide it."

I looked straight ahead as we approached the house, feeling now as if ants were running under my skin. My mother parked the car in the same spot Jack had left his on our previous visit and turned off the ignition. Rebecca's car was nowhere in sight.

"She's here," my mother said. "She's waiting for us."

I knew she wasn't referring to Rebecca, and I flinched, remembering my last visit and knowing there'd be no alcohol and no Jack this time to act as a buffer. My mother surprised me by taking my hand with her gloved one. "Together, we are strong enough to fight her. Remember that."

I studied her for a moment. "Then why didn't you stay? Before, when I was small. You keep telling me that you didn't leave because of me. Was it because of her? Because you couldn't fight her and I wasn't strong enough to help?"

She squeezed my hand. "There's so much I still need to tell you, Mellie, and I will—soon. I just don't think you're ready to hear it yet."

I pulled my hand away. "I'm almost forty years old, Mother. How much older do I have to be before you can trust me with the truth?"

Her eyes darkened. "It's not the truth I don't trust you with. It's your fear. You can't be afraid of what you don't know."

I shivered inside my coat. "Now you're scaring me. I'm not at all sure I want to do this."

"You must, Mellie. I'm here, and we will face this together, or we will never be free."

I noticed again how pale she looked, how tight her skin seemed to stretch over the fine bones of her face, realizing how she'd been that way since she'd touched the journal. When she put her hand on the door latch to open her car door, I placed my hand on her arm.

"There's something else that's been bothering me."

She looked at me and I noticed the dark circles under her eyes.

"I don't think I put the journal in the kitchen. I'd been reading it in my room before I went to sleep, and I left it inside the drawer of my bedside table. I might have moved it, but I don't think I did."

Her brows furrowed. "Why do you think it was moved?"

"Rebecca told me that I shouldn't let you touch it; she'd had a premonition and told me that it could be dangerous for you. I wasn't sure I believed her, and besides I couldn't see you willingly touching it again, but I kept it hidden from you and out of sight just in case. I wouldn't have brought it to the kitchen."

She nodded. "This other entity wants to use the journal to reach me in a negative way. She saw how the journal writer used it to communicate with me, and she saw an opportunity. It's a—portal of sorts. A way to communicate with those like us. But you have to make sure that you don't get the wrong spirit on the other end." She glanced toward the house. "Come on. Let's see if anyone's home."

I followed her out of the car and up to the steps leading to the wraparound porch. After not receiving an answer when I'd called earlier, I didn't expect anybody to be home. So I was surprised when I heard footsteps approaching the front door.

A plump woman in her late sixties with white hair and large blue eyes greeted us enthusiastically when she opened the door.

She introduced herself as Mrs. McGowan, then said, "You must be Melanie and her mother. I got your message that you were on the way. Come in, come in! What a day it's been for visitors!"

"Excuse me?" I asked.

"A reporter from the *Post & Courier* was here. She left about an hour ago. We must have been in the attic when you called and left your message."

I shared a glance with my mother. "Was her name Rebecca Edgerton?"

"Blond and perky?" Ginnette added.

"Yes, that was definitely her. Sweet girl. Is she a friend of yours?"

"Sort of. Yes, actually. We're working on a project together. As you've already gathered, I'm Melanie Middleton and this is my mother, Ginnette. When I was here before with Jack Trenholm and spoke with your husband, he showed me the portrait of the girl with the locket and we've been trying to determine her identity. Jack mentioned that you'd discovered some information in your attic that might be useful to us."

She put her hand to her chest and actually fluttered her eyelashes. "That Jack. Such a charming man. We've spoken on the phone several times, but I haven't had the pleasure of meeting him in person. He's promised to stop by and try some of my blueberry cobbler."

"He did mention that," I said as I followed my mother over the threshold. She gripped my arm as we stood in the foyer, and I knew that she'd felt the icy wind at our backs, too.

Mrs. McGowan shivered as she closed the door behind us. "Come on in. I've got a nice fire going in the family room. And I still have all the papers out that I was showing Rebecca, so no more trips up to the attic." We followed her, staying close together, then shrugged out of our coats before sitting on the sofa Mrs. McGowan indicated. "I just put a kettle on to boil, so if you'll excuse me, I'll go make us a nice pot of hot tea."

"We don't want to put you out," my mother began.

Mrs. McGowan waved away her protests. "I enjoy the company. And I just took out a batch of Scottish shortbread that I would love to share." She patted her ample waist. "George and I certainly don't need to be eating the whole thing." She laughed as she walked out of the room. Calling back to us, she said, "Feel free to look around, if you like. The portrait you were talking about is in the dining room off the entrance hall."

My mother stood and held her hand out to me, but I didn't stand immediately. "I've already seen it, and I don't want to repeat the experience, thank you."

My mother squatted down in front of the sofa. "Mellie, it's not going to go away just because you like to pretend it isn't there. It will be worse for you if she senses your fear." She stood again, and held out her hand. Not completely convinced that I was doing the right thing, I allowed her to pull me to my feet.

I led the way to the familiar spot in the dining room where I'd last seen the portrait. I stared at the girl with the familiar features, focusing on the heart-shaped locket with the initial *A* engraved in the middle. It was clear that there had to be some relation to the two girls in the other portrait, but that only added to the confusion. She couldn't be a Prioleau, but the family resemblance was there. And the other portrait had been found in my mother's attic, adding to the assumption that they were family members. Not to mention the fact that I bore a strong resemblance to them as well. I hoped Mrs. McGowan could shed some light into the murky corners of my family's past—and that Rebecca hadn't made off with the evidence again.

Ginnette. I startled at the sound of the voice that was now so familiar to me. But the relief that she hadn't been saying my name quickly evaporated when I realized she was speaking to my mother.

My mother reached for my hand, as if it were the most natural thing in the world. Her eyes were wide, but not with fear; it looked a lot more like determination. Her breaths were quick and shallow, and I looked at her with alarm. "Are you okay?"

She nodded. "She's trying to get inside my head, but I won't let her. Don't let go of my hand." She closed her eyes tightly and shook her head, as if she were answering a question I couldn't hear.

A cold wind circled us, slicing the air between us like a steel knife, sliding between our joined hands. I thought I heard a voice telling me to let go, but I couldn't be sure. Nausea rose in my throat as the putrid smell of dead things from the sea flooded my nose. Panic strangled the words I struggled to say. "I don't know how to do this. I don't know what to do."

Her voice was firm, calming me. "Just be strong. Don't listen to the voice, and keep telling yourself that you're stronger than she is. That *we're* stronger than she is—but only if we work together. You're not alone anymore, Mellie. I'm here."

Our eyes met, and I knew she was talking about way more than the mere matter of evil spirits. I looked away quickly, feeling the encircling cold as it continued to search for a way in. My mother's gloved fingers lifted from my hand, one by one as if being forced by unseen fingers, and for the first time I saw the fear in my mother's eyes.

"I'm stronger than you," I said out loud, grabbing my mother's hand with both of mine. But my grip was weak—my fingers boneless—and I felt her hand slipping from my grasp.

"*We* are stronger than you," I shouted and my grasp tightened.

"We are stronger than you," we shouted together, then stood still as the cold dissipated like a whisper, leaving only the faint scent of the ocean to remind us that she'd been there at all.

"Tea's ready." We both turned with a start to see Mrs. McGowan holding a tea tray brimming with mugs, spoons, and a plate of shortbread cookies.

"Let me take that," I said, taking the tray and feeling my mouth start to water at the sight of the cookies. My shaking hands were the only reminder of what I'd just experienced, and I tightened my grip on the tray to keep the mugs from jostling against each other.

We sat down and waited for Mrs. McGowan to add lemon and sugar to the tea. My mother and I each took four cookies, making our hostess regard us with a raised eyebrow. "I could go get more from the kitchen," she suggested.

"No, but thank you," I said, washing down my last bite with a sip of tea. "We must have both missed lunch." *Or fighting spirits burns a lot of calories.* I smiled. "And I must apologize again for showing up on such short notice. We were just, um, trying to show up at the same time as Miss Edgerton to make it easier on you."

"It's really no problem, dear. I love to help other people who are as interested in history as I am, and I don't get enough company as it is, seeing as how we live so far off the beaten path."

My mother leaned forward. "Melanie mentioned that you've been searching through the old documents of the Crandall family, who owned this house before your husband's family acquired it during the 1930s. We were hoping that you'd discovered the identity of the girl in the portrait."

"I have actually, and that's just what I was discussing with Miss Edgerton."

My heart beat a little faster. "That's wonderful. Could we please see what you found?"

"It would be my pleasure. I believe I mentioned to Jack on the phone that I remembered about some sort of family tragedy that occurred in the late 1800s, but I couldn't recall what it was. Most of what I have is in letters between Crandall family members in Connecticut and the branch who migrated down here to the coast of South Carolina."

She stood and began to rummage through a neat pile of yellowed envelopes stacked on the coffee table. "I've read through all of these so I'm fairly familiar with them. It's a bit like eavesdropping on history." Mrs. McGowan looked up at us with a wide smile. I stole a glance at my mother and wondered if I was wearing the same tight-lipped grimace she was in an attempt not to appear impatient. I glanced down at her crossed leg and watched as her foot bounced up and down.

I made a point to still my own. "It must be fascinating," I said. "So what did you find?"

Mrs. McGowan finally pulled out an envelope and carefully slid a fragile letter from it. "The letter is from William Crandall, of Mimosa Hall, to a Mrs. Suzanne Crandall of Darien, Connecticut, sister-in-law of Josiah mentioned in the letter and aunt to the girl in the portrait. I've gathered from other correspondence that William is the cousin of Suzanne's husband. It's rather sad, I'm afraid." She slipped a pair of reading glasses out of her pocket and put them on. "I'd rather it not be handled too much, at least not until I can get it into an archival album, so I'll read it aloud to you."

At our nods, Mrs. McGowan cleared her throat and began to read.

September 29, 1870

Dearest Suzanne,

It is with great sadness that I must tell you the news that weighs heavy on my heart. The ship carrying Josiah and your sister Mary, along with their daughter, Nora, has been lost at sea. We were hoping that their delay was for other reasons, but when a week went by past their expected arrival, we made enquiries into the whereabouts of their ship. The last contact with the captain and crew was when they dropped anchor at Wilmington, North Carolina, before heading down the coast. The captain was advised to delay his departure as a terrible storm was being predicted, but he felt confident that he could get ahead of it. Alas, it does not appear to be so as no sight has been made of the ship, its captain, crew, or twenty passengers. The only sign of the ship's fate is the discovery of the ship's figurehead on the beach at Edisto Island.

My heart breaks over the loss of your sister and her husband, and their little Nora, just an infant, lost forever in the clutches of the sea. I have taken the liberty of having a memorial service said for them, and have placed a marker in the family cemetery here.

How fortunate for young Alice, to have fallen so ill as to make her unsuitable for travel and thus to have been left behind in your tender care. She was spared the same watery fate as her parents and twin sister, and for this we must be grateful, even as our hearts grieve.

Your cousin,
William Crandall

Mrs. McGowan folded the letter and replaced it in the envelope. "I'm a little bit of an amateur genealogist and have been working on the Crandall family tree with information gleaned from these letters. Nothing serious, mind you, but just something that sparked my interest." She began rummaging through a stack of papers that had been placed inside a large three-ring binder.

My mother and I shared a glance before I asked, "So who is the girl in the portrait?"

Mrs. McGowan looked up at us, seeming confused for a moment. "Ah, yes. That's Alice Crandall. Daughter of Josiah and Mary, and twin sister to Nora, the child who perished on the ship with her parents. She remained in Connecticut, raised by her aunt Suzanne, until she was thirteen and the family moved down here to South Carolina. Alice lived here until she died in the 1920s, mercifully before the family lost the house and property during the Depression. Her son, Bill, had to deal with that."

I'd been hoping that one of the names would have had an *R* or *M*, something that would fill in a piece of the puzzle instead of adding to it. I would have even been willing to suggest that the Crandalls and their tragic story had nothing to do with us, that the girls and their identical lockets were merely coincidence.

My mother turned to me. Speaking softly, she said, "But then the girl's spirit wouldn't have followed us here."

I stared at her for a long moment, wondering if she'd even realized that I hadn't spoken my thoughts out loud. Maybe all mothers and daughters were like that, but I'd never had the chance to learn.

I turned back to Mrs. McGowan. "I'd like to see a Crandall family tree, if you have that handy."

Her forehead wrinkled. "That's what I've been looking for. That's odd. It was right here. I was showing it to Miss Edgerton, so it couldn't have gone far." She continued to flip through the binder. "I'm wondering if she accidentally picked it up with her things when she left."

Again, I shared a glance with my mother. "Probably. When I see her, I'll ask and let you know." I stood. "We can't thank you enough, Mrs. McGowan, for your time."

"And your cookies," added my mother as she stood, too. "You've been most helpful."

Mrs. McGowan escorted us to the door. "I've enjoyed it. Please come back anytime you want to discuss more of the family's history. It really is quite interesting. And bring Jack." She smiled and handed us our coats.

"One more thing," I said. "Do you have any idea of the name of the ship that sank with all on board?"

She shook her head. "No. It was never mentioned in any of the letters. Only that it sank in 1870 somewhere along the coast between North and South Carolina."

I nodded. "Well, that's a place to start. Thank you again," I said before turning and leading my mother from the porch.

We paused at the car, facing each other over the roof. My mother said, "Well, that wasn't a complete bust. We know the girl in the portrait is Alice Crandall, and she had a twin named Nora who went down with a ship in a storm in 1870. And that whoever is haunting the house on Legare is connected to this house in some way and wasn't very happy to see us today." She looked up as a heavy cloud lumbered its way over the sun. "We also know that for some reason Rebecca is reluctant to let us see the Crandall family tree."

I groaned in frustration. "None of this makes sense. I'm beginning to believe that none of it is even related to anything else."

My mother opened her car door. "Let's go eat dinner and we can discuss this more. I saw a nice seafood restaurant about five miles down the road on our way in."

I studied my mother, noticing the graying sky behind her head, and the way the fading light darkened her eyes, making them look more like mine. I sighed, realizing that regardless of the new yet tentative bonds that we'd begun to forge, there would always be parts of my life that my mother had opted out of; parts that would always be irretrievable. But along the way, those things had somehow begun to lose their significance. "I'm allergic to seafood, Mother. I had a severe reaction to shrimp when I was eight years old and I haven't touched it since." This wasn't completely true, as on my doctor's recommendation I'd tried it again as an adult and I'd had no reaction, but the small child in me wanted my mother to know that she hadn't been there in a moment when I'd needed her.

She was silent for a moment, her eyes sad as she contemplated me. "There's something you need to know, Mellie. . . ."

Her words were drowned out by the sound of an approaching car. We turned and I recognized Jack's black Porsche, puffs of dirt and gravel thrown behind it like exclamation points.

He pulled up next to us in the driveway, then climbed out quickly. Ignoring me, but with a quick greeting to my mother, he said, "Rebecca's already gone, I assume." He wore an unbuttoned and wrinkled oxford cloth shirt thrown over a white T-shirt, and he was still sporting a five o'clock shadow. I wanted to say that he looked disheveled, but the only thing that came to mind was how much he looked like he belonged on a magazine cover.

I faced him. "She left about an hour before we got here. How did you know she was here?"

"Yvonne called me, trying to reach you. Your cell phone must be out of range. She told me about the window and your grandmother, and how Rebecca has the folder with the information Yvonne had meant for you, and that the Crandall family tree is missing from the archives. I wanted to find Rebecca to set the record straight."

"Us, too. That's why we came here. And guess what. Mrs. McGowan can't find the Crandall family tree that she was working on, either. It went missing somewhere between the time Rebecca got here and the time she left. Go figure."

He narrowed his eyes at me. "I'm sure there's an explanation. Sometimes Rebecca gets really caught up in a story and she does—irresponsible things."

"Like stealing the journal from my kitchen? That's more than irresponsible, Jack. It's a criminal offense. And she's not returning any of my phone calls."

He rubbed his hand over his jaw and when he looked at me again, his eyes were hard. "I'll get to the bottom of it." He glanced at the house. "Did Mrs. McGowan have anything interesting to show you?"

"Besides the missing family tree? Yes, actually." I quickly filled him in on the identity of the girl in the portrait and the ship lost at sea.

He was thoughtful for a moment. "You said the ship was lost in 1870, correct?"

"Yes. Way too late for my ancestors—the supposed wreckers—to have been involved, if that's what you're thinking."

He raised both eyebrows. "The ship was lost off the South Carolina coast, and the figurehead was found not far from your family's plantation on Johns Island. It's a bit of a coincidence, don't you think?"

My mother stepped forward. "But surely our family's financial and social positions were secure enough by that time that such drastic actions weren't necessary."

Jack shrugged. "All I'm saying is that the ship went down near Johns Island. If any salvaging was done by anybody, it would have been a crime of circumstance seeing that it was Mother Nature who sunk the boat. The Civil War devastated the finances of many of Charleston's upstanding citizens, and the market for sea-island cotton, not to mention the difficulty in cultivating it without slave labor, would have made a huge cut in the Prioleau family fortunes. Who's to say that they wouldn't have seen an opportunity and taken advantage of it?"

"It's possible, I suppose," I admitted reluctantly. I didn't want to be related to anybody who could profit from another's loss. "But it still doesn't bring us any closer to the identity of the girl on the sailboat that was sunk nearly sixteen years later."

"Maybe it was Alice on the sailboat," Jack said.

I shook my head. "No. Mrs. McGowan said that Alice moved from Connecticut with her aunt to Mimosa Hall when she was thirteen and lived there until she died sometime in the 1920s. But she wore an identical locket to the one worn by the unidentified girls in the portrait in my mother's house. And if a girl named Meredith lived at Thirty-three Legare, then I have to assume it's probably her in the portrait with the *M* locket on."

Jack approached the car. "Not to confuse things"—he began as he reached into his back pocket and brought something out, keeping his fist closed over it—"but aren't you curious what Yvonne was so eager to tell you?"

"Yes, of course." I'd nearly forgotten the reason Jack was at Mimosa Hall in the first place.

"She found a casualty list from the Charleston earthquake of 1886." He paused for effect. "She found a listing for Meredith Prioleau. Missing, presumed dead. Her last known residence was Thirty-three Legare Street."

My mother stepped forward. "But why isn't this Meredith anywhere on our family tree?"

I rubbed my temple, feeling the beginning of a headache. "We found a calling card with Meredith's name and address in the journal, and the casualty list also gives her address as Legare Street. If we can make a leap of faith and say that she was probably the journal writer, I think we can assume that she's the girl in the portrait, too."

Jack nodded, his expression unreadable. "That's what I was thinking, too, until I picked this up today after having it cleaned."

A cold gust of wind caught my hair as Jack placed the gold locket and chain in my hand. At first I didn't recognize what it was because it now gleamed in the fading light.

My gaze met his. "I don't get it."

"Look closely."

Giving up on vanity completely, I squinted my eyes, staring at the single letter in the middle of the locket. Even in fading light and without glasses, it was clear to the naked eye that the last leg of the letter *M* had been added at a later time—and that the original letter on the locket had been an *N*.

I held it up to my mother, who had already slipped on her reading glasses. Slowly she raised her gaze to both of us. "This is just a shot in the dark, but since it's the only thing we have to go on right now, could the *N* have been for Nora?"

I'd been thinking the same thing. "But how could the locket have ended up in the sailboat sixteen years after Nora died? And why was it altered?"

After a final look, I slipped the locket into my purse as Jack scratched his head. "Look, why don't we all grab a bite to eat so we can discuss everything, see if we can reach any conclusions?"

Avoiding my gaze, my mother smiled brightly at Jack. "Thanks so much, but I need to get back home. But you and Mellie will certainly be able to figure things out without me."

"You can't go alone, Mother. I'll come with you."

"I'll call your father. He'll come."

I wasn't sure if that made me feel better or not.

She continued. "I'll be fine. You two go on."

It was clear she was trying to push me together with Jack, but I was equally sure that he wasn't too thrilled with the arrangement either.

As if the situation were settled, she returned to her car and opened the driver's-side door. Before she got in, she said, "One more thing, Mellie." She paused. "We made the ghost mad today. We showed her that together we're stronger than she is. She's going to try even harder now to separate us, to diminish our power. We need to find out who she is soon."

"Or what?"

She shook her head, the wind loosening the French twist and blowing her hair around her face, making her look vulnerable. "I don't want to find out."

She got in her car and with a brief wave, headed out of the drive.

Without a word, Jack opened the passenger-side door and indicated for me to get in. As he slid behind the steering wheel, he sent a glance in my direction. "Glad to see you didn't come back for more of a sampling of Mr. McGowan's brandy." His lips turned up at a memory he apparently didn't see the need to share with me.

About half an hour outside Ulmer, we pulled into a roadside restaurant advertising fried chicken, fried okra, and fried pie—my three favorite food groups—and settled into a booth in the corner. The restaurant smelled of stale smoke and grease, and an underlying aroma of beer and late nights that emanated from the bar and lit jukebox. I surreptitiously pulled out an antibacterial wipe from my purse and rubbed down the plastic red-and-white-checked tablecloth before pulling out a clean one to wipe my hands and vinyl booth cushion, seemingly held together by short strips of duct tape. I offered a wipe to Jack but he declined with a raised eyebrow and slow shake of his head.

The waitress came and took our orders and then, unnerved by Jack's pervading silent perusal of me, I pulled out a notepad from my purse. I drew two columns and as many rows as would fit on the page, then began filling in everything I'd learned since my mother first returned to Charleston and told me that I was in danger. Everything I still had questions about I put in the right column. Everything I had answers to I put in the left column. By the time I was finished, I'd run out of room in the right column and I had only two items in the left column: Meredith Prioleau wrote the journal and presumably the same Meredith Prioleau was listed as having lived at Thirty-three Legare Street and was reported as missing following the earthquake of 1886.

I held my pen poised above the pad, then looked up at Jack, wondering why he hadn't added anything or at least said something annoying. He was still shaking his head.

"What's the matter?"

His eyes met mine. After a moment he said, "You."

"Me?"

Again, he contemplated me in silence. "Yeah, I'm wondering what in the hell I'm doing here with you."

I hid my hurt with a frosty smile. "I assume because Rebecca isn't returning your phone calls and you didn't have anybody else to harass. Besides, I thought you were looking for research material for your next book. I know you'd never help me for purely altruistic reasons." I stared pointedly at him, hoping to remind him of the first time we'd sat in a similar restaurant eating barbecue shrimp while he lied to me and told me he was interested in everything but the diamonds that were hidden in my house.

Jack leaned forward, his eyes flashing, but he seemed to hold himself back from saying what he wanted to—something he might regret. Instead, he signaled for the waitress. "Make our order to go, please."

The waitress dropped the check on the table and as Jack reached for it, I placed my hand on his arm. "Are you still angry with me for the stupid things I said to you the night of the house tour? I already apologized for that, didn't I? And I truly am sorry. I thought we were friends again, Jack. Have I done something else to make you mad?"

The waitress reappeared with three grease-stained bags of food and a cardboard container with our two Cokes. Jack took one of the Cokes out and left it on the table before grabbing the bags. "The car only has one cup holder," he said in explanation before standing and moving toward the door.

I grabbed the remaining drink and followed him outside into a night that smelled of rain.

We drove the entire way back to Charleston in silence, without even the radio. I didn't dare open one of the bags despite the tantalizing aroma and my grumbling stomach, which I'm sure Jack heard over the roaring of the engine.

The sky opened up with a torrential downpour somewhere between Ruffin and Osborn, precluding me from speaking. I was miserable, wanting him to talk to me but dreading what he might say. I was afraid of him not being in my life anymore, but terrified of what he'd need me to do to keep him there.

My foot began to keep rhythm with the fast pounding of the windshield wipers until Jack put a hand on my leg to get it to stop. His touch was electric, sending little fires through my bloodstream as it traveled up my leg and back—like mercury in a thermometer—before settling somewhere in the pit of my stomach.

He must have felt it, too, because he let go quickly and returned to staring ahead in silence as he drove through the pelting rain.

We pulled up to the curb on Legare Street in front of the house, relief flooding me when I saw that the outdoor lights were on along with the majority of lights inside. I wondered fleetingly if my mother had done that for me, or for herself.

I turned to Jack. "Thanks for the ride. Do you by any chance have an umbrella?"

He turned to me with a slight smile that barely resembled the ones I'd grown so used to that I now missed them. "No. Actually, I don't. Never figured I'd melt."

"No, you wouldn't," I said under my breath. I thought of my hair, my suede jacket, and my Kate Spade pumps and frowned. Eyeing the large paper bags with the now-cold fried food, I said, "I don't suppose you'd let me take the food out and use the bags for cover."

He was looking at me with an odd light in his eyes. His voice was so soft that it was hard to hear over the splatting of rain against the car roof. "Go ahead and get wet, Mellie. Do something unscheduled and unexpected for a change."

"If you'd just let me use one of those bags . . ."

He didn't let me finish my sentence. Instead he took my head in his hands and crushed his lips to mine. I was so shocked at first that I didn't move. And then I felt his hands in my hair, and the roughness of his chin, and the way his lips fit mine as if they were supposed to be together. I closed my eyes and I think I sighed as I pressed back and gave in to the fire that had begun to lick at the base of my spine.

I jerked back, suddenly remembering whom I was with, and who I was, and that I had a reason for not kissing Jack but with only a fuzzy recollection as to exactly what that might be. Panicking, I grabbed the door handle and hurtled out into the pouring rain, slamming the door before running for the front gate. I managed to unlatch it and had reached the top step before Jack caught up to me.

He pulled me into his arms and pressed me against the front door so that I felt the entire hard length of his body against mine, and I shivered despite the heat that seemed to resonate through every limb. Those same limbs no longer seemed able to support me, and I reached my arms around Jack's neck, allowing him to press me into the door so I wouldn't fall.

His lips were hard and insistent and I found myself opening to him, losing myself in the strength and warmth that was Jack. I closed my eyes, tasting rain and skin and Jack, seeing behind my eyelids a kaleidoscope of colors I hadn't known existed.

Then, inexplicably, he stopped and pulled back, his eyes dark and unreadable. We were both breathing heavily and I was perilously close to asking him to do it again.

"And that, Melanie Middleton, wasn't an almost kiss. That was the real thing." He turned the doorknob, and pushed open the door, revealing Sophie, Chad, and both of my parents standing in the foyer—suddenly trying to pretend they'd been doing anything other than listening.

Like Rhett Butler dumping Scarlett O'Hara at Ashley's birthday party, Jack made a formal bow—which managed not to look ridiculous even though he was dripping wet—said his good-byes, and left without another word.

CHAPTER 23

I woke up hearing someone calling my name, the smell of gunpowder, and the sound of clinking metal floating in the air like an afterthought.

"Wilhelm?" I called out softly.

My door crept open as an icy finger of air stole into the room.

I slid out of bed, careful not to disturb General Lee, and walked out into the hallway, my sock-clad feet padding softly on the wooden floor.

I saw a shimmer of light at the bottom of the stairs, and paused as I watched Wilhelm's progression toward the kitchen. I ducked back into my room to retrieve the flashlight I now kept on my nightstand and then, without giving myself time to rethink my actions, I hurried down the stairs, following him into the darkened kitchen.

"Wilhelm?" I shivered, the pervading chill in the room permeating the flannel of my nightgown. I turned my flashlight on and scanned the kitchen, taking in the closed door to the back staircase and the gaping hole behind the fireplace.

Cautiously, I moved forward, shining my flashlight into the secret room. I caught a flash of curling gold hair under a Hessian's tricorn hat, then climbed into the fireplace and through the small opening, shining my flashlight on the beamed ceiling on the carved words.

"*Gefangener des Herzens,*" I said. I looked sideways at Wilhelm and saw that he was smiling. "What's so funny?'

Your accent. It is really quite bad.

I almost made the mistake of looking directly at him, but managed to sigh heavily. "Prisoner of the heart," I said. "What does it mean?"

That is not why I brought you in here.

I kept my eyes focused on the beam. "Then why? I've already looked in the chest. It's empty."

You have not looked everywhere.

"I don't know what you mean. Where haven't I looked?"

He walked slowly to the corner of the room, his boots thudding softly against the dirt floor. *Here. You have not looked here.*

I moved my flashlight to the corner, the light shining through him, and illuminating nothing but brick wall and dirt floor. "There's nothing there," I said, feeling impatient.

Look harder.

I stepped closer, moving the flashlight in an arc, catching more of the bricks and dirt and his shiny black boots but nothing else. Frustrated, I repeated, "There's nothing here."

"Wilhelm."

I moved the flashlight back to the opening, watching as my mother crawled through it. From the corner of my eye, I spotted the soldier placing his hat against his chest and bowing. *Ginnette.*

She came to stand next to me. "Did you ask him what he meant by 'prisoner of the heart'?" Her warm hand found mine and I realized she wasn't wearing her gloves. In unison we both turned toward him and for the first time in my life, I saw him in solid form; I could see the blue of his eyes and the pink, ridged scar on his temple. I could even see the repaired hole on his jacket sleeve and the cleft in his chin. My mother squeezed my hand and I knew she noticed, too.

Our gazes met and he seemed as surprised as me that he was still there. And then he looked at my mother and his expression softened. *It has been too long.*

A soft smile illuminated her face. "Tell us, Wilhelm. Why are you a prisoner of the heart?"

I cannot tell you. It is my shame.

I stepped toward him, still holding my mother's hand. "We could never pass judgment on you. You're our protector, and you've saved me more than once. I can only feel gratitude toward you."

Because you do not know.

"What was her name?" my mother asked. "The girl who held your heart captive."

Look harder. In the corner.

"We will. But first we need to know her name."

I could feel his spirit wanting to leave, but my mother and I held him in place, unwilling to let him go until we had an answer.

"Tell us her name, Wilhelm. Is it the girl who wrote the journal?"

He smiled. *Meredith. No. It was not Meredith. I saved her when she was a baby.*

"Then who was she?" I asked.

"If you tell us, we can help you find forgiveness. Help you move on from this place," my mother added.

His eyes emptied of light. *I am destined to protect the women in your family. Meredith showed me how. And now it is my penance.*

"For what?" I asked.

His sigh echoed in the cold, empty room, settling in our ears and our hearts. *For my betrayal. For allowing her to die.*

"How did she die?" I asked.

She drowned. I did not know she was on the ship. I did not know to save her.

"Who?" My mother's voice was barely a whisper.

Catherine.

We exchanged glances and when we looked back at Wilhelm, he was gone.

"Who is Catherine?" Ginnette asked.

I closed my eyes, trying to see the Prioleau family tree in my mind, knowing that Catherine was one of the names on the earlier part of the tree. I'd studied it so many times that I nearly had it memorized. "She was Joshua's daughter. I remember her because she died so young, nineteen or twenty, I think. And also because it was on my birthday, July fifteenth. She lived here right after the Prioleaus purchased the house in 1781. Right around the time the British troops abandoned the city, which lends credence to Rebecca's assumption that Wilhelm chose to stay behind in Charleston. Maybe he was in love with Catherine and he willingly remained for her."

"He wouldn't have been a prisoner if he stayed here willingly. Maybe

Wilhelm was here in secret and her father found out, or he knew all along, and forced Wilhelm to stay as an unpaid worker in return for keeping him hidden, and for room and board. And Wilhelm did it, but only because he loved Catherine."

"But she died. Because of him," I said slowly. "She was on a ship that sank, and he was there but didn't save her because he didn't know she was on it." *They were wreckers, Mellie. Your illustrious ancestors started out as wreckers.* Jack's words taunted me, but I couldn't—wouldn't—jump to conclusions without some kind of proof.

Our gazes met for a moment and I watched as her eyes widened. "We both saw him, and he was solid. He was stronger and we were giving him that strength because we were together and wanting him here. We're an amazing team, Mellie."

Before I could decide if I agreed or should resent what she said, she tugged on my hand. "Come on, let's go."

"To where?"

"To turn on the lights. I don't want to be stuck in here in the dark just in case you know who decides to pay us a visit. I doubt that she will because we're both here, but I'd like to be safe. I don't think Wilhelm would be able to return so soon; it would have taken most of his strength to appear that solid for as long as he did."

She stopped to allow me to exit through the opening first, then followed me. I waited with my eyes focused on the closed door leading to the back stairs until she flipped on the light. Our gazes locked again. "How did you know I was down here?" I asked.

She shrugged. "Mother's intuition, I suppose. I awoke and knew somehow that you weren't in your room. I went downstairs and followed the sound of your voice."

As she spoke, I looked around at the mess in the kitchen, the workers' tools strewn over the floor as they awaited my decision as to what to do next. My gaze rested on a shovel that lay on the floor with the pile of removed bricks.

I walked over to it and picked it up. "We need to go back in there."

"What for?"

"Wilhelm keeps telling me that there's something in that room. And tonight, when he first brought me in there, before we asked him about

Catherine, he told me that I need to look harder. He kept indicating the far right corner. Maybe there's something buried under the dirt."

Ginnette pursed her lips, unsure. "Can we wait until daylight?"

"Could you sleep knowing that a possible answer to the thousands of questions we keep asking ourselves is just as far as a quick dig in the floor?"

She took a deep breath. "You're right." She moved toward the opening and flipped on her flashlight. "I'll hold the light while you dig."

For the second time that night, I climbed through the opening. While my mother held the flashlight, I began digging in the hard, compacted earth. It was made more difficult by the fact that I couldn't stand completely upright, and by the back pain I experienced from the first jarring blow of trying to dig the shovel vertically into hard ground.

Getting the hang of it, I began to scrape the ground with the shovel, lifting off one thin layer of dirt at a time. My mother suggested calling Jack for help, but my reaction was the same as hers when I suggested we call my father instead. So I slowly dug a shallow hole in the corner of the hidden room until my neck and lower back were nearly numb.

I was unaware of the passage of time, but when I didn't think I could take one more pass at the impacted earth, the tip of the shovel nicked something solid. I glanced at the glare of light behind which I knew my mother watched. "Come closer and shine it down here."

She did as I asked and we both knelt on the cold dirt, staring down at whatever it was that I'd hit.

"It looks like bone china. Maybe a handle of some sort."

I nodded. "I was about to say the same thing. But I'm afraid I'll break it if I continue digging it out with the shovel." I sat back on my haunches, dropping the shovel and rubbing my face. "I'm going to go grab one of the hammers and one of your grapefruit spoons. I can use the claw back of the hammer to dig around the perimeter of the china piece, while you use the grapefruit spoon for the close-up work."

She frowned. "Sophie was just telling me how valuable the family silver I found in the attic is. I wonder what she'd say."

"I wasn't planning on telling her," I said, raising my eyebrows meaningfully. Standing again, but remembering to keep my neck bent, I said, "I'll be right back."

My mother stood at the opening waiting for me to grab the items, and then we returned to the shallow hole in the corner. We placed both of our flashlights on the ground, their beams illuminating our workspace. We worked for almost an hour, digging out a spoonful at a time, uncovering a delicate china teacup. By the time we realized we'd loosened the dirt around it enough to be able to pull it out from its prison, our anticipation was almost palpable.

Sinking back on my haunches, I turned to my mother. "I suppose you don't want to be the one to touch it first."

She shook her head. "Not yet, anyway."

I nodded, then slowly sank both of my hands into the shallow hole and lifted out the blue-and-white china teacup. Looking over our discovery to my mother, I smiled. "It's intact. I think it might be Delft."

She leaned over to see it better. "Hold it down here, Mellie, so I can shine my flashlight into the bottom. I think there's something written on the inside of the cup."

I lowered the cup so that it rested on the ground, but kept my hands on it to steady it. Our heads nearly touched as she shone the arc of light into the cup, allowing us to see the bottom.

An imprint of an old-fashioned triple-masted schooner, once used as fast-moving cargo ships, filled the bottom of the cup. Printed in a semicircle under the picture of the ship were the words "Ida Belle."

Our gazes met over the cup. "What do you think this means?" I asked.

"All I can say for sure is that this was most likely from a china set made for and probably used aboard a ship called the *Ida Belle*. And it means something to Wilhelm, and he wants us to know what it is." She paused for a moment. "We can summon him, Mellie. And ask him."

I shook my head. "He'll fight it. He's ashamed to tell us, but he's given us enough clues to figure it out ourselves. And it will take too much of our strength to summon him now."

"You feel it, too?"

I nodded. "Ever since we started digging, I feel as if she's been watching us, feeding us hatred. She's waiting. Waiting to make her move. We need to be ready."

"Yes." I watched as a shudder racked her body. "It's cold in here. Let's take the teacup and get some sleep. I'll leave the connected door open between our rooms."

She didn't ask or make it a suggestion, because she seemed to know that I'd want it opened just as much as I would be too embarrassed to acknowledge it. "All right," I said, walking past her with the teacup held gingerly in my hands. "If it makes you feel better."

She didn't say anything but I thought I saw her smile as I stepped through the opening into the kitchen, feeling her close behind me.

The doorbell rang the next morning around eight o'clock. I'd already been up and dressed, organized my closet, and done an unsuccessful Internet search for the *Ida Belle*, so I rushed down the stairs to reach the door before it awakened my mother.

My father stood on the front step with a bouquet of pink roses and something else tucked under his arm. "Good morning, Melanie. I brought something for you, and I figured I should bring something for your mother, too."

"Hi, Daddy." I opened the door and allowed him into the foyer. "Mother's still sleeping. Follow me to the kitchen and we'll put those flowers in a vase next to the others." I raised an eyebrow, seeing if he'd caught my sarcasm. Since he'd begun to re-landscape the yard and garden, the house never seemed to lack for flowers—pink roses in particular. I had deliberately tried not to pay attention to the amount of time my parents spent together, but I couldn't help but notice that my mother seemed to spend a lot of time at restaurants around town discussing the garden with my father.

He handed me the flowers and I took them to the sink to cut off the stem bottoms before making room for them in the overflowing vase on the table. He walked over to the fireplace and peered inside. "Your mother told me about this room. Shame you didn't find anything useful after all the trouble."

"Actually, we did. Mother and I did a little digging last night and found a teacup, apparently from a ship called the *Ida Belle*. Haven't had any luck discovering anything about it, yet, but I've only just started."

"You should give Jack a call."

I felt the color rushing to my cheeks, remembering the previous night and all its witnesses. "I don't think he really wants to talk to me."

He raised his eyebrows and stared pointedly at me. "You might be right, Peanut. He sure didn't seem to be wanting to do a lot of talking last night."

I held my hand up. "Stop, okay? You're not really the relationship expert, are you? Besides, I don't know what that was about. All I know is that he's really angry with me and hasn't been answering my phone calls. Last night was just an aberration."

"Is that what they're calling it nowadays?" He walked toward me, pulling out whatever it was that he'd been carrying under his arm. "Anyway, he came over this morning and gave me this to give to you."

He held out Meredith's journal and after a moment's hesitation, I took it. "He gave you this? Where did he get it?"

"Apparently from Rebecca's condo."

"She gave it to him?"

"Not exactly." He cleared his throat, embarrassed. "Rebecca wasn't there."

"He broke into her apartment?" I found that hard to believe, even for Jack.

My father began to studiously examine the roses behind me. "Actually, he had a key so he let himself in."

I licked my lips, wondering if there was anything I could say to that and decided that there really wasn't. I looked down at the journal. "So Rebecca did take it. Did Jack tell you why?"

My dad shook his head. "No. But he did mark a couple of pages that he wanted to make sure you'd read." He reached over and flipped the journal open where a small slip of paper had been stuck and I began to read.

W showed me the secret room behind the wall in the kitchen pantry. I had to wait until R went for a stroll with C because she cannot know about it. Everything that is special to me, my cat for instance, my favorite book, or my prettiest dress, she finds a way to destroy. So I have stopped sharing things with her, even this discovery of a secret room in a house she has lived in all of her life. I am glad she cannot see W, because then she would find some way to make him go away and I would be all alone.

W kept telling me to look harder, to find what he wants me to find, but all that I saw in the room was an empty sea captain's chest. I think W is purposefully obtuse, wanting me to figure it out on my own. He says it is because of his shame, that he cannot stand to disappoint me by telling me what he did. He will only confess that what is in the room will be the thing that will illuminate the truth, and maybe even free him from his prison. But I need to solve this for myself—if only I could. I am so confused; W told me that he saved my life and that in return, I could save his.

I looked up at my father. "Did you read this?"

He nodded. "Didn't make a lot of sense to me, except for maybe the hidden room. I'm assuming this room used to be the pantry. Who's W?"

"I'm not sure," I said slowly. "But I think the teacup is what he wanted her to find."

"And how would you know that?" he asked in the way I'd grown familiar with—his warning signal that I couldn't answer with something he would refer to as "hocus-pocus."

Instead of answering, I handed him the journal. "What was the other page Jack wanted me to see?"

With a pointed look, my father took the book and opened it to the inside back cover where we'd found Meredith Prioleau's calling card. Somebody—and my bet would be on Rebecca—had pried off the rest of the glued page, exposing an ink drawing of an angel head and wings, the bottom of the body disappearing in a triangle. I looked up to meet his eyes. "It's an image from the window. Look."

I went to my purse on the counter and pulled out my cell phone where I still had the photo of the window. "It's not really clear, but when I zoom in on that section it's obvious it's the same thing."

He took the phone and stared at the picture of the window, then back to the page. "What in the world is it?"

"I don't know. But it seems that Meredith—whoever she is—might have known about the window and the hidden images. Or somebody else drew the image inside the journal much later because the journal predates the window." I rubbed my temple, trying to get the facts to shuffle into an order I could understand.

My dad scratched his ear, a familiar sign to me that he was about to tell me something I didn't want to hear. "Mellie, Rebecca was here a couple of days ago. I was working in the garden and she was asking me a lot of questions about the flowers and plantings and what I had planned. But whenever she thought I wasn't watching, she was taking pictures of the window. Lots of pictures."

"Who was taking pictures?" We both turned around to see my mother standing in the threshold with General Lee in her arms. She put him down and he ran to his newly installed doggy door.

"Rebecca," I answered. Then I held up the journal. "Jack got the journal back from Rebecca and gave it to Daddy." I turned the journal around to show her the drawing. "It's on the page that was glued to the back cover."

She stepped closer but didn't touch it. "So you're thinking the writer knew my mother, and knew why the window was changed."

"Yes."

She nodded, thinking for a moment. "What about the ship? Have you had a chance to go online?"

"I did, and I got a lot of hits related to baby names, handmade soaps, and an Iowa family genealogy. Just nothing that could have been the ship we're looking for."

"You should call Jack."

I looked at my father, then back to my mother, wondering if they were conspiring against me. "No. I shouldn't call Jack. As I explained to Daddy, Jack doesn't really want to have anything to do with me." I caught them exchanging a glance over my head.

"I'm going to call Yvonne at the historical society and see if I can come in this morning."

My dad reached into his coat pocket. "One more thing I brought for you, Mellie. I found this with all the other pictures I took from the house. I was going through them again last night and I came across this one and thought you might like to see it. I remembered you telling me that you wished you had a picture of Rose as an adult, so when I saw her name written on the back of this photo, I knew I had to bring it to you."

I flipped the photo over, expecting to see a short, fat woman with a cane. Instead I saw a picture of a tall, lean, handsome couple dressed in clothing from the earlier part of the twentieth century, smiling at the camera and standing on an embankment in front of a very tall waterfall. I turned the photo over and read in faded blue ink, "Rose and Charles Manigault, Niagara Falls. Honeymoon, January 1900."

I looked at my parents. "Come with me," I said before leaving the kitchen and heading toward the drawing room where the portrait of the two girls still sat against the unpainted wall. I held the photograph in my hand up to the portrait, comparing them. "Now I'm positive that the girl wearing the *R* locket can't possibly be Rose." I continued to compare the two girls. Although separated in age by at least five years, I could see that the shape of the face of the girl in the portrait was rounder, her shoulders wider, her eyes harsher. The young woman in the photograph had a light about her, an aura that made you think she was your friend. And I remembered what I'd thought the first time I'd seen the shorter girl in the portrait, how her eyes held a secret, a secret I didn't necessarily want to know.

Then my gaze shifted to the other girl in the portrait, the one wearing the locket with the initial *M* engraved on the front and saw again the widow's peak—a widow's peak just like the one my mother and I had, and a pair of eyes that tilted up at the corners.

My mother looked at me and I knew her thoughts echoed mine. "But she could definitely be her," she said, pointing to the taller girl—M as I referred to her—who stared back at us from the canvas with eyes that were identical to my own.

CHAPTER 24

As I drove to the historical society library on Meeting Street, I dialed Mrs. McGowan's number one more time, hoping I wouldn't get the answering machine again. As I dialed the final digit, a new call came in and I sighed with relief when I recognized the McGowans' phone number.

"Hello—Mrs. McGowan?"

"Yes, good morning, Melanie. I'm sorry I didn't call you back sooner, but I've been out in my garden. My camellias are simply beyond gorgeous this year. I'll be happy to send you home with a clipping next time you're here."

"Thank you, Mrs. McGowan. That would be lovely. But what I'm calling you about this morning is the Crandall family tree. Have you had any luck in locating it?"

"No, dear. And I have looked all over for it. Did you ask Miss Edgerton?"

"I haven't had a chance to. But I really need to know if a name appears anywhere on the family tree. I'm just looking for any connection, by marriage or by birth. You mentioned to me that you'd created the family tree by going through the family letters you found in the attic, and I was wondering if it would be possible to do it again."

After only a short pause she said, "Of course I can. When would you need it?"

I cringed, hating myself for doing this. "As soon as possible—like today? I wouldn't need anything detailed, just the name and how the person is related to the rest of the Crandall family."

There was a longer pause this time, and then she said, "I can do it, but I'm going to ask you for something in return."

"Yes?" I asked, dreading what was coming next because I could think of only one thing that she might want that I might be able to give to her.

"Could you bring that lovely Jack Trenholm here so I could meet him? I've read all of his books, and he sounds so charming on the phone. I really would love to meet him in person."

I groaned inwardly. I would have to ask Chad or Sophie or even either one of my parents to ask him, but I figured who got him there wasn't important; Jack Trenholm showing up on Mrs. McGowan's porch step was.

"Sure," I said. "I'd be happy to."

"Okay, then. I'll get to work right away, as soon as I get these camellias in vases. They really are lovely. It would be super to bring Jack now when the weather's mild and I can show him my garden."

"I'll see what I can do." I gave her the name I'd originally come up with on a whim, until it seemed that the more I thought of it, the more certain I was that I was right. "Just call me on this number as soon as you have the information. If I don't answer, that means I'm still at the library and I won't be able to talk, so if you could please just leave a detailed message."

"All right," she said. "And I hope that one day you'll tell me what this is all about. I'm very intrigued."

"It's a deal. Thank you, Mrs. McGowan." I flipped my cell phone closed and tossed it into my purse just as I pulled onto Meeting Street. Lacking the Jack Trenholm touch, I once again had to search for a parking spot, finally finding an open one several blocks away. I was panting by the time I returned to the Fireproof Building and climbed the steps.

Yvonne was waiting for me as usual in the reading room and greeted me with a smile. I smiled back and said, "I'm assuming your good mood means that you were successful in finding the *Ida Belle*."

"You've yet to stump me, Melanie, but you're welcome to keep on trying."

I sat down at the table and she surprised me by sliding over a laptop.

"It's my personal computer. I bring it here sometimes so I don't have to walk around so much. I have access to all the library's databases. Not that I needed them for this search."

I sent her a questioning look. "What do you mean? I didn't turn up anything on my preliminary Internet search."

She flipped open her laptop. "You'll have to excuse the slowness. It's an old laptop and I have a really slow connection." She mashed on the power button and I heard the computer come to life with a slow grinding noise, like gerbils on a spinning wheel. Yvonne continued. "The Internet is a great thing, but only when you use it correctly. You have to know how to narrow down your query first, before you can expect to find the results you're looking for." She leaned forward, peering over the tops of her bifocals. "Jack taught me that, by the way."

I gritted my teeth, then squinted to see the laptop screen better.

"You'll get wrinkles," she said without looking at me as she started typing slowly, just using her index fingers. Being a fast typist myself, I had to restrain myself from asking her to move aside to let me type.

"We know the *Ida Belle* was a three-masted schooner, which more or less gives me a time period to work with. Logic would tell us to start looking here in South Carolina, and then extend our search to North Carolina and Georgia and so on until we find what we're looking for."

She pecked a few more keys on the keyboard and I had to dig my fingernails—what was left of them—into my palms to keep from reaching over and doing it myself. "What a lot of researchers overlook is the variety of museums we have nowadays—science, technology, art, history, that sort of thing."

I leaned forward. "So you did a search on nautical museums."

"Uh-huh," she said as she triumphantly hit the ENTER key. "And I got a hit on the *Ida Belle* when I visited the North Carolina Maritime Museum Web site."

I stared at the screen as an image slowly emerged like a secret not wanting to be divulged. I stared at the very familiar image of an angel with long, flowing hair and abundant wings, re-created on the computer in all of its three-dimensional glory. Instead of the familiar flattened image on stained glass, this was carved wood, with weathered and chipped paint that spoke of untold stories. "What is it?" I asked.

Yvonne twisted the laptop toward me so I could see it better. "It's the figurehead from the *Ida Belle*. It was found on Edisto Island. The storm that sank the ship most likely sent it there, but there's no way of knowing."

My head felt like it was filled with effervescent bubbles rising to the surface as I realized I'd just made a considerable discovery. I just had no idea yet what it meant. "Does the site say anything else about the shipwreck?"

Yvonne nodded. "There was a link to another page that was all about shipwrecks including the big ones like *Titanic* and *Lusitania*. But there was a small footnote about shipwrecks off the coast of the United States and one of them listed was the *Ida Belle*, which included a note about the cargo and a link to the passenger list. You might not have seen it when you did your preliminary search because it was listed under its original name, the *Victoria*. It was sold and rechristened a year before it sank, and named after the wife of the ship's captain. I actually came across that little gem by accident in a book we have here in the archives, naming every ship whose port of origin was Charleston. That's how I knew to search for the *Victoria*."

"Do you have the passenger list?"

With an admonishing glance for doubting her abilities again, she slid over two pieces of paper. "I printed these from the Web site."

I found the three names easily, listed near the top: Josiah Crandall; Mary Crandall; Nora Crandall, infant. All had "Darien, Connecticut" printed next to their names. Slowly, I flipped to the next page, which appeared to be a photocopied page of an insurance claim made by a Suzanne Crandall for jewelry amounting to the total sum of twenty thousand dollars—a nice bit of change now, but almost a fortune for back then.

Moving my hand up to my face so Yvonne couldn't see, I squinted to read the fine print on the claim. It read like a laundry list: emerald-cut ruby cocktail ring surrounded by twelve diamonds set in gold; one diamond butterfly hairpin with three large diamonds set in platinum; sapphire-and-diamond chandelier earrings, pierced, with matching sapphire-and-diamond collar necklace consisting of . . .

I sat back, my eyes hurting from squinting, and my head spinning. *Sapphire-and-diamond chandelier earrings, pierced, with matching sapphire-and-diamond collar necklace.*

Quietly, I said, "I'm betting the jewelry wasn't found on the bottom of the ocean floor."

My phone buzzed and I looked down to see that someone had left me a voice mail. Turning to Yvonne I gave her an impulsive hug. "You are worth your weight in gold, Mrs. Craig, and I will be thinking of ways to thank you for the next decade or so."

She looked up at me in surprise as I slid back my chair. "I've got to go. I'll give you a call later to tell you everything." With a quick smile and a wave, I left the room, running down the steps and nearly tripping in my hurry to listen to my voice mail.

I hit the button on my phone and held it up to my ear, realizing that I was holding my breath only when I began to feel faint. Taking air into my lungs again, I began to listen.

"Hello, Melanie, dear, this is Mrs. McGowan. I think I found what you were looking for. Alice Crandall, who as you know was the twin of the girl Nora lost in the shipwreck and who moved to Mimosa Hall when she was a teenager, had a son and a daughter. The daughter, Allison, married a John Edgerton. Descendants of Allison and John live not too far away in Summerville, although I've never met them. I'm curious, Melanie, if this family is any relation to your friend, Rebecca? I'm assuming that's why you wanted to know, although I'm surprised she didn't mention it when she was here and saw the family tree. If you need any more information, please call me. And I look forward to meeting Jack and seeing you again soon. Good-bye."

I stood in the middle of the sidewalk as people brushed by me, too stunned to move out of the way. Rebecca was related to the Crandalls of Mimosa Hall, and to the girl in the portrait, Alice, but had kept the information to herself. And I had every intention of finding out why. As I walked to my car, I dialed her numbers again, receiving the expected voice mails, then started dialing Jack's cell before I could talk myself out of it. I hung up before the first ring. I wasn't sure where our relationship—whatever it was—stood after the previous night, when he'd kissed me in the rain. I was planning to never mention it, in the ridiculous hope that he might have forgotten about it. Still, despite everything, he was the first person I wanted to talk to about my recent discovery, and since I wasn't too far from his condo, I decided to just show up. Besides, I doubted he'd answer his phone and I'd already had a lot more luck begging entry on his doorstep.

I parked my car in a nearby garage and was pleasantly surprised to see the entry door to his building propped open to allow a moving company easy access to move in furniture from a large truck parked at the curb in front. Smiling as if I belonged there, I walked past the moving men to the elevator and confidently hit the button for the top floor. I relaxed only after the door opened on Jack's floor and I exited the elevator, waiting for it to close behind me for good measure.

My smile faded, however, when I reached Jack's door. It wasn't closed completely, as if maybe he'd been bringing in groceries and had to close the door with his foot and hadn't noticed that it hadn't latched.

I knocked and waited and when I didn't hear anything, I knocked again and called his name. After about a minute, I pushed open the door a little wider and called his name a little louder. I was about to leave when I noticed that his bedroom door was closed, and I thought that he might be sleeping or taking a shower and that he probably wouldn't mind if I sat and waited for him.

Leaving the door slightly open—for no other reason than to prove to him that that's how I'd found it—I walked into the main living area, forcing myself not to make any judgment calls about the mess or to start cleaning anything. My gaze settled on the glass-and-bronze dining table that had been cleared of its iron candelabras and centerpiece bowl— they'd been carelessly stacked in a corner of the dining area—and was covered with stacks of books and what looked like photographs organized in some kind of a pattern. Thinking to myself that since it was out in the open it couldn't be private, I walked closer to get a better look.

I moved around to the other side of the table to examine the photographs and had to stare at them for a long moment until I could tell what they were. They were apparently the pictures Jack had taken at my grandmother's grave the day Rebecca, Jack, and I had gone to St. Philip's cemetery. He'd blown up each of the photographs and cropped them so that each word was separated into its own rectangular picture. I looked at them closely, trying to see anything new or telling from these photographs, but I was unable to do so.

I looked to the last row of photographs, which weren't from the tombstone but of the stained-glass window as seen from the outside at the precise moment the sun hit it correctly to illuminate the hidden image. This picture, too, had been separated into individual photographs. I recognized portions of what I knew now to be the figurehead, and the house, and the oak tree. But he'd also taken the odd border that encircled the entire window and cropped it into individual photographs, laying them out so that they appeared to be in the order in which they appeared in the window. I stared at the pictures closely, noticing that some of the seemingly random markings were thicker and larger than the others, and I wondered if Jack had noticed it, too, and what he thought it meant.

I walked to the other end of the dining table to where the stacked books, some lying open on top of each other, were arranged. I peered at several of the titles, realizing with a start that they all had something to do with ships, shipwrecks, and the maritime history of the southeastern United States. I picked up the top book and scanned the open page. At the bottom were three paragraphs that had been highlighted with a yellow highlighter. Bringing it close to my face and squinting so I could see it, I read the passage three times, just to make sure that I'd read it correctly.

The entire passage concerned the disappearance in clear weather of a British schooner bound from Charleston to Boston in 1785. It was last seen near Johns Island on the fifteenth of July, and no further news of the ship or its crew and passengers was ever heard again.

I pressed my hand to my chest, realizing that it was the sound of my heart beating that I was hearing echo in the quiet room. *Catherine.* Wilhelm's Catherine had died in July of 1785. I remembered the date because it had been on my birthday—July fifteenth. I remembered what Wilhelm had said about her—how she died. *She drowned. I did not know she was on the ship. I did not know to save her.*

I flipped the book over to read the title: *Pirates of the Land: Eighteenth- and Nineteenth-Century Wreckers along the Southeastern Coast of the United States.*

I was distracted by a noise coming from Jack's bedroom—a low throaty chuckle that didn't sound like him at all. I took a step toward the bedroom and that's when I noticed the woman's high-heeled shoe, a pair of stockings, and a purse lined up like a bread-crumb trail that stopped directly in front of the bedroom door.

The pink patent leather high-end purse was familiar to me, and as I stared at it the door handle turned and the door opened to reveal Rebecca Edgerton clad in nothing else but one of Jack's oxford cloth shirts.

She seemed as surprised to see me as I was to see her, but she recovered more quickly. While I stood there with my jaw hanging and trying to think of something to say, she retrieved her clothing from the floor and managed to look almost professional when she addressed me.

"What are you doing here?"

I wanted to ask her the same question, but since neither one of us really had the right to ask it, I didn't. Nor did I answer her. Instead, I took a step forward, my anger at her subterfuge fueled by the fact that she'd just emerged from Jack's bedroom wearing nothing but his shirt.

Jabbing a finger in her direction, I said, "How dare you ask me questions! You're the one that needs to answer quite a few—like how long you've known you're related to the Crandalls of Mimosa Hall—and the girl in the portrait. I just haven't figured out why you'd want to hide that little gem from me, but I'm working on it. And I want to know why in the hell you picked my mother and me for this little game of yours."

She frowned and looked confused and for a moment I almost believed that she didn't know. But then I remembered how she'd been avoiding my phone calls and how she'd taken the journal and I narrowed my eyes. I wasn't fooled, regardless of what was about to come out of her mouth.

"I don't know what you're talking about, Melanie. I'll admit that when I saw my last name on the Crandall family tree, I was intrigued, but I didn't know of any connection before that. I was as surprised as you."

"So surprised that you stole the folder with the family tree that Yvonne meant for me and 'accidentally' picked up the one Mrs. McGowan had prepared? Do you think I'm stupid, Rebecca? I know all of this is related somehow and I've got a strong feeling that you know how. But you're holding out on telling me for whatever reason." I drew a deep breath, my anger sucking all the wind out of my lungs. "But I will find out—without your help."

I held up my hand. "Don't bother saying anything. It's all going to be lies and I don't have the time to listen to it." I pulled my purse strap over my shoulder, prepared to leave. "Just know that my mother is off-limits to your questions from here on out. Please don't darken our doorstep again. You will not be welcome."

I turned to leave, eager to get out of there before I saw Jack or started to cry—or both. I'd only felt this humiliated and betrayed once before—and Jack had been involved then, too. Then I'd believed he was interested in me when all along he was out to find the treasure hidden in my house. I felt the same way now, except this time I had only myself to blame for forgiving him once and letting him back into my life.

I'd made it to the door before I heard Jack call my name. "Mellie, wait."

I jerked open the door and turned around to find Jack in jeans and an inside-out T-shirt, his hair wild. "Why? So you can humiliate me some more? How long have you and Rebecca been laughing behind my back? Is that why you didn't return my phone calls? Because you and Rebecca had decided to work together and leave me out?" I felt the tears in the back of my throat, but I swallowed them back, not wanting to give him the satisfaction.

"It's not like that at all. This"—he waved his hand behind him, but I wasn't sure if he was indicating Rebecca or the mess in his condo—"was just something that happened." He stepped forward and when I looked him in the eyes, I could almost believe him. Quietly, he said, "I promised you before that I would never lie to you again. And I haven't."

Our gazes locked. I did remember his promise. I even remembered that I had believed him. But when I looked at him, I couldn't help but think of our kiss and I wondered if he recalled the way the rain tasted on our lips, how our bodies seemed to fit, and how empty the days were when we weren't together. And I wondered if I was the first person he thought of calling whenever he had something to say, too. I'd been denying all of it in a stupid bid for self-preservation, and I realized that he might have been doing the same thing.

I looked over his shoulder to Rebecca, who stood watching us with an unreadable expression on her face. I turned back to Jack. "One of you is lying. The very first time I met Rebecca she showed me a picture of my mother wearing an heirloom necklace and earrings. The same jewelry that was listed as belonging to Mary Crandall and lost with the sinking of the *Ida Belle*, the boat carrying them from Connecticut to South Carolina. Rebecca wanted to know where the jewelry came from, using the pretext of being a journalist and writing a story about my mother. Don't you see? She's been lying to me since the beginning. She wants something from me, and she's using you to get it."

Rebecca moved forward and put her hand on Jack's arm, pulling him back. "Let her go, Jack. She needs to calm down so she can begin thinking rationally again. She's too distraught to see reason at the moment and it's no use talking with her."

I kept my eyes focused on Jack. "Ask her why she was taking pictures of the stained-glass window at my mother's house. We both know it's a clue to something, and I have a feeling Rebecca's figured it out. Or maybe she's already told you and you're holding out on me. Whatever. Just know that I don't trust her and by association I don't trust you, either." I clenched my eyes, unable to look at him anymore. "And I cannot believe that you'd sleep with her."

His eyes hardened. "I believe that would be an instance of the pot calling the kettle black, Mellie."

I flushed, knowing he was referring to Marc Longo and our brief encounter before I'd learned the truth about Marc's involvement in the search for the missing diamonds.

"But you're wrong about Rebecca," he said. "She came here to tell me about her discovery—how her family is related to the Crandalls. It's purely coincidence that there's a connection with your family."

I smirked and gave in to the impulse to roll my eyes. "The one thing that I have learned from you, Jack, is that there's no such thing as coincidence." I walked out of the door but turned around one final time. "I never, ever want to see you again. And I really mean it this time." Then I walked to the elevator and pushed the button for the lobby without looking back once.

CHAPTER 25

I drove directly to my office, hoping to lose myself in my work as I'd always done when faced with personal problems. In my career life, I was strong, confident, and successful—all the characteristics I lacked in my personal life. At least in my office I could pretend that the two overlapped and I was as good at dealing with other people as I was with selling houses.

Nancy Flaherty greeted me with a bright smile when I entered the lobby, her mood having improved with the return of warm golfing weather. I noticed she wore leather golf gloves as she gripped the receiver of the office phone and she caught me staring at them.

"My kids gave me new gloves for Christmas and I'm trying to break them in. I keep dialing the wrong extensions, so I apologize in advance if you get the wrong caller." She replaced the receiver then leaned forward, trying to get a good look at me. "You look awful, Melanie. Have you been crying?"

"No. Allergies."

"In January?"

I narrowed my eyes at her. "Are there any messages for me?"

"Yes. I've put them on your desk. Two are from Jack, two are from the Dembrowskis—the couple from Poughkeepsie double-checking the time for the showings tomorrow and also verifying that you're on the same page with them about not wanting anything older than five years."

I frowned. "Anything else?"

"Yes. Sophie called. She knew you'd be in the library so she didn't want to call you in case you'd left your phone on. But she wants you to call her as soon as possible. Says she's found something you'll be interested in hearing."

"Thanks, Nancy," I said as I handed her my coat, feeling slightly better now that I was in familiar territory. "One last thing. If Jack calls, I'm not here. I'm never speaking to him again."

"Still? Or is this a new time?"

I pretended I hadn't heard her and headed toward the back of the building. As soon as I got to my office, I called Sophie. She answered on the third ring.

"Hey, how are you?"

I stared down at the phone. "I'm okay. Why are you asking?"

She didn't answer right away. Then, "Jack called. Said you might be calling."

"Did he tell you anything else?"

"Not really. Just that you might not be inviting Rebecca to any birth-day parties. Please tell me that he and Rebecca . . ."

"I don't want to talk about it right now, okay? Maybe later, after I've had a few days to add perspective, but not right now."

"Do you want me to send her name in to the American Association for Nude Recreation as a possible future keynote speaker?"

Despite myself, I smiled. "Thanks, Soph. You're a good friend. But that's all right. I think I can handle this one. So," I said, eager to change the subject. "What did you want to tell me?"

"I found Meredith."

"What?" I pressed the phone closer to my ear to make sure I was hearing her right.

"I found Meredith. And I wasn't even looking for her."

I waited for her to explain, having learned through experience that if I didn't ask any questions, she'd eventually get around to telling me what I wanted to hear.

"Do you remember me telling you about the fund-raising they're doing at St. Philip's to restore some of the older markers?"

I had no idea what she was talking about, figuring it had been couched between the mind-numbing requests for more money or the hiring of another specialist. Or maybe she'd mentioned it right after she suggested we make the Legare Street house a museum to restored sound—as in no electricity, running water, or anything else that could be heard from the inside of the building that would make one think, God forbid, that they were living in the twenty-first century. "Uh-huh," I said into the phone and waited for her to continue.

"Well, I've been going through all of their oldest records to at least determine what some of the dates on the stones would be, or even if the full inscription was recorded in the church's records. And guess what I found." She was so full of excitement that I pictured her holding her breath in puffed-out cheeks.

"Meredith?" I ventured.

"Oh, right. I already told you. Only it wasn't actually Meredith, but a memorial marker." The rustle of paper crackled through the phone. "Let's see—right. Here it is. The memorial marker was installed in 1890 by Rose Prioleau in memory of her cousin Meredith Prioleau, who went missing and was presumed perished in the earthquake of 1886. An obituary was included, presumably for the church bulletin. It stated that Meredith was a distant cousin who was adopted by Rose's father—her mother having already died—and raised as a sister to Rose after Meredith's parents perished in a shipwreck."

"Wow." I sat back in my chair. "Did it make any mention as to what might be on the marker?"

"No."

I tried to hide my disappointment. "Damn. Because knowing my family, I wouldn't be surprised if some sort of puzzle piece was put on that marker."

"You didn't let me finish, Melanie. I said there was no mention in the records of what was on the marker. But you interrupted before I could tell you that the marker itself is still there and all I had to do was cross the street to read it."

I leaned forward, my elbows on the desk. "What did it say?"

Again, I listened to the rustling of papers. "It reads: 'Meredith Prioleau, born 1870 and died 1886.' There are no other words, but there is an engraving of a heart-shaped locket that's identical to the one your father gave you. Except . . ." I could imagine her frowning as she squinted at her notes.

"Except what?" I prompted.

"Except that this one has the initial *R* on it."

I let the words sink in for a moment. "An *R*? Are you sure?"

"Yep. It's as clear as day."

I chewed on my bottom lip, watching as two lights appeared on my phone, indicating waiting calls. "Can you meet me for dinner tonight to discuss all of this? I really need somebody to talk to and I'm not speaking to Jack as long as I live."

"Again?"

Ignoring her comment, I continued, "My schedule's pretty packed but I think I can get away at five. We can go over all of the possibilities. . . ."

"Melanie, I'm sorry, but I can't. I've got a date."

I stopped in midbreath. "A what?"

"You know, a date. What normal people have when they're not pre-occupied with work and hunting ghosts."

"But with whom? And what about Chad?"

"It's, um, actually, with Chad."

"You're going on a date with Chad?"

"Um-hm. We decided to test the waters and go on a date. Dinner and a movie. He's found a really cool theater in North Charleston that only screens foreign films and we're going to try and catch a few."

I shuddered silently at the thought of sitting in a darkened theater with a bunch of people who preferred art films and movies with subtitles. They probably all wore Birkenstocks, too.

"Wow, well, um, you two have fun. And let me know how it goes."

She sounded almost giddy, which made me smile. Dr. Sophie Wal-len was not a giddy person as a rule, regardless of how she dressed. And if Chad made her giddy, then I'd have to say that we were on the right track.

"I will," she said. "How about dinner tomorrow night? We can talk then. Maybe figure out what the memorial marker means in relation to everything else."

"Sure," I said, knowing that I couldn't wait that long. We said our good-byes before I slowly hung up the phone.

Ignoring the waiting calls, I sat staring into open space, going through my options of people who would make a good sounding board for all the wild theories I had sprouting in my brain. I even considered calling Marc Longo before good reason set in. I still wasn't sure how much I trusted him, and I didn't want to use him as a Jack substitute, especially when I was sure that Marc would fall short.

The last person's name who filtered through my brain was my mother. I remembered how we'd stood together in the hidden room and spoken to Wilhelm, and how I'd felt stronger with her by my side. I wasn't sure if she could help snap a few puzzle pieces into place, but she was a Prioleau after all, and puzzles were as much a part of the gene map as long legs and a penchant for sugar.

I pressed the button on my phone for the front desk. "Nancy, could you please take messages for my waiting phone calls and cancel and re-schedule my appointments for the rest of the day?"

Instead of seeming annoyed, her voice sounded almost hopeful. "Oh, do you have a date?"

I frowned at the phone. "No, Nancy, I don't have a date. Why do you ask?"

"I can't imagine any other scenario that would make you cancel your appointments."

"I've got things to do at home, that's all. And I don't think the world will grind to a halt in my absence."

"My, my. I think somebody's grown up. It's about time you realized that, Melanie. I'm thinking you should take up golf. You know, find something relaxing to do when you're not working."

"I don't think I've gone that far, Nancy, but thanks. I'll keep it in mind." I hung up the phone, then headed to the reception area to grab my coat.

Nancy stood, revealing the red argyle pants I'd seen before. "Don't forget. You have a closing at nine o'clock tomorrow morning. Let me know if you need to reschedule that, too." She smiled and waved her gloved fingers while I smiled halfheartedly. For the first time since I could remember, the thought of closing a deal elicited no physical re-sponse: no heart-thumping, blood-pumping release. I refused to think about the reasons why, but I was pretty sure that in the back of my mind somewhere I was thinking of Jack Trenholm and blaming him for messing with the order of things and rearranging my life from the way it should be.

∽

I was surprised to find my father's truck gone and no painting vans parked outside the house. Mercifully, the fuchsia hues of the entranceway as well as the Nero-esque ceiling mural in my bedroom had been banished under historically accurate (at least in color, if not in process) paint. But we'd found it increasingly difficult to get painters to come back, regardless of how much money we offered to pay them. The revolving door of painting professionals kept telling us stories of paint cans overturning, brushes being thrown, and cold hands pushing them from behind.

I opened the front door, smelling the scent of fresh paint, and feeling again a throbbing sensation in my bones, like the heartbeat of the old house. I closed the door behind me, listening to the hollow thud echoing off the bare floors. I stayed where I was, unsure of what to do next. My mind reeled with loose pieces of information, like confetti in a parade, and I found myself seeking the one person I'd never thought I would.

"Mother?" I called out.

"In the kitchen," came the answer, and I quickly walked to the doorway where the hideous swinging doors had thankfully been taken away. My mother sat at the table with her back to me, staring out the window. She wore her gloves, and the journal lay on the table.

"I need someone to talk to," I said quickly, as if I'd forget all the words if I didn't.

"I know."

She turned in the chair and looked up at me, and I saw that her eyes were sunken in her face, her skin nearly translucent over the fine bones of her face.

I approached her with alarm. "What's wrong?"

She shook her head. "She's very strong, Mellie. I feel her reaching for me."

I sat down across from her, pulling the journal away. "Stop. You're making yourself ill."

Speaking as if I hadn't said anything, she said, "She's very near. I think she knows that you're too strong, so she's going after me now. I'll be fine. I've fought her before. I just need to—rest." She closed her eyes and her body swayed in her seat.

"I'm taking you up to your bedroom so you can lie down. Where's Daddy?"

With her eyes still closed, she answered me. "He went to Summerville. To get clippings for the garden . . ." Her voice trailed away, and for a moment I thought that she'd fallen asleep sitting up. Then she opened her eyes and smiled at me. "I haven't been alone. Wilhelm's been here. He won't show himself, though. He's ashamed. Of what he did to Catherine."

She frowned as she looked at me. "What about you, Mellie? You look so sad."

Just her compassion was enough to make me want to cry. I shook my head. "I don't want to talk about it now." I didn't ask that she not answer the phone or door if Jack called or came by because I was pretty sure that he'd do neither.

I stood, then moved to her side. "Come on. Let's go upstairs. You need to rest."

She didn't argue and allowed me to help her stand. Pointing at the journal, she said, "Bring that up, too."

I hesitated only a moment before sticking it under my arm, then helped my mother up the stairs. I was surprised at how heavily she leaned on me, how frail she appeared, and I felt a tremor of apprehension. The whole house seemed to breathe with it, blanketing the air with stale fear.

As she sat on the side of her bed, I knelt to take off her shoes, then helped her slide under the covers. I moved to take off her gloves, but she shook her head. Tucking the covers around her, I said, "I spoke to Sophie today. She found a memorial marker for Meredith, installed by Rose Prioleau in 1890. It listed her birth year as 1870 and the year 1886 was listed as her year of death."

"So she was sixteen when she died."

"Yes, but . . ." I thought for a moment, sifting through the puzzle pieces, selecting and discarding them just as quickly. "The girl found on the *Rose* was older."

Our gazes met, and she lifted her eyebrows. "Did Sophie find anything else?"

I nodded. "Rose's father adopted Meredith when Meredith's parents died in a shipwreck and raised her as Rose's sister."

"Well, then. That explains a lot, doesn't it?" She pointed to the journal that I had placed on the nightstand. "I found something out today. An entry that you probably read before but didn't mean anything. I bet it will now." She reached across the journal and clumsily flipped through pages until she reached the one she sought. "Read this entry." She handed the journal to me and I began to read.

Father has a surprise for both of us for Rose's birthday. I already know what it is, though, since Father borrowed my locket to have a duplicate made—but with R's initial instead of mine. She wants to be just like me, and it scares me a little because sometimes I believe that she wants to become me. She likes to make me sit down next to her in front of a mirror so she can see how we are almost like twins. It is only when she stands or tries to walk that our differences are visible. She played a little joke on C last week, when she had me sitting in the drawing room and pretended to be her when he came in. I agreed only because it is so difficult to deal with her anger when things do not go her way, but now I fear that she will want to pretend to be me the next time he calls. I will have to send him a warning, so he will not give anything away.

I thought for a minute, tapping my fingers against the yellowed page. "Rose married a man named Charles, four years after the earthquake. Four years after she left Charleston to travel Europe with family friends."

"Four years is a long time. Long enough for people to forget the physical differences between two girls who resembled each other so much that they might have really been sisters." My mother's gaze met mine. "We are not as we seem."

I pressed my fingers against my temples. "No, I suppose we're not. So who are we?"

My mother sat back against her pillows. "I've seen the pictures of Rose and Charles on their honeymoon, and I've seen the portrait of the two girls. And there's the fact that the girl found on the boat had a hip joint problem. If I were a gambler, my bet would be on Meredith being our ancestor—whoever she really was."

She licked her dry lips and I gave her a glass of water that sat on her nightstand. With narrowed eyes, she regarded me over the glass. "The question then is how Meredith supposedly died in 1886 yet gave birth to my mother in 1900."

"Then if Meredith wasn't the one found on the *Rose*, who was it?" I probably knew the answer, but until my mother spoke, I held out hope that I was wrong.

"Everything points to Rose. She wants us to ask, but we're not ready to speak to her yet."

"Why not?" I asked, the small yet heavy feet of fear marching down my spine.

She took a deep breath, as if to draw in strength. "The forensics report showed that her skull was cracked, as if she'd suffered blunt-force trauma. She has reason to be angry. To want revenge. And that makes her very dangerous."

"But why us?"

"Because this was her house, her birthright. But instead of living here, and having children and grandchildren living here, she ended up at the bottom of the ocean, wearing a locket that wasn't hers, while someone else lived the life she was supposed to have."

I sat down on the bed, feeling sick. "There's more to this that I only recently discovered. Alice Crandall—the girl in the portrait at Mimosa Hall—is Rebecca Edgerton's great-great-grandmother. The sapphire-and-diamond jewelry that your mother gave you originally belonged to Alice's mother, who went down on a ship in 1870. When Rebecca saw a photo of you wearing the necklace and earrings, she knew there had to be a connection. That's why she approached us in the first place."

A soft smile lit her face. "So if the jewelry was recovered, then a baby might have been, too. A baby wearing a heart-shaped locket, identical to the one her sister Alice wore except with an *N*. And then it was simply a matter of changing the initial on the locket and renaming her Meredith."

I shook my head. "I can almost feel sorry for Rose. Her father finds a baby and brings her home, then asks Rose to accept her as her sister.

Except the imposter is more beautiful, and perfectly formed, and loved to sail like their father. It must have been difficult for her."

My mother closed her eyes and I took the glass of water from her. I straightened my back as another thought occurred to me. "Does this mean that we're descendants of a murderer?"

My mother shook her head. "Don't say that. We don't know the circumstances. And from reading the journal I can't help but believe that Rose had a hand in her own undoing."

I sat up, remembering something I'd heard. I turned to tell her, but her eyes were closed, and for a moment I thought she'd gone to sleep. But she opened them, touched my arm, and said, "Tell me."

I somehow didn't find my mother's ability to read my mind as disturbing as I probably should have. "Wilhelm told me that he saved her, the writer of the journal. If our assumptions are correct, and it was Meredith—or Nora—then maybe he was the one who found her after the shipwreck. Maybe she managed to survive the sinking and somehow ended up on shore."

A small furrow formed between her brows. "But he would have been dead for one hundred years by the time of the shipwreck."

I sent her a sardonic grin. "Right. Like we wouldn't know how that works." I sighed. "From what I've read in the journal, Rose couldn't see Wilhelm, which probably meant that she didn't have a sixth sense, which would make it likely that no one in her family did, either. But I've heard stories. . . ." I looked down to make sure she was still awake and found her gaze focused intently on me.

"Go on," she said, her voice soft.

"I've heard of instances," I continued, "where spirits can make themselves known to others by expending all of their energy for a brief moment."

"Who told you that?"

"Grandmother Sarah."

A soft smile lifted her lips. "I've seen it happen. Usually it's when the spirit is making his final good-bye to loved ones, or during an emergency when a life is at stake."

"Like when a baby is in danger of drowning."

My mother nodded. "Wilhelm said that he protects us in reparation for what happened to his Catherine. And why he continues to protect the women of this family—Meredith's descendants."

"Wilhelm told us that Catherine drowned." I frowned, remembering the books on the table in Jack's condo, regardless of how much I wanted to forget that entire scene. "Jack believes that the Prioleaus in the latter half of the eighteenth century might have been wreckers. Their plantation on Johns Island would have given them access and opportunity. Whether or not they lured ships up onto the rocks or were simply opportunists feeding off of a ship's bad luck, it's entirely possible that they built their fortune on the misfortune of others." I swallowed, trying to bury my humiliation at the mere thought of being in his condo while he and Rebecca were back in the bedroom. "He marked a passage in a book that concerned the disappearance of a British schooner in 1785 off of Johns Island. The passengers, crew, and cargo were never seen again."

"And 1785 is the year Wilhelm's Catherine died."

"I thought the same thing. And I keep thinking about the carving in the beam in the hidden room: 'prisoner of the heart.' Rebecca mentioned how some Hessian soldiers were hidden by Charleston citizens when the British fled the city. What if Wilhelm was held prisoner here in the house in exchange for doing some dirty work for the family, like scavenging cargo?"

My mother nodded, her eyes never leaving my face. "And even if the ship was wrecked by Mother Nature and not by intervening human hands, no mercy was shown to survivors, as they would be witnesses to the scavenging."

I thought for a moment, almost hearing some of the puzzle pieces clicking into place, and feeling dread as I reached a probable conclusion. "So if Wilhelm was doing his job, and scuttling cargo from a ship that his Catherine was on—but didn't know it—and she drowned while he did nothing to save her, his guilt would have been unbearable."

"So he spends his centuries making amends for the woman he loved but couldn't save." My mother turned her face to the side, revealing the black-and-blue imprint of a human hand.

I stood, staring at the bruise. "What happened?"

She struggled to a sitting position. Her face was nearly as pale as her pillowcase, and she tried to hide it with her hand. "I told you. She's getting stronger. She's trying to weaken me so that she can then go after you."

"Why were you trying to hide this from me?"

Her eyes were hard. "Because I didn't want you to feel fear. Fear is what will make you weak; it is what she will be looking for. It is what will allow her inside your head and she will win." She leaned toward me and grabbed my arm. "She can hurt you. Her hatred is that strong."

"What does she want?"

She didn't answer right away. "I don't know."

"Yes you do." I leaned closer to her and she met my gaze again. "Why won't you tell me?"

"Because I feel your fear right now. She's near. Can't you feel her? She's waiting for her chance."

I backed away. "I don't want this. I've never wanted any of this. Why can't we just walk away—leave this house to her?"

"You know that you can't. She's followed you before, and she won't rest until she's won. Until . . ." She stopped speaking, her chest rising and falling in shallow breaths.

I glanced sharply at her. "Until what?"

Instead of answering, she laid her head back on the pillow and closed her eyes. "Get the door."

"I didn't hear . . ." Before I'd finished my sentence, the front doorbell rang. I moved to the window and looked out onto Legare and saw Jack's black Porsche parked at the curb.

"It's Jack," I said, unable to keep my voice steady.

She took a deep breath. "You should let him in."

"No. You don't know what he did."

She opened her eyes halfway. "I suppose I do, actually. But you should still let him in. He needs your help."

"I can't. . . ."

She sat up on her elbow, her eyes angry. "He's going to need you soon as much as you need him now, so go answer the damned door and stop arguing with me."

My eyes widened. I didn't remember my mother ever yelling at me, and despite the anger I felt, there was something comforting in it, too. Like she and I were growing accustomed to our roles and didn't need to make nice anymore.

Without a word, I went downstairs, taking my time, making him wait. And the whole time I was trying to figure out what my mother had wanted to tell me, and wondering if I should tell her that I felt Rose's presence now, as close as a scarf about to be squeezed tightly around my neck.

CHAPTER 26

I stood inside the door for a long moment before finally unlocking it and pulling it open just enough to frame my face.

Jack was clean shaven and his hair wet as if he'd just stepped out of the shower, reminding me of an altar boy or a boy presenting his best face before being scolded by his mother. His clothes were cleaned and pressed and he smelled of soap and shampoo and that other unnamable scent that I just referred to as Jack.

"Are you sure you've got the right house? I thought Rebecca lived in Ansonborough." I was proud at how even my voice sounded, not giving away any of the hurt and humiliation that seemed even worse now that I was facing him again.

"Look, Mellie, I'm sorry. I'm sorry you were in that situation; I can't imagine how embarrassing that must have been for you."

"Embarrassing? Walking down the street with the back of my skirt tucked into my panty hose is embarrassing. That scene in your condo was . . . mortifying. And degrading."

"Degrading?" He raised his eyebrow and I sensed his anger. "It would only have been degrading if you and I were involved in a relationship, Mellie, and you made it perfectly clear to me that you didn't want one. I'm certainly no saint, but I would never cheat on a committed relationship. Your apparent disinterest led me to assume that I was free to pursue other interests. So I did. You can't have it both ways, Mellie."

I wanted to slam the door in his face, but I couldn't. Because there was no escaping the fact that he was right. I just needed to make sure that

whatever happened next I never let him see how much I hurt or regret-
ted missing my chance to lose some self-control.

"Can I come in, please? I have something to show you."

I opened the door a little wider. "Can you just show me out here so
that you can be on your way?"

Without saying anything else, he reached into his back pocket and
pulled out a gold chain. He held it up in front of me, the sun's reflection
off of it like a conspiratorial wink. I squinted to see it clearly, to make sure
that I'd seen what I thought I had. Hanging from the center of the chain
on a tiny gold loop was a golden heart locket with the initial *A* engraved
in the middle of it.

I stepped back in surprise and Jack took the opportunity to push the
door open farther so that he could move inside to the foyer.

"Where did you get that?" I asked, although I was pretty sure I already
knew.

"Rebecca left it on the floor of my bathroom. I'm thinking it fell off
as she was getting dressed and she doesn't know that it's missing yet."

I decided to ignore the implications of why Rebecca might have been
getting dressed in his bathroom. My eyes met his. "It's Alice's, isn't it? And
if Rebecca's had it in her possession, then she must have known about the
connection between her family, the Crandalls, and the Prioleaus."

He nodded but I wouldn't drop his gaze.

I crossed my arms across my chest, my anger a welcome cover to the
crushing bruise around my heart. "Did you know?"

He shook his head. "I probably figured it out at about the same time
you did. And I'm telling the truth that I didn't believe Rebecca knew
anything before that, too."

"Is that why you brought the locket, then? To prove to me that you
weren't lying?"

"Partly."

"Only part?" I wanted to slap down the part of me that felt a rising hope.

A corner of his mouth twitched and I was happier than I'd admit to
see something of the old Jack. "You know I can't leave a good mystery
alone. And we do work well together."

I curbed my disappointment. "Just don't ask me to work with Rebecca."

He didn't answer right away. "Fine. I don't know what she's up to, and she's probably already figured some of this out, but I'm sure it's not as bad as you're thinking. Regardless, I won't make you work with her if that's what you want."

I stared at him for a long moment. "Why Rebecca?" I said the name with the same distasteful inflection most people reserved for names like Hitler or bin Laden.

"Why Marc Longo?" he mimicked in the same tone of voice.

Despite myself, I smiled.

"Truce then?" he asked.

I could think of a million reasons to say no, including his ability to lure me into doing things I really didn't want to, but I could see in Jack's eyes that I'd already been shot, bagged, and my head mounted over his fireplace. "No" simply wasn't an option. "Fine," I said, sighing heavily. "At least until we can figure out all of this."

"And then what?" He sounded almost hopeful.

"Then I can move back into my Tradd Street house, and you can get back to writing your historical true crimes. We'll send Christmas cards for a while, and I'll wave to you from a distance when we see each other at the annual Oyster Festival at Boone Hall Plantation that Sophie will make us buy tickets for each year until we're too old to walk without assistance."

He smiled, but his eyes didn't. "Great. Then we have a truce." He drew a deep breath. "So let's get busy." He reached into another pants pocket and pulled out a stack of photographs and began laying them out on the foyer floor. I recognized them as the pictures I'd seen on his dining room table. The last thing he pulled from his pocket was a folded-up piece of paper that he straightened and placed on the floor above the photographs. I knelt to see better and realized that it was a handwritten version of the verse on my grandmother's tombstone, and that each line had been numbered, and each letter had been numbered from left to right starting at the number one at the beginning of each line. Someone had highlighted what seemed like random letters with a yellow highlighter.

When bricks crumble, the fireplace falls;
When children cry, the mothers call.
When lies are told, the sins are built,
Within the waves, hide all our guilt.

"What is this?" I asked.

"I'm not sure. I think I've figured most of it out, but I need you to help me with the rest."

I tried not to grin like an idiot and kept my gaze focused on the verse. "Show me how far you've gotten."

He set up the photographs of the lasso-like outline that encircled the verse on the grave marker and the stained-glass window in the same order as they appeared with the top, two sides, and the bottom forming a circle. He pointed to a gap between the top of the left side and the upper line. "See how there's a separation here? That makes me think that they're in order from number one to number four, starting at the top and moving clockwise around the circle." He slid the paper with the gravestone rhyme next to the photographs. "Notice how there are four lines on the marker. Since the border appears on both the marker and the window, I assumed it wasn't a coincidence."

"Since there's no such thing as coincidence according to the Jack Trenholm school of thought."

He didn't smile, and I hoped it was because he was remembering when I'd last said that to him, when he was defending Rebecca as I confronted him with the evidence of her connection to the Crandall family.

"Exactly," he said through narrowed lips.

"There's something in the journal, too," I said. "How the soldier—Wilhelm—would tap on the glass four times, always by the quadrant where the depiction of the angel's head is."

"You didn't tell me that."

"You've been avoiding me."

Clearing his throat, he pointed to the photographs again. "Remember how I noticed that some of the weird marks in the border were larger and bolder than the rest? Like here." He indicated the top border where the second and fifth black marks stood out from the others. "I played with it a bit until I figured out that they corresponded to a word in the rhyme. For instance, the second and fifth words in the first line are 'bricks' and 'fireplace.'"

My eyes met his and I felt a surge of adrenaline. It had been this way between us before, when we'd worked together to solve an old cipher. "That's really good," I admitted.

"I know."

Our eyes met again and I couldn't help but roll my eyes to disguise my smile.

"Going around the border, these are the words that I picked out."

He flipped the paper over and I read the words out loud. "Bricks, fireplace, the, sins, within, hide, our."

He glanced up at me and I found myself staring at his lips and remembering our kiss. I looked back at the words, struggling to speak past the lump in my throat. "Obviously, they're scrambled. Have you been able to make any sense out of them?"

"Not yet. That's why I came here. You're really good at creating order from chaos."

"Thank you," I said. "I'll take that as a compliment." Without waiting for him to respond, I stood and went to the kitchen to pull out two notepads and pencils. When I returned, I handed him one of each. "There're only seven words. Create as many sentences as you can using those words—making sure nouns, verbs, pronouns, etcetera are all in the right place so that they're forming coherent sentences."

"You don't need to tell me that, Mellie."

I shrugged. "I'm sure I wouldn't know that. You seem to have an appalling lack of judgment."

He didn't say anything as he sat down on the floor beside me. Then he leaned over and whispered, "Marc Longo."

I pretended I hadn't heard him as I began to write.

> Our bricks hide within the fireplace sins.
> Sins within our bricks hide the fireplace.
> The fireplace sins hide within our bricks.

I glanced over at Jack, who'd made equally nonsensical sentences. With a sigh, I returned to my word bank and studied them again, the words

seeming to twist and warp on the page, teasing me. I closed my eyes, seeing the words like metallic glints against my eyelids, on what seemed like
a scrolling marquee. I focused on the words behind my lids, then popped
my eyes open to stare at the paper again. I squinted, trying to get them to
lie flat, focusing on the nouns and verbs in a final attempt to wrestle them
into some kind of a coherent sentence. I blinked, then sat up, eyeing the
words again and seeing how obvious they were, and wondering why they
hadn't been as obvious to me the first time I'd seen them.

With a firm grip on the pencil, I wrote, *Within the fireplace bricks our
sins hide*. Putting the pencil down, I said, "I think I've got it."

Jack stood and I handed him my notepad. He read the words out loud.
"Within the fireplace bricks our sins hide." His eyebrows knit together. "I
think you're right." His gaze met mine. "But which fireplace?"

I thought for a moment. "All of the fireplaces in this house are brick,
including the one in the kitchen. But we've already examined every inch
of it. If there's anything else hidden there, we would have found it by
now."

"And what sins can you hide?"

I shook my head. "I don't know. But since the words appear on a window my grandmother installed, as well as on her grave marker, I'd say it's
fairly safe to assume that the sins directly relate to her and her family."

"The Prioleaus."

"Or not. Meredith Prioleau was born Nora Crandall."

Jack raised his eyebrow. "Something else you forgot to tell me."

"Not exactly. You were—busy, if you recall. That's why I went to your
condo, to tell you what I'd learned."

He didn't say anything in his defense, so I continued. "My mother and
I believe that the infant Nora Crandall wasn't lost at sea, but was rescued
by a member of the Prioleau family, perhaps by my great-great-grandfather, and raised here as a distant cousin to Rose. They changed her name
to Meredith, and treated her as Rose's sister."

"Which would explain the change in the locket initial. And why
Alice Crandall would have an identical locket."

"And," I continued, "Rose's father had one made for Rose, which is
how she ended up with hers. Apparently Rose felt quite a bit of jealousy
for Meredith, always wanted what Meredith had."

Jack was frowning at something I'd said.

"What is it?"

"Rose's locket. We've found the other two, but where is the one with the *R* on it?"

"Hold that thought," I said, and went back to the kitchen to retrieve the photograph my father had found of my great-grandparents on their honeymoon.

Jack flipped it over to read the names, then studied the sepia-toned faces. "I don't get it. What does this have to do with Rose's locket?"

"It says it's Rose, but it's not. The woman in the photograph is tall and slender. Look how tall she is in comparison with her husband and the horse behind them. And she doesn't have a cane. The remains discovered in the sailboat were of a person who was no more than five feet two inches, and who would have walked with a limp."

"So who do you think it is in the photograph?"

"Meredith. I'm sure of it."

"But if Rose is the one on the sailboat, why was she wearing Meredith's locket?"

Quietly, I said, "Within the waves, hide all our guilt."

My legs were getting cramped as I knelt on the floor and I moved to stand. Jack extended a hand to me and I paused for a moment before taking it.

He didn't let go of my hand right away, but stood close to me, a look of hard concentration on his face. "If you're right, then somehow during the earthquake of 1886, Meredith and Rose swapped identities. But how? And why?"

I shook my head, gently untangling my hand from his. "I don't want to speculate. I don't want to think that my great-grandmother was a murderer."

"A locket could be hidden within a fireplace brick." Thoughtfully, he added, "Within the fireplace bricks our sins hide."

We stared at each other as a strong gust of wind pushed at the house, making the front door shudder. The chandelier above our heads swayed, the mirrored glass tinkling gently like a muted conversation.

"A bad storm's coming in this evening," Jack said. "A nor'easter. It's going to get pretty nasty on the coast."

A breath of cold air descended on me and I shivered, but Jack didn't seem to feel it.

He looked at me oddly. "You do realize that all this means that you and Rebecca are cousins."

The thought had crossed my mind, but I'd avoided thinking about it, much as a person avoids muddy puddles on a city sidewalk. "I suppose you're right. I guess that explains her ability to see things in dreams. But the rest of her," I shook my head, "comes from a completely different gene pool."

I thought for a moment he would laugh, but instead he focused on something behind me. Clutching his arm in apprehension, I turned.

My mother appeared at the bottom of the stairs, her hand trembling on the newel post. "Rebecca's in danger. We need to find her—quickly." A streak of lightning illuminated the graying sky outside, shooting white light across her face, making her seem transparent.

"How do you know?" I asked, but I could see the journal tucked under her arm, and I knew.

"Meredith," she whispered as her knees gave way and she ended up sitting on the bottom step.

I moved to sit next to her, and put my arm around her narrow shoulders. "You're not going anywhere, Mother. You don't look well."

Despite her diminished appearance she trembled with anger as she faced me. "Don't tell me what to do. You need to listen to me, and do what I say. And we must find Rebecca. Rose is with her, and Rebecca doesn't know how to fight back."

I wanted to argue with her until I realized that her fury was directed against someone or something that meant me harm, too. Relenting, I asked, "Where is she?"

My mother's eyes were blank and we both turned to Jack.

"She left shortly after Melanie did, and I haven't heard from her since. I've called her cell phone a couple of times, but it keeps switching to voice mail." He pulled his phone out of his pocket and dialed before raising it to his ear. He waited for a long minute before snapping it shut. "Still no answer."

"Where would she have gone?" I asked out loud as my eyes settled on the journal still tucked under my mother's arm. "Can I see it?"

My mother relinquished it with what seemed like relief. I opened it to the back cover that showed the illustration of the angel head. "Maybe this might tell us."

Jack approached as I opened my cell phone to the picture of the stained-glass window that illuminated the hidden picture. I pointed to the angel. "This was the other thing I came over to show you today. It's a picture of the figurehead from the *Ida Belle*, the ship carrying Nora and her parents from Connecticut to Charleston. The figurehead was the only part of the ship that was ever recovered—and they found it on Edisto Island."

Jack's gaze met mine. "Which is very close to Johns Island."

I nodded. "I think that the way the figurehead is situated in the picture, with it half turned, could mean that it's pointing to something. See?"

With my fingernail, I indicated the bottom of the triangle made by the angel's hair and wings. "The tip is missing, as if it's buried under sand, which I think indicates land. My father told me that he saw Rebecca taking pictures of the window, as if she might have figured this out, too. The picture of the figurehead from the boat is on the Internet, so it's more than possible that she discovered it. And what it might mean."

Jack pointed at the depiction of the house in the picture. "Do you know the location of the old Prioleau plantation on Johns Island?"

I frowned, thinking. As a Realtor, I'd sold a lot of houses on the island, and I was familiar with all the golf communities and the names of the neighborhoods named after the former plantations upon which they were built.

"Belle Meade," I said. "It's a golf club community now. I know where it is, but I haven't been to the house since I was a little girl. My grandmother Sarah took me."

My mother's voice was strained. "I can find it. If you can get me into the neighborhood, I'll know where to go."

The house shook as a large roll of thunder launched itself at the earth, making me shudder. Heading out to an old ruin in a thunderstorm on pure speculation didn't sound like a good idea. "It's practically gone. Hurricane Hugo took off the roof and toppled chimneys, but local preservationists wouldn't let them bulldoze the rest. It's taped off to prevent trespassers because it's not safe."

"Chimneys?" Jack asked, and I jerked my head toward him.

I nodded. "There were at least three fireplaces that I can remember. But the largest was in the main room of the house, what used to be part of the original farmhouse."

"She could have figured out what we have, and decided to search for whatever is hidden in the fireplace," Jack said.

My eyes widened. "Like Rose's locket."

Rain pelted the house as bright forks of lightning illuminated the gray world outside the windows. I wanted to suggest that Rebecca and Rose might be evenly matched, but from looking at my mother's drawn face I realized that the situation was much more serious than I wanted to think.

"We need to go. Now." We both faced my mother, who was gripping the newel post and trying to stand. I wanted to tell her that she obviously wasn't well, but her obstinacy and determination reminded me too much of myself.

I walked toward my mother and helped her up. "Let's go, then. But I'm driving. Jack's car is too small, and you can barely stand." I grabbed my purse from the hall table and carefully led her outside while Jack closed the door firmly behind us just as another flash of lightning illuminated the sky like an omen.

CHAPTER 27

We headed toward US Highway Seventeen South and the Ashley River Bridge to the road that would lead us onto the island. Bohicket Road was a narrow two-way thoroughfare canopied by old oaks and sweeping Spanish moss. It was ethereal and magical in the sunlight, but in the height of a thunderstorm it brought to mind the presence of things that went bump in the night.

Against my better judgment, I let Jack drive my car so I could sit in the backseat with my mother, who appeared too weak to sit up on her own. She rested her head on my shoulder, and I recognized the scent of her shampoo as the one I used. I remembered recognizing the same scent on Rebecca. I recalled, too, Rebecca's ability to see things in dreams, and the way her hands had seemed so familiar to me, and I shook my head, castigating myself for being so oblivious. But as I sat in the back of the speeding car, listening to the storm whipping at the windows and feeling the weight of my mother's head on my shoulder as if it were the most natural thing in the world, I realized that being oblivious was sometimes just another form of denial.

I navigated from the backseat, directing Jack to turn onto an unmarked road. The community was so exclusive that the residents believed that if you didn't know it was there, you had no business being there. When we reached the security gate, I showed my Realtor credentials to the guard and with a few odd glances at my mother and me in the backseat, he opened the gate and we drove through.

The asphalt drive was still dry, the storm behind us but approaching quickly. Ginnette lifted her head, sensing the change in direction and pointed to an unpaved road that led to the right off of the main road. "That way. Follow it through the woods until you reach a fork in the road, and go right. If you go left, you'll end up in the old family cemetery."

Her voice held a note of panic in it and I glanced at her, only to find her looking past my shoulder, into the darkening woods. I followed her gaze, seeing the fading NO TRESPASSING signs and broken, rusted chains that had once blocked access to the road. "She's there," she said quietly.

"Rebecca?"

"Both of them." Raising her voice, she turned toward the front seat. "Hurry, Jack. You must hurry."

I listened as the bottom of my car scraped rocks and tree roots, trying not to imagine the repair bills. Within ten minutes of entering the front gates, we emerged into a clearing, the darkness of the woods behind us and the roofless ruins of an old plantation house looming in front of us against the darkening sky. And there, parked under the shelter of a towering oak with a heavy shawl of Spanish moss, was Rebecca's red Audi convertible.

The distant rumble of thunder reminded us that we needed to hurry. Jack exited the car, then opened the back door. Our eyes met above my mother's head, and his worried expression mirrored my own thoughts. Gently, he helped her out and as I followed, I sniffed the air.

"Do you smell that?"

Jack and Ginnette turned to me, matching looks of alarm in their eyes.

"It's smoke. Wood smoke, not burning leaves," I said.

The three of us turned toward the house. Jack was the first to spring into action. Addressing me and my mother, he said, "Stay here in the car. If I'm not out in ten minutes, use your cell and call 911."

I wanted to argue with him, and insist that I go in, too, but I was reluctant to leave my mother by herself, knowing that in an emergency she wouldn't be able to move quickly enough to get out of harm's way. I nodded my assent, and watched as he jumped over rotting steps to the front porch, then through the gaping hole where a front door had once guarded the entrance. I looked down at my watch, and began to time him.

We resettled ourselves into the backseat of the car, still smelling smoke but not yet seeing any signs of fire. Swallowing heavily, I turned to my mother. "Rose can't actually hurt anyone, right? I mean, she gave us bruises, but that's all. Right?"

My mother took my hand and I noticed that she'd removed her gloves. "I need to tell you something, Mellie. Something I probably should have told you long ago."

I glanced down at my watch. *Two minutes.*

"About why I left."

Slowly, I turned my attention to her. I'd waited years for this moment, years of uncertainty, and questions, and hope, and grief, yet now that it was here, I could only feel panic. I'd based my entire life on certain assumptions, and if I suddenly learned that they weren't true, then where would that leave me?

I couldn't meet her eyes and instead focused on the trees behind her, and the way the wind tortured the leaves into pulling away from their stems and into the gathering maelstrom.

"Your grandmother, as she lay dying . . ." Her voice broke and she took a moment before continuing. "I was there. She told me . . ."

"That we aren't as we seem," I interjected, wanting to interrupt her so she couldn't tell me what I was afraid she would.

"Yes. But that's not all." Gently, she placed her fingertips on my jaw. "Look at me, Mellie, and listen carefully. Your grandmother didn't trip. She was pushed. By the same spirit that haunts the back stairs today. The spirit that was made stronger when they pulled her remains from the sailboat."

"Rose," I whispered.

"Yes." Her voice was so soft that I had to lean down to hear her over the rising wind. "I was pregnant . . ."

"I don't want to hear this," I said, wanting to push her away, to leave the car.

"I know. That's why I didn't tell you before. But you need to hear it now. Your fear gets in the way of your strength, Mellie. You need to be strong. We need your strength."

I closed my eyes, trying the deep calming breaths Sophie had been trying to teach me for years. Then I opened them again, and glanced at my watch. *Five minutes.*

"Listen to me, Mellie. I had a miscarriage. A baby boy. The trauma of seeing my mother die like that, and Rose's taunting voice. I—I lost the baby because of her." She squeezed my hands and made me look at her again. "I didn't want to lose you, too."

I shook my head, but I couldn't look away. "But you did. You left."

"I had to. Don't you see? You were too young to fight her. She knew that as you grew, you would get stronger. And that if we worked together, we could defeat her. Send her away forever. But she wanted to make us pay for what Meredith did to her, although I didn't understand her reasons at the time."

"You could have told me then. I would have understood." Tears fell on our clasped hands, and I was surprised to see that they were mine.

"You were seven years old, Mellie. You couldn't have understood. And it would have been cruel for me to make you. We were a beacon for her, the two of us together. Being with you was dangerous—for both of us. But you were more vulnerable."

"I wasn't going to stay young forever. I grew up. I grew stronger. You could have come back and we could have fought her together."

"No. You needed to overcome your fear. We were like a bonfire in the darkness for all spirits. Good and bad. You had your imaginary friends, remember? But there were other spirits in the house you avoided, who made you crawl into bed with me or your grandmother each night. You didn't recognize that being able to see them and communicate with them gave you power over them. So they took advantage of you, fed on your fear. I couldn't let that happen with Rose. She killed your grandmother, and my baby. I had to dilute our brightness, until you understood your strength. And I wasn't going to let her hurt you, no matter how much it hurt me to lose you." Using her thumbs, she wiped the tears from my cheeks. "I told you that before. Do you remember? That sometimes we have to do the right thing even if it means letting go of the one thing we love most in the world. I wanted you to remember that. Did you?"

I did remember; I remembered lying in my darkened bedroom with my eyes half closed in sleep while she said those words to me. I might even have listened better if I'd known that I wouldn't see her again for more than three decades. But I closed my eyes and shook my head in denial, trying to cling to everything I'd once known as truth, regardless of how wrong, and stubborn, and irrational I was being. This was the woman I'd taught myself to hate, to forget, to pretend had never been in my life. I'd learned to resist everything I'd ever inherited from her. But she'd just told me that she'd let me go to save my life, and I'd spent that same life hating her, and wanting to be as far away from her as a person could go. Shame settled on me like a bird; I could still function, but every time I'd turn my head I'd see it.

Pulling away, I fumbled for the door latch on the other side of the car and threw myself out onto the gravel and dead leaves. I had to hold on to the door to keep the wind from slamming it shut. The smell of smoke was stronger now, and I could see wisps of smoke coming from the back side of the house. I looked down at my watch one more time. *Ten minutes.*

I tossed my cell phone onto the backseat, ignoring her look of anguish. "Call 911," I shouted over the roar of the wind, my words splattering against the car like raindrops. "I'm going in to see if Jack needs me."

She leaned toward me and I had to struggle to hear her over the din of the approaching storm. "It was your fear when you were a little girl that threatened to be your undoing. You can't afford that now, do you understand? Don't listen to her voice, and keep telling yourself that you're stronger than she is. The second you begin doubting yourself, you let her in."

I stared at her, wanting to ask her the question teasing my lips, but I stood paralyzed, not yet ready to relinquish the hold I had on the person I thought I was.

"Yes, Mellie. You can do it. But run. Run fast. She's near."

Our gazes held for a brief moment before I turned and headed toward the house, jumping over the rotting steps as I'd seen Jack do just as a large roll of thunder shook the ground.

I stepped through the doorway, finding it hard to distinguish the inside from the outside in the roofless foyer. Green vines crept up what remained of the old plaster and rotting wood. Wide-planked oak floors, with termite holes and missing joists, created a sort of minefield to cross to get to the back of the house. I looked down through a hole to the brick pilings of the foundation, seeing if Jack might have missed his footing. A once-majestic staircase rose to emptiness in front of me, the banister and newel posts long since lost to Mother Nature or vandalism.

Ragged fabric hung at the open windows where not even a shard of glass interrupted the complete desolation of the house's facade.

"Jack!" I called, then coughed as I sucked in a lungful of smoke-filled air, wondering if I was imagining the unmistakable sound of crackling fire.

"Mellie, back here. Be careful where you step—but hurry."

Moving quickly but carefully, I made my way through the front of the house toward the back, calling to Jack twice to reorient myself. The lightning was quickly answered by thunder, a celestial duet announcing the storm's approach. In the dim light, I stepped through a beamed opening onto a brick floor, and apparently into an older part of the house. Most of this roof was still intact, partly I assumed because it was lower and thus spared the strong hurricane winds that had destroyed most of the house.

I squinted into the darkening light, seeing the huge fireplace I remembered at one end of the room, with two figures huddled on the ground in front of it. "Jack," I said, stepping forward.

"Be careful. There're loose bricks everywhere."

I moved closer, studying the fireplace that had once dominated an entire side of the old farmhouse kitchen. But where the chimney should have disappeared through the roof, the roof was gone, and the fireplace itself disintegrated in a pile on the floor that Jack was leaning over.

"What is it?" I asked, moving closer still until I caught a movement from beneath the rubble. "Oh, my God," I said, kneeling by Rebecca's head, the blond hair now matted with blood. Her body from the waist down was covered with a large slate slab, and Jack appeared to be holding it off of her body.

"What happened?"

Rebecca groaned, her face a white mask of pain.

Jack answered, "She said that the mantelpiece just suddenly dislodged itself, slipping from the wall and falling on her along with a lot of the fireplace bricks. I think her leg might be broken."

Rebecca screamed and I thought at first that something else had begun to fall. We both followed her gaze to see the other half of the room, mostly rotted wood timbers, explode into flame as a flash of heat and light washed over us.

I looked to Jack, knowing he had the training to figure out our next move.

"We've got to move fast; the wind's feeding the fire and we don't have time to wait for the rain." He coughed, the smoke thick and heavy. "Rebecca, I'm sorry, sweetie, but this is going to hurt. Hopefully, you'll faint so you won't feel anything."

I didn't have the heart to look at Rebecca's face to see how she took the news. I was too busy watching the wall of flame consume the walls.

Jack continued. "On the count of three, I'm going to lift this slab as much as I can so you can slide Rebecca out from under it. Can you lift her?"

I nodded, my eyes tearing from the smoke, then moved my arms under her shoulders. She didn't say anything and I wondered if she'd already fainted.

With his eyes on me, he counted, "One, two, three!"

Grunting, he managed to lift the slab enough for me to slide Rebecca out until she cleared it, then Jack let the slate crash back to the brick floor. Rebecca screamed, and the sound was nearly buried by another clap of thunder.

The flames licked closer to us and had almost reached the threshold of the hallway from where we'd come—our only exit from the room.

"Hurry," I yelled at Jack, who was kneeling next to Rebecca and gently lifting her in his arms. Her jeans were bloody but she was still conscious, biting her lip to keep from screaming, and I felt a grudging admiration for her. The backs of my hands stung and when I glanced down at them, I saw them crisscrossed with bloody scratches that I didn't remember getting.

As Jack began carrying her to the exit, Rebecca struggled in his arms. "Stop!" she yelled, pointing a scraped and bloody finger back toward the fireplace.

I turned and saw a dark wooden cigar box partially buried under a pile of bricks. The words from the puzzle echoed in my head. *Within the fireplace bricks our sins hide.* I paused, imagining time pausing, too. Before my name had even passed Jack's lips, I ran to the box, extricated it, then followed Jack across the threshold just as a roaring whoosh of exploding timbers filled our ears and the remaining roof crashed down onto the spot where we'd been just seconds before.

Placing my shirt over my nose to help filter the thick air, I carefully followed in Jack's footsteps until we emerged onto the porch and into a nearly blackened world as the sky opened up on us and began to pour down sheets of rain.

We paused for a moment as we tried to catch our breaths. Jack turned to me, his eyes lit with fury as the rain slid down his face. "That was really stupid, Mellie. You could have been killed." He was trembling, and I knew it was more than just anger.

Despite the situation, a glimmer of hope emerged somewhere in my chest. Before he could read my thoughts, I ran past Jack to the car and threw open the back door so he could lay Rebecca down across the backseat. I stood staring into the car as he approached with Rebecca, not quite comprehending that it was empty.

I pulled back to allow Jack room, then began frantically looking for my mother in the vicinity of the house, heedless of the mud and rain. "Mother!" I screamed. I ran to the side of the house that was now a blackened, smoldering shell, feeling the odd mixture of heat and ice on my face at the same time. I ran around to the front of the house, jumping up on the porch and sticking my head inside the opening. "Mother!" I screamed again, feeling a terror I hadn't felt in a very long time—not since the morning I'd awakened to find her gone.

I jumped back onto the gravel, then jogged around the other side of the house until I'd reached the back. Sour gums and tall, spindly pines huddled together near a muddy path that led to the creek, the rising water already at the top of the cord grass. "Mother!" I shouted, looking frantically for any sign of her.

A strong hand grabbed hold of my arm and pulled me around. I faced Jack, and it wasn't until he shook me that I realized how very close to losing control I'd come. I still held the box, and felt something shaking inside. I was breathing heavily and it took me a moment to catch my breath. "My mother. She's gone. She was here when I came into the house. I gave her my phone. . . ." I stopped, realizing how useless it was talking out in the rain.

Jack's voice was strong and reassuring. "If she went inside the house, we would have seen her. She probably went back to the gatehouse to get help."

I allowed him to lead me back to the car. He opened the passenger side and put me inside, putting his hand on my head like cops do on television shows. My teeth chattered, from fear or cold I wasn't sure. Then he stripped off his button-down, leaving him in just a T-shirt, and ripped it into shreds before wrapping two of the strips around Rebecca's leg to try to stanch some of the bleeding. She didn't cry out although I could see how much pain she was in from the way her lips drained of color, making her even more doll-like.

After Jack slid behind the steering wheel, I turned back to Rebecca, impressed by her stamina. "Are you okay?" I managed to ask.

She nodded and I saw that she was shivering, too. "Hang on." I leaned over and pulled the trunk lever before flinging open my door. I ran to the trunk and retrieved one of the blankets I always kept there for emergencies, huddling over it to keep it dry, then returned to the car, slamming my door behind me. Leaning over the seat back, I opened the blanket and laid it on her, then used my purse to make a pillow. She smiled her gratitude and closed her eyes.

I turned to Jack. "I told my mother to call 911, but I don't know if she did." At the mention of my mother, a large tremor shot through me. Jack put his arms around me and began rubbing brusquely. "Not to alarm you, but I hope she did because my phone is out of range here."

"We've got to find her, Jack. She's not wearing a coat, and it's raining pretty hard." I realized I was babbling, but I was unsure how to express concern for a woman who only months ago I had liked to pretend didn't even exist.

"We'll start driving back to the gates, all right? We can't delay too long, because we need to get help for Rebecca. I have to go slowly in the mud, anyway, and we'll both be looking, so we can't miss her."

I nodded and he started the engine, flipping on the high beams, although they did little more than reflect the rain that seemed to come from the heavy clouds as if being poured out of a pitcher.

He drove slowly, as he'd promised, and we scanned the area on both sides of the car. I tried to tell myself that he was right, that she'd probably gone to the front gate to ask a guard to call an ambulance and a fire truck, although with the deluge of rain I felt confident that the latter no longer mattered.

The front right tire fell into a hole and I listened as Jack gunned the engine, then rocked it into reverse before shooting us forward again.

"Stop," I said, rubbing the window with my sleeve to clear the fog on the inside. We'd come to the fork in the road that my mother had pointed out to me earlier—the path that led to the old family cemetery. I closed my eyes, blocking out the fear and the cold and the sound of the storm, and tried to listen to the quiet place inside of me that my grandmother had always told me was there if I only took the time to find it. I needed to now, since everything else—my control, my organization, and even my spreadsheets—were completely useless to me.

I pointed down the road. "She's there. She went to the cemetery." I looked back at Rebecca. Her shivering had slowed with the car's heater blowing full force, and she'd managed to prop herself against the side door. Her color hadn't improved but at least she was still conscious.

"Yes," she managed from a dry mouth. "The cemetery. I saw Ginnette there. In a dream. I didn't know what it meant, until now." Lightning shot across the sky, making her skin and eyes look jaundiced. "She's—not alone."

Jack didn't wait to be persuaded. He pushed down hard on the gas pedal, and we lurched forward, but I wasn't paying any attention to the sound of rocks grating against the metal of my car. All I could think about was that my mother was in trouble, and she needed me.

I remembered the box in my hand again, and looked down at it. "Is Rose's locket in here?" I turned to face Rebecca in the backseat. "Is that what you were looking for?"

Rebecca groaned as Jack hit a pothole, jarring her injured leg off the seat. I helped her right herself, struggling against the jolting car. She shook her head. "I wasn't sure what was in there. I just knew that the figurehead in the window pointed to the house. And the code in the window and on the gravestone, about the sins hidden in the fireplace bricks, it had to be in the house."

I flicked open the latch on the box, then lifted the lid, pulling it back to allow the feeble light to show me what was inside. Blinking up at me was an emerald-cut ruby cocktail ring, and a diamond butterfly hairpin—both items I remembered from the insurance claim from the *Ida Belle*. They'd been lost along with the sapphire-and-diamond necklace and chandelier earrings that were now in my mother's possession.

I held the box up to show Rebecca. "You did all of this for the jewelry? If you'd just told me, I would have given it to you."

She shook her head, wincing in pain as she did so. "I wasn't looking for hidden treasure, if that's what you mean. I wanted—my heritage. There's an oil painting in my mother's house of my great-great-grandmother—Alice and Nora's grandmother. In it, she's wearing the sapphire-and-diamond necklace and earrings. When I saw your mother wearing them on television, I needed to find out how you came into possession of them. I thought"—she took a deep breath, as if riding a tide of pain—"I thought you knew, that you were hiding the truth deliberately."

I brought the box back to my lap and shook my head. Then, looking down at it again, I noticed a tarnished silver baby rattle, nestled amid the jewelry. I held it up to my face and rubbed the handle with my thumb, exposing a monogram: *NSC*. I didn't know what Nora Crandall's middle initial was, but I would bet everything I owned that it started with the letter *S*.

I closed my eyes for a moment, realizing that Jack's theories about my ancestors were at least partially correct. I opened my eyes and spotted one more thing at the bottom of the box, a yellowed piece of paper that looked as if it had been torn out of a book.

Using my short and torn fingernails, I worked at the edge of the paper to release it from its snug fit, managing to pull it off the bottom of the box without tearing it. Carefully, I unfolded it once, then turned on the overhead light. It was written in the same handwriting as the journal, and I realized with a start that that's where it had probably come from, but the page had been removed undetected. Moving it closer to the light, I began to read out loud:

> It is now two days past the great earthquake that struck Charleston. No one knew for certain what it was at first, and Rose and I thought that a bombardment had started again from the dreaded Yankees that poor Father always talked about. But Father has been gone now for almost a year, and I am glad that he is not here to witness my shame.

I am putting this all down on paper, to record the truth, to ensure that future generations will not be led into thinking ill of me. The truth always has a way of coming out, and this is my way of recording events so that they be known in their entirety. Later, when I have figured out everything, I will leave a trail to this place to be discovered in due course.

Everyone is calling the earthquake a disaster, and there are few who would disagree. Yet I call it a fortuitous event; an event that allowed me the chance to right a wrong, and to hide my sins.

On the morning of August 31, Charles was scheduled to call on Rose and to take her driving. We have been putting off telling her the truth about us, knowing how miserable Rose would make our lives if she knew. For that reason alone, we delayed letting our feelings be known, biding our time until the right opportunity presented itself.

It was a hot summer day, so I had given the servants the day off, knowing Rose and I would need nothing except for our dinner, which Cook promised to return to prepare later that day.

Earlier that morning, Rose cornered me in my sitting room, insisting that we play a trick on Charles. I didn't want to, knowing that it could only lead to disaster, but Rose was insistent in the only way she knows how, like a spider ready to bite. I agreed, and was surprised when Rose made me swap lockets with her to complete the deception. She then settled herself on the settee in the drawing room until Charles called, whereupon Rose began to build her web.

I stood outside the door, listening, and realized shortly afterward that Rose had suspected all along, and was only waiting for Charles to admit it and embarrass himself. And then go after me.

I could not listen anymore and escaped up the back servants' stairs, collapsing into tears of despair at the top. Charles is my one true love, and of all the things I have given up for Rose, he could not be one of them.

I heard them arguing, and then the front door slammed and I waited, knowing she was going to look for me, and dreading the confrontation that would follow. I huddled where I was, hoping against all hope that she would not find me in the servants' wing. But like all evil, it finds what it seeks.

Despite her small stature and deformity, she has an almost inhuman strength. She hauled me up by the elbow and slapped me, drawing blood from my lips. I told her that I was sorry, that we had never meant it to happen, but then she turned the tables and began accusing me of stealing everything she had ever had—her father's affections, her friends, even the clothes on my back and the food that I ate. She had me pressed against the stairwell wall, and that is where I was when she spotted the *R* locket she had given me to wear. Her face contorted into an expression of pure hatred, and she accused me of wanting not only what she had, but to be her. And she was going to tell the world that I was not a Prioleau at all, that I had been found on a beach when I was a baby and adopted by my father as a companion for her. She told me about the jewelry and the baby rattle that was found with me, which she now kept in a box in her dressing table because it was her insurance if she ever needed to keep me silent, her payment for having been forced to share everything with me since she was a girl.

I told her it was all lies, and that I would gladly relinquish everything if she would just let me leave with Charles. Her anger consumed her at my ready answer, and she grasped for the locket around my neck and pulled. It was clear to me that her intention was to propel me down the stairs. But instead, the unthinkable happened. The chain snapped in her grasp and she fell backward down the stairs, somersaulting until she reached the floor below, her head bent at an unnatural angle.

I ran from the house, and caught up with Charles and brought him back to the house, where I confessed everything to him, including the fact that I was not a distant cousin as I had always been led to believe. It was us together who decided what we would do, and we promised to each other that we would never regret any of our actions.

We placed Rose's body in a trunk we found in the attic and loaded it into Charles' carriage and brought it to Belle Meade. It was my idea to use the *Rose* as her coffin. We loaded the trunk onto the sailboat, then I took it out to deep water where we scuttled it. Charles followed me in a rowboat, and took me back to shore, where we looked back across the smooth ocean to where our sins lay hidden within the waves.

And then the earthquake came, and it was such an easy matter to claim that I was Rose and that Meredith had perished. With all of the destruction and chaos, nobody seemed to notice anything different than they might have otherwise. There were no other heirs, yet if Rose had known the truth of my origins, I was afraid others might as well and I would lose everything that I loved. Everything that my adopted father had loved and had wished for me to have.

I plan to go away for a time, so that people will forget the differences between Rose and Meredith, and come to accept that I am Rose. If I'm gone for long enough, I can claim that I sought treatment for my affliction and can now walk unassisted.

Charles will wait for me, and when I return, we will be married and we can put the past behind us. I can only pray that Rose has forgiven me. But forgiveness never came easily for her, and I can only hope that her vengeance cannot reach beyond the grave.

My one regret is that we sent her to her eternal rest wearing my locket, and I in possession of hers. I found it at the bottom of the stairs with the broken chain where she'd dropped it, and I had a horrible premonition that she would want it back. Although she claimed everything I owned was rightfully hers, she took great pride in her locket. I suppose it is because it was given to her by her father, who showed her little affection, but regardless it is hers. And I have no doubt that if she is able, she will come back for it.

I looked up, and saw that we'd reached the clearing my mother had spoken about. We'd climbed to higher ground, so there was no standing water, and tall pines sheltered the twenty or so graves within the boundary of a peeling wrought iron fence. Through the filter of the rain, I saw the shadowy ghosts of Prioleaus long since gone, but their attention wasn't focused on me.

I shoved the page back into the box and slammed it closed. "I know what she wants," I said, my mind suddenly clear, the remaining puzzle pieces suddenly snapping into place.

"What who wants?" Jack looked at me as if I were hallucinating.

"Rose," I said as I opened my door. "Pop open the trunk." I turned to the backseat to check on Rebecca. Her skin shone with a cold sweat, but her eyes were open and regarding me quietly.

With a quick nod, she said, "Be careful."

I ran to the back of the car and retrieved the shovel that I kept in my trunk for times when I needed to put up my own signage for open houses. I ignored the look on Jack's face as I passed him with my shovel.

"Mother!" I called, my words stolen by the wind. But it didn't matter because I'd already seen her; I'd followed the ghosts of the ancient Prioleaus to where my mother knelt in front of a small marker in the corner, digging into the moist earth with her bare hands. I ran toward her. "Mother," I called again, and this time she looked at me.

She was soaked through and shivering, her lips tinged with blue. I knelt beside her and took off my sodden sweater, then threw it over her shoulders thinking it had to be better than nothing. "What are you doing?"

We both turned to look at the marker: MEREDITH PRIOLEAU. B. 1870 D. 1886. But this marker, unlike the memorial in St. Philip's cemetery with the heart locket and the initial *R*, had no further inscription. Meredith had assumed, correctly as it appeared, that anyone who'd made it this far would have figured it all out by now.

Ginnette placed a cold and trembling hand on mine. "We must hurry. She's here. She's here now, and her anger is feeding her hatred." Her troubled gaze met mine. "She doesn't want to go, not while we're still living."

I stood and placed a hand on her shoulder and helped her stand. "Step back." She saw the shovel I held and took a step backward. "You should go to the car," I said. "The heater's on and it will get you out of this freezing rain."

She shook her head, wet strands of her hair that had fallen from her chignon whipping her cheeks. "No. We can only do this together." She suddenly pitched forward as if unseen hands had pushed her, and I managed to break her fall before she hit the ground. "Hurry, Mellie. Please."

While she huddled nearby, I lifted the shovel, but stopped midstrike, surprised to feel resistance. I turned, and saw Jack with his hand on the handle. "Let me do this. Stay with your mother."

I stared at him for a moment as the rain cascaded down his face and plastered his shirt to his chest. I started to argue that this was my battle and he'd already opted out, but he leaned forward and kissed me hard on the mouth, surprising me into making me let go of the shovel. He sent me a dark gaze before driving the shovel into the wet and weeping earth.

I knelt by my mother and put my arm around her, holding her close. Unseen hands pulled at our hair as the wind and another unknown force pushed at our backs. I struck out a hand, angry that she wouldn't show herself. "Stop it!" I screamed to the pelting rain.

Ginnette grabbed my hand and squeezed it. "Focus, Melanie. I need you to focus. I can't do this without you and she knows it." She closed her eyes tightly, and I saw how rivulets of water clustered on the tips of her eyelashes before spilling over. "We are stronger than you," she said loudly, then said it again, squeezing my hand.

"We are stronger than you," we said in unison as Jack dug into the mud, unearthing a hole that quickly filled with water. I felt my mother's warmth and her strength at the place our hands were joined, noting that the torturing hands had gone. A sense of triumph filled me, and I squeezed my mother's hand tighter as a sign of victory while I turned to her with a smile.

But her face was drawn and ashen, and she was looking past me to where Jack had stopped digging. "No, Mellie, not yet. Don't let your guard down. She's waiting!"

Jack shouted, and I turned from my mother in time to see him hold up what appeared to be a square ivory box. I watched as he held it up so the rain could rinse off the dirt, then pried open the lid. He dug his fingers inside and held up the locket, the broken chain dangling between his fingers.

Dropping my mother's hand, I reached for it.

"Mellie, give me your hand!" I could barely hear my mother's voice as she shouted over the renewed force of the wind.

As I turned I heard Jack call out a warning and from the corner of my eye, I saw the flash of light hurtle down from the sky, striking the earth in front of me. I watched in horror as Jack and my mother were knocked from their feet, then realized that I was already on the ground, my mouth tasting dirt and burnt ions. A warm trickle oozed down my forehead and right before I closed my eyes, I realized that I must have hit my head on a stone.

I lay on my back as the rain poured down, but it wasn't touching me.

I felt dry, and warm, as if I'd been pulled in from the storm and wrapped in a soft blanket, and I heard my grandmother nearby, telling me to get up. Groggily, I turned my head, a blood-searing scream in my ears, and I saw Rose. Her skin was white and waterlogged from being on the bottom of the ocean floor for so long, her eye sockets empty but projecting rage. Small fiddler crabs scuttled in and out of her mouth and empty eyes, scavenging for food.

The screaming evaporated into a high-pitched whine, and was replaced by her voice, the same terrible voice I'd heard in the kitchen. *She left you, Melanie, because she never loved you. She is jealous because you are stronger. Go to sleep, Melanie, and let me take care of her. Let me punish her for what she did to you.*

I turned my face from the stench of rotting sea creatures, toward the sound of my grandmother's voice calling my name. And then I heard my mother's voice, edging its way out from my past. *Sometimes we have to do the right thing even if it means letting go of the one thing we love most in the world.* Closing my eyes and blocking out the sounds of all the voices, I searched for the dark quiet inside of me, and remembered my mother's words. And after more than thirty years, I understood. Finally, I understood.

I stuck my fingers into the earth, trying to claw my way from the hideous apparition, but I couldn't move. I scratched harder, trying to crawl away, screaming and screaming as her icy breath brushed the nape of my neck. A door appeared in the darkness, with fingers of light escaping around the edges like a halo, and I struggled to a stand, suddenly certain that if I reached the door, the evil I felt at my back would go away, and I wouldn't need to be afraid anymore.

"Mellie!" somebody called in the darkness, but I wasn't sure who.

I was moving in slow motion, trying to reach the door. I kept my gaze focused ahead of me, knowing that if I turned I'd see Rose again and that if I had to look in her eyes, I would die. I scrambled toward the door, but instead of moving faster, I was swimming in a sea of black fear, roiling up against my skin like thick crude oil, the smell hot and rancid and stinking of rotting fish.

"Mellie!" I recognized my mother's voice this time. In my fear and need to escape, I'd forgotten she was there; I'd forgotten what she'd told me about fear and strength and our need to fight together.

I stopped struggling, staring at the door that seemed no closer and panting as if I'd run for miles.

"Mellie," my mother's voice called again, but not as strong this time. Almost, I thought, as if she'd given up.

The evil thing moved behind me again, telling me to go to the door. To open it where I'd find safety. But I felt my mother's presence, too, and it was stronger, and sweeter, and full of truth, and I stopped struggling, and I remembered her telling me not to listen to the voice. With one last look at the door and its beaming light, I turned around ready to face the encroaching darkness that nipped at my heels.

The first thing I felt was the icy rain, hitting my face as I stared up at a nearly black sky. I sat up, catching sight of Jack, who was struggling to stand. Frantically, I searched for my mother and found her crumpled on the ground near Meredith's marker. As I forced myself to stand, I felt something sharp biting into the skin on my palm. I glanced down at my closed fist and slowly opened my fingers, one by one, revealing the dull glint of a gold locket.

The light shimmered around me, the air viscous like embryonic fluid feeding me the strength I needed and holding me together as I moved toward my mother. I placed my hand on her back, relief flooding me when I felt her take a breath. She moaned and turned over, looking up at me with glassy, feverish eyes.

"Thank God," she said, and grasped my hand and I felt the fizz of electricity shoot through me and back to her. She didn't let go, even as I pulled her to her feet and we both looked up at the sky and the funnel of mud and leaves that circled above our heads. I made to jerk back but my mother held on, and I knew that I couldn't let go ever again.

"Give it back to her," my mother shouted over the increasing wind. "Give it back to her, and tell her to find the light. To leave us in peace."

I looked down at the locket in my hand, then drew my arm back and threw it as hard as I could toward the funnel of air. A sound like the screeching brakes of a train pierced the air as the locket evaporated into the spinning cloud of debris. Every hair on my body stood on end as I held my ground and didn't look away.

"Go!" I shouted. "Leave now. Find the door and the light and leave this place forever. You have what was yours. Now go."

The air hummed with electricity as the funnel whirled faster and faster, sticks and leaves whipping at my face, but I didn't back down. "Be gone!" I shouted and the funnel exploded into a million balls of light and ice, spraying us with hail and knocking us back to the ground.

We lay there, breathing heavily, the air suddenly clear. Above us, dark clouds unfurled around the rising moon, wiping away the storm clouds as if an eraser had swept over the horizon. In the distance, I heard the call of sirens, relief consuming me now that help was on its way and I didn't need to fight anymore.

Jack staggered toward us, his face determined and I managed a thumbs-up before I lay back on the ground next to my mother, tasting rain and dirt and the metallic tinge of electrified air, and I knew that somehow I had found the strength she'd known I had all along to save us both.

CHAPTER 28

I placed the last suitcase in the trunk, then tucked General Lee firmly under my arm before shutting the rear trunk of my rental car, my own car still in the shop undergoing massive body repairs. I only wished there was an equivalent in the human world, as my mind and body still felt bruised and battered, although it had been two weeks since the night of the storm.

I stared up at my mother's house, no longer feeling the undercurrent of a pulsing heart or dreading opening the front door to whatever might be lying in wait. I drew in a deep breath, taking in the warm air that was scented with the promise of spring. Although the official start of the new season was still a few weeks away, the gardens of Charleston were already pregnant with emerging bulbs and bud-laden stems, holding their secrets for just a little longer.

The front door opened and I watched as my mother emerged from the house, followed closely by my father carrying a breakfast tray. After a night in the hospital, where it was determined that she was suffering from nothing more than poor blood iron, she'd returned to her old self. Well, almost. Because the woman who looked at me now wasn't the same person who'd once hesitated before touching me or watched me with guarded eyes. I found myself sometimes missing the old version of herself, as now she felt no need to hold back when it came to mothering me. She felt free to comment on everything from my hair, makeup, wardrobe, dog-training methods, and diet without reservation. And although I pretended to be annoyed, I didn't really mind it. I suppose because regardless of a woman's age, she will always have the need to be mothered. Some things remained off-limits, however, such as Jack and my relationship with Marc Longo, if only because such things were unexplainable.

As I approached the garden, I watched as my father settled my mother in a wrought iron chair—discovered in the attic along with the matching table and other chairs—then draped a blanket gently over her shoulders. He then proceeded to place dishes and silverware onto the table, and a vase full of pink roses nearest to my mother's chair.

It was hard not to roll my eyes, but I managed. Despite coming to terms with my mother's new presence in my life, I hadn't yet managed to reach that point with my parents' burgeoning relationship. Now that I understood my mother's reasons for leaving all those years ago—although not completely agreeing with them—I could stand back and view the events of thirty years before more clearly. My father—whose alcoholism had done much to tarnish his image in the intervening years—was no longer the knight in shining armor that I'd envisioned as a little girl. Instead, I'd begun to see him as my mother had: intractable and closed minded when confronted with things that didn't work inside his world order.

Granted, he'd seen much more of the world than I with his years as an army officer, but I was his daughter and my mother supposedly the love of his life. And I couldn't help but think that he should have pretended to accept, or at the very least condoned, the fact that my mother and I could see things that he could not. Maybe if she'd had his support in that darkest point in her life, she wouldn't have felt the need to abandon us both.

He looked up and smiled as we approached, and General Lee wrested himself out of my arms to receive a table scrap from my mother. I was still his favorite human, but he was easily enticed with food offerings. Unfortunately, he didn't possess the family gene for a high metabolism, and he'd started to bulge out of the argyle sweaters that Nancy continued to knit for him.

My mother held up her cheek for me to kiss and my father enveloped me in a bear hug before I sat down in an available chair. "The garden is lovely," I said, admiring the burgeoning knot garden he'd been reconstructing from old photographs, and the neatly clipped boxwoods that lined the brick patio area. The dormant annual beds still slept, waiting for their place to shine within the coveted gates of a Charleston garden.

"If I can get your mother to agree, I want to move the fountain to the back, so it can be enjoyed from the kitchen. I think Sophie's gotten to her, though, as she's resistant to alter anything that was original to the house."

I took a donut from a plate and eyed it thoughtfully. "Which means you'd need to have a consent form signed by God and witnessed by the Board of Architectural Review to allow it to happen. Better think of a plan B, Daddy."

He poured a cup of tea for my mother, then slid a plate with a donut on it in front of her. I almost stopped him to ask for ID and find out what he'd done to my real father.

My mother turned to me. "Don't forget your coffee cup—the one with the sales graph on it. I put it on the kitchen counter so you wouldn't leave it behind."

"It's not like she's going away forever, Ginny. She'll be back."

"I know. It's just that I think she'd want to say good-bye before she left. To the kitchen," she added slowly, her eyes heavy with meaning.

Both my father and I regarded her silently. Slowly, I slid my chair back and rose. "Well, then. I guess I'd better go get it."

I left them to finish their breakfast in the garden, then entered the house through the front door. I smelled the hint of gunpowder in the air, and I began to realize what my mother had meant. We'd discussed Wilhelm's presence in the house, and how he'd remained earthbound for us, but that it was time to set him free. I hadn't understood at the time that she was allowing me the chance to exercise my newfound understanding of my psychic abilities.

"Wilhelm," I said out loud, summoning him. I closed my eyes, focusing inward, finding the power I was only beginning to comprehend—and appreciate—although I wasn't sure if I'd ever get to that point. "Wilhelm," I said again, opening my eyes. He stood in front of the stairs, his boots shiny, his hat tucked under his arm, and his musket gripped in his left hand. He bowed, and looked me in the eye. My gaze traveled down to his boots and that's when I noticed that I couldn't see through him anymore. It was as if in discovering my own strength, I'd given some to him.

You look beautiful this morning, Melanie. More so than yesterday, but not as much as tomorrow.

I smiled. "Did you used to say that to Catherine?"

A mischievous smile crossed his face. *You are very clever, Melanie, because you are correct. Catherine was very beautiful. You remind me of her. But perhaps you already knew that.*

I blushed, remembering how he'd kissed me, feeling foolish that I hadn't guessed why. I considered him for a moment, thinking how he'd carried his musket for over two hundred years in penance for an event he'd had no control over. His presence had been a warm memory of my childhood; his help in protecting me from Rose had probably saved my life more than once. But it was selfish to expect him to wander this house aimlessly, mourning for his lost love. It was time to say good-bye.

Swallowing the thickness in the back of my throat, I said, "She's waiting for you, Wilhelm. On the other side. She wants to be with you again."

His eyes were unsettled. *I went back for her. Into the water to be with her forever. But instead I stayed there by the shore for long years, watching for ships. Guiding them away from danger. Until baby Nora, and I came here. I don't know how to leave this place.*

"You were a good protector, Wilhelm. But you're not needed here anymore. It's time to go, to find Catherine at last. I can help you. My mother said that helping you leave can be as simple as letting you go."

I want to. I do not know how.

I remembered the door, and the bright light behind it. For me, the door had been closed, but for Wilhelm the light would be burning brightly, the door leading to it opened wide. "Look for the light. It will show you the way."

But who will take care of you?

"My mother and I will be together, and Rose is gone." I smiled, trying to appear more confident and sure than I felt. "We'll be all right. But it's time for you to move on."

His face began to glow as a smile transformed his face. *I hear Catherine. I hear her calling me.*

"Follow her voice. She'll lead you to the light."

He stepped toward me and I looked into his eyes, seeing the flecks of brown in them that I'd never noticed before. He leaned down and kissed me gently on the lips. *Good-bye, Melanie.*

I heard a quick intake of breath and I turned to see my father standing inside the door, watching us and I realized that he could see Wilhelm as clearly as I did.

Wilhelm straightened and clicked his heels together before placing his tricorn hat on his head. And then, with military precision, he saluted my father, then slowly began to fade away until nothing was left of him except the faint whiff of gunpowder smoke and the warm tingling on my lips where he'd kissed me good-bye.

I pulled into the driveway at my Tradd Street house, squinting to see if I'd really seen a banner strung across the front door. I hoped they hadn't used masking tape since that might ruin the ridiculously expensive paint that Sophie had insisted I use because it had been blended to perfectly match the color of the original used more than one hundred and fifty years before. Every time Sophie mentioned touching up the paint on the door from workmen bumping it or from the sun fading it, I just heard the huge ch-ching of a cash register. I kept threatening to replace it with a storm door with plastic windows just to see her look of horror.

I grabbed General Lee from his car seat and slowly walked through the garden to the piazza, listening to the soft trickle of the fountain. I stood back to read the sign: WELCOME HOME, MELANIE! I smiled, figuring it had to be Chad and Sophie. I didn't know anybody else whose enthusiasm reached out to somebody who'd been staying only blocks away while her wood floors were being refinished. I paused, my smile fading. Then again, I couldn't help but wonder if they'd found something else in the house that would require not only a prolonged absence, but also a huge outlay of funds and they were trying to soften me up before felling me with the news.

Dispirited, I turned the handle and opened the door, prepared to be pelted with confetti or at the very least a work order and deposit check that needed to be signed immediately. Instead, I was greeted with silence and an empty foyer. I put General Lee on the floor and he scampered to the back of the house in the direction of the kitchen. After dropping my keys and purse on the hallway table, I moved inside, smelling the reassuring odor of wax and fresh wood—a tangible reminder of all the money it had cost to restore the floors. But from what I'd seen, they looked beautiful and would serve as the perfect backdrop for the home I hoped to create when all the work was finished. Whenever that would be.

I was about to head upstairs to my room when I spotted wrapped packages on the dining room table. Warily, I approached, then peeked at the tags, which were all addressed to me. Feeling somewhat despondent, I sat down and began opening them.

The first was from Jack: a small blue T-shirt, apparently for General Lee, which had splayed across the back, BITCHES LOVE ME. I tried not to laugh, and ended up sputtering instead. I still wasn't sure where Jack and I stood. We'd seen little of each other since the night of the storm, and I knew that he'd joined Rebecca at her family's summer home on Pawleys Island for a few weeks while she recuperated. I'd visited her in the hospital, where I'd been forced to sign her pink cast and listen to her call me "cousin."

I'd returned the box of jewelry to her and called it even. She didn't argue, and instead began talking about hosting a barbecue to introduce me to the rest of the family. I remembered the days when I thought of myself as an only child as a bad thing, and found myself thinking of them with nostalgia.

There was a gift bag with tissue that held a can of paint, to "touch up the front door" as the tag read, from Sophie and Chad, and a tube of Chanel lipstick in hot pink from Rebecca—her favorite color, which she thought would look great on me, too. There was also a framed oil miniature of Belle Meade as it must have looked in the early 1800s, with only the words "thank you" written on the card in Rebecca's rounded, girlish handwriting.

The sound of voices and a door slamming brought me into the foyer again in time to see Chad, Sophie, and Jack coming in from the kitchen. They all stopped when they saw me, and it was apparent from the looks on their faces that they'd been discussing me. Or the house. Or both.

"What's wrong?" I asked, secure that whatever it was it couldn't be the roof because I'd already paid to have it replaced.

"Did you see your gifts?" Sophie asked, pointing to the dining room.

"Yes, actually, I did. Thank you. I think the T-shirt might be a little small on me, Jack, but I'll give it a try."

He raised an eyebrow and sent me his killer grin, and I almost forgot that we were wrong for each other and that I'd practically thrown him into the arms of another woman on purpose.

I faced Chad, knowing he'd be the easiest to crack. "The floors look beautiful. It's hard to believe that you did them all by hand without an electric sander."

I saw the alarm in his eyes and knew that I had him. I zeroed in for the kill. "So, what's wrong with the house now?"

Without looking at Sophie, he said, "There's a pretty thick crack in the bricks on the back of the house and Soph thinks there might be something wrong with the foundation."

I stared at him and blinked soundlessly for a good minute, having absolutely nothing to say. They all began talking at once, but I held up my hand. "I'm going upstairs to change, and I might even lie down a bit. I need a little time to recover first before I can listen to any more."

I'd barely taken a step toward the staircase when the knocker sounded from the front door. When nobody else moved, I made my way to the door and pulled it open.

Amelia and John Trenholm, Jack's parents, stood on the piazza, looking uncertain and trying to see past my shoulder. Amelia smiled tentatively. "Hello, Melanie. I'm glad to see you looking so well. Is Jack here? We've been trying to find him, but he's not at home and he's not answering his cell. We were driving by and saw his car outside."

I pulled back, opening the door wider, just as I caught sight of the third person standing on the piazza with them. She was a young girl of about twelve or thirteen years old. She wore platform shoes, low-rider jeans, halter top, heavy blue eye shadow, and was at that moment sticking a wad of bright pink bubble gum on one of the front columns of my house.

She turned to me and smiled and my eyes widened. The girl had black wavy hair and dark blue eyes, but it was the dimple in her left cheek that gave her away.

"Jack," I said slowly. "You might want to come out here."

He came to stand next to me and had opened his mouth to say something when he caught sight of the girl and stopped.

Her grin widened when she saw him, and I knew the effect wasn't lost on him, either.

"Hello, Daddy," she said, leaning nonchalantly on the railing. "Surprise."

I looked from the girl's multipierced ears to Jack's astonished face and suddenly having a cracked foundation didn't seem like such a big problem after all.

"I'll let you talk in private," I said before sweeping back into the front hall of my Tradd Street house, smelling the scents of varnished wood and new paint that reminded me I was home, then closed the door behind me.

Photo by Marchet Butler

Karen White is the *New York Times* bestselling author of more than twenty books, including the Tradd Street novels, *Dreams of Falling*, *The Night the Lights Went Out*, *Flight Patterns*, *The Sound of Glass*, *A Long Time Gone*, and *The Time Between*, and the coauthor of *The Forgotten Room* and *The Glass Ocean* with *New York Times* bestselling authors Beatriz Williams and Lauren Willig. She grew up in London but now lives with her husband near Atlanta, Georgia.

CONNECT ONLINE

karen-white.com
facebook.com/karenwhiteauthor
twitter.com/KarenWhiteWrite
instagram.com/karenwhitewrite